a girl like me.

by
GINGER SCOTT

ISBN: 0-9990464-1-1

ISBN-13: 978-0-9990464-1-8

For Helen.
The most bad-ass young woman I know.
Love you to the moon, girl.

O, when she's angry, she is keen and shrewd!
She was a vixen when she went to school;
And though she be but little, she is fierce.
~The Bard

CHAPTER 1

When I was little, still in grade school, right after my mom left, I had these dreams that she had just gone to the store to pick up something my dad had forgotten. My dad and I were always sitting at the table, sometimes playing a game, other times just talking. The feeling was so alive, so real. It was…normal. I'd wake up in this distorted existence where everything was okay. Sometimes that feeling would last almost a full minute. It always disappeared, but I'd go to sleep the next night whispering prayers—to whomever it is that puts dreams in heads—to let me have that one again.

It would never come when I truly wanted it.

Over the years, I had that dream less and less. I think it was maturity killing silly, childish fantasies. It's been three years since I felt my mom's presence in my slumber, and the memory of that dream had almost left me completely.

Last night, though—she was here.

Here.

Kyle and I arrived at Grandma Grace's house in Tucson after an all-night drive that turned into morning, then afternoon. I needed to see her, and my heart and head were acting together when I hatched the late-night plan to hit the road with the only friend I have who would embrace my wildest and craziest ideas. Kyle has been through it all with me—literally from the bottom to this rocky journey back up. When I asked him to drive me here, to see my grandma and get answers about my dead mom, he merely motioned toward the truck, keys in his hand, ready to drive. And when I added in the bit about also wanting to find Wes, Kyle didn't flinch, indulging my hopes and not once questioning me. Kyle loves me more than I deserve, but I will never tell him that. I'm selfish, and as much as my heart belongs to Wes, Kyle's friendship also makes me whole.

I called my dad from the road when we were too far away from home for him to stop us, and he reluctantly called ahead to Grace for us. This was after chewing my ass out for about thirty minutes and demanding we turn around and come home. I left out the part that our drive home would take twice as long…because *oh yeah, and we plan to look for Wes, because I believe he's alive and he's sent me cryptic messages. Sound good?*

The drive took nine hours; by the time we arrived at the small brick home—surrounded by cactus and shadowed by a mountain scarred with blackened earth from a recent fire—the sun was just beginning to set over the peak.

Our greeting was awkward. Grace pulled me in for a hug, but her hands never came to a rest on my back, her touch stilted—guarded. She made a pallet on the floor in her sewing room for Kyle. She led me to a spare room with blank walls and laced curtains at the end of the hall, and when my head hit the pillow, my eyes closed easily from exhaustion.

That was more than twelve hours ago. I'd give anything to close my eyes again, but it's too late. They've opened, and that feeling from the dream…it's already gone.

My body aches from the long ride in Kyle's truck and the hard mattress beneath me. I roll to my side and pull my knees to my chest, one at a time, removing my prosthetic and stretching my body as I kick away the heavy quilt I slept under. I half expect the sensation of phantom pain to kick in, but it hasn't for weeks—at least nothing like when I first lost my leg in the bus accident.

The door to my room is slightly opened, and I strain to see what I can of the house beyond it through the four-inch gap. When the door pushes toward me, I startle and sit up quickly while my mind registers that it's only Kyle.

"There's breakfast out there," he says, stretching his arms above his head, his fingertips nearly grazing the ceiling-fan blades above him.

"What time is it?" I press my palms into my eyes, forcing out the puffiness.

"Eleven," he says, his mouth ticking up on one side while my eyes widen. "Yeah, we slept for fifteen hours."

"So, doesn't that make it *lunch*time?" I say, tugging my fingers through the knots in my hair.

"Yeah, but Grace…or your grandma, or…what do I call her?" Kyle asks.

I shrug. She's really a stranger, other than the few times I saw her when I was a kid.

"All right, well…Grace…she said she always wanted to make you breakfast, so…"

Our eyes meet as his words trail off, and I instantly wonder if what Grace told Kyle was a lie. I was so brave in that field, when I held that photo in my hands, sure I'd find Wes and some long-lost connection with a woman I barely know. I'm not brave now. That dream took away my faith when the warm feeling left me.

"Kyle, maybe we should just—"

A woman with a long, gray ponytail tethered at her neck and dirt-stained garden gloves covering her hands fills my doorway, and I pause mid-sentence. I didn't really look at Grace when we arrived, and the image in my head was something daintier, or maybe polished, at least. The person smiling at me right now is miles away from that version. This Grace is tough, a thick body that looks like it could carry fifty pounds without breaking a sweat, despite the wrinkled arms that dangle at her sides.

"Bacon's on the table. I'll wash up and join you both in a minute, but feel free to start without me."

Her smile lingers on me a few extra seconds before she spins from the door and disappears down the hallway. Kyle and I both look at the spot she just left. I don't breathe until I hear a door close.

"She looks like me."

Kyle lifts his eyes to mine, a small chuckle escaping with the lift of the left side of his mouth.

"I bet she swears like a sailor, too," he says.

My eyes slit and my lips pucker a second before I throw the down-filled pillow at his face.

"Oooph, that's it! You owe me a piece of bacon," he says, zinging the pillow back at me. I catch it on my lap and sneer at him one more time. "Right...because you talk like an angel."

"You bet your ass I do."

Kyle cranes his neck to make sure the coast is clear before flipping me off and leaving me alone again in my room. I laugh hard enough that a sound escapes me, and hearing it makes my smile grow. I can do this. There are things I want to know—I *need* to know.

After spending a few minutes stretching my limb, I put on my prosthetic and work my way to the bathroom to freshen up. We drove straight from the flower field. I was too afraid that my dad would notice if I stopped back at home. Maybe I was afraid I'd change my mind about this trip, too. Now, five hundred miles away from home, toothbrushless, clean underwearless, and—I tuck my chin to my left shoulder and sniff—deodorantless, I think the next leg of our trip in the truck is going to be a rough one.

I make do with what I can find, splashing water on my face and rubbing a finger full of toothpaste around my mouth. By the time I feel clean enough to leave the bathroom and head to the kitchen, Grace has joined Kyle at the table. Her smile catches me off guard; it's the same one as before, almost like she thought I'd been a made-up story all these years and is only now finding out I'm real, as if the other times we were together were delusions.

"Here," she stands, the squeal of her chair against the tile making me flinch. "I have a plate for you."

I take the dish from her hand, my eyes not able to make it fully to hers. I'm intimidated.

"Thank you," I say.

"Grace, what's in these eggs? I mean, serious...these are pretty much the best thing I've eaten in my entire life," Kyle says in-between bites.

"It's just a little bit of pepper jack. I find it gives them kick," she says, that last word coming out a little louder than the others.

"I just hope it doesn't give me gas," Kyle says through the side of a full mouth. I kick his chair hard enough that it scoots to the side an inch or two.

"What?" He looks up at me with his shoulders drawn up and eyebrows pinched.

My eyes fall closed and I shake my head. My face feels hot.

"Nothing," I whisper, recognizing the feeling that made me scold him. I want Grace to like me. It's the same desperate feeling I used to get when the kids at school would stare at me when something embarrassing happened—when I sat with Christopher...*Wes*.

I fill my plate with two strips of bacon and a scoop of eggs before taking a seat next to Kyle. Grace pours a glass of orange juice for each of us while I pick at my food, nibbling at the edges of a piece of bacon.

"Thank you," I say as she finishes pouring. I glance up at her, but immediately look back down at the bacon in my hand.

She slides the pitcher onto the table next to my plate, and without pause moves her left hand to my shoulder, resting it on me gently. My pulse quickens.

"Josselyn." I swallow hearing her say my name. Somewhere deep inside me, I think maybe I remember hearing her say it before—a long time ago. My lips tight, I look up at her again and smile through my fear of rejection. She moves her fingertips to my chin, tilting my head up just enough that I have to look her in the eyes, and my breath grows choppy with my nerves.

"I have missed you so much."

I bite my lip the second it quivers, but she sees right through it, her hand sliding to cup my cheek as she reaches up with her other hand, too.

"You grew up so beautiful," she says.

I force myself to breathe in slowly, looking for the lies in every word. I can't see them, though. All I see is a reflection, my future. My eyes are blue because of hers.

"Thank you," I whisper.

A gentle chuckle shakes her shoulders before her fingertips fall away from my skin. My heart now kicking steadily, I hide my nerves behind my appetite, cleaning my plate and taking seconds.

Kyle and I both help Grace clean up the kitchen, and we follow her to a back patio that looks out over an open stretch of desert. We sit on a wicker sofa while she sits in an iron chair across from us.

I keep glancing to Kyle nervously, not sure how to transition into the millions of questions I want to ask. I should have practiced with him while we were on the road, but I didn't think I'd need to. I was so sure of myself until I was faced with the real thing. Every time Kyle raises his brow, urging me to speak, I want to kick him. He finally rolls his eyes and looks out at our view.

"It's pretty out here," he says, and I breathe out a laugh through my nose at his small talk. His foot nudges mine, chiding me.

"I sure like it. When Zeke passed away…that was your grandpa. He died just before you were born," Grace says, filling in the gaps. "I wanted something simpler than living in California. It took a year or two to work out, but eventually I bought this place with the money I got from his pension, and when the house sold in Pasadena, I moved here."

She moved away.

"It made it awfully hard to see you, though," she says, almost as if hearing my thoughts. I start to nod slowly, not expecting a reason, but she isn't done. "Your mom and me…"

She holds her mouth half open, eventually pushing her tongue into one cheek and nodding as she looks just below my eyes. She stands, holding up a finger. When she steps toward the back door, I get up to follow her, but she shakes her head.

"I'll be right back."

Kyle and I sit in silence for nearly a minute before I speak.

"I'm scared," I admit to him.

He reaches down to where my hand rests between us and threads his fingers through mine, bringing my knuckles to his lips, kissing them.

"Don't be," he says, squeezing once before letting go.

Grace steps back outside a few seconds later with a metal tin. She pops the lid off as she sets it on the glass table between us, and I lean forward to look inside.

"I have more things I'd like to give you, but it's been so long since I've gone through the old things in boxes that I'm not sure what everything is anymore," she laughs, and I catch the vibration. She's nervous, too. "I put this together when your dad called so you'd have something to take home with you."

She reaches in, pulling out an old Polaroid photo, and even though it's faded, I recognize the pink knit cap on my baby head immediately. I've seen photos from this day, just not this one.

"You were there when they brought me home?" I bring the picture close so I can take in the details of a tiny me cradled in a younger Grace's arms.

"I sat through thirteen hours of labor waiting for you," she laughs. "I wasn't going home before the good part."

This time when I look up, I meet her gaze and hold it. A warm feeling rushes around my insides, almost like the one from my dream, but better—this feels more permanent. I lean forward and reach into the box, taking out a golden pin shaped like eagle wings with a propeller in the center, the metal a little tarnished at the creases.

"Air Force," Grace explains. I nod. "Your grandfather was a lifer, which meant we moved around a lot when your mom was little."

The next photo I take out is of my mom as a teenager. She looks about my age, and she's standing in front of an old Volkswagen Beetle, holding keys out toward the camera. Her hair is curly and she's wearing flip-flops, swim trunks, and a bikini top, her face freckled from summer sun. She looks happier than I ever remember her. I see the difference in her eyes— there's a light there, one that by the end, was never there for us.

"That was when we bought her a car. Her seventeenth birthday," Grace says, taking the photo from my hands and leaning back in her seat to look at it closely. Her smile is faint, and I can tell there's sadness mixed in her thoughts. "We moved around so much, your mom never really had any roots or real friends. When we got to California, Zeke was finally put in a permanent position, and I just wanted her to have *something*. She was so happy that day. I think it's the last time she and I truly got along until you were born."

"Why didn't you get along?" I ask, my courage growing.

Long seconds pass before she puts the picture down. Our roles reversed, Grace keeps her gaze from me this time, instead leaning back again in her chair and looking off to the side, toward the charred mountain.

"That happened last summer," she says, bypassing my question to instead talk about the landscape. I feel my chest constrict, but I hold in my sigh. We all have things that are hard to say. My mom isn't easy for me to talk about either.

"Wildfire?" I ask, indulging her.

"Arson."

I look back to the mountain after her quick answer, this time with new eyes. I'm not sure how big an acre is, but I'd guess what I'm looking at equates to hundreds.

"It's hard to believe a single person can do so much damage," I say, my eyes tracing along the blackened, jagged rocks and small signs of new growth that pepper the mountainside. I look back to Grace, and her eyes are waiting for me. They're devastated—raw at the edges and black in the center—as if she'd just talked to the living dead.

"I know you came here for answers, and I want to give them to you, but..." Grace's words stop, her lips parted.

I sit back and fold my hands in my lap to show her I'm ready. She closes her eyes for several seconds, probably praying for strength. I wait until she's ready.

"Sometimes, Josselyn, things just are what they are. There isn't some great reason, or some moment of redemption that makes all of the hurt and suffering right again," she says, closing her mouth after that last word, a heavy breath pushed from her nose.

"Was she ever even sorry?" I ask, letting go of that final thread that held on to hope that there was a reason for it all...that my mom left because of money, because she and my father fought, because she was depressed. She left for a man, a man I hate deep in my soul.

Turns out the answer was always simple—she was selfish.

"I think she was," my grandmother finally answers, and it takes me a minute to remember what I asked. "I used to offer to send something along with my cards or letters. I'd offer to call your father and set up a visit. Oh...how we would fight about it. She was adamant that she had made her choice, and that your dad would never forgive her, but I don't know."

I don't know either. If it were now, I think maybe my dad would be open to talking at least, but then... *no*. The wounds were too fresh.

"I think it was more than guilt that made her lash out at me. Your mom always had this idea in her head about what her life would be like, but that's not how this works."

"How what works?" I ask.

Her head waggles as she holds her palms out to her sides and says, "Any of it."

No. I guess it's not. If that's how life worked—precisely the way a person wants it to—then I'd still have my leg, and Wes wouldn't be...wherever. And my mom...

She'd probably still be gone.

"Some people are just built differently," Grace says, her eyes shifting to the dark scene in the distance. "When your mom found out about the cancer...she walked out into the desert, and dropped a match."

Arson.

"Your mom could be awful when she didn't get her way. That...that's why we didn't get along. For years, I would just take the abuse—let her rail against me for everything. Every time she was the new kid at school, that feeling she would get—the fear of being new? My fault. When a boy she liked, liked another girl? My fault. Every single time we moved—my fault. I was a military wife, and that was just the way our life worked as a

9

family. I couldn't let it be Zeke's fault. So…I let her blame me. And when your dad started drinking, and things started unraveling with their marriage…"

"That was their fault," I interrupt.

Her eyes blink slowly above her tight-lipped smile in agreement.

"It was, but your mom couldn't see it that way. She blamed me for every wrong turn in her life. And eventually, I refused to be her whipping post," Grace says. Her shoulders rise and fall with labored breath. "I didn't talk to her for years. I had no idea where she'd gone when she left your dad. I didn't know Kevin at all. I had to let her go; let her try and force life to work the way she wanted it. And then she got sick. Kevin took a job in town, I think, so she and I could be close."

"She came to you," I say.

Grace nods.

"I think maybe it was the first time she felt utterly powerless against something, so she took it out on God. She burnt his beauty to the ground. The official report blamed it on lightning from one of the monsoons, but I found her rocking in the garage, dirt on her boots, and the box of matches in her hand. I never told anyone. Not even Kevin."

Grace's gaze drifts beyond me, and after nearly a minute of silence, her eyes still lost in nothing, I start to worry until she finally speaks.

"Your mom was convinced that she was born to be the villain," she says, her focus sliding to me until our eyes meet. She leans forward and pushes the tin toward me again, then stands and moves toward the door, stopping to turn her head before moving inside.

"I'm going to run to the store, pick up a few things for you and your friend, for your trip in the morning. Maybe look through that while I'm gone," she says, her fingers rapping on the wood frame of the doorway. "I'll tell you anything you want to know."

I watch her disappear before turning my attention to the tin in front of me. I lean forward and snag the edge with my fingertip and drag it closer, then sit, frozen while I breathe and wonder what else I could possibly ever want to know.

"You all right?" Kyle's voice is soft and sleepy. I shouldn't have dragged him through this with me, but I was too scared to do it alone.

"I'm not sure…I think maybe…no, I'm not," I say, scrunching the shoulder closest to him.

"What can I do?" he asks.

I tip the container forward slightly, and the photos and trinkets inside all slide toward me. In a short time, Grace managed to pack a lot of things into this tiny box. Funny how they look different to me now, though. The specialness is all worn off.

"Why don't you get a little more rest in my room?"

Kyle waves off my suggestion, acting tough, but I know he's tired. And he needs to drive several miles tomorrow, and I'm not entirely sure where we're going.

"You know you slept like shit on the floor last night," I say, pointing as I catch him mid yawn. He contorts his mouth into a smile, but a guilty laugh breaks through.

"Fine, you're right. You all right alone?" he says, standing up from the wicker sofa. It crackles with the release of his weight.

I tap my finger on the tin.

"I think I'm gonna go through more secrets and memories," I say.

"Right," he nods, leaning forward and kissing the top of my head. "Wake me up after an hour or so. I don't want to throw my body's clock out of whack."

I nod *yes* and wait until I'm sure I'm alone to bring the tin into my lap. The first thing my eyes notice is an old leather keychain—Volkswagen. I pull it out and rub my thumb into the logo patch, noticing the places where it's worn deepest. My touch on top of hers—our fingertips the same size.

When I drop the keyring back into the box, it lands on another photo that slid sideways, the edges poking up. I pull it out next wanting to make sure it isn't bent, and I nearly dismiss it as another family photo taken on the day I was born, when a face catches my attention.

The eyes are the same, and the smile. I could chalk facial features up to a coincidence—so many of us have near twins out in the world. But it's the cane—the one he's using to stand while he holds me in his other arm—that won't let me move on.

My gut tells me the man in this photo is Shawn Stokes. He knew me. He was there—on this day. I stand, carrying the tin with me inside and setting it on the kitchen counter, moving to the best light to study the photo more closely. The longer I look, the more positive I am it's him.

Within minutes, I begin to pace, waiting for my grandmother to come home. I only hope that of all of the things Grace said she would tell me, this is one she can.

CHAPTER 2

"How did my parents know Shawn Stokes?"

Grace is barely inside the house before I pelt her with my question. Her body shielded by a half-dozen plastic grocery bags hanging from her arms, I can't read her face, but the way she's paused—frozen—speaks volumes.

"Why is Shawn Stokes in a picture with me and my parents?" My question lingers a second time, and I wait until Grace begins to move again, taking a few of the bags from her arm as she ambles into the kitchen.

I wait impatiently as she begins unpacking bags of chips, bread, snacks, and other essentials—things she's bought for Kyle and my road trip, and I want to appreciate how kind she's being, but all I can do is bounce on my legs, anxious to know what that photo means. She's working on the third bag when I tug it away from her.

"Grace, please," I say, my heart now pounding so hard my hands tremble with the beat. I know I'm not adopted. My dad had a paternity test done after my mom left, and I've seen photos of her pregnant with me. I've heard the story about the long hours in labor. I'm theirs…genetically. But then how does Shawn fit into our little family photo?

My grandmother pulls a chair out from the table, patting the one closest for me to join her. For the first time since I've been here, I notice her eyes fall to my leg as I slide into my seat.

"That was from the bridge." Her eyes flit to mine waiting for my confirmation and back to my leg.

I nod.

"I saw it on the news, and I called your dad. He gave me a few updates as you recovered," she says.

"I've learned to live with it," I shrug. "I've been working with a trainer...to compete again. I play softball."

Her lips stretch and curve on the ends, and I'm suddenly filled with this need to defend myself, to explain that it isn't just a cute hobby for me. Competing is life.

I lean forward on my elbows and look at her sideways, square in the eyes. "I'm good."

The curve of her mouth pulls into her cheeks and her eyes crinkle at the edges.

"I hear you're *really* good," she says, sliding her hand palm-down along the table closer to me.

I'm not used to affection like this, and my reciprocation is slow and awkward, but when her hand grips mine, my fingers seem to automatically know how to hold her back. Her hand is cool, her skin soft, age spots and blue from veins coloring the top. I wonder if this is how my hands will look one day.

"I promised you I would tell you everything I could, but some things might be better left in boxes," she says, holding my hand a little harder, perhaps feeling my urge to run. I don't blink as I stare at her eyes—this piece of the puzzle is too important to forgo just because of a little pain.

"I'm prepared," I say.

She reaches forward with her other hand, and I mimic her movement, turning in my chair until she's holding both of my hands. It's the most uncomfortable position I've ever been in, being touched like this, but I think maybe it's more for her than me, so I breathe deeply and take it.

"I shouldn't have put that photo in the box. I didn't realize, but I suppose...I suppose it's too late. And maybe you really should know the full story. I take it by your question, you remember Shawn?" Her head falls to the side and her eyes soften.

"He's…" I'm not sure what he is—he's important; he's a clue; he's Wes's uncle…sort of. "It's weird, how I know him, but he was the caseworker for a guy I know that was adopted. He's also the boy's uncle…his brother adopted my friend."

She nods, almost as if she already knew this part.

"Am I…adopted?"

The question stumbles from me sloppily, sounding ridiculous in my ears, but I'm relieved when my grandmother laughs in response anyhow. The breath I had been holding rushes out, and I laugh sadly with her.

"Sweetheart, no. Though, perhaps after the things I've told you today, you wish you were," she says, letting go of my hands and leaning back, her eyes still on mine. "No…you weren't adopted. But…those first few years…they were…rough."

My brow draws in.

"I think your mom thought having you would be the missing piece…solve all of her problems, end the fighting with your dad," she says.

Except for that last argument, I don't have vivid memories of my parents fighting. I recall yelling, sometimes. I'd usually busy myself, or go outside. I was avoiding without even realizing it. There were a lot of times when the two of them were apart, too—my dad working late, my mom going to bed early. And there were periods where they wouldn't talk to each other at all—sometimes for days. They were good at pretending for me, I guess.

"Shawn was your neighbor, at least until you were about two, maybe three, and you spent almost every day during that time at his house."

I scratch away inside my head, desperate for something that recognizes what she's saying, but I can't find a single thread—I don't remember anything from then. The photo of him, his face—it isn't familiar because of those years, it's only familiar because of now.

"It was a long time ago." She chuckles. She must sense my frustration at not remembering.

"Didn't he go to work? Did I go with him? Did I sleep there?" I ask my questions in a rush.

"Sometimes," she says, applying that word to all three. "He had an extra room. You liked it when he had other kids, clients that he needed to find homes for. There was this one boy..."

She leans back and shuts her eyes, tilting her chin to the ceiling, smiling through a breathy laugh, and I know...

"You were both maybe two, and you fought over every toy that man had in his house. But you'd cry, and that sweet boy," she pauses to chuckle again. "He'd always give you your way."

Everything inside my chest is heavy, doing a slow slide down my ribs on the inside, my body sinking, my shoulders falling. I feel sick.

"Do you remember his name?" My pulse pounds in my ears.

Grace's mouth scrunches just before she speaks. "Josselyn, I hardly remember what day of the week it is."

My pulse stops.

"But I'll tell you this...I've never seen a pair of bluer eyes on a child in my whole life." Her hands flatten to pat the table to punctuate how special this boy's eyes were before she gets up and busies herself putting away her own groceries and packing a travel bag for us.

My lips quiver with his name, and I almost don't want to say, because it would be just one more strange thing, but at the same time—I have to know. "Wes," I hum.

My eyes wide on her back, I wait for any sign that I'm right. She keeps unpacking and moving things from one bag to another, and disappointment starts to wash through my veins when she pauses and bunches her brow, a box of crackers in her hand.

"You know, maybe...that sounds right. It was something short like that. How amazing that you could remember!" She titters, returning to her work.

I don't remember. It doesn't mean I don't know it in my gut, though.

"Do you know where Shawn moved to?"

It's been years, probably fifteen, but on the off chance...

"I didn't know him very well. Your mom and he were pretty close, I guess. When she was at home while she was on bed rest, pregnant with you, he would stop by and check on her. It turned into a daily thing, and your dad didn't really mind because Shawn…well, he wasn't really the hunk-type, and your dad was so worried about her pregnancy—you, my dear, were not easy." She glances over her shoulder at me, her mouth tucked in on one side and her eyes squinted.

"Nothing new there." I laugh, standing from the table, fairly confident that I'm going to end this trip with the full picture of just how poisonous my parents' marriage was, but not a single clue that will help me find Wes.

I leave Grace to finish in the kitchen and make my way to the spare room. I'm careful with the handle as I push it down and slide the door open, but Kyle's awake on the bed, hands folded behind his neck, elbows out, knees bent as he rolls his head to the side to watch me come in.

"It's creepy as shit in here. I think I was better off in that sewing room on the floor," he says, scooting backward and propping himself up on his elbow. I lay down next to him in the same position, and he reaches up and tucks my hair behind my ear then lightly pinches my chin as he smiles at me.

"I don't know what I was thinking with any of this," I say, blinking once, my mouth a hard line to match my hardening heart.

Kyle squints at me, then rolls to his stomach folding his hands under his cheek, resting his head sideways as he studies me.

"You were thinking that you'd just do this all yourself," he says.

I roll my eyes and puff out a breath.

"Do what myself?"

Kyle's body rises with his deep breath, and the smile fades from his eyes and mouth.

"Nobody's really looking for him. They've all given up. But not you." Kyle reaches toward me again, giving my chin the same pinch as before. He leaves his hand there and stares at me through dozens of breaths. "I believe you."

I suck in my lip at those simple words. I'd told Kyle everything I could remember, about how Wes caught the rock, about how strong he was, how he never had more than a scratch or two, and how I got the mysterious texts. It sounded insane as I spoke the words to him, and he never responded out loud. He just listened.

And he drove. He drove me here.

"You think he's alive?" My lips quake when I speak, and my eyes pool, so I smoosh my face against the cool sheets to hold it together.

Kyle brushes my tangled hair away from my face again, this time cupping my cheek.

"I do," he says. "And we're going to find him."

I reach my hand up to cover his and whisper, "Thank you."

We were supposed to go to my mom's grave today. I don't want to anymore. I buried her a long time ago, really. This trip was more about Grace, I think. Or at least, it's become more about her...her and me.

I sit up and rub my palms against my eyes, wondering if Kyle and I will ever get to sleep tonight before we wake up early tomorrow to start our trip to nowhere. I know Shawn doesn't live far from Bakersfield, because he made the drive to pick up Wes's things. I'm hopeful that asking around at a few places, maybe convenience stores in small towns, might give us a tip. I don't really have a solid plan beyond that, but I'm going to keep looking for as many days as Kyle is willing to drive.

"Josselyn," Grace says, her voice soft behind me, the tone delicate...cautious. She has something bad to say. I turn to see her standing in the now-opened doorway. She moves closer to me, handing me the small bag of toiletries she assembled. I take it from her and offer a crooked smile, my guard heightened behind my expression, though— waiting for the shoe to drop.

"Kevin," she says. My body starts to tremble with adrenaline. "You should see him."

"No." I can't even mask my cold, immediate response. I feel bad when Grace flinches, but no...Kevin is the devil. Forget my mom. Kevin is the villain.

I notice Grace's eyes shift to Kyle. She exhales and bunches her lips in thought, and before I can shift my position enough to block her view,

Kyle engages.

"Why?" he asks.

"It doesn't matter, why, Kyle." I swivel fast and my eyes bore into him, my teeth clenched so hard my jaw pops.

One blink and a tilt of his head only pisses me off more.

"We're not seeing Kevin," I say, drawing my line, which Kyle steps over immediately as he gets up from the bed and walks closer to Grace.

"Do you think he could tell her things, too? About her mom?" he asks.

"Maybe," Grace says, pulling her lips in tight.

"I think I've learned enough for this trip. I'm full. All filled up," I say, standing to join them, three of us in a standoff at the doorway, arms crossed over our chests—two against one.

The more breaths that pass with absolute silence between us all, I can feel Kyle's loyalty practically in a tug of war next to me. I'm ending it here. I'm ending it all.

"Whatever it is you're looking for, sweetheart..." Grace speaks before I have the chance. It's the first time she's not said my name to me, and it wasn't a condescending voice. There's no demand in her tone, no authority. It's something I've seen so little of lately. It's faith. "Maybe it's closure between you and your mama. Maybe it's something else. That's not for me to know, but Josselyn, you'll never be at peace until you've turned over every rock in your journey."

"Kevin's one hell of a rock," I say.

She smiles while Kyle breathes out a laugh.

"Yes, to you he is. But he's not a horrible man. I've come to like him over the years, and..." she holds up a hand, knowing where my gut is leading my mouth. "You don't have to ever like him. You are right to feel that way, and your circumstances lend to it. But he is a piece of your puzzle. And maybe...just maybe...he knows something you need to know."

My eyes flit to her and I search her face for more meaning behind those words. Why did she choose *those* words?

"Where is he? I'm...I'm not saying we *will* see him, I'm just...if I decide to, how far out of the way is he?" My hands start to tremble at the thought of seeing Kevin—his face from one of the worst days of my life is permanently etched in my memory. I've tried to erase it for years, but it's always there—lingering, like a demon that shows up in dreams to steal pieces of my soul.

"He's near the university. He took a job there, which is the only reason your mother and I reconnected as much as we did. I'm sure if it were up to her, she never would have set foot in the same state I'm in."

Grace doesn't wince. There aren't any tears when she talks of my mom. She shrugs, as if she lost a two-dollar bet on a horse race. But when I stare at her long enough, drilling down deep into her eyes, waiting for the moments where the façade breaks…just a little…I see it. My mom— she left her, too.

And it hurts.

My grandmother leaves Kyle and me alone, asking that I "think about it." Kyle doesn't prod, even though I can sense the voice in his head that's trying to send me a signal, willing me to see Kevin. I don't make my decision until morning, when Kyle and I are packing the truck and winding up the charging cord for our phones that we have to share.

"I don't want to stay there long," I say.

Kyle doesn't turn around. He continues fitting bags and boxes in the back of his truck, making sure the food is kept cool in the small space behind the seats.

"All right," he says, again without looking.

I smile as I watch him—my best friend. He doesn't want me to run.

"All right," I echo, my lip curling on the right as I lift the case of water to the tailgate for him to slide toward the cab.

After hugging Kyle, Grace meets me at the passenger side of the truck. She waits until Kyle's door is shut, then hands me a small paper along with an envelope. I can tell without peeking inside that it's filled with money, and I instantly refuse.

"Take it," she says, folding my fingers around it, covering my hands with her own. I notice the similarities when we touch, the same wrinkles

I'll probably wear one day. "I wrote down directions to Kevin's. And there's two hundred dollars in there, for emergencies or maybe…maybe you two stop and have a nice dinner on your drive home."

My closed lips bend and my cheeks dimple with the automatic smile. My dad was right about this one thing—he knew I would like Grace.

"Thank you, Grandma," I say, and I can tell leaving her with that word, calling her that, was important the moment she embraces me, pulling me tight against her as one hand cradles my head as we hug.

"I love you, sweetheart. And your mama did, too…in her way," she says quietly in my ear.

I nod, sniffling as I step back from her and climb quickly into the cab. I smile through the passenger window and press my hand against the glass to say goodbye, but Kyle can hear the change in my breathing, and he recognizes what I need. As he backs out of the driveway, he holds my other hand, and when we're out of Grace's view, he squeezes it tight while I let the tears run hot along my cheeks. I feel it all for three blocks, maybe four, and then I put the hurt back away, drying my face on my arms.

"Where to?" Kyle asks.

Unfolding the paper Grace gave me, I get my bearings and figure out we need to turn left to get to the highway. I guide Kyle along the thirty-minute drive that brings us close to the city. I find the exact house on my phone's map, and it doesn't take much longer for Kyle to park us across the street from it a few minutes later.

Turning the ignition off, Kyle lets the keys dangle as he sits back and stares out the window with me. We wait for minutes in silence.

"I know you don't want to push me," I say. "But you're going to have to. I don't want to do this."

"Then we'll just go," he says, quickly.

I roll my head to the side to look at him as he does the same.

"You don't mean that," I say.

He shakes his head and smiles faintly.

"No," he says. "I don't."

My eyes on my friend's, I breathe in deep several times, trying to fill my lungs and make my chest iron—willing myself stronger.

"I hate him," I say.

"I know," Kyle answers.

I nod, just glad that he's given me permission to still feel this way.

"Right," I say. Marching orders to myself.

I open my door as Kyle does the same, and together we walk without stopping until we're in front of a blue door with a stained-glass center. I press the doorbell button before I chicken out, and within a blink, I see movement behind the colored glass. My right hand starts to tremble and my left frantically searches for my friend's. Even when he holds it, I still shake uncontrollably, but the moment the man with gray hair, cut short like a military general, opens the door, my tremors stop.

His features are similar to my memory of him, but he's worn. His eyes have circles under them, deep with sags, and his cheeks are fuller. He's growing a beard, and he's traded the Cal State sweatshirt for a deep-blue collared shirt with his name embroidered over his heart: KEVIN TOWLE. I never even knew his last name. I chuckle lightly to myself, smirking as I pronounce it in my head—*towel*.

As terrified as I was just before the door opened, Kevin is twice as afraid now. His face pale, he hasn't taken a breath in the several seconds he and I have just stared at one another. He recognizes me—that much is certain. I'm not sure how, though—I look nothing like that child he destroyed with his inability to keep his dick to himself and out of my parents' marriage. We didn't send my mom photos.

"Did Grace tell you I was coming?" My voice comes out strong, and getting through this first hurdle bolsters my confidence even more.

Kevin's head shakes rapidly as he sucks in a sharp breath through his nose.

"No." His voice is weak, so gravelly, just that single word makes him cough.

"Can I come in?" I'm growing bolder.

Kevin nods, pushing the door wide as Kyle and I step inside. The house looks like my mom. It's the Kristina Winter's touch—I recognize it in the pale colors on the walls, the white furniture throughout the house, the wooden floors chosen in a shade to hide the dirt. It's a small space— a historic home on an immaculate street with driveways filled with expensive cars. It's nothing at all like Bakersfield. I bet she was happy here.

"It's nice," I say, spinning to look at Kevin. He's leaning against a wall near the doorway. *He's afraid to let me too far inside.*

"We renovated when we moved in," he says, his voice fading into the sound of him clearing his throat.

I breathe out a short laugh and turn to look around some more, finding my own way through the hallway to a small sitting room across from the kitchen. Kevin has no choice but to follow, and Kyle stays by my side.

My hand grazes along the arm of a cream canvas sofa, and I close my eyes picturing the yellow and green one we have at home—holes taped closed on the corners, wooden legs scuffed from cleats and vacuum cleaners. Our couch is older than I am, and this one looks like a showroom piece. I decide I don't want to sit on it.

"I'm not sure why I'm here really," I say, folding my arms over my chest and shifting my weight. My eyes move to Kevin in fits. I can't seem to look at him long.

"Your mom...she wanted to see you..."

I chuckle.

"No, she didn't," I say through a tight smile that hides the bile taste forming at the back of my throat.

Kevin's eyes sag and he moves to a chair across from the couch. Sitting, he brings his elbows to his knees, leaning forward as he clasps his hands together, fidgeting. I notice the gold band he's still wearing, and I have to look away again.

"She did...at the end. I know..." he stops to exhale, and the sound brings my gaze back to him. It's his turn to look somewhere else. Eyes on the floor now, he continues.

"I know it was probably too little too late, but when Kristina was sick, she did a lot of...I don't know...soul searching I guess?" He looks up, and for the first time our eyes lock, and the jolt of it presses my heart fast against my bones.

"It was too late," I say, pushing my voice to be strong, to hide the crumbling inside.

"I know," Kevin responds in a whisper.

I cross the room to the kitchen side and drag my hand along a smooth, granite counter, then open a cabinet door to see stacks of patterned dishes inside. A set.

"Can I get you something to drink?" Kevin asks. I pause with my back to him and my fingers curled around the handle of a drawer.

"I'm fine, thank you," I say, pulling the drawer open to see shined silver spoons, knives, and forks. I let go and give the drawer a tiny push and watch it close the rest of the way on its own.

"I'm fine, too. Thank you," Kyle says. I smile with my face away from them because I know my friend could be dying from thirst and he'd turn down Kevin's offer just to show solidarity with me.

"You know the molding around our kitchen floor is missing?" I turn to face Kevin again, meeting his eyes. His mouth is turned down, sour because I'm making him feel uncomfortable. "Yeah, it's funny—my dad and I were trying to fix the sink once, and we didn't turn the water all the way off, so the whole room just flooded," I say, laughing through my words. "Nearly a decade and we still haven't replaced the wood."

Kevin blinks slowly, and his mouth remains a straight, emotionless line. I lean into the counter behind me, resting my palms on the edge, and stare at him while my teeth chew at the soft tissue inside my lip. A minute passes without a word, and then...

"I'm not going to apologize," he says, and my heart begins to kick wildly, the rhythm felt in my stomach, my toes, my fingertips.

"I didn't come here for one," I spit back, my fingers on my right hand tapping along the underside of the counter where I grip it. It's true; I didn't come here seeking that. It doesn't mean he shouldn't say sorry, and it doesn't mean I don't want him to grovel and beg for forgiveness. I just don't expect it.

Kevin's eyes move to my leg, and I wait while he stares. He won't ask. I'm sure he's heard from Grace.

"I loved her. And your dad is a drunk who didn't treat her right," he says, eyes flitting to mine again.

My breathing picks up speed at the mention of my father. Months ago, I would have agreed with him. Hell, I would have high-fived him and probably run away to live here instead of in the misery that was Bakersfield, but that was before…before *everything*.

"*Was* a drunk," I say.

Kevin's eyes glower.

I shrug my right shoulder and push away from the counter to come back to the sitting room. "He got sober. I lost my leg. He and I are closer now, and you are still a homewrecker," I say, every word feeling as good as I'd imagined it would.

"You feel better?" Kevin stands, running his hand through his thinning hair. He's still trembling, though not as much.

"Nope," I shake my head.

We both avert our eyes for a few long seconds, and eventually Kevin leaves the room, heading into a bedroom in the back.

"This was a mistake," I say to Kyle while we're alone.

"You keep saying that about everything," he smirks.

"Shut up," I say, tugging the collar of his T-shirt and motioning for him to follow me back toward the front door.

Kevin cuts us off on our way, an old yellow envelope in his hands.

"Before you go," he says, fidgeting with it before finally handing it to me.

I don't reach for it right away, not sure I want to know what's inside. Like coming in here, looking in there might just make me feel worse.

"Take it," he says. "They're pictures, mostly. A lot of them of you. Your mom sorted them, and she could never throw them away. She kept them in this envelope, and you…you should have them. They mean something to you, or maybe they will. I don't know."

I grip the envelope and hold it against my chest, nodding as I look down to our feet.

"All right," I say.

"Joss, I wish I had more to give you. I wish I had more to say, but I just…I don't," Kevin says. "I'm not sorry I loved your mom, and I don't regret my life with her. But I am sorry you were hurt as a result. I can say that."

I pull in my lips and suck, fighting the urge to tell him to go fuck himself.

"All right, then," I decide on. It's laced with an F-U, and that's enough.

Kyle opens the door, and I follow him back out to our truck. Kevin doesn't linger to watch us leave, and I hear the door close behind us after our first few steps outside. We don't speak for several miles, not saying a word until Kyle pulls onto the highway, pointing us back toward home. I don't even want to search for Wes anymore. I'm no closer than I was days ago. I have nowhere to begin.

"Where to?" my friend asks.

"Home," I say, sighing as my head nestles against the window.

"Okay," Kyle says, turning on the stereo, searching for any decent station to come in. He settles on an alt rock one.

We drive the straight line through the desert for almost an hour before I move. I think about closing my eyes, but sleeping on the road has never been easy for me. I feel the sun's heat against the glass, and it grows warmer every minute until I have to move my head away. My eyes catch the envelope that I've wedged between the doorway and the seat, so I reach for it and pull it into my lap.

"You sure you want to open that now?" Kyle asks.

"Why not," I shrug.

Kyle turns his attention back to the road while I slide out a stack of photos and cards, setting them on top of the envelope. I flip through several photos first—most of them baby photos of me, or pictures of me as a toddler. One of me covered in mud makes me laugh and I hold it up for Kyle to see.

"Ha, even then—always willing to get dirty," he laughs.

I sneer at him, but pucker my lips in a tight smile and put the photo back in the stack on my leg. I flip through a few cards, next. They're birthday cards for me that my mom never sent—one for twelve, one for thirteen, and finally one for eighteen. I open that one because my birthday was two weeks ago, which means she bought this one in advance...before she died.

The message inside is short, but her handwriting is still the same. I let my thumb follow the curve of her *J* as I read.

Dear Joss,
I wish I got to see you turn eighteen. I could never explain, but I just had to. I was suffocating. Never because of you. I hope you do something big with your life.
Love,
Mom

The words should make me cry, but they don't. I read the note twice and feel nothing. I don't bother with the other birthday cards, and I gather everything into a pile and push it back inside. My fingers feel something along the inside as I do, though, and I take one last envelope out to look at. It's a letter, addressed to my mom. There's no name, but the return address says LAKE ISABELLA.

The paper is crisp and yellowed at the edges as I pull it out, so I unfold it carefully. The writing is faint pencil that's been smudged in a few places, but I'm able to make out the words at the top.

Kristina,

I heard you and Eric divorced. I'm very sorry. I hope I'm not intruding, but I tracked down your address online. I hope this is the right one. I wanted to make sure you were all right, and I wanted to make sure Josselyn was taken care of. I worry about her, with Eric's drinking. Please do let me know if there's anything I can do to help, especially with Joss. I love that girl as if she were my own.

I hope you find much happiness.

Your friend,
Shawn

I grip Kyle's arm instantly and sit up straight in the seat, flipping the page over and looking for more. That's all he wrote, but that's enough. The envelope—that's enough. I let go of Kyle, who has now stopped on the side of the highway, other cars whizzing by at high speeds.

"It's him," I say, unfolding the letter again and pointing to the name.

Kyle squints to look at it, then takes it in his hand.

"Shawn…that…you think it's *that* Shawn?" My friend's eyes widen on mine.

"It has to be," I say swallowing hard and looking at the address on the envelope, my hands shaking as I try to type the numbers in on my phone's map. Kyle plugs the charger in to his truck and gives me the other end so I don't run out of juice. Shawn was always home for Wes. When foster families gave up on him, he'd end up back in Shawn's care. The man has been Wes's one constant—as a social worker, and as an uncle who knew Wes belonged with the Stokes family along with Levi and TK.

"Lake Isabella," I say.

"That's so close to home," he says.

I nod, my stomach fluttering, my pulse racing throughout my body.

Kyle shifts the gear and looks over his shoulder, pulling us back onto the highway, his foot heavy on the gas. I watch his speedometer approach a hundred before he eases off, but he doesn't let up much.

He believes it's the right Shawn, too. And even more—he believes we're close.

We're close to finding Wes.

CHAPTER 3

It's night by the time we near Lake Isabella. Not even early night. It's late. Just after ten. My needs won't wait until morning, though. I wouldn't be able to sleep if I were forced to. Kyle doesn't ask, either. He lets me navigate him directly to the address on the envelope.

The homes around here are rather random, and the roads are just as bad. We wind along a dirt road closer to the lake when we eventually spot a mailbox with the right numbers to match the address on my envelope.

"You think this is it?" Kyle asks as he pulls to a stop, his tires kicking up a cloud of dust that fogs our view of the small gray trailer about a hundred yards away.

I take a deep breath and blow it out, letting my lips make a flapping sound as I raise my shoulders.

"That didn't sound confident," Kyle laughs.

"It's not," I chuckle back.

Kyle eases his foot from the brake and the truck crawls closer, crunching along the ground underneath us. I turned the radio off about an hour ago. My nerves couldn't handle sound any longer. Now, the sound of the tires rolling seems deafening.

Kyle stops about halfway between the mailbox and the mobile home, shifting to park and then turning the truck off. I flex my fingers then form a fist, trying to push feeling to the tips. My heart starts to pound loudly in my ears, and I swallow once because I'm starting to feel nauseous.

"I don't see his van," I say, pausing to stare at our destination for another minute. "There's a ramp, though. The last time I saw Shawn, he was in a wheelchair. He would need a ramp."

"Yeah…he would." Kyle folds his arms over the steering wheel and leans forward, squinting. "There's a light on; you can sorta see it through the blinds."

I nod, my head shaking vigorously.

"We should go knock," he says.

I nod again, but I don't move. For almost a full minute before he opens his door and turns to me, Kyle lets me sit still, except for the trembling in my legs.

"I can do it. If you want."

I shift to the side and meet his eyes, a voice inside of me screaming, "Yes, please!" I eventually shake my head, though. He can't do it. This…it needs to be me. All of this needs to be me. This is my quest for answers, and I need to be the one marching toward the people who can answer my questions.

"Okay, but I'm coming with you. This is the kind of place where people have bodies preserved in freezers covered in weeds in the backyard," he says as he steps from the truck, watching me and waiting for me to do the same.

"Encouraging," I deadpan.

Kyle's lips pucker a smirk.

One more breath, and I exit quickly, shutting the truck door before I have a chance to back out. I meet Kyle by the front of his truck, and without thinking we both link hands, his squeeze tight—reassuring. Our feet crunch along the loose gravel and dirt that lead us here, and we keep a slow but steady pace up the ramp until I'm faced with a vinyl-covered door. My eyes run along the NO SOLICITING sign taped above the chipped-gold doorknob, and I instantly concoct a lie in case whoever answers this door isn't Shawn. We'll say we were lost or that someone gave us the wrong address.

I look at Kyle and nod, my teeth clenched and my jaw locked with nerves as he nods back, raises his hand and knocks on the door. The knob jiggles when he does, and within a second or two I can feel the deck beneath us vibrate from movement inside the home.

My eyelids sweep closed, and I don't let them open until I hear the door opening. When my eyes meet Shawn's, I'm not sure if I should cry or scream. He doesn't speak right away, but he leans his weight back into his chair, his head falling slightly to one side as his mouth curves into a slight grin.

"Josselyn."

I'm rushed all at once with everything I've learned over the last forty hours. He's said my name before—many times. He wrote my name to my mom. He fed me, clothed me, soothed me, watched over me. Why are he and I so intertwined? Why have I never known this connection?

"Can I come in?"

I feel Kyle's hand let go of mine, but move to my lower back. As it does, Shawn's attention flits to him.

"Shawn Stokes," he says, reaching his palm for my friend.

Kyle looks to me first, and I nod. He lets his hand drop from my back and brings it to connect with Shawn's, his eyes narrowed.

"Good to meet you, sir."

Shawn's mouth tugs up higher on one side as he chuckles at my protector. When he lets go from their shake, his hand moves to his right wheel, and he turns it enough to unblock his entrance.

"Come on in," he says, holding his palm open and gesturing inside.

I pause for a second, and in my hesitation, Kyle's hand returns to my back.

My eyes focus first on the brown sofa against the wall across from me. I head there quickly, my legs shaking. I sit down fast, leaving enough room for Kyle to sit by my side. Shawn reaches out and grabs a band on his door, pulling it closed, then smirks when he faces us.

"Sometimes I can't reach the damn door to shut it. I believe you'd call that there one of those life hacks," he says, laughing lightly. I join him for a second, but mostly from nerves.

Our eyes quickly settle on one another. *How many times have I looked into these eyes as a baby?* I study him as he studies me. While I explore his face

32

for any trigger of a memory—other than the time I met him at the Stokes's house—I feel as if he's flooded with memories from looking at me. His eyes dazzle, slight wrinkles on the sides, his cheeks puffed out and pulled high with the smile that slowly forms on his mouth.

He looks away and pushes into his kitchen, pulling a few glasses from a drying rack on the counter. My gaze drifts.

"Can I get you guys something to drink? Juice? Or I have some tea. I don't think I've got any soda, sorry."

"I'll take a water, thanks," I say.

"Make it two," Kyle adds.

My focus dances around the room. It's a simple home—one main living space that consists of this couch, a television and a reading lamp, bleeding right into a kitchen area with a small card table pushed up against the wall. No chairs, and nothing on the floor except for a few plastic bins stacked near the television. A wide doorway to my left leads to what looks like his bedroom and probably bathroom. As for the floorplan, it's essentially two squares attached by a door.

The walls, however, tell a much different story. They're filled with organized clutter—glass cases mounted with comic books displayed, figurines lined on shelves, signed drawings framed and bunched together, superhero costumes pinned to the walls in the shape of the man or woman who they were probably made for.

I don't stop darting my eyes around the room until Shawn is in front of me, holding out a glass of water.

"Thank you," I say, taking it into both of my shaking hands. Unable to fight the urge, my eyes move back to the various displays. Shawn hands Kyle his water, which he removes from the cup holder affixed to the side of his chair, then twists so he's sitting directly across from me. He follows my gaze to the wall of costumes, and begins to chuckle.

"It's a hobby. I've been obsessed since I was a kid. When my dad died, I inherited his collection. Most of the costumes were his," he says.

I nod slowly and pull my lips in, smiling, mostly to be polite. Shawn holds up a finger and moves over to the stack of bins, pulling the one on the top into his lap before pushing back to me. He starts to rifle through a few cards and small booklets, finally pulling out a wax envelope and handing it to me.

My brow bunches and I look to him for permission before opening it.

"Sure, go on. But just hold it by the edges," he says.

With tentative fingers, I bend the flap and reach inside, pinching a piece of film reel. I hold it up to the light to see if I can make out the action happening in the four or five frames.

"They all look about the same. It's a hiccup worth of twenty-millimeter from one of the first prints of *The Shadow*. I got that last week at an estate sale. That little piece right there is worth a couple thousand bucks."

My fingers shake when he tells me that, so I work the strip back into the envelope and return it to him.

"I'm sorry, I don't know what *The Shadow* is," I say, tucking my hands under my thighs to ease the trembling.

Shawn pulls the bin close to his stomach and curls his hands over the rim, shaking it with his laugh.

"No, I suppose young kids like you wouldn't know anything about that," he says, his eyes coming back to that comfortable rest on me again.

I look down to my lap and start to pick at the nail on my left thumb. Kyle slides his foot into mine, and I glance up at him to see him nod slightly.

"Something you come up here to talk about? The way I figure, you must have gone through a bit to find out where I live, maybe some trouble to get here, too, this late at night and all." Shawn breaks our short silence. Kyle nods to me again.

I draw in a deep breath and leave my chest full as I turn back to our host. He knows what I'm here for. He knows everything I now know— I'm sure of it by the way he's studying me. It's like a force field has been removed.

"I found this…I was visiting my grandmother, and she gave me a few of my mom's things," I say, sitting up enough to slide the photo of him and me out of my back pocket.

His eyes warm and a tiny gasp escapes him, his smile growing fast as he takes the photo into his palms before removing a pair of glasses from his pocket and sliding them on his face.

"Would you look at that. There's hair on my head," he says, belly shaking again as his throat crackles with laughter. He turns his mouth into his sleeve to cough, but quickly returns to examining the photo.

My foot begins to tap the longer he stares at the pair of us without speaking, but I wait. He isn't denying anything. He's just not explaining.

"You were so small," he finally says. My foot pauses with my toes in the air, heel to the floor. "Did you know you were born three weeks early?"

I blink once…twice.

"No," I say.

"You were," he says, glancing up at me over the rims of his glasses then down to the photo. He holds it for a few more seconds before giving it back. "You were this tiny little thing. Skinny arms and legs. You grew strong, though. It seems like it only took you days to make up what you were missing."

Shawn's eyes travel down to my leg then blink back to my face. He begins to nod slowly, I presume applauding how far I've come with my prosthetic and rehab. I am stronger. I'm stronger now than I ever was.

"You were our neighbor…that's what Grace said." My words are coming more easily, yet still not easy enough.

"I was. I probably should have said something when I saw you, but I don't know…it didn't seem like the time, and a person doesn't really remember things from when they were two."

His eyes linger on me when he's done answering. Every time he stares, his mouth ticks up just a hint. It's how I know we're both playing a game. He's trying to unearth exactly how much I know, or *think* I know, about Wes and what he can do, while I'm trying to find the right words to get the answers I need. The thing about games, though…I don't lose them.

"You took care of Wes when I was little," I say, sitting up a little taller. I see Kyle shift a bit in my periphery. He already knows these details. We talked about them as we left Tucson.

Shawn brings his hand up to his face, leaning his elbow on the arm of the chair and holding his knuckle against his bottom lip. His mouth twitches again on one side.

"You remember."

I hold his stare for a few seconds, deciding whether it's best to lie and say I do or stick with the truth. Eventually I shake my head *no*.

"I don't," I say. "I wish I did."

His lips pucker, suppressing a chuckle that his body shakes with.

"You two have always had this...connection."

I can feel the crease form between my brows when Shawn says this, and he holds up a finger, winking as he backs away and rolls down the hallway.

"I don't think I trust this guy," Kyle whispers as he leans into me.

"He knows something. Just play along," I say back, my voice hushed.

I spend the next minute or two it takes Shawn to find whatever he's looking for in the back room bouncing my left leg up and down. My right one hurts, and I haven't stretched like I should, or like my body is used to, so I rub my thigh and press on my quad muscle with my thumbs.

"We need to get you home," Kyle says, less quiet.

"We need to find Wes. That's our priority," I snap back, shutting my mouth when I hear Shawn approaching.

Kyle looks to our host then back to me, nudging me with his elbow until I meet his eyes. His brow lowers slightly, and his lips pinch at the corners, stretching his mouth into a tight, straight line. I shake him off. I know he's worried about me, but this is more important. It just...is.

"I'm glad I kept this," Shawn says, moving close to me again.

His thumb is marking a page inside a leather-bound photo album. He flips it open in his lap then turns it to face me. I recognize the bricks— the curve of the grass and line of rose bushes that still exist next door to my house. The grass has died some over the years, and the bushes bloom less, but it's still the same.

"You were one, maybe just a little older," he says. My hand moves in to the photo as I pull the book closer to me, my finger tracing the spot where the little boy's hand is holding mine. "You'd just mastered walking, but that wasn't enough for you," Shawn chuckles. "You...you were born to run."

My heart kicks at those words. As if it weren't already, somehow the air inside this small space has grown thicker—the atmosphere more serious. I can hear Kyle's heavy breathing. He's skeptical. I'm not. And Shawn is right. I *was* born to run. I was also born to fight.

"How did Wes end up with you?" I ask, not able to take my eyes off the photo. Both of us barely a hair on our heads, Wes's small hand is wrapped around mine, holding me steady as I walk toward a red wagon. I remember that wagon, yet this moment...I can't find it inside. It's gone.

"Not everyone is meant to be a parent," Shawn says.

I breathe out a punctuated laugh.

"That's true," I say, running my fingertips over the photo one last time before giving the book to Kyle so he can see. "Some people can learn, though."

"Not in Wes's case," Shawn says.

I pull my bottom lip between my teeth and hold it as my gaze moves back to Shawn. I think about the boy I remember—about Christopher. He's gone through many sets of people not meant to be parents.

"Why didn't you place him with Bruce earlier? Why go through so many foster homes first?" I ask, tucking my hands back under my thighs.

Shawn exhales as he leans back, weaving his fingers together and resting them on his bulging belly, the cream-colored T-shirt stretched tight around his frame and the denim button-down unable to close around his body.

"I hadn't really thought of it. My brother and Maggie had never talked about wanting kids, and to be honest, we weren't really close."

His response surprises me. I don't know him well, or his brother for that matter, but the few times I was with Wes's family, they always seemed warm and kind. And I never heard anyone say anything bad about Shawn.

Except, of course, when Wes told me he was dead.

"You and Wes..." I begin, but stop. I don't know how to ask him what happened, why Wes would say he was dead, especially when every fact I've learned so far seems to point to Shawn being the only constant person Wes could rely on until he was adopted. My usual directness feels like a misstep right now. I decide to take another approach.

"Why didn't you just adopt him?" I ask. Shawn's eyes haze just enough that I notice. A sort of darkness comes over him, and the way his mouth is caught somewhere between the straight line and a hint of a smile makes my arms and legs feel restless. I stand to give myself space, walking around the room to look at Shawn's collection more closely.

"I kept him as long as I could," he says once my back is to him. "But like I said—some people just aren't meant to be parents."

I twist and peer at him over my shoulder. His eyes are waiting for me.

"He wanted to stay with you," I say.

Shawn nods, confirming what I'd always thought. Wes must resent him for putting him through those years with the foster families who were cruel to him.

I turn my focus back to the framed prints of rare comic books, some dated back to the fifties. I only look at them briefly though, closing my eyes and balling my hands into tight fists in my pockets. It's why I came here. I have to ask.

"Is he staying here now?"

I don't turn to see his response. Without looking, I know his eyes are hazed as they were before. I know the not-quite-there smile is on his lips. I know my friend is nervous for me, for us. I know that I'm only getting pieces—half-truths. But I also know he won't lie. Not completely.

"He is."

My eyes open, and the first thing I see are a pair of eyes on a damsel in distress. It's a comic I don't recognize—the hero only outlined in shadows, standing on top of a building while the woman is being dragged on her back by something evil holding her tightly around the wrists and dragging her along the ground below. Her eyes are blue. Her hair blonde. We're glaring right at one another, only me...I'm real.

"He's alive," I say, my fists tighter in my pockets, my eyes unflinching on the drawing in front of me.

Shawn is quiet for several seconds, and eventually I have to turn around. My craving to see him, to see his expression, is too strong. The smile is waiting for me, and his eyes lock onto mine the moment our gazes connect. His head tilts to one side and his lips raise the tiniest bit more.

"Of course he is." Shawn waits patiently for my next question, and I file through my options. I want to win this game. I need to come out of this with Wes. It's not enough to just know that he's safe. I need *him*—to be able to feel him, talk to him. I need the safety that comes with his arms around me. No matter how strong I am, I'm not strong enough.

I begin to open my mouth to speak when Shawn starts in before me.

"You were looking at that story. The one on the wall," he says.

I shake my head and pull my brow in tight in frustration.

"Yeah, umm, I was, but…"

"That one's mine," he says.

I turn to look at it again, only glancing, then face him, folding my arms over my chest.

"It's nice. Where's Wes?" I'm done solving riddles.

"Look at it again," he says, nodding to the wall behind me.

I sigh heavily, stomping my feet to turn and face the framed book again.

"The girl," he says. My lips part and my pulse starts to race. "That's you."

My breathing picks up, and I'm not able to speak quickly enough to keep Kyle in his seat. He's next to me in a fraction of a second, not looking at the image I'm staring at, but looking at me.

"Let's go," he whispers. I shake my head *no*, tiny movements, just for him.

I reach up and put my hand on the button to open the case, glancing over my shoulder.

"May I?" I ask, my fingers trembling along the glass covering.

"You may," Shawn says.

I pull the book from the small clips holding it, but I keep my back to him, my reaction private as I look at the details of the drawing. The girl is maybe my age, perhaps a little older. She's wearing a white dress with short sleeves, nothing I would normally wear, but her right leg is shaded differently, a curve rounded just below the knee. She has a prosthetic.

"When did you draw this?" I ask.

Shawn doesn't answer, and the more time that passes, the harder the waves of nausea hit. My heart starts to flutter irregularly, and my hearing begins to fade in and out.

"Joss, you're pale," Kyle says, sliding an arm around me, holding me up on my weakening legs. He steadies me and guides me back to the couch, brushing the loose hairs from my face and tucking them behind my ears. My eyes struggle to focus on him.

"I'm going to get you more water," he says, waiting until I offer a nod.

Kyle takes the glass from the sofa arm and walks into the kitchen, filling it quickly and rushing back to my side. I take it in two shaking hands and gulp nearly two-thirds of it down. I've never been one to panic. I'm not panicked now. But I think I am a little bit scared.

"I hadn't seen you in years," Shawn begins. I bring my eyes to his, forcing myself to look—to read him for signs, for any doubts or holes. "I'd gotten a call from Wes's foster parents at the time that he was in the hospital, and things with him seemed strange."

"The Woodmansees," I hum.

"Yes," he says.

"How...strange?" My words are slow, careful. I'm not sure if any of this is a trick, where truth ends and fiction begins.

"The doctors wanted to do some studies on him, because his brain was injured but not in the way it should have been. He had some short-term memory problems, but the place where he took the impact—from the accident...?"

I nod slowly to him.

"Wes should have had major loss of motor function. Instead, he barely had a bruise on his head."

40

I nod again. I knew this. Even without Wes telling me these details, I always knew. He wasn't hurt when he should have been. He's *never* been hurt from the traumatic things he's been through physically. He isn't strange, he's…

"That's when I knew I had been right," he says.

"Right…" I echo, my mouth growing sour. I swallow, hoping to ease the tightness in my throat, but it doesn't help.

"I filed to take him back into my custody, to find him other arrangements, which is what the Woodmansees really wanted when they called. They didn't want the responsibility. Wes lived with me for another short period—weeks, maybe a month. And that's when I made that." Shawn points to the book in my lap, and my eyes follow, looking back down at it.

"You drew me with one leg," I say.

"I did," he says. I look at him, the smile now gone. His eyes slanted, his fat cheeks drooping with the corners of his mouth. I hold his stare.

"I knew your story the moment I held you in my arms, your tiny fingers wrapping around one of mine and your blue eyes open on the sky. I swore to your mom that day that I would always protect you. One look and I knew you would need to be saved. But I was weak—my body would not hold up to time. You would need a hero."

"Wesley," I croak, looking back down at the art on the cover.

"Yes," Shawn says.

I exhale heavily before looking Shawn in the eyes again. "Who is Wesley Stokes…really?"

The smirk begins to snake its way back along his lips and a breathy chuckle falls from his mouth. I'm not sure what I'm expecting to come from his mouth in response.

"You know exactly who he is, Josselyn," he says, his brown, sunken eyes unrelenting with their hold on mine. I dare him back, holding the stare until I realize exactly what he's saying without him finishing the word completely.

"*Super…*"

My head falls to the side and my mouth twists, one eye closing more than the other. I'm pretty sure Shawn is crazy. Not just wild with ideas, but legitimately and certifiable. Wes cannot stay here. I'm not sure how this book was made, or if he even drew it. Maybe it's something he found that reminded him of me, or of Wes, but I'm done buying into this fantasy. I toss the book on the table and stand with Kyle by my side.

At first Shawn's eyes look pained, and his mouth opens, gasping that I'd actually doubt him, but within seconds, he starts to laugh.

"Oh, I didn't mean that literally. He's not *really* some caped savior," Shawn says.

I roll my eyes and laugh once, hard, as I walk across the room, getting myself closer to the door. Shawn turns, his gaze following me while I walk.

"Those guys are all fictional, genius fantasies dreamed up by artists better than me long ago. There's a difference. Wes…he's real," Shawn says, and I pause because as much as I had just convinced myself that this was all a delusion, there's truth in what Shawn just said. Wes *is* real.

"I want to see him," I say, looking to the door, half expecting Wes to open it any moment.

"I'm not so sure he'll come home knowing that you're here," Shawn says.

"Why?" I ask. "He misses me. He *wants* me to find him. He…he left me this."

I pull the photo I took of the peonies from my back pocket and hold it out flat in my palm. Shawn's eyes narrow on it, and his mouth curves on one side, which makes my chest beat with hope.

"Look, here," I stammer, turning the photo in my palm to show him the words Wes wrote—a small note that promised he would be watching. Pushing the photo back in one pocket, I pull my phone from the other. I slide to my messages, to Wes's number and the image he sent me of my photo and where to find it in the field. And then I unclick the case on my phone and pull out the delicate ticket I keep hidden behind my phone. That ticket, the same one I'd given Wes as a child, is what gave me faith in the first place and led me to meet Shawn at the Stokes house. It was the beginning of everything, the start of real hope.

He takes my phone in his hand, the same smirk on his face, only his lip twitches a little higher. I wonder if he's proud Wes reached out to me, proud that his protégé doesn't want to abandon the girl he's supposed to save.

"Why would he send me these messages? Why would he lead me here if he didn't want to see me? Why wouldn't he just come home?" My palm trembles as I take my phone back from Shawn. His eyes crinkle at the sides as he looks at me, his head cocked to one side.

"Because he doesn't want the story to end," he says. I turn my head toward him, my chin falling to my chest. "My book. I wrote everything in there, and I haven't been wrong yet."

My eyes narrow, and after a few seconds I look back to the book on the table, the image suddenly more vivid and familiar. It's me—someone is hurting me. It's a moment that I have not yet lived. The very idea that Shawn knows exactly what's going to happen to me, though, is too impossible.

I turn my focus back to Shawn.

"I write my own story," I bite. "And tell Wes that I'm not leaving until he talks to me. I'll wait outside."

Kyle takes my hand as we leave, and I purposely slam the door closed behind us. I march to the truck, not letting go of my friend until I reach the handle of my door, and before I can push it down to open it, I fall apart.

"I got you," Kyle says, his arms quick to hold me, turning me to face him so I can bury my face in his chest.

"I won't leave until I see him, Kyle," I say, my words a blubbering mess against my friend's T-shirt. "That man…"

I start to shake my head, and Kyle holds me tighter.

"I know, Joss. This is fucked up. And I know. He's just some crazy guy, who is messing with you…with Wes," he says, his hand cupping my head to soothe me. I nod against him, agreeing.

"Wes has to come home with us," I say.

"I know," Kyle repeats. "He will. We'll wait for him."

I suck in air hard and fast, holding my breath and forcing the tears to stop. I push my palms into my eyes and let the air fall from my lungs, a fast rush through my mouth and nose. Nodding to my friend, I pull the truck handle and open the door, climbing in while Kyle waits at my side, his eyes studying me for any sign that I might lose it again.

"I'm good. I just needed to get that out. I'm…I'm good. Come sit with me," I say.

He stares into my eyes for a few seconds to read me, to make sure I'm being honest.

"I swear," I say, reaching up to press my hand flat on his chest.

Kyle grabs it and squeezes it tight, nodding and backing away to close my door. I watch him walk around his truck, and I count in my head just as I would when I had to survive one of my father's drunken rants. I wait for the calm to wash over me as Kyle climbs inside and turns the key enough to kick on the radio. I roll my window down and look out at the stars, drawing in a deep breath in search of a familiar scent—wishing we were in the flower fields instead of here.

I wait to feel like I'm right, and Shawn is wrong.

But I never do. Not completely.

And that terrifies me, because…maybe I'm crazy, too.

CHAPTER 4

Kyle's eyes aren't closed, but they're not fully open either. They haven't been for the last hour. My eyelids are heavy, but I force them to stay open just enough that I can catch any sign of movement before or behind us.

It will be morning soon. The sky is still dark, but the horizon has a glow that draws a fine line along it. The sun is coming, but Wes still isn't here.

"I'm sorry I made you do this," I say, my throat sore from saying words and fighting fatigue.

"You don't make me do anything. You never have," he says, forcing his eyes wide and wrapping his fingers around the steering wheel to stretch his arms. His mouth contorts with a heavy yawn, and he twists to face me, grinning through the end of it.

"I make you do all kinds of stupid things," I say, smiling as my head falls sideways into the fabric of the headrest.

"Yeah...you do," he says through crooked lips. I reach forward to punch him, but my tired arm only results in my fingertips slapping against his arm.

"That was pathetic," he teases.

I laugh for a few seconds, but the giddiness quickly fades, and I end up staring at my friend in silence for nearly a minute. He lets me, looking back into my eyes. Somehow, we're talking without words.

"I love him...Wes...I..." I stop speaking, pulling my lips together tight. I know Kyle knows, but with these last few days, this trip and how close we've become—closer than we've ever been—I just need him to

45

know my heart is still lost.

"That's not why I keep driving this truck, Joss," Kyle says.

A heavy breath falls from me, and Kyle reaches for my hand. I give it to him, watching as he turns it over and kisses my knuckles.

"I didn't do this in hopes that I could somehow win you over and take Wes's place. I did this because you and me…we do these things for each other. No matter what."

Kyle's eyes stay on mine, and I know by looking at him that what he said was true. He isn't trying to make me feel better. Kyle is maybe the greatest friend to ever walk the earth. Somehow, I got lucky enough for him to be mine.

"You think Wes can fly?" I ask.

Kyle's expression breaks, his mouth tugging high on one side as his chest jerks with a hard laugh.

"Yeah, and he probably wears tights under everything. And I bet he came to this planet in a pod," Kyle jokes.

"Oh my god, I'm in love with a pod person!" My laughter grows to hysterics, and my side starts to ache with a cramp from laughing so hard.

Kyle and I don't stop for several minutes, throwing out ideas like laser vision, magnetic hands, stretchable skin, and invisibility. As much as each concept is making me laugh at the absurdity of it all, it also makes my stomach twist, because whatever this really is, it's more fucked up than some superhero tale. I'm the key player in some man's mind game. So is Wes.

My mouth aches from laughing, and the curve starts to settle back into a frown. The world outside of Kyle's truck is starting to glow, not golden, but blue—it's that brief color that happens just before the sun crests. I watch as Kyle's face illuminates with it. His smile is gone, too.

"Let's go," I say.

"You sure?" my friend asks.

I stare out at the open road that stretches and winds for miles in both directions. Nobody is coming. And I'm not going back into that trailer.

I nod, and Kyle waits for a few seconds, giving me a chance to change my mind. He twists the key, and I sink into the seat, turning the air blower away from my face so I can fall asleep for the hour-long drive home. We make it a mile before I yell for him to stop.

"Jesus Christ, Joss...one of these days you're going to get us killed while I'm behind the wheel! What?"

Kyle's truck has barely finished skidding to a stop by the time I have my door open and I begin to run. I hardly hear him call after me as he climbs out from the driver's seat. If I were looking, I never would have seen him. I'd given up. The universe didn't want me to.

Parked a mile away from us, probably waiting there for hours, Shawn's van is shrouded by overgrown brush and a busted-up sign used to mark peak boating hours on the lake. To anyone else, it would look like an abandoned, beat-up vehicle left hidden to spare the world of how unsightly it is. But I know that van. And I know it still runs just fine.

He doesn't bother to turn the lights on, but I wish he did. If the lights of the van were blinding me, I wouldn't see his face looking back at me through the glass, everything around us growing more golden by the second with the sun's rise.

I've been obsessed with the thought of finding him, with the idea that he's alive and fine and surviving...somewhere. It is literally the only thing that made me fight so hard when I started rehab with Rebecca. Maybe it was seeing Shawn's collection, hearing his theories—experiencing his delusion. Whatever it was, something snapped as the stars began to disappear, and now I'm angry. I'm angry because I need Wes—and he isn't where he's supposed to be. He led me here, gave me all of this...*hope*...and yet he's hiding. Why would he hide?

"You fucking coward!" I scream, picking up a heavy rock from the side of the road and throwing it at the van. I manage to dent the bumper, but I won't be satisfied until I break glass, so I pick up another.

"Stop it, Joss!" Kyle growls, grasping my elbow before I can send another stone at my so-called superhero.

"He's fucking right here, Kyle! He's been here...right here!"

My face is hot, and I'm panting. My knees feel shaky, and I grab my friend's bicep, gripping it hard. My eyes are set on Wes, but my weight is held by Kyle.

"He's right here," I quiver.

Kyle doesn't speak, but I can feel his arm muscles tense around me. If he were face to face with Wes right now, he'd hit him. I'd let him.

"Why won't you move?" I yell. Kyle's hold on me loosens, and eventually his hand falls away as the blood rushing through my veins strengthens my body once again.

I take a few careful steps forward, the ground uneven from large gouges left in the dirt road from trucks driving through when the earth was wet. The closer I get, the more defined he is. His eyes, blue as ever, don't even blink. His chest rises and falls in a slow, even rhythm.

He wanted me to find him.

I move closer to the van, and I notice how hard he works not to look at my leg, so I stop near enough to see him—for him to hear every word—but far enough that he has to look at all of me.

"Is it this?" I shout, my finger pointing down at my prosthetic that's visible below my knee. I've gotten so used to it that I don't even get self-conscious wearing shorts anymore. My legs have never been in better shape thanks to the workouts with Becca. I still fight through doubts, but I'm getting better at not setting limitations. I'm learning to prove people wrong.

"Are you hiding from me because you think you did this?" My voice carries, echoing off of the tree-and-wood cave Wes has backed himself into. He just stares at me through it all. He's not even afraid of being seen. It's like he's torturing himself.

He's torturing me.

I begin to laugh, the breathy kind tainted with disgust, and I stop with my eyes square on his—my tongue held between my gritting back teeth. Slowly, my mouth falls closed into a clenched smile as my eyes become slits.

"You didn't do this. Life...life did this! Life just does things sometimes, and our job is to figure out how to cope."

I step closer, my fingers now on the curved hood of the van. It's covered in a layer of dirt, which makes me wonder where he's been. Was he looking for me?

"You know how I cope with the shit in my life, Wes?"

I drag my hand along the front of the van until I get to the mirror of the driver's door where I wrap my fingers around the chrome. His window is rolled down. I want to reach through it and touch him…*feel* him…hit him. My chest starts to pound so hard I'm sure it's making my entire body tremble. I hold on to the van harder, my grip so strong I feel as if I could rip the mirror right from the door.

"I get up every day, I go to rehab and work my muscles to exhaustion, because of you. I hear your voice, whether you speak or not. I feel you. I'm alive…because of you. I…*cope*…because of you, Wesley Stokes. It has always been you—always."

My lip starts to quiver, and the tears fill my eyes fast. I wipe my forearm across my face, but it does little to stop the shaking in my chest. I'm going to cry, and I'm going to be honest through it all. I thought I'd forced Kyle to drive all this way so I could find Wes and bring him home, but that's not why at all. I thought that was why, and maybe it was at first. And then I found out he *chose* to stay away. He could come home today. He could have come home yesterday…months ago. But he chose to stay away. So now, I do this so I can be the strong one—so I can move past needing someone to take care of me.

I do this to win.

"You're just like the rest of them," I say, sucking in hard and fast, working my shoulders straighter. I stand taller. "You left. Just. Like. She did."

Through everything, Wes has sat perfectly still—the only movement the slight turn of his head and blink of his eyes, rarely, as he followed me. But those words hit him hard. His nostrils flare, and that line along his jaw flexes. I remember those subtle movements from the first time I saw him—at least what I *thought* was the first time—on that pitching mound. His jaw tightened every time I frustrated him, too…every time he fought to keep me safe and I ran toward danger.

That's what this is. He actually believes the crazy man in the trailer, and he thinks I'm being reckless. He believes the delusions because some man who was obsessed with my mother drew a bunch of pictures on paper.

My chin sinks toward my chest as I move the few remaining feet until my palms are resting on the open window cavity. I couldn't look away from the blue if I tried. Our eyes are magnets, and the bond is electric. There's also something different, though. Every other time I've stared into those eyes, they've always looked back at me as if they were made of steel—unbreakable and unafraid. Right now, those eyes are shattered.

"Come home with me."

I hear the words leave my mouth—no longer the angry voice willing to throw away everything my heart swears by. One look from my boy—*my hero*—and everything that a breath ago was tough and determined becomes soft. I'd only be pretending I didn't need him, and I'm not so good at lying anymore. I don't want to need him, and I hate that I do.

Wes's eyelids close, and my chest fills with hope that's dashed just as fast as it comes.

"I can't."

My mind tries to make sense of his words while his face contorts, his mouth pulling tight with pain, his eyes creasing on the edges as he squeezes them shut tighter. If the words are so painful to say, I wonder why he would say them.

"No." My voice crackles when I speak.

Wes's lips part and his eyes follow open. We stare at each other for long seconds in an impossible standoff that I'm certain is not based on reality. It's based on coincidence.

"I won't come back, Joss."

My heart bleeds. I feel it. I swallow, and my lips grow numb, tingling with urge after urge to yell something—anything—that might sink through the bullshit that's clouding him.

"You know that fortune-telling isn't real, right?" I wait for a reaction from him, but all I get is the tilt of the head, and more sad, blue eyes. "Crystal balls…fortune cookies…those booths people spend hundreds of dollars in at the fair just so they can get a glimpse of what their lives will be. Will they have kids? Will they meet the right man this year? Will they get that new job? It's all bullshit. It's a scam, Wes, and Shawn is feeding it to you for free just so he can…what…control you and watch you dance? I don't understand, Wes. Why are you letting him tell you how your life goes?"

"It isn't my life I'm worried about." A shiver crawls down my spine, and it's as if Wes can see it. His eyes move from mine for the first time in minutes, trailing along my face and neck, like a paintbrush soaked with color making strokes to fill in my form.

"If you're so worried about me, then why won't you come home?"

His eyes come back to mine with that question, and a heavy breath escapes him, his lips—those lips that I only want to kiss, if he would just let me—they're turned down on the corners.

"I've done nothing but hurt you, Joss," he says, his head shaking as he speaks. He actually believes it, that we're some disastrous formula. His logic makes me laugh, and I step back, letting my fingers fall away from his door as I bend over and laugh harder.

"You have been the only thing that's kept me alive, Wes. *Twice*," I say, my laughter cutting short the moment I speak. Four feet of morning dawn, warm air growing warmer by the minute, is all that stands between us, yet it feels as if there are mountains and valleys, raging rivers and fire.

I feel for the photo in my pocket, and for a few seconds, I hold it between my thumb and finger, my arm behind my back. My jaw grows hard the moment the truth washes through my mind. Wes didn't send me those messages, and he didn't leave me this photo. Shawn did. He wanted to keep his precious story going.

"You have no idea about this, do you?" I say, a sad, breathy laugh escapes my lips as I pull the photo out, pinching it on the bottom and holding it for Wes to see. His eyes pain quickly then flutter closed as his chin falls to his chest. "I came here looking for you because I thought you missed me. I thought you *needed* me…wanted me. I thought we were this crazy kind of love that defied everything bad in life. But you didn't want me at all, did you? Shawn did. He wanted me for his collection, to add more pages to his crazy, fucked-up narration about my life. And you—"

My breath breaks, my chest shaking hard as the tears are hot with their threats in the corner of my eyes.

"You never wanted me to know. You never wanted to see me again." I wait for any sign that I'm wrong, but Wes's only movement is the slight rise in his head, just enough to look up at me and stare right through everything I just said. The corners of his mouth turn down, and with one blink, his focus is somewhere other than me.

I hear Kyle's weight shift behind me, his footsteps coming closer, but I don't move from my position. I stand and stare Wes down, waiting for him to snap out of this trance. More than a full minute passes with no words at all, and he never flinches. He doesn't look at me again until Kyle reaches me and rests his hand on my back. His head moves at that touch, and his eyes widen for a beat. He doesn't like seeing me touched.

"You don't get to talk to me. If this is what you're deciding, then you need to disappear. Your parents, Wes…your brothers…they are…this has ruined them. They've fought so hard to even entertain the idea that you're gone for real. If you're not coming back, then you need to stay away from us all. And you can't stay here, because I know you're here. It's too close. You don't get to keep me from getting over you. That's cruel. If I want to love someone, you have to let me. If I need to move on, then you need to allow that to happen."

I lean forward a few inches, and through gritted teeth, I yell the rest.

"And if I find trouble, let me have it. I'll handle life on my own from here on out. You, Wesley Stokes, are no hero. You're just a fucking asshole!"

I turn fast, my eyes catching Kyle's, and he falls in step with me, his fingertips grazing along my shoulder blade as we take long steps back toward his truck. When I feel his touch fall away, I turn to see him striding back to Wes. I pause, but I don't stop him as he marches back to the spot

I was standing, reaches inside the cab and punches Wes in the face.

Wes just takes it.

I let him.

And when Kyle makes it back to where I'm waiting, we both turn our attention to his truck, climbing in and buckling while the wheels are already in motion. Neither of us speaks until the lights of Bakersfield are in view.

"School starts tomorrow," Kyle says.

I wait until he pulls up to my driveway, and I stare out at my dad's car, the garage left open, my gear stacked in the corner. Our dead yard, punctuated by a crooked mailbox, and paint chips falling from the trim of the house.

"Some fucking life," I say.

My front door opens, and I can make out my dad's form behind the screen. He repaired it last week. I helped. It was nice. It will have to be enough.

I open my door and grab the envelope and box from behind Kyle's seat, turning to my friend who looks at me with eyes that say he doesn't know what to do.

"I'll be fine," I say, and his head falls to the right while his lip quirks on the opposite side. "Yeah, okay, so maybe I won't, but whatever, right?"

He nods once, smirking.

"Whatever," he says. "Pick you up at seven?"

"Whatever," I repeat, chuckling as I slam his door shut and walk through the dead grass that leads to my front door.

Kyle's motor kicks in as he pulls away, and my dad pushes the screen open slowly, his eyes meeting the memories in my hands first then moving to my face.

"Grace gave me a bunch of Mom's shit to look through," I say, leaving out the part about Kevin and tracking down Wes. My story would sound crazy—and it wouldn't be wrong. It is crazy.

My dad doesn't say a word, only holds my things for me while I move into the kitchen and begin pulling out meat and cheese from the fridge to make a sandwich. After a few seconds, he makes his way into the kitchen with me, his hand frozen above the counter with the envelope from Kevin, and the tin from Grace propped against his side. He's staring at the open end of the envelope, and my stomach sinks, knowing what's inside. He shouldn't see any of it, but I won't hide it from him either.

"It's mostly photos. Some birthday cards she never sent," I say, keeping it off hand and pretending that it doesn't mean much to me. I'm not sure any of it really does.

I turn when my sandwich is made, sliding the plate on the counter and leaning forward, propping myself up by my elbows to eat. It takes my dad eighteen seconds to finally set my things down. I know because I keep count with chews on my sandwich. He knows I'm lying, but he also knows it's for his own good. Sober isn't easy without adding the baggage of betrayal and heartbreak.

"You were right about Grace, though," I say through a full mouth. My dad blinks himself out of his daze, finally switching his focus from the packages of photos and letters to me. His mouth curves in a forced, closed-lip smile. "Grace," I repeat.

"Oh, yes…I'm glad you got to spend time with her," he says, his mind only half invested in our conversation.

I take another bite and watch him closely before answering. He's twitchy, but he isn't drunk. I can feel that he's not entirely here, though.

"I am, too. She made the trip worth it," I say.

He nods, his smile meeting his eyes this time as he steps around the counter toward me, leaning over to kiss the top of my head.

"I'm glad that dumbass Kyle didn't drive you into the Grand Canyon," he says above me, squeezing my shoulder once before moving to the coffeemaker to brew himself a cup. He's replaced alcohol with caffeine. His breath smells, but not like reeking of whiskey or bourbon.

"We didn't drive that way," I say, laughing lightly.

"And that's probably the only reason he didn't drive you off a cliff," my dad jokes.

He keeps his back to me, and I can tell he'd prefer to end this subject on that note—Kyle and his driving. We don't need to get into the details and memories of Mom.

"Yeah…you're probably right," I say, my eyes lingering on the back of my father's head. He's staring straight ahead, no longer with me.

He's with her.

"Hey, I'm gonna shower and rest for a while, maybe take a nap. I'm three days old on everything," I say, still no response from my dad. I back away to the hallway, stopping just before he's completely out of sight.

"Dad?"

He turns slowly, coffee mug in his hand, and begins to take a sip when our eyes meet, stopping when the hot liquid hits his tongue.

"Right, yeah. Shower's all yours," he says.

I smile as I turn, but it falls away the second I'm out of view. I left this house in the middle of the night in search of answers, and days later, all I have is pain and regret. I crawl up on my bed and lift my leg, pulling off my prosthetic and stretching my quads and hips that ache from atrophy.

I lay still for several minutes, fatigue hitting me full force, finally. I'm considering postponing the shower for a nap when a familiar sound hits my ears. Our front door slams shut, and my dad's car engine never roars. Nearly five minutes pass without a sound, so I finally lift myself and move to my window, looking out to see his car unmoved from the driveway, and my dad nowhere to be found.

Dread I haven't felt in months drowns me in a flash. I move to my doorway, using the wall for balance, and I hop to the end of the hallway. My mouth waters with the urge to vomit when I realize the envelope is gone. I left it there, trusting that my dad wouldn't look. I didn't want to make it seem like I was hiding something. But I am. And I should have.

So much progress, and all it's going to take is a few Polaroids and an unflattering letter from a crazy man that used to live next door to undo everything.

My eyes zero in on the tin still setting on the counter, so I maneuver my way across the room to grab it, tucking it under my arm and taking it back to my room. I open it and feel around for my grandfather's pin, then fall back and hold it over my head, my thumb running over the tiny dents in the metal from the years he wore it on his chest. I bet these wings went to war.

I pin it to my T-shirt and cover it with my palm. If it's war everyone wants from me, then it's war they'll get.

Sleep comes fast, and I embrace it. I won't dream tonight. I won't let myself. In fact, nothing happens to me without my permission from this point on.

CHAPTER 5

The pain is there this morning…where my lower leg used to be. It's worse than normal, if normal is a thing, and it makes me slow to get ready. I have to let Kyle in while I finish brushing my hair and teeth, and he takes over my half-eaten cereal bowl for me while I search for my shoes.

"I don't think I have ever seen you without a Pop-Tart in the morning," Kyle says, slurping the last drop of milk from the bowl before setting it in the sink.

"We're out. Apparently, Dad isn't shopping anymore either, because we're out of pretty much everything. You mind running me by the store on the way home?" I ask, sliding my left heel into one of my favorite pair of Vans.

"Sure, but don't you have rehab?" Kyle grabs my bag for me while I jerk my right shoe into the correct position, and I look down at the laces for a few extra seconds, avoiding him.

"I'm not going," I say.

Kyle laughs immediately, but he stops when I adjust my posture and look him in the eyes. I reach for my bag, but he swings it over his shoulder and glowers at me, moving toward the back door and holding it open for me to follow. I drag slowly by him.

"That's your plan, huh? You're gonna just quit on shit again? Maybe pick smoking back up, mix some pills with a few shots of whiskey, start dangling out of cars, and maybe nosedive off a bridge? Fuck, Joss, you make it really hard to be your friend sometimes."

I stop a few feet away from his truck, but he keeps going, swinging my bag around his body and tossing it into the back.

"I don't need your shit, Kyle!" I shout, but my words are cut off when he slams his door closed and quickly turns over his engine.

My standoff is short-lived, mostly because Kyle won't make eye contact with me, so I walk to the passenger side and get in, clicking my belt angrily and nestling into the corner of the seat, against the window, because I don't want to be near him.

I expect his driving to be just as rushed—quick turns, hard stops—but that's not the case. Kyle drives calmly, even though I can feel the words he's not saying pounding inside of him, begging to come out. We pull into the school without another word between us, and I unbuckle and fling my door open without pause. Kyle remains still, though, and just before I slam my door closed, I catch him rubbing both hands over his face.

"What?" I huff.

His hands fall away and he rests his head sideways against the seat, tired eyes looking at me. "What are we supposed to do now?"

My brow draws in, and I squint one eye, irritated, not yet over my rush of angry emotions, and my leg still firing pain signals to my brain.

"We go to fucking class, then we go home, and I pull out my Jose shirts and I put one on and see if I can pick up some extra shifts, start back early."

"Not that," Kyle says, his eyes fluttering with his words as he shakes his head.

I hold the frame of the door opening and lean on my good hip, shrugging.

"What do we do with all of this fucked up shit we know? Wes…his brothers. How am I supposed to walk into that school, slap hands with TK and Levi, and pretend the last two days didn't happen? How is that okay? Their brother is alive, and I'm not supposed to say a word? What's *your* plan, Joss? How are you going to lie to them?"

My breath draws in slowly through my nose, and I force myself to unclench my teeth and let my jaw relax. I roll my shoulders and let go of my hold on Kyle's truck, taking a full step back with my eyes squarely on my friend's.

"I'm not," I say, then slam his truck door closed before I walk around his truck to his side, reach into the back and grab my bag.

I start to walk toward the main hall doors swiftly, but my speed is no match for Kyle's, and I feel his hand slide around my bicep to slow me.

"You can't just walk in there and tell them, Joss. I agree they need to know, but this has to be handled the right way. You can't…"

"I'm not stupid," I say, shirking away from his hold. I continue to move toward the doors, but not with the same determined march as before. Kyle's right.

I stop when we get to the main building, and instead let my bag slide from my shoulder to the ground while I sit on the short wall that leads to the gym. My eyes move to the baseball field on instinct. It's empty, and my gut twists at the thought of no longer seeing Wes standing out there.

Kyle sits on the grass across from me, pulling his knees up and resting his elbows on them, his back leaned against the opposite wall.

"My dad took off last night. I don't think he came home."

Kyle's face falls, his shoulders sagging as the air leaves his body. He knows my worries.

"That doesn't necessarily mean he's drinking again, Joss," he says, but his mouth pulls tight on one side after he speaks, because he knows it also very well might.

My gaze drifts back to the field again.

"I don't think I can handle it all—if he is drinking? I'm barely holding on, and that…I can't go back to that," I say.

Kyle doesn't respond. He doesn't have to. We sit out here—in the periphery where no one pays attention to us—until the bell rings. No longer able to pretend, we both stand and pick up our bags, then wait for our friends to walk up the hill from the weight room. My father made it to the gym for workouts, but then again…he always did. He never let the guys on his team down. And even though he isn't coaching them now, they're still his guys.

The boys pound knuckles and ask TK questions about football while

Taryn slides her arm through mine and walks alongside me to the stairwell. She glances at me, a signal asking if I need her help, but I smile with tight lips and shake my head.

"If you knew the exercises Rebecca had me doing, you'd realize stairs are like kid's play for me now," I chuckle.

I don't show off, even though I feel the urge to. I take the stairs one at a time and hold the rail on the side. I'm careful—just like Wes would want me to be.

"How was Grace?" Taryn asks the moment we settle into our seats in the biology lab. I wonder if Wes would have been in here, too.

"She was…" I slide a new spiral notebook from my bag before hanging it over the back of my chair. I breathe out short and fast through my nose when I turn back to face the table, flipping to the first page and writing the date.

"She was actually great," I admit, smiling on the side closest to Taryn. My friend mimics my expression. And responds with "Yeah?"

I nod and look down at the paper in front of me, pressing my pencil along the holes by the spine to draw tiny dots. "She gave me some of my mom's things…pictures, mostly," I say, biting at the inside of my lip, physically forcing myself to stop from sharing more.

"Was she glad to see you?" Taryn rests her head on her hand, looking at me sideways, and I meet her eyes.

"Yeah," I nod again, breathing out a small laugh and letting my smile grow until it scrunches my cheeks toward my eyes. "I think she was really glad."

"Then it's good you went," she says.

I can tell a part of my friend is hurt that I went to Kyle instead of her, but I needed my rock. There are some things—some of my ugliest parts—that Kyle will always understand best, maybe even better than Wes.

Mr. Dickerson clears his throat as he switches off the lights and closes the classroom door, so I straighten in my seat and ready myself to take notes as he flips on a projector and begins reviewing classroom procedures. I need to do well this year, preferably all *As* to prove that I'm not the poor student my transcripts reflect. But paying attention proves impossible, my mind drifting with every new point our teacher reviews. By the time class is over, I've managed to write down two bullet points, neither with complete thoughts or sentences.

I pack my things and wear my smile for my friend before we split up. I have algebra next—alone and in a class where everyone is a full grade behind me, and the eyes are on me the second I walk in. I recognize Bria from softball, so I take the seat next to her, near the wall and the back of the classroom, away from everyone's view. It doesn't stop people from looking though. I expected it—my story was all this town had to talk about for the summer, and most of the people in here don't really know me very well; they only hear the stories.

"I'm glad you're in here," I chuckle, sliding out my same notebook and turning to the next page, writing the date again with the intention of scribbling more relevant things down this period.

I glance back to Bria, and she smiles and raises her eyebrows, her voice no doubt choked off by the awkward questions now following me everywhere I go. My smile falls to a flat line and my eyes move down to the floor. I nod slowly, wondering how many times I'll have to do this today.

"It's okay to talk about it," I say, twisting my head sideways. She bunches her lips, pretending not to understand. "My leg. I know you want to ask, and it's perfectly okay."

Her cheeks become pink as she blinks quickly, looking down at her own pen and paper.

"Go ahead," I say, turning my body and extending my prosthetic toward her. I wore shorts today, hoping to get most of the questions out of the way. I notice a few students nearby glancing over their shoulders, too, so I begin to talk a little louder. "It only hurts sometimes, and it's mostly my other muscles feeling overworked or nerves that are sorta getting…I don't know…*tangled* I guess."

"Does it…like…feel different?" Bria winces at her question, embarrassed, so I try to set her at ease.

61

"I know what you mean. Of course it feels different, but you mean have I gotten used to it, or like when I walk, do I notice one leg isn't real," I say, more students turning around. A few get up from their seats at the front of the class and step closer so they can see.

"Can you run?" asks a girl sitting on the other side of Bria.

I nod and smirk, because I can, thanks to Rebecca. "I'm still pretty fast," I say.

"Do you have one of those metal ones?" a guy asks, standing to look over Bria.

"A blade you mean?" I ask. He nods. "I do. I only got that recently, and I'm still working with it. It's what I'll compete in."

"Are you going to run this year? Like track or cross country?" Bria asks. I pull my legs back under my seat and wink at her.

"Nope," I say. I keep my smile on my face, my lips tight trying to hold the laughter in as I look up at the teacher now writing notes on the white board. I can feel Bria's eyes on me still, though, so I lean sideways enough that she can hear me, and I whisper. "I'm going to be the state's number-one prospect."

I flit my eyes to hers, and catch her eyebrows lift with a flash as her mouth curves up a hint. I wink again, then look back to the front as I write down the first bullet point about when assignments are due. I'm already one up on my biology attention span.

English is another repeat of algebra, and I answer mostly the same questions to an entirely different group of students. I have weights after lunch, then government and photography, so if I'm lucky, I'll get most of the show-and-tells out of the way today. Only one person has asked to see how it works, so I did a demo right before lunch.

McKenna is in my English class, and other than my close friends, she's the only person who has asked about Wes. I told her she probably knew more than I did, because of my rehab work keeping me busy. I thought she'd gloat about it, even though it was a complete lie, but she didn't. Instead, she gave me a quiet nod of acceptance before walking to her seat on the other side of the room.

When the lunch bell rings, I pull my phone from my back pocket and start to text Kyle, hoping he's up for driving off campus for lunch. I'm not really up for spending my lunch on display, too. I stop when I see dozens of missed texts, though. Several are from Taryn, but the most recent one is from my dad.

My heart thumping with fear, I walk quickly, slipping into the restroom near the end of the hall where few people go. I lock myself in the last stall and hang my bag on a hook, leaning against the wall while I cup my phone in both hands. My fingers tremble, and I hesitantly slide the message open, preparing myself for the kinds of messages I used to get from my father—the pleas for help, the rants about my mom, the blaming and the hate.

Call me. Now!

My heart races faster, not sure if his words are a good sign or a bad one. My eyelids sweep shut as I press the CALL button and hold the phone to my ear.

"Joss?" I hear Taryn's voice shout through the bathroom door. The phone still ringing, I unhook the latch on the stall door and step out so she can see me. Her pale face is only outdone by the brightness of her white eyes, her legs teeming with energy as she practically bounces on the balls of her feet, her mouth wide, like an *O*, and her chest quivering as she struggles to breathe.

"Josselyn, come home," my father says in my ear. "It's Wes…"

My pulse stops, and the world goes quiet. Taryn is in shock, her arms waving at me to hurry, but my legs won't move. They're practically vibrating from my confusion and the jolt of adrenaline that hit me all at once.

"Josselyn," my father repeats. "Someone…somehow…they found him."

I breathe.

I hang up.

I run.

CHAPTER 6

I ride with Taryn, but text Kyle while we're on the way. He's already left school with TK and Levi, and when we turn the corner at the Stokes' street, I see Kyle's truck parked several houses away. News trucks line the road, and a few orange barricades block the street from traffic. Taryn begins to ask me where she should park, but I'm already out of the car before she can finish.

My father is pacing on the other side of the street, and I jog over to him, my eyes scanning through the growing crowd for Kyle.

"What's going on?" I ask. My dad holds up a finger, and I realize he has his phone to his other ear.

"Right, thank you. Just for today," he says, hanging up and gawking at me with an open mouth, unsure of what to say.

"I got a sub, for the rest of the day, I just…the school understands," my father says.

"Have you seen him?" My eyes blink slowly, like shutters on a camera, taking snapshots of every breath, every sound—every lie.

"Not yet," my dad says. "I'm not even sure he'll come home tonight. Bruce and Maggie must be with him. We had the TV on in the weight room, and it was on the news. We all just left. I haven't seen the boys yet to ask them any questions."

"I'll find Kyle," I say, sucking in a deep breath, turning quickly and rushing closer to the chaos.

I feel like a fraud, my muscles all working in unison to act with surprise and shock. I check my expression in the reflection at a squad car's window as I walk by, just to make sure I look the right amount of worried and elated. I'm neither.

I'm…confused.

Yesterday, he was never coming home.

Today, he's magically *found.*

I spot Kyle standing in the carport, typing frantically on his phone, and I call his name. He looks up and waves his phone at me.

"I was just texting you," he shouts.

I lift a line of caution tape and bend to slip underneath, but a police officer holds up a hand and crosses the street in my direction.

"Miss, I'm sorry, but this is a private residence, and you can't…"

"She's family," Levi says, jogging over to me and lifting the tape higher so I can pass.

"Thank you," I say, hoping I'm still making the face I was when I checked a second ago.

"We haven't seen him yet. His parents went to the precinct a while ago," Kyle says, turning to walk backward as we get closer to TK and Levi. I slow when he does, and he drops his voice to a whisper. "Apparently, Wes was staying at some church shelter in L.A. when he woke up yesterday and remembered who he was."

"Fuck, seriously?" I know my expression won't pass now, so I turn my head enough to hide behind Kyle.

"Joss, what the hell? Are we supposed to just go along with this?" Kyle asks. I shrug, but really, it's not like Kyle hasn't lied before. What's one more secret to keep?

"Joss, hey," Levi says, palming his phone and opening his arms to hug me. I practice looking surprised while my face is against his chest, and when I step away from his hold, I feel pretty confident I can bluff my way through the next five minutes at least.

"What have you heard?" I ask.

"I guess Mom and Dad went to get him from the county hospital. They said something about being worried about head trauma, maybe some nerve damage that affected his short-term memory. I guess when

65

he was little, before they adopted him, he was in a pretty bad accident," Levi says.

I flit my eyes to Kyle's, and my breath stops. It doesn't take much for me to relive that day, and I see it happen in my head a thousand times before Levi actually says it.

"I guess some dude ran his car into a house, or something crazy like that, almost hit his own kid," he says, and only then do I realize that Taryn has walked up to stand beside me. If I stop this now, it's nothing more than some piece of gossip Levi heard. Taryn won't ask questions; she knows I don't like to talk about it. I feel her fingers tickle against mine, and I know she's prepared to change the subject for me, but it's too late. Levi is able to sneak in one more sentence—the only words that can undo so very much.

"Wes pushed the kid out of the way, I guess, but not before the car clipped him on the side of the head," Levi says. My eyes are locked on Kyle's, but I feel Taryn's thoughts next to me. I hear her breath fall away, the tiniest gasp escaping her lips. She's put the puzzle together.

"How awful," Taryn says, and my eyes fall shut with relief. Her fingers reach to mine again, and I squeeze them this time.

"You have any idea when they might get here?" Kyle asks, and I turn, opening my eyes to look directly into Taryn's. I'm instantly a child, and she's my friend who tells everyone what to do. I need her to tell me what to do. I need Wes, but at the same time I'm so angry at him for staying away, for shutting me out, for changing his mind without preparing me.

"Mom said she would send a text when they were on their way. I hope those cameras stay away," TK says.

I turn to look over my shoulder, at the line of media trucks, reporters with phones out sitting on sidewalks, snapping pictures as they type their stories on tiny keypads. I'm sure this story is already trending on Twitter.

"Not a chance," I say, remembering a scene so very similar nine years ago. I was the one they were trying to take pictures of, and Wes—he shielded me.

"Maybe if we pull the truck out and park it there," Levi says, pointing to the small space in front of a squad car at the end of his driveway.

"They could pull all the way up to the door that way," Kyle says. "I'll move my truck, too. Maybe we can block off some of their view."

Both boys pull keys from their pockets and jog over to their trucks while TK moves to the center of his family's lawn, cupping the screen of his phone to be able to see it under the bright noon sun.

"You've never kept something from me," Taryn says quietly. My heart begins to pound, even though I knew this was coming. I knew I'd have to tell her one day.

"I know," I say, drawing in a full breath through my nose and holding my lungs full for several long seconds. I shut my eyes again briefly as I exhale, then I turn to my friend and look her in the eyes. She's hurt, and I can tell, but her eyes also reflect my own. She's just as confused as I am.

"Taryn…" I begin, only to be cut off by TK's rush toward us. He pounds his palm against the hood of the boys' truck as Levi backs out, then holds a thumb up, his cheeks puffed from the elated smile spilling across his face.

"That them?" Levi says, hopping out of the truck and rushing over to us.

"Yeah, got it. We're here, and the driveway is clear. Come in from the north, and maybe we can keep the news cameras out of our business," TK says, ending the call a second later.

His eyes bounce from Taryn's to mine, and eventually to his brother.

"They'll be here in two minutes," he says, his chest rising and falling at a rapid pace. Everyone's is—even Taryn's. Every heart in this small circle is beating fast, and everyone's skin is tingling, their muscles flexing with adrenaline and their spines soaked with the kind of magic a child feels when they think they've heard Santa Claus outside.

Everyone feels it. Everyone…but me.

My stomach sinks, and my mind races from thought to thought, wondering how I'll react when I see him, whether or not I should pretend or run. I spin mentally from how to handle Taryn—what to say and how to apologize for leaving her out of my secret—but ultimately, everything brings me back to this…to right now.

My friend has let go of my hand, moving to TK and linking her arm through his, and I can't help but feel hurt that she's abandoned me so quickly. I suppose I deserve it.

I turn to the scene behind me, reporters still quiet, unaware of the story that's about to pull into this driveway and splash across their channels at five o'clock or paint their front pages in the morning. My dad is leaning on the front bumper of his car, his arms folded over his chest, one hand's fingers tapping nervously on the forearm of the other.

Everyone wants this to happen right now, this way—everyone, but me.

I don't know what I expected…that I'd find Wes, our eyes would meet, and hand-in-hand we'd walk home together, no questions, no spectacle about his return. Right now, this way—it's the *only* way this could happen.

"They're here," TK says, reading a message on his phone.

Everyone moves toward the house, and I follow a few steps behind. My eyes go to my dad first. He pushes away from his car, standing and moving his hands to his pockets, his eyes roaming along the roadway, waiting to see the Stokes's car. I follow the line of his gaze and hold my breath, my focus fixed on the corner. A few reporters have caught wind, and they've moved away from their trucks, pushing against caution tape and breaking it in other places.

The car turns the corner, and my mouth becomes sour.

"Stay back!" an officer shouts, holding his palms out toward what has grown to a group of seven reporters. The group doubles in a breath, and in another, there are twenty people pushing against the arbitrary line the police drew in the middle of the Stokes's yard. Feet are trampling flowers, and camera posts dig into the ground while shutters begin clicking. The words of a handful of reporters begin to run together, each beginning nearly the same.

"The boy was thought dead."

"A missing Bakersfield teen is coming home."

"For the parents, a miracle has happened."

It's all just the soundtrack that floods my ears as Bruce drives slowly toward his home, wanting nothing more than to make his family whole again and hold onto his boy forever. A boy he told me himself is special.

A boy I know is special.

"They call him a hero…"

It's those words that stand out, the ones from a blonde woman standing in front of a camera closest to me, words that remind me of similar ones I'd recently heard from Shawn.

"You would need a hero."

My mind recalls what Shawn said, and I repeat it now to myself, my lips muttering silently as the tires dip at the driveway's edge, the car squeaking as axles bend. Wes is wearing a hat pulled low over his brow and one of his father's coats with the collar flipped up high.

When Bruce kills the engine, the media begins to rush forward, and that line the police thought they drew is instantly erased. I'm shoved by a camera-wielding shoulder, and Wes's brothers are both shouting, holding their arms out, trying to protect Wes from being seen. It's all so impossible. Those pictures of me in my driveway, the wreckage my father made, will live on forever on websites and in clips people cut out from papers, excited that their little town was famous from some tragedy.

Everyone will see Wes—the teenaged hero who has finally come home. This will follow him for weeks, maybe months, until something sexier, more tragic comes along. And even then, it will be revisited. His first Christmas home, his graduation, wherever he goes to college—every move he makes is news now.

I'm engulfed in a sea of reporters—lights and flashes—when Bruce exits his car and holds open the back door, trying to block everyone's view of his son. I stand on my toes and see the top of Wes's head followed by the deep brown of the jacket he's wearing. He moves, protected by his family, and by Kyle and Taryn, toward his home.

He shouldn't risk being viewed, but I know why he does. He slows, and his family does the same as he moves his hand from shading his eyes and scans the thick crowd now filling his family's property. Eyes so blue blink from the flashes, and his lips part, almost as if he wants to say something. I know what it is—he wants to call for me. I shift in the crowd, and I rest my hand on the shoulder of a cameraman in front of me. Ignoring his grumbles, I lift myself higher until his eyes find me in the madness, and I'm suddenly hit with a wave of fear.

His mouth shuts, but he takes a few seconds to look me in the eyes. Hundreds of pictures are taken, and photographers shuffle and move to get the best shot of a face so perfect that it will never leave my memory.

Wes is home. I should feel something. I should be happy and relieved. But he said he would never do this, and his uncle told me why.

What happens at the end of the story, Wes?

I blink and look down, and when I glance up again, Wes and his family and my friends have all gone inside. The cameras stop, falling away from shoulders as men and women retreat back to their vans and cars. They won't leave, not for hours. They'll sit out here and wait for a blind to open, for someone to come out that door and give a statement. They'll pounce on Taryn and Kyle when they leave, and they'll start knocking on doors to ask neighbors for their opinions, as if any of them could possibly speak on Wes's behalf.

My feet begin to retreat before I fully decide, so I listen to my instincts and play the part of a curious on-looker until I reach my dad. He nods at me, but I only glance and tilt my neck toward his car, urging him to get inside.

He waits while I buckle up, and when I'm done, I twist to look at him.

"I'd like to go back to school," I say, my eyes flitting to the steering wheel then back up to my father's face. His brow draws in, and he holds my stare for a few seconds before nodding once and pulling his mouth in on one side.

"All right," he says, turning over the engine and buckling his seatbelt before shifting into drive. He doesn't move right away, and I sigh in anticipation of his question.

"You can miss a day of training, you know. And school, for that matter," he says.

"I'll come back later," I say, sitting tall in my seat and glaring at the empty street ahead. I want to leave everything behind me…just for a little while.

"I figured you'd want to be here. I mean—" he starts to speak, but I break in.

"I figured you were done sneaking out to drink at night and crying over old photos of Mom," I spit out. My words are cruel, and I regret them almost the instant they come out, but I can't be here. Not right now. And I can't ignore the fact that my dad was gone, and he has a history of disappointing me.

We sit with the motor humming for several seconds, and I blink as I look straight ahead, fighting my father's silent pleas to look him in the eyes. If I do, it will break me.

"I don't know what's going on with you, Joss, or why you feel like you have to pretend that what just happened doesn't mean something to you, but I'll respect your wishes to leave now. But don't open old wounds only to cover up new ones, not when I've been working so hard," he says, and I can't help myself. I twist, my fist holding onto the seatbelt that crosses my chest as I stare into my dad's stubborn eyes.

"Where'd you go last night, Dad?" I ask, knowing I won't get an answer. My father's mouth remains a still, flat line. His jaw flexes, and I catch the movement in his cheek, which makes me breathe out a laugh. I fall back into my seat the right way and let go of my belt. "That's what I figured. I'll quit hiding things when you do."

My dad sighs heavily, but eventually he eases his foot off the brake and gives his attention over to the road. He drives me to the front office, parking at the curb to walk me inside and sign me in. I left my things in Taryn's car, so I'll need to borrow a camera for photography, but I already missed my weight-training class and most of government.

"I'll pick you up and take you to Rebecca in an hour," he says, his words spoken over his shoulder as he walks through the glass door, getting in his car, and driving away.

If it weren't photography, I'd walk out of the office and turn the wrong way, heading to one of the empty lots across the street, hidden by overgrown bushes and trees. I wouldn't smoke because that shit was really hard to quit, but I'd hide. I'd sit there in silence without anyone's questions but my own.

But I don't want to miss photography. I love it too much. And fuck Wes Stokes if he thinks he can take that away from me, too.

CHAPTER 7

"I can't believe I'm saying this to you, but you need to slow it down. You're pushing too hard."

Rebecca leans over the treadmill and hits the down arrow, slowing my run from a sprint to a comfortable jog. It takes a few seconds for my heart rate to catch up to the pace I just put my legs through, but after running what was maybe my best mile time ever, I'm no less wound up than I was the moment I came in here.

My dad dropped me off. "Some place he needed to be," is what he said. I didn't ask for details, and he didn't give any. I'm sure I won't see him tonight, though. My only hope is that he's spending all of this time with Meredith, the older woman he met in his support group that's become my father's closest friend. I've thought about calling Grace. I'm not sure where she and my dad stand with one another, but I know one truth about it—neither has ever disrespected the other in front of me. Grace talked about my dad's drinking, but she never blamed him for his disease. There's a certain respect there that must come from both being hurt by my mom.

My face is hot, and I'm sure my cheeks are bright red. The treadmill slows to a walking pace, so I work to lengthen my stride, stretching out the muscles of my legs while I work to regulate my breathing again.

"I don't know what brought this power surge on, but you keep working out like this and we're gonna have to start thinking about putting *you* in the Iron Woman," Rebecca laughs.

She tosses me the hand towel and I wipe the sweat from my face and neck. The machine stops completely and I lean forward, stretching the backs of my legs, feeling the burn on my hamstrings. Rebecca folds her arms and looks at me over the top of the treadmill.

"It's really something when you think about it," she says.

"What?" I chuckle.

"How far you've come," she says, winking as she pushes back from my machine and walks to her binder and gym bag resting on the windowsill.

I pull my lips in on one side and look down at my feet, legs bent forward at a hard angle, flesh on one side, metal and fiberglass on the other. My limbs work in unison to stretch in a position that only a few short months ago would cause me to fall to my knees. Today—best mile time *ever*.

My smile grows, and I laugh to myself as I step away from the machine and grab my water bottle from the window. After guzzling down nearly a third of it, I untie my hair and roll it into a knot, fastening it to the top of my head to cool down my beet-red neck. I'm soaked with sweat, and I feel terrible that Kyle has to put me in the cab of his truck, because I'm definitely ripe.

"There's someone I'd like you to meet," Rebecca says. She stares at me for a second, a proud smile hitting her lips, curling, and eventually dimpling her cheek.

"Why do I feel like you're fixing me up?" I chuckle.

"No, it's just…I'm genuinely proud of you. And when I set this up a couple months ago…don't take this the wrong way, but I wasn't sure you'd be ready," she says.

I bite my bottom lip and squint at her, tilting my head as I screw the cap back on my water bottle. Now I *really* feel like I'm being set up.

I wait while Rebecca reaches into her bag, fishing around for her wallet. When she finds it and unsnaps it, she pulls out a card, but quickly hides it under her palm, her hand over her chest.

"I would be there with you for the entire thing, and I'd be a part of the story, too…" she begins, and the moment she says the word *story* my head rushes with a fluttering feeling and my knees begin to feel weak. Shawn saw my whole story. Wes doesn't like the end of my story. That comic book Shawn drew—about my story—hasn't been wrong yet. Everything I burned calories and sweat to avoid for the last two hours comes barreling back into my head, and I miss the rest of Rebecca's point until my focus returns on the business card now in my hand.

"*Girl Strong*," I read the words. I glance at the name and title: EMILY COORS, MANAGING EDITOR. "As in…the magazine my dad used to buy for me when I was a kid?"

My brain somehow switches to the present, to the very real present with unbelievable opportunities. This is life, with potential.

"That's the one," Rebecca giggles.

I look back down at the card, no longer able to hold back the grin that pushes into my cheeks. My chest flutters with giddiness.

"They were going to do a story on just me, and after we started working together, I called them with this idea," she says. My grin now locked in place, I look up at her again, so very ready to hear more. "Your story is so inspirational, Joss. I know you don't like to think of it like that, but truly—there are little girls out there who are born with deformities, or who lose limbs or have disabilities that they think limit them. You prove that all wrong. I want people to read that story, to see your face and what you can do. What do you think?"

My lips part with an exhausted breath, my body coming down from my workout as my heart kicks with this news. While Rebecca's right, attention like this isn't really my thing, having people notice my work is.

"I've never thought of myself as a role model. In fact, a year ago I was probably very much an *anti*-role model." I laugh out my words, but settle into a serious mode quickly. I swallow at the honor and enormity of this, and my breath catches as I think of Rebecca's belief in me. Looking back down at the card imprinted with a magazine that has featured every major female Olympian since 1981, I nod and let my smile grow again. "Hell yeah, Becs. You just tell me what I need to do, where I need to be, and when."

"Awesome," she says, her hand wrapping around my very tired bicep. It grows rigid, and I look up to meet her eyes. "But seriously, you can call me *bitch* before you call me *Becs*, got it?"

I stare her down, and hold my laughter in. We've grown so close during our time together. Rebecca has become family to me.

"So I can call you bitch?" I tease.

"Only if you want me to push the up arrow on the treadmill next time," she says, letting go of her grip on my arm and pointing with two fingers from her eyes to mine.

"Whatever," I laugh, running the towel over my face one more time and staring at the card as I make my way to the locker room.

I text Kyle just before I get in the shower, and he's sent a message back by the time I dress and gather my things to meet him out front. I read it as I walk through the gym, stopping to hug my first trainer, Stephanie. I'm not a hugger, but Stephanie is, and when I hated everyone for a while there, she was persistent on being my friend. That kind of tenacity deserves a hug, I figure.

My phone is in my palm as I walk away from her workstation; I stop about ten paces from the door as I read Kyle's words.

I'm sorry. She made me do it.

I blink once before looking out the glass door to the parking lot, at Taryn's enormous Crown Victoria. If there were a backdoor to this place, I'd consider escaping through it now, but since that isn't the case, I grip the *Girl Strong* business card in my hand and remember that not everything is terrible and uncomfortable. That thought carries me to Taryn's passenger door, but it does little to help me breathe the suffocating environment that welcomes me when I climb inside.

"We're going to talk," she says, turning her key, shifting and backing so fast that her wheels spin out enough to fishtail her giant automobile.

"Kay, sounds good. Favor though?" She brakes hard and I fly forward, dropping the card to the floor between my feet when my palms flatten against the dashboard to keep me from smashing my face in. I grit my teeth, but sit back in the seat after picking my card up. "Mind if I buckle up before you go all demolition derby?"

I buckle fast because I pretty much know she's going to peel away again, and she does just as I hear my belt click.

"Demolition derby implies that I'm going to crash into someone, which I'm not," she says, stopping hard at the first light. I grip my seatbelt and cough as it locks against my chest. "I'm merely going to drive angry."

"Awesome," I mumble.

I figured Taryn was pissed. I understand it, and I know that all of the shit I'm going through doesn't really cancel out her feelings of being left out from my circle of trust. It's going to be hard to explain—perhaps impossible—but I'm going to try.

I rehearse it all in my head during the jerky drive home, but I'm no clearer on where to start when she stops at my curb and kills the engine. I glance sideways, hoping to see a smile on her face, or something soft that says, "I'm going to forgive you; let's just move past this." Instead, she's sitting with her back pressed hard against the seat, her arms locked, and knuckles white.

"Christopher."

I breathe out a laugh and smile on the side hidden from my friend. It's like reliving everything I went through, the suspicion and eventual reality.

"Yep."

I keep my eyes trained ahead on my street. Cars parked along the curb on either side, tires in front yards, a mom with her child splashing in a baby pool three houses down.

"When did you know?" Taryn asks.

"The moment he stood on the mound at the elementary school," I admit, turning enough in my seat to look at Taryn.

She chews at her bottom lip, her teeth sawing at it while her eyes squint as she draws from the memory of that day.

"Does your dad know?"

"No," I answer. "Nobody knows, except for Kyle, and now you."

She nods, but still doesn't look at me. The guy who drives the jacked-up truck that rumbles so loudly we can feel it in our ribs revs his engine a few houses behind us, and we both turn to look. When I twist back around, I watch her, and I know she can feel me.

"So he, like…saved you twice then, huh?" she says, resting her hand on the back of her seat and laying her chin on top.

"Taryn…"

Her body relaxes with a slow exhale, and finally she rolls her head to the side and looks me in the eyes. They're glassy, and I feel like shit.

"I wouldn't have told anyone. You could have trusted me, and I wouldn't have made fun of you," she says, sniffling through her words and running her red eyes along her sleeve.

I rest my head sideways to mirror her.

"I know," I say, reaching forward to touch her. She lets her hand fall down to mine and we lock fingers.

"That's some fucked up shit," she says, laughing through tears.

I laugh, too.

"T, that's not even close to how fucked up this shit gets," I say, closing my lips into a tight smile that eventually rests in a straight line. "Come inside so I can change, and I'll fill you in. I want to check in at the Jungle Gym, see if I can start back early. I want to buy a car, and Rebecca said a friend of hers owns one of those hand-control businesses that retrofits cars so you can brake and control the speed with your hands. Anyhow, they could maybe set me up for cheap."

My friend nods with a smile. We both leave her car, and the rumbling truck down the road, for the quiet of my bedroom. It takes me five minutes to change. I spend the next hour telling Taryn the unbelievable story that is my life.

And in the end, there are three of us who now need to lie to the faces of people we love—all because Wesley Stokes came home with a story that's so much better to believe.

CHAPTER 8

I miss mopping the floors at night at the Jungle Gym. I've been back to work for exactly four days, and I've already been vomited on, threatened by an angry mom whom I didn't give the correct change to, and offered sixteen babysitting gigs that I wouldn't take if I were desperate. I go there right from school. I work, I go to rehab, and I go to bed. Homework gets done in the morning just after I run, or in study hall. Sometimes at night, but once a procrastinator…well, some habits are hard to quit. Turns out quitting smoking was easier than quitting putting off algebra.

My self-inflicted packed schedule does mean one thing, though; I haven't seen one of the Stokes boys in days.

Things will be harder soon. Wes hasn't come back to school yet. Taryn said his parents were being cautious and over-protective because of how much attention they're still getting and everything Wes has been through. They worry about his health. They've had tests and scans done, made visits to neurologists—all resulting in a clean bill of health.

If they only knew.

Every day, at least one media truck is parked on his street. I don't linger, and I always run by quickly for fear that he'll be outside and we'll have to interact. So far, I've managed to avoid him for four complete days. Taryn says I need to forgive him, and even though Kyle doesn't say as much, I know he wants me to as well. They've both spent a lot of time with him over the last few days, but always with the rest of the family, so Kyle hasn't been able to talk about what really happened with him.

I don't want to talk. I'm not sure I ever will. Taryn begged me to go to the Stokes house with her yesterday after my job. I went to work out with Rebecca instead, even though I have questions—*a question, really*—why did you come back if it puts me in danger? Thing is, I can't ask that question without getting past the fact that he never wanted to see me again. I think about it every goddamn night when I look at the photo I picked up in the field, my photo, which has forever been contaminated by lies scribbled in marker by a delusional nut job.

I still can't seem to throw the photo away, though. And it's not because I took it. It's because, ruined or not, the memory from the day I took it still feels special. The only boy I've ever loved drove me to my favorite place, and he laid his shirt on the ground so I could take a picture. That was maybe the most honest moment I've ever had with anyone, and I want to protect it from all of my damn doubt. That moment meant something.

I deleted the texts from Wes. Not all of them—just the ones I knew were from Shawn. I've put a few small details together. I'm pretty sure Shawn picked up the photo when I saw him at the Stokes's house as he was collecting a few of Wes's things. I also know that he's the one who paid to keep Wes's phone line open under the pretense that maybe somehow Wes's phone would work and he'd be able to reach out to them from wherever he went. I learned that little tidbit when I filled Taryn in on everything. She told me it was something TK mentioned. They all talked about what a miracle it was that his phone somehow worked enough after being soaked in the raging river, and after months of hiding out in a church shelter, that authorities were able to help him charge it to call his family to come take him home.

Miracle.

Man-made.

Seat of your pants cover-up operation.

All I can think about now, staring at the stupid photo with stupid words written on the back in stupid marker, is what trouble they both must have gone through to construct the fabric of this latest lie. Clearly, it's the exact same phone model he had before—but more than that, I wonder if Wes bothered to truly run the battery down before slipping into that shelter and claiming to have had a jolt of memory. I wonder if he just picked any old shelter, or if he vetted them, knowing one day he might need to return just like this.

And of course, I wonder if he's back because he senses that my story is about to end—just like Shawn warned.

"Don't be stupid, Joss. You're better than that," I whisper to myself. Superheroes aren't real, and there isn't any trouble that can be worse than what I've already survived.

I flip off my light at that thought and fall back into the softness of my bed, untangling my blanket enough to flop it across my stomach. The air from my fan blows the loose strands of my hair around my face, and I count on the tickling sensation to keep me awake a little while longer. I still need to shower, and my leg needs to breathe. I worked my quads hard tonight. We're going to start working out on the field more, getting me ready for the season—for the scouts.

The familiar sound comes just as my clock flips to ten thirty, so I hold my breath and listen to the routine. My dad's keys jingle, the back door creaks then slams shut, and the motor of his car purrs while the headlights shine through my window for exactly eight seconds as he backs out of our driveway and goes...*somewhere*. He isn't drunk when he comes home. Or if he is, he's been hiding it well. History has taught me that my dad is poor at hiding his addiction, though, so apparently, he's good at hiding something else.

I wait for ten or fifteen minutes before I finally make my way to the shower and get ready for bed. While I untangle my wet hair with my fingers, I slide open a message from Kyle on my phone.

House is free tomorrow night. We're going to watch TK play, then kick it here for a little after party. I'll drive.

TK's playing football. Taryn has not stopped bragging about her boyfriend and how amazing he is. It kinda makes me want to take up football just so I can get better at it than he is to shut her up, but that's just my bad attitude talking—the part of me that's all screwed up from falling for a boy.

A boy who is apparently the chosen one without a cape.

I write Kyle back.

Who's coming to this party?

I toss my phone on my bed while I slip from my towel and balance to pull my favorite T-shirt over my head. I run my fingers along the threadbare patch over my stomach where the blue waves of Huntington Beach are so faded that the color is actually more of a gray now. One day I'll have to throw it away, but I plan on watching it fall apart. I love the water, and this shirt reminds me of a happier place.

My phone buzzes, so I slide back into my bed, rolling to my back and holding my phone above me.

Everyone's coming.

I stare at Kyle's response for nearly a minute, until my fingers start to tingle from falling asleep hovering above my head. My hands flop to my sides, my phone clutched in the right one when I feel it buzz again. Unable to resist, I lean on my elbow and look.

It's a big deal to our friends. To TK. You should come.

And before I can begin typing, another comes through.

You can't hide forever. You're doing the exact same thing he did.

My lips push tight at the corners, and my eyes haze as I zero in on that last part.

I'm coming.

I send the first part, but hold my thumbs poised over the keyboard while I think about Kyle's accusation. I'm not hiding. I'm right here. If Wes really wanted to see me, all he'd have to do is knock on my door. He's avoiding me just as much as I am him, and really, he's made it pretty clear that I was never supposed to see him again. I type.

And there is nothing the same about me and Wes.

I plug my phone in and flip it over on my night table, done defending myself. But for the next hour, I toss around my sheets, unable to sleep. I get lost in the pattern the slits in my blinds make on my ceiling. The streetlight out front flickers, and it's been doing that for nearly a year without anyone bothering to repair it. By now I find it comforting—I don't think I want it to change.

I knew I had this week to pretend. Maybe next, if I'm lucky. But Wes will come back to school soon. My father will still love him. And now Dad feels beholden to him for saving me and trying to rescue him. More than anything, though, is the way my heart will break every single time I see the blue of his eyes. I will always want to go back to before, to un-know what I know, or travel back in time and have him fight like hell to get back to me.

I'm not sure when the shadows on my ceiling completely disappeared, but I blinked and everything was suddenly black in my room. The streetlamp finally quit on me, too. I chuckle at the thought as I stretch my arms above my head and exhale heavily.

I have never been afraid of the dark. When I was really young, I'd always win hide-and-seek games because I'd bury myself in the depths of the darkest spaces. When I slept at Taryn's house, she always wanted to keep a light on. When we were here, I'd torture her by making everything as dark as possible. She told me stories of ghosts and spirits to try to scare me into turning the lights back on, but nothing made me flinch. My pulse never raced in blackness.

But something about tonight is off.

I sit up, but keep my head low, my mind suddenly filled with worry that someone will see me through my window. I stare at the cracks in the blinds, watching for movement, but the only thing that I see is the gentle sway of the vinyl slats caused by my ceiling fan. I swallow quietly, slide from my bed, and lay low on the floor, dragging my body with my arms, my prosthetic just to my right. I rest with my back against the wall just below my window and pull my leg back on, my movements are unhurried and silent. It feels like it's been a minute since I took a breath.

Turning slowly, I pause when my eyes find a small opening where my blinds meet the inside of my window. It takes me a few seconds to adjust my focus through the small space, but when I do, I'm able to make out the form of a car parked outside my house on our side of the street. It's the kind of car that doesn't belong here—black or dark blue in color, a curvaceous body that screams Porsche or Camaro—and no one inside.

My mind starts to betray me, and for a second, I think I hear two men talking, but when I turn my head and cup my ear toward the window, the only sounds I notice are the repetitive clicks of my fan blades.

Leaning forward, I grab my phone from my night table and open it, ready to call for help. I don't though, because really—it's just a car on the street. For the next hour, I lay on my arm, which is resting along the windowsill. I look out through the bottom of the blinds, a cap from one of my old water bottles wedged in the space to keep a small slit open for me to spy. It's a pendulum of me convincing myself to go back to bed one minute and committing to standing guard the next.

When my clock flips to midnight, though, I roll my tired eyes and curse Shawn Stokes for getting to me, too. He's already corrupted Wes with his theories. I hate that I've given them as much of me as I have.

My finger wraps around the cap and I start to slide it out, for some reason still not ready to break my cover. Eyes trained on the plastic piece, I have it nearly out when my finger stops, catching the falling blind as I see a body rush past my window, only a few feet from my house.

I catch my own gasp, sure the immediate pounding in my chest will give me away to whomever is outside. Surely it sounds like the bass in one of my favorite songs. I slide my phone in my hand, maneuvering it while my eyes remain focused on the scene outside. My breath is ragged, and my jaw is clenched so hard my teeth might crack.

I'm about to hit the emergency button for 911 when two men come into view at the end of my driveway. They point to a house across the street, and I hear them laugh. They look like they're in their thirties, but I'm not sure—their details aren't defined because of the lack of light. I'm able to capture enough that I see one of them pull out his phone and hold it to his ear. He holds up his other hand and gestures toward the car, and within a breath, they both climb inside and drive away.

It takes me another hour to find feeling in my fingertips and to ease the nausea in my stomach. By two in the morning, I'm fairly certain they were looking for another house—maybe a party or friend's home. I justify that a nice car like that wouldn't be interested in doing something bad in a neighborhood like mine. There's nothing to gain here. Nobody with anything worth any value at all.

By three in the morning, I become certain that I made the whole thing up. I'm sure there was a car, and maybe people. But they were just outside. Nothing strange happened at all. I'm exhausted, and maybe my emotions are a little ragged from the last few weeks…and months. I roll my eyes as I finally make my way back to bed, and I lie back after plugging my phone into the charger again.

I'm almost convinced.

Only…the light outside. It's back on.

CHAPTER 9

TK is wasting his time playing football at this school. We've never been good. And as good as he is, he's only one guy. He can't do everything. Though, he sure as hell tries.

"Baby, you were so amazing out there. They just need to get you the ball more," Taryn says as her boyfriend finally comes out of the locker room.

Kyle, Levi, and Wes have been waiting for us in the parking lot. I followed Taryn to the locker room with the hope of talking her into just taking me home, but she didn't drive. She rode with Wes and Levi. I rode with Kyle. And I know exactly how the next fifteen minutes is going to play out—they're all plotting to get us alone together in the same vehicle. I'll walk first.

The game was a decent enough distraction from him, but my eyes must be trained when he is anywhere in my vicinity, because despite forcing Taryn to sit several rows away from the boys, I found Wes in every crowd he was in for four quarters of football.

During the first half, it was much of the same he's experienced for the last week. It's the hype and frenzy of the lost boy found. Girls came up to him all night, giggling and asking him questions about coming home. A few teachers stopped to see him, along with the cop that patrols the parking lot and stands during our home games. I couldn't hear a word from where I was sitting, but I could tell from the slight movements Wes made, and the few times his lips opened and closed that his answers were all short. Of course, everyone would understand and leave him, figuring the stress of it all is still so hard. He's just trying to get back to normal, find his way after being so lost. He's...*fragile.*

But I know better. He's just trying not to make his lie so big he can't control it.

"What'd you think, Joss? How'd I look out there?" TK brushes his arm against mine, his other slung around Taryn's neck as we walk out into the parking lot toward the two trucks—my only two options.

"You play football about as good as you play baseball," I say.

TK chuckles.

"I'm gonna go ahead and pretend you're paying me a compliment, Cherry," he says.

I turn to walk backward and flip him off. He knows I hate that nickname, so he saves it like a right hook, when he has no other way to get back at me for teasing him.

Taryn recalls a few of her favorite plays as we walk, feeding her boyfriend's ego while forgetting to mention the two dropped passes that, frankly, he should have caught. All I hear in my head, though, is the conversation about to happen about me and Wes. Someone will need to ride in one car, and then someone else will need to be with Kyle, or someone forgot they needed to pick up whatever at the store, and then *bam*—I'm alone in a truck with Wes.

The boys are all leaning on the front of Kyle's truck now, their arms folded, heads turning as each takes a turn speaking. Still several feet away, I consider bolting—just sprinting the entire way home, crawling into my bed and waiting for a weird car to show up and the streetlamp to go out. I'd rather feel afraid than angry and hurt. A few more steps, though, and I've come too close to find the courage to run. The part of me that wants to end up in a truck with him, that wants to be forced together, to talk, to scream and shout—that piece of me has taken over driving my body. The hurt part is too weak to fight.

My eyes find his even in the dark. Our faces are the same—flat mouths, heavy eyelids; the weight of things both said and unsaid pulling us down.

"Shoot, TK...I forgot the beer at my house. Can I just go with you to get it?" I breathe in as Taryn speaks, my eyes still on Wes's.

"I was going to swing by the store, too. My dad hasn't gone shopping, and there ain't shit to eat in my house," Kyle says.

Before Levi can make the suggestion, I roll my eyes and walk up to Wes, pinching the long sleeve of his gray ringer-tee as I walk by, jerking it lightly then letting go.

"Just drive me to Kyle's and save them all this embarrassing," I stop, turning to face my friends while I walk backward to the passenger door of the Stokes's truck, "and very poorly scripted and performed scheme to get me and you alone in a truck together."

"Oh, Joss...we didn't," Taryn starts, but I cut her off, one foot in the truck already.

"Save it, T. You did. I knew you would. Whatever, just get the beer there, and buy me some fucking Reese's." I slam the door closed, and a blink later Wes does the same.

"Just drive," I say, glancing at him before shaking my head and pulling my buckle in place.

He's just as silent, and he does as I ask. Or maybe it's what he intended, too. Our friends are predictable, and I'm sure his brothers are prodding him to reach out to me. I'm sure everyone's confused, wondering why I'm not glued to him, afraid to let him go again. They have no idea that glued to me is, apparently, the last place in hell he wants to be.

Wes is quiet as he drives out of the lot. Our friends pull up beside us, and Levi screams from the back of Kyle's truck, standing and holding on tight to roll bar along the cab. Kyle glances my way as he waits for traffic to stop so he can turn. I let my head fall against the window while I stare at him.

"Sorry," he mouths, and I can tell he genuinely is.

Taryn leans forward to look at me around Kyle, and I can tell she's not sorry at all. "Talk," she mouths. My eyes glare, and after a slow blink I face the front, intent on letting her worry about how pissed I must be until I get to tell her to her face.

I hear every sound in the cab, many of them familiar, and my fingers roam from my legs to the seat on either side of me. The fabric is worn, just as I remember; the rattles all sound the same, and there's a torn piece of cardboard wedged where the windshield meets the dash. I remember when Wes put it there to dampen a vibration that was driving him nuts. I'm tempted to pick it out.

We pull up to the light for the road that leads to our neighborhood, and because I'm incredibly unlucky, it turns red and Wes doesn't make an attempt to run it. The longer I sit here, surrounded by the visuals, sounds, and smells that made me feel so safe once, the more I want to kick the door open and run. I test the theory, moving my hand to the window, running it down the door panel and resting my fingers on the handle.

"It's locked," Wes says.

His voice touches me everywhere, but I manage not to let it show on the outside. I let my grip slide loose, but I keep my gaze away.

"Of course it is," I say back. I wonder if my voice has the same effect on him.

The light changes, and the truck crawls forward. My eyes close and I imagine the next few hours of my life. If it's anything like this short ride in his truck, it will kill me.

"Take me home."

I can feel the groove form between my brows when I say the words. It hurts to ask. It hurts to be here. It's so painful that a part of me wants to believe and stay the course, to see if there's a miraculous shift between us that takes us back. But things like that aren't real. Just like superheroes aren't real.

Villains.

That's the only thing out of all of this that exists, and I'm surrounded by them.

We get to my street and Wes stops. The motor gurgles, and we both breathe long and slow draws, each waiting for the other to do…*something*. Anything!

Several seconds pass, and I notice the headlights of another car flash in my passenger side mirror. The car behind us slows the closer they get, and I give in and turn to look at Wes.

"What are you doing?" I ask, my words overlapped with his.

"Have you ever teeter-tottered?" he asks.

I stare at him for a few seconds, glad the car behind us finally passes. It was making me anxious. Now we can sit here and stall—that's what this is…stalling—for a few more minutes.

"What?" I ask, finally.

"Teeter-totter," he repeats, meeting my eyes. Blue. So unbelievably blue. "You know, like…"

Wes holds one hand up and stretches his fingers wide, twisting his palm from one side to the other.

"I know what a teeter-totter is." My mouth is a flat line.

His eyes leave mine as he turns to look back out his window toward a small park where the weeds grow high and where teenagers have melted garbage cans and picnic tables with lighters and cigarettes. I've contributed my share to the vandalism. In the thick of trash and a forgotten youth, the orange metal seat sticks out from a dirt circle that once held sand.

"I have never been on a teeter-totter," he says, breathing out a chuckle as he brings his hand to his mouth, resting his weight on his palm, gazing out at the park I played in for years—until the neighborhood turned and my life slid off tilt. I wonder if Shawn brought us there ever when we were small. I wish I could remember any of it.

"You probably just don't remember," I say, my voice softer, even though my arms cross my body to stand guard. I still want to go home.

"I'd remember. Trust me," he says, pulling his hat from his head and running his hands through hair that's become thicker—longer. "Nobody would take the other side. When I was with the Woodmansees?"

He turns to me again, the look in his eyes a reflection of the lost boy. It's that look right there that always finds a way in—it shows up in my sleep, in my daydreams. It lulls me now.

He chuckles a little more before turning back toward the playground equipment.

"I would sit there on one end, kicking my legs as hard as I could against the ground, trying to lift myself up. The other end was never heavy enough, though," he says.

"That's sad," I say, and my words come out careless. I'm hardened, because my lonely boy didn't want to come back to me. I gave him a friend. I gave him my heart—every little piece of me. It wasn't enough to make him want to come home.

I expect Wes to shrug me off, to start the truck and turn my corner and drive me home, tired of this push and pull. Instead, he turns off the engine, kills the lights and opens his door, stopping just long enough to speak over his shoulder.

"Come on."

His door shuts and I sit motionless while he pushes his hands in the pockets of his perfect jeans and glances both ways before jogging across the street. His hat low on his brow, I breathe in at the silhouette of his form as it walks away. He's like a ghost, like a hologram that isn't really here. Only part of him is here. I want the whole thing, though. More than that, I want *him* to want to be here…completely.

He stops at the teeter-totter, pulling up on one end, the creaking sound deep and loud enough to hear a hundred feet away in his truck. He stares at me for a few seconds before gesturing with his hand for me to come. More of me wants to than doesn't, so I give in and leave the shelter of his truck, not bothering to check for traffic when I walk toward him. I notice his mouth raised on one side as I step closer, and I shrug.

"What can I say. I'm a rebel," I say, gripping the other end of the long metal beam and swinging my prosthetic leg over. The balance is a little awkward, but I'm strong enough to manage. Wes waits as I adjust, his eyes lingering on mine briefly, then flitting to my stomach and eventually my legs, a slight curve to his lips.

"You are much more than a rebel," he says with a shake of his head as he swings his own leg over and balances us both.

Knowing he has me by a good twenty-five pounds, I push up quickly from the ground, lifting myself high in the air as I watch Wes fall hard on his ass. It was mean, but it felt good.

"Yeah, I'm a real bitch, too," I smirk, winking.

Wes chuckles, moving one hand to his ass while he shakes his head.

"Normally, I'd argue with you about that, but that hurt like hell, so I'll let you have this one," he says, kicking up hard enough that my real foot finds the ground.

For several minutes, we work together like this, Wes pushing up with more thrust while I merely lift myself back up. The entire time, our eyes are locked. We study each other, and the longer I look at him, the more my emotions mix into a dangerous cocktail and the less I understand about anything.

"Kyle and I used to come out here and do this when my parents were fighting," I finally say.

There's a brief pause in Wes's movement, and he holds us even for a breath.

"It's no big deal. I was just sharing," I say. "You know, just filling this fucking awful silence."

His head falls a tick to one side and his mouth pulls in on the corner. Sympathy. I stretch my left toes so they touch the ground and push up a little, signaling that I don't want to dwell on this.

"Was that before or after I knew you?" he asks.

This time I pause, letting him do all of the work while I tuck my chin in to glare at him, my toes barely tickling the ground.

"You know better than to ask me that," I say.

The small rocking halts completely, and I pull my legs up so my shoes rest on the long metal shaft that's balancing us.

"I don't remember much about when we were little, when I was…with Shawn the very first time," he says, glancing down so all I can see is the brim of his hat and his parted lips as they take a heavy breath.

"I don't remember any of it," I say.

His head tilts up and his eyes find mine through the shadow of his hat, his mouth a crooked smile.

"We were babies," he shrugs.

I hold his stare for a moment, waiting through the twisting feeling my insides get from being so close to him.

"We were never really babies, Wes," I say, and his brow pinches.

"You were a superhero, and I was just awesome," I add, shrugging again and smiling on one side.

Wes chuckles and pushes up again lightly, taking control of our sway as he floats me to the sky then brings me back to earth gently.

"I swear I'm no hero, Joss. I know what Shawn said, but I can't do what he thinks I can," he says, and I can't help but see a slideshow in my mind of all of the things Wes *can* do. I let my legs fall back to the sides, and I lean forward, gripping the bar with a jerk that makes Wes stop our movement.

"Then why'd you come back at all?"

I glare—my face hard and my eyes demanding to just cut through the damned bullshit. His expression morphs slowly. The ease of a moment ago sliding away, fluid, until his mouth rests flat, his head shifts slightly and his eyes—those ever-powerful eyes—hold me hostage.

"Just because I'm not who he says I am, doesn't mean he isn't," he says.

A swift kick hits my ribs on the inside, a sharp breath that I didn't take, my heart recognizing my worries and my doubts and that place where they intersect.

"He's a crazy man, Wes," I say, and I watch his chest fill with air slowly before his head shakes *no*.

"He lives in a trailer by the lake, in a house filled with toys and fantasies, and he...he abused you, Wes," I whisper, saying what I really felt when I walked into that place with Kyle days ago. "Not...not physically, but emotionally, *yes*. He did Wes, and I don't know why you can't see it. He filled your head with these insane thoughts and theories that will hold you back and keep you from truly living."

Wes's eyes move from mine to the ground, and eventually his head shakes.

"Joss, there are many things that Shawn did to me that aren't…that aren't right," he starts, and I take in a sharp breath, my mind racing ahead somewhere I hadn't expected. Wes draws in his mouth on one side and quickly shakes his head at my assumptions, though. "No, never physically. Like you said. Emotionally, though…yes, I will agree. But his visions? Joss…there is too much truth to those, things that have happened and that I've seen that I can't disregard."

"So then why bail on me?"

I hold the bars tight and lean back as far as I can, my body balanced over nothing, one slip and I will fall to the ground, probably hit my head. Is that in some drawing somewhere? Does Wes rush to save me, catching me just before my head busts wide open? I tilt my head to the dark sky and smile, just a bit.

"He saw your leg, Joss. He saw water. He saw a bus. Damnit, Joss." His tone is harsh, like the night I fell from a speeding car, and it snaps me from my trance. I sit up to stare into his eyes, and there's a story hiding in them, one where words are missing—where characters die. "I went to Shawn when I climbed from the river. I ran the entire way, in the downpour. He was sitting in his living room with the door open, just watching and waiting for me because he knew what had happened. He knew when the first raindrops fell. And he knew I would give in and come to him."

My stomach sours. Lips bent down, the bottom one quivering, I lean forward and hold tight, slowly moving my right leg over the bar, all of my weight balanced on my good left limb. I can feel my pulse in my guts, like a steady churn that's killing me from the inside. Wes holds himself up, waiting until I let go of my end before setting his down gently and standing on the opposite side of the teeter-totter.

I fold my arms over my chest, tucking my fingers under each elbow.

"I'm stronger than I was before," I say.

Wes's brow draws in and his eyes fall to my feet, his lips pulled in tight as he shakes his head.

"I should have never let this happen to you," he says, his voice soft, not quite a whisper.

"I'm stronger," I repeat. I wait until he inhales and flits his gaze back to mine. I nod once and lift my eyebrows. "This was happening whether you were here to fix it or not. And while I would give anything to have my leg back, I'm so grateful for the strength this experience has given me. I'm so strong, Wes. You have no idea."

He doesn't blink, and we remain quiet, our eyes locked, while a line of cars drives along the road behind me. Others coming home from the game, maybe even friends who are going to Kyle's house.

"If I wasn't here, maybe you would have been somewhere else. Maybe you wouldn't have been on that bus," he says.

I let that thought soak in for a beat, and quickly dismiss it.

"Then that means I would have quit, and my dad would still be a drunk, and he and I would still be doing nothing but hurting one another. I'm not sure what's worse," I say.

His jaw flexes at my argument, and he draws in a quick breath through his nose, blowing it out as his eyes move to the scene behind me. I turn when I hear whistling. Levi and TK are both standing in the bed of Kyle's truck now as they pass by slowly, teasing us. I chuckle and shake my head as they turn down the street after mine and head toward Kyle's house.

"What if I can't stop what's next?"

I watch Kyle's taillights fade in the distance while I think about Wes's words.

"What if…" I stop, twisting again to face him as I speak. "What if life is better happening just however it's meant to?"

His swallow is slow, and the movement in his neck forces his chin to rise. He doesn't respond, so I twist my lips and quirk a brow, ready to gloat and tease that maybe I'm right. But he doesn't let me.

"It's not," he says, and my breath stops. I blink once. "Your life…it's not better the way Shawn sees it."

My cocky smile and confidence fades. Wes tucks his hands in his pockets and looks down at his feet, punching the toe of one shoe into the dirt, tearing out a weed. His head looks up at me again with a snap.

"I came back because I have to try," he says.

"Even though the crazy man in the trailer says you fail." I breathe through my nose, my front teeth closed tight.

He nods slowly, and I breathe out a laugh, tucking my tongue in my cheek and looking the opposite way. A breeze picks up and the tips of my hair tickle my bare arms. My legs feel chilled, goosebumps on one, and imagined cold on the other. I nod slowly, my mind made up the same way it does every time I work through this crazy scenario on my own. I turn and begin to walk back to Wes's truck, and after a few steps, he follows me. I climb in on my side, and he does on his. We both buckle, and he turns the key waiting for me to tell him where it is I want to go.

"Let's just go to Kyle's," I say.

His body relaxes, his posture less perfect and his arm muscles less flexed. Probably, because I'm being agreeable. Only I'm not. I don't agree with any of this. I've never liked people telling me what to do.

"And just so we're clear," I begin as he turns down the next street toward Kyle's house. I sense his glance at me. "I believe in free will. *I* get to decide how this goes. And I have also decided that both you and your uncle don't know shit."

The truck rolls to a stop with my last word. I unbuckle, happy to leave things there with Wes. I'll go inside, get a beer, and tuck myself in my favorite chair, ready to get back to the life of a young girl—with friends, and laughter, and a dad that, while he disappears, isn't throwing up in the front lawn anymore and calling on me to come clean it up.

"My father," Wes says, just before I slam my door to a close. I freeze, turning quickly to meet his gaze, a million thoughts about those words all trying to line up and make sense out of them.

His tongue is held between his teeth as he breathes out hard, once.

"Shawn. He's…he's my father."

I stare at him, half hoping for a laugh to leave his lips next. This is a joke. He's seeing how far this can go before I give up. When he doesn't break, instead pulling his mouth into a tight line and slowly shaking his head, I know that I'm waiting for nothing. There's nothing more. That's it. Shawn is his dad. And this is all so incredibly fucked up.

I let the door fall closed and I watch him for a few seconds through the window of his truck before I turn and head inside where I find my beer and my favorite chair. My friends are all laughing. But this is nothing like the life I had before or imagined I'd have again. This is a mess. And it hurts.

And I'm sick of it.

CHAPTER 10

A year ago, I would have spent a party after a football game at Kyle's either sick in his bathroom, passed out on his bed, or standing on his coffee table singing the lyrics to my favorite rap songs. I wouldn't stop until four in the morning—annoying the shit out of everyone drunk and dizzy from not being able to hold their liquor like I can.

Last night, I walked home after being at Kyle's for only an hour.

Wes let me. But I heard his truck pull up outside around two, and when I finally fell asleep, I know it was still there.

My dad wasn't home when I came in, and this morning, his car still isn't in the driveway. Wes is gone, though. No more watchful eyes over me when the sun comes up, I guess.

On my way to the kitchen, I rub the sleep from my eyes with my fists, and I'm staring into the pantry filled with empty boxes when I hear my dad's car pull up the driveway. A second later the back door opens.

"You're up early," he says, his voice accompanied by the rustling of plastic bags.

"Please say you bought Pop-Tarts," I say into the barren shelves in front of me.

"And milk. And eggs. And some of those...what are these called?"

I close the pantry door to look at my dad.

"Pomegranates," I respond, taking one in my hand and tossing it in the air a few times.

"All I know is you better not drop it. Those things are a nightmare to clean up. You dropped one of those seed things on the floor a few weeks ago and I stepped in it," he says, and I chuckle as I pull out a plate and slice into the fruit with the only large knife we own.

"I thought that was blood on the floor. My bad," I say, pulling out a section and popping it into my mouth.

"I guess you don't want Pop-Tarts now then?" he says, holding a box of strawberry ones toward me. I snag them and rip the top open in one movement, unwrapping the pastries and biting one in half.

"I can eat both. Two different kinds of carbs," I say through a full mouth.

My dad rolls his eyes, then turns to the groceries he brought in and begins putting them away. He's wearing his usual pocketed sweatpants and dry-weave T-shirt, and I notice that his elbow is wrapped up with some gauze.

"You donate blood?" I say, pointing to his arm as he turns around.

"Huh?" he says, stretching out one arm then the other, finally noticing the bandage. "Oh! No, it's nothing. I burned my elbow being stupid."

He stretches his arm out a few times, proving to me that it works, then goes back to tidying the kitchen. There's something about it that I can't let go, though.

"What'd you burn it on?" I ask.

His back to me, he doesn't answer right away. Instead, he rinses out a few cups, putting them in the dishwasher, wiping down the counter and faucet, and folding the damp cloth on the counter next to the sink. He sighs heavily, leaning forward with his palms flat on the counter, and eventually his head falls forward, chin to his chest.

"I didn't burn it."

I knew that was the case. I tear a paper towel off and wipe the fruit juice from the corners of my mouth. My dad turns around and folds his arms over his chest, resting against the counter.

"It really isn't that big of a deal," he says, his mouth hesitant to say more words. I tilt my head and pull in my lips, and he takes another long breath before swallowing hard.

"You got into a fight," I answer for him.

We stare at each other, and after a few seconds, he blinks. I breathe a sad laugh through my nose and push back from the counter as my eyes close, the legs of my stool screeching as they drag.

"Was it at Jim's?" I quirk a brow, standing and finally meeting his gaze again.

His mouth pulls in tight, as if he's made a solemn vow not to break under my interrogation. His silence speaks volumes.

"Awesome," I say, pushing my plate toward the center of the counter, no longer hungry.

I turn to head back to my room, and I make it to the hall before my dad speaks.

"It's nothing to worry about, Joss. Really," my dad says.

I raise up two fingers, a peace sign, but keep walking to my room. I turn to shut my door, but my dad has followed me down the hall, and he's gripping the frame of my doorway with trembling hands. The tremors are slight, but I see them. I've been trained to look for them, and as he speaks, I can't look at anything except his shaking fingers.

"What are you up early for?" he asks.

"I'm going to get some work in at the field today. And I picked up a shift at the Jungle Gym after lunch," I say, finally looking him in the eyes. They're desperate.

"You didn't tell me you wanted to do some fielding. I don't have anything going on, though. If you give me a few minutes, I'll go with you; hit you some hard ground balls," he says.

"It's fine. Kyle's coming." *You're lying to me, and I don't want you there.* The hidden meaning behind my words must shine through, because my dad backs away silently when I look away, and by the time I change and come out of my room again, he's gone.

I grab my things from the rack my dad installed last month in the garage and zip up my bag, stopping to grab a water bottle from the tiny fridge in our garage. I look at it long and hard, feeling the cool air hit my knees. Those shelves used to be full of beer. My dad never preferred beer, but he'd drink one in the morning sometimes, to cut the hangover. The only things in there now, though, are sports drinks and water.

Slamming the door shut, I pull my phone from my pocket to check the time. I lied to my dad—Kyle isn't coming. I hadn't planned on calling him, and now that I see it's barely after seven, I know that option is gone. I was going to go alone anyhow, but for some reason, my chest burns and my stomach twists because my dad offered to help and I turned him away.

"Fuck." I kick the door of the fridge with my metal blade, denting the corner, and I chuckle at my own outburst. "I'm just like you, damn it. Just…fucking like you," I say to myself.

I pull my father's school keys from the hook and pocket them with my phone, resolved to walk to school and set up the tee to work out on my own, like I planned all along.

I live in my own world during the walk, kicking out every thought that tries to take up space in my head—my dad, my mom, Grace, Shawn, theories…*Wes*. That last one is impossible, though, and even if I could avoid thinking about Wes and what he said, I can't avoid the boy. From a thousand yards away, I know it's Wes sitting with his back against the backstop. He's a speck, yet I know.

I don't slow, walking to my destination as if he weren't there at all, but I never take my eyes from him. His hands rest loosely over his knees, and even from this far away I swear I can see him breathe. I start to sync my own breaths with the steady drum of my heartbeat that I'm also sure matches his. His hat sits high enough on his head that the shadow doesn't reach his eyes, which means he sees me. His leg shifts, one falling straight and the other pulling in closer to his body, and his head tilts to the side. The movements are small and thoughtful, but I catch them all. He's wearing the gray shirt with long, blue sleeves that he wore under his uniform last season. I remember how it feels, and my fingers tighten their grip on the handle of my bag in response.

He's breaking me just by being, and it isn't fair.

Wes is standing by the time my feet hit the dirt of the infield. I purposely look away as I walk up, hoping that maybe he'll get scared and leave, but that was a silly theory—Wes doesn't get scared.

"So...you're here," I say, dumping my bag near the dugout before moving to the bench to adjust my leg and wrap my thumbs and fingers in tape.

"Thought you might need someone to take care of blister protection," he says, lip raised on one side as he walks across home plate and steps into my space.

My teeth grip the edge of the tape and I tear it, patting the loose end down and moving to the next finger.

"Nah, I'm all good. I can tape myself," I say, ripping for the next finger.

Wes pauses at the dugout entry, leaning back on the brick wall and kicking the toe of his shoe against the chain-link gate across from him. His shoes look brand new, and I feel my lip tug higher at that observation. I look up at him as I twist a piece of tape around my pinky, and he smirks under his hat.

"Stubborn," he says.

"Yeah, well, I like to be predictable," I say, tossing the roll of tape toward my bag as I stand.

I continue as if he isn't here, but I know he won't leave. He's moving back in, trying to find the ease we used to have. Part of me is dying for it, too. But I can't forget the look on his face when I held up the note I thought he had left, and I can't forget that sick feeling that took over when I realized those clues were never from him, that he didn't want to be found.

"How often have you been getting work in out here?"

I roll my eyes at his question since my back is to him. He follows me to the storage room at the back of the dugout. After I open it with my father's keys, I toss them to him.

"Hold those. If I lose them I'm as good as dead," I say, and there's a sliver of a pause after that word—*dead*—when we both stop breathing and lock eyes.

"Sure," Wes finally says, putting my dad's keys in his pocket.

I start pulling out the nets and the tee, and Wes takes the heavy things from me. If he's going to be here, I might as well benefit from it, so I let him prep my hitting station while I pull out my training bat and the new one my dad bought online when I said I was going to play again.

"I've done some basic fielding. Lots of running, and hitting indoors, over at the cages on central. I've worked with Kyle a bit, and my dad. But I have a trainer," I say, stopping when I realize Wes has finished with my net, and he's staring at me, eyes somehow reflecting the blue of the sky to be even more brilliant.

"What?" I ask.

I know what. What makes me weak. It hurts to fight it, but it also hurts to give in.

His left eye crinkles as his cheek lifts and his lip raises in a half smile. His head shakes slightly. "Nothing, it's just…you're a goddamned force to be reckoned with. I'm…I'm proud of you, is all." His teeth grip his bottom lip briefly when he's done, and I feel my body rush with the tingle of adrenaline, a blush that is innate for me when it comes to this boy.

"Thanks," I say, opting for grace over saying something cruel.

Wes nods toward the tee, dumping out the bucket of balls, swinging it upside down to use as a stool and placing the first ball on the tip for me to hit.

"Come on, let me be useful. I'm out here," he says.

My eyes squint and I exhale a short sigh, but I step up to the tee and line up my feet and bat. I cock my arms back and focus on my technique—leg, hip, lower body twist, hands inside, hit. I let the sound of the ball cracking off my bat sink in while Wes puts another ball in place for me.

"You never did say *why* you were out here," I say, waiting for his hand to be out of the way before swinging again.

Wes lifts another ball, rolling it in his hand and grinning before looking up at me.

"Last night, when you left early? Kyle gave you shit, and you said you had to get up early to practice before work," he says, putting the ball in place then tapping his finger against his temple. "I locked that little bit of info in here."

I study him, fully aware that my lips hint at a grin. I feel the smile wanting to come out, but I hold it where it is—at a fraction. My eyes blink and focus back on the ball, and I swing again.

"I left a little after you did, so I could make sure I got up early, too," he says, and I let my bat fall to my side while he loads the tee. I wait for him to add more to his story, to tell me he sat outside my house, but he doesn't, so I test him on it.

"You went home and right to bed then, huh?" I ask, bringing my bat back to my shoulder.

"Yep," he says.

I freeze in my stance and move my eyes from the ball to Wes, his focus on the ball he expects me to hit, the next one already in his hands.

"You liar," I say, and his eyes flit to mine. I swing and crack the ball, then drop my bat back down to lean my weight on the handle. "You sat outside my house. I saw you."

Our eyes lock and in a breath, our mouths have matching smirks.

"I did," he admits without much fight.

I wait for Wes to place the ball, swinging through it when his hand moves away, trying to think of nothing but the work—my goals. It's impossible, though. There's too much when I'm near him. My mind won't focus, instead spinning out of control with questions and conversations I have with myself, because I don't want to have them with him. I avoid them, because every single question leads to a bottomless pit, and I don't want to be trapped in something dark again.

"You haven't asked," he says, palming the next ball—holding it hostage.

My lips smile tightly to cover my gritted teeth.

"Asked what?"

I know what. About the bomb he dropped. I haven't asked, because I think maybe I knew. Just the same, I don't want to know. My opinion of Shawn has plummeted. I don't want to think of the two of them sharing traits.

Wes rolls the ball from his fingertips back into the bucket, and I fall back a step, defeated and frustrated. My stomach clenches as Wes rubs his palms over his cheeks and chin, leaning forward and glaring at me at the same time. My bat resting on my shoulder, I give in, exhaling slowly and letting my eyes linger on his blue.

"Why didn't you tell me earlier?" I ask.

"Because I hated him…I *hate* him."

His answer comes fast, and it jars me. It is the opposite of everything I've known of Shawn through his eyes. I thought he was beloved to Wes—the man who rescued a lost boy and gave him love when his foster parents wouldn't…over and over again.

"He told me to get me to go with Bruce and Maggie, after the hospital. I didn't want to leave, because staying with Shawn had always felt like home. But he said I was supposed to be with them," Wes says, his voice breaking with a betrayed laugh.

His eyes look down at the ground between his feet before his head turns sideways, and his eyes shift back to me.

"I was a one night stand with some woman he paid. She left me on his doorstep," he says, mouth tugged in on one side. "He said I wasn't born to live with him, though."

His eyes linger on my face, and I fill in the blanks.

I would need a hero. That's what Shawn had told me, and he wanted to make sure that Wes was close by.

"Why Bruce?" I ask.

"It wasn't so much Bruce, as it was Maggie," he says, adjusting his position on the bucket, stretching to one side. "Maggie has family close by—a sister. They'd talked about moving here a lot."

"And you would be near me," I say, barely above a whisper, my eyes blinking to the empty dugout while I process. I can see just enough of Wes to tell he's nodding in agreement.

I am a job. I'm *his* job.

After several seconds of processing, I reach forward and grab my own ball from the bucket, putting it in place and swinging hard. I'm about to do it again, but Wes anticipates and slides one in place before I have a chance.

"Quit helping me," I say, bringing my bat forward gently and tapping the ball from the tee like a pool cue.

Wes picks the ball up and puts it back, so I repeat my movement, knocking it to the ground again. The routine goes on a few more times, each time Wes placing it down more sternly, and me jerking the ball away with my hand as he replaces it with another one. In some other life, this would be cute flirtation—we'd both be giggling, and end up with our hands tangled and our lips locked.

But that's not what this is. This is me trying to prove something, and Wes trying to prove me wrong.

"Gah!" I gasp, tossing my bat end over end to the ground next to Wes.

Turning my back to him, I take a few steps away, into the field, then dig my fingers into my hair, pulling the band from my ponytail and spinning to look him in the eyes. He's still sitting on the bucket, a ball in his hand, and unsurprised eyes staring right back at me. My chest thumps in frustration, and a few seconds pass before Wes leans forward slowly and sets the ball from his hand on the tee. My eyes zero in on it, and we both remain silent for nearly a minute.

"Why didn't you want to come back?" I ask him without looking at him directly. I avoid his eyes, and I give him the security of knowing I'm not seeing through him when he speaks. I just need this answer. I need it more than I need air.

"I never said I didn't want to come back," he says, his voice low and quiet.

I wait, my eyes still on the tee and the ball he sat there for me to hit. After several seconds, Wes's hand interrupts my trance as he reaches for the ball again, taking it away from my view. I won't look at him, but I can see from my periphery that he's struggling. His elbows are on his knees, and he rolls the ball in his hands, over and over, as if one of these times the right words will be written between the stitches for him to read to me, satisfying the hole in my heart.

"I said I *couldn't* come back."

"You said you wouldn't," I interject. My eyes flit to him, but I look away quickly. "Wouldn't…it's…it's different than couldn't."

Wes stands, his shadow crossing my line of sight, but I remain focused. My hands are fists at my sides, and my pulse is drumming. I'm hot, my hair starting to stick to my shoulders and neck, but I leave it wild. *I'm wild.*

"I thought if I stayed away…if I wasn't a part of your world, then maybe the bad things would stop," he says.

I breathe. My chest lifts. It falls.

"It hurt," I say, finally breaking and looking him in the eyes. He's leaning against the dugout fence, his hands to his sides, a ball still clutched in one, and his head leaning to one side. "When you didn't come home; when you were missing…it hurt. When I found out you were alive…"

My mouth quivers a smile that only lasts for a breath at the memory of hope. I take a few steps closer, feeling the tightness in my hands as I squeeze them. I clench so hard my nails cut into my palms.

"When I found out that the texts and the note…that they weren't from you…" My head shakes. Wes stands tall, but I hold a hand up to stop him from moving forward. I don't want him close—not while I say this. My eyes lock with his.

"It broke my heart. It broke it," I wince. "But so help me, Wesley Stokes…you will not break my spirit."

I shake my head, and pull my lips in tight.

"Go home, Wes," I say.

He doesn't move, so I utter it again.

"Go home. I can do this. I can do it all—on my own," I say. "I do not need a hero."

His head falls to the side again, and his eyes begin reflecting the morning sun. I know if I stepped closer I would see the redness in them. I would see the tears forming. I stay where I am because I need to be strong. I can't let him in, not even the slightest bit. He will just leave again when he thinks his work is done.

Wes holds my gaze until the glossiness disappears, finally stepping forward and dropping the ball from his fingers into the bucket and my dad's keys in the grass by my things. Stopping there, he lets his arm dangle limply over my equipment, small twitches firing away at his fingers, itching to go against my wishes. His breathing is slow, and his lashes blink in a steady rhythm with his thoughts as he looks at the ground. A small gasp leaves his mouth as his lips part, ready to speak, and my chest is slammed with a kick of hope that he's about to say something that will make everything I'm feeling go away, that will take us back to the beginning or the middle—*to before.* Then my heart fights back, pushing that hope right out into the open, away from me.

Wes's heart…it pushes too. His eyes close and his fingers curl, perhaps ridding his hand of the temptation to touch me. His mouth closes, too—washing away the desire to kiss mine.

He takes a few slow paces toward me, still not looking me in the eyes, but stops when I tuck my chin and move back in reaction. His stare goes to my hands, still holding on to themselves with all of my strength.

"I know you don't need a hero, Joss. You are the strongest person I know. Even so, I can't help myself. I never could. And not because someone told me I was supposed to, either."

His head lifts just enough at that last word, and with a single blink, his eyes are back on mine. I count the seconds that we both stand still. I count both hoping my number is small, and that it also goes on forever.

I get to seven, and Wes's eyes finally move to the ground.

Eight, and he closes them as he nods.

Nine, his fingers flex at his side, his will too weak to hold his hand up any higher to say goodbye, his heart too guarded to speak again—guarded like mine.

By ten, his back is to me. I don't move until I lose my sight of him from the corners of my eyes. I don't turn to look at him fully until he's a shadow. And I never cry. Not once. Because I don't need a hero…because I'm a liar, to myself more than anyone.

A hundred swings turn into two hundred, and eventually, my blistered hands cannot swing anymore. I pack up my equipment, putting away the pieces that stay at the school, and then begin my slow walk home so I can get ready for my job.

I busy myself through every step by thinking about the math—how many weeks until I have enough to buy some piece-of-shit car that's new enough for Rebecca's friend to alter. I pull my phone out and flip through used-car postings, wishing I had the cash now. When my feet hit the familiar territory of the sidewalk outside my house, I put my phone away and look toward home. My head lifts just in time to see Wes's truck turn the corner up ahead.

He was waiting for me—seeing me home safe.

And I hurt all over again.

CHAPTER 11

Sunday mornings at the Jungle Gym have become a bargaining chip. The first four hours are a glorious peace fest, as quiet as my school library, which has also somehow become one of my favorite places. I don't always study there, but I go there almost every morning. I like the regulars—a girl named Lana who I think might actually already have half of her college credits done; the two guys in the engineering club; Meagan, who's obsessed with poetry; and Monk. I think Monk's real name is Collin, but he's been Monk ever since I can remember. He's always been a foot taller than everyone, and he's the only other decent player on our football team. He's shit at school, though, so he has a tutor who studies with him every morning.

It's the same at work on Sundays. The first two hours are taken up with opening the place, counting the register cash, and pre-ripping wristbands so when the place gets packed in the afternoon, staff can just slap one on a kid's arm and let them run off to play. The rest of the morning is nothing but the regulars—the few families who don't go to church, the mom with triplets who constantly looks like she's about to pass out, and the woman we all call Grandma. She brings her grandson Emmitt in, and she always has a pocketful of candy. It would be creepy if anyone else did it, but when it's a seventy-year-old grandma in overalls, somehow it becomes endearing.

"Sundays are so slowwwww," Taryn says, pulling herself up to sit on the counter by my register. Her feet kick out until they brush my hip, so I time it just right and grab one, threatening to tip her backward. She jerks free, then scowls at me, tucking one leg under the other.

"Just trying to keep things interesting for you…you know…make the time pass," I laugh.

"By cracking my head open in the lobby?" Her eyes roll.

"You don't know that it would have cracked. Maybe you would have bounced," I say.

"Ha ha," she says.

Before the accident, I usually worked Sundays alone; at least until we unlocked the doors. Our boss decided I needed company, though, and as much as I love Taryn, sometimes I miss the silence of those first two hours on my own.

Especially when she uses our time to talk about Wes.

"So, did you guys, like…officially break up or whatever?"

She throws the *whatever* in to make it sound like she's just chitchatting. It's irritating.

"I don't want to talk about it," I say, punching in the code to open the register so I can make the last deposit drop in the safe before our shift ends.

"Geesh, fine," my friend huffs, sliding from the counter and reaching over my arm into the register to grab her time card. "Just save it all for Kyle," she mumbles just loud enough for me to hear.

"Taryn, I told you…it's not like that. I said I was sorry," I say, starting over counting out the twenties in the drawer.

"I know," she says.

I count out two hundred in cash and tuck the money in an envelope, ready for the safe. When I look up, Taryn is tapping her pen on her time sheet and staring at me.

"What?"

She shrugs in response, so I walk to the back room and drop the envelope in the slot on top of the safe. When I come back, though, she's still staring at me.

"Seriously, either harass me or don't. I can't do the creepy, staring shit," I say.

"You've changed," she says.

"Gah," I breathe out, rolling my eyes and going back to my work at the register.

"I don't mean your leg, I mean…I don't know, like…you had this light for a while and now it's just, like, gone," she says.

"Oh, you mean the bright light I had when my dad used to call me from the bar at three in the morning?" I lean my hip into the counter and fold my arms, staring her in the eyes, my mouth a hard, flat line.

"No, Joss," she sighs. "Not then. Just…"

"You mean Wes," I fill in, shaking my head and turning back to my work. I pull out the schedule for the next week, and I count the hours. At this rate, I might be able to afford a car by the time I'm forty-six.

"It means something that he did come back," she says, and I do my best to not acknowledge her. "You know he thought of you. He missed you, and he wanted to come home, but he was afraid something bad would happen."

Taryn knows everything Kyle knows. But neither is aware of Shawn being Wes's father, and I'm not sure they understand the extent of how crazy he is.

"You talked to him about me?" I finally ask.

Her mouth twists on one side and her eyes look down as she draws in a deep breath.

"I just think you two are meant for each other," she says.

"Taryn," I say, punching out my employee number on the register and stepping to the side so she can do the same. "Soul mates is a lovely theory. It's a stupid theory…but a lovely one."

"He just wanted to keep you safe," she says as we walk through the back hallway. "That's…that's romantic."

"That's lunacy. And he wanted to hide…and never see me again. That's what he wanted. Let's be real," I say, pushing my ass into the back door and holding it open for my friend.

We walk to Taryn's car, and I wait while she unlocks the doors.

"Besides," I chuckle to myself. "If Wes's mission in life was to keep me safe, then why does he park outside my house at night to stand guard when nobody is there, but the night two dudes were creeping around our front yard, he's nowhere to be found?"

Taryn halts from getting into the driver's seat, her eyes snapping to mine and her lips parting in surprise. She's about to buy into the crazy.

"No, forget about it, don't get all freaked out," I say, shaking my head and pulling my door open. "It was nothing. They were lost, looking for a different house."

I get in and curse myself for saying anything.

"You talked to them?" she asks.

I put off answering while I buckle, but she's not buckling and starting the car. I'm a fucking hostage.

"No, T. I didn't talk to them." My words are snarky.

"Then how do you know they were looking for a different house?" she asks.

I shrug and look out my passenger window.

"I could just tell," I lie.

Truth is, I made that theory up and sold myself on it. Those men haven't been back, and the light hasn't stopped working again since that night. No more rabbit holes for me.

Taryn doesn't dig into it more, and she drops the topic of Wes and me and happily ever after—instead, talking about doing it with TK in the back of the truck out in the desert. For once, I'm happy to get these details. It's better than the third degree.

"Who's visiting you?" Taryn asks, drawing my attention to my driveway as we turn onto my street.

There's a gray sedan parked at our house. My arms start to tingle with an unexpected dose of adrenaline, so I squeeze them and rub up and down, pretending I'm just cold. It's probably because we were just talking about the strangers in my yard, but the scene we pull up to at my house has my heart beating a little faster.

I get out, and Taryn follows a few steps behind. My eyes roam over the car, and I look in the back and front windows as we walk toward my open garage. Whoever is here, they're inside…with my dad.

"Maybe Meredith got a new car," I suggest.

"Your dad's sponsor?" Taryn asks.

I nod, satisfied with this theory, too, even though Meredith is on a fixed income and the car I'm looking at wouldn't be in her budget. It's not fancy—probably five or six years old. But it's too much for a Social Security check alone.

I'm hesitant when I twist the handle on the garage door, pushing it open lightly to keep it from creaking.

"Hello?" I call out when I step inside. Taryn moves her hand to my shoulder, hiding behind me.

"We're not at a haunted house," I say over my shoulder.

"Yeah, well, weird shit happens to you. I need time to run," she says.

"Nice," I say, shaking my head.

I drop my wallet and phone on the counter and walk farther into the living room. I don't even hear my dad, let alone a visitor.

"Dad? You home?" I call out.

His car was in the garage, and his keys are by the sink. My throat starts to close as another wave sends shivers along my skin just as I hear a thud in the backyard.

"He's hitting something against the back wall," Taryn says, her finger pushing a few of the blinds back so we can see.

She pulls the sliding door open.

"Mr. Winters?"

My dad loses his grip on whatever he was banging against the wall, and the heavy sheet falls into the dirt.

"Aww hell," my dad says, running his wrist along his forehead, wiping away the sweat. He puts his hands on his hips and exhales, looking down at what looks like a car floor mat.

"You detailing cars now or something?" I step through the doorway next to Taryn, and my dad chuckles at my question.

"Well, it was supposed to be a surprise, and I mucked up the floor, so I wanted to shake them out for you, but…" He stops his words, pulling his lips into a tight smile as he reaches into his pocket, pulling out a small ring with a key on it. "She's all yours."

He tosses the key to me and I snag it in the air, staring at it for a few seconds in my palm while my dad steps back to the mat and bangs it against the wall a few more times.

"That's as good as that's going to get," he says, walking back toward the door through the garage. He stops and looks at me over his shoulder; I glance up from the key resting in my hand. "Well? Come on. Let's take her for a spin."

My dad walks to the car, tugs open the door and kneels to slide the mat back in place.

"Holy shit. He bought you a car, Joss," Taryn whispers, leaning into me as we both drag our feet slowly through the garage, around my dad's car to what I guess is now mine.

"I…I have no idea what to say," I stammer. My eyes blink a few times, trying to make sure what I'm looking at is real. "Dad, this…we can't afford this. It's too much."

"I've been working at night," he says, and I freeze, my lips parted and my head tilted slightly while my mind catches up to his words.

"That's where I've been. I didn't want to tell you, or make you feel bad. Money was tight, and I just…I wanted to be able to do some things for you, so…I restock the tack and feed store out on old forty-seven every night. It's not forever," he says, waving his hand and shaking his head in response to my falling face. "And don't feel guilty. You'll need to buy your gas and pay for insurance, but I wanted to do this. I…I *needed* to do this."

I swallow the lump in my throat and look back to the key in my hand.

"Dad, I…"

My father's hand rests on my shoulder and I look at it first, then up to his gaze. His smile slides in place and he draws me into his arms for a hug.

"That was worth it right there," he says in my ear. "It's nothing special, but it's yours."

I back away from his arms and look at my car. *My car!*

"It's about eight years old, sixty thousand miles, but it was owned by an older woman and she took it in for every oil change and…" he leans forward and sniffs, smiling on one side, "she didn't smoke. My guess is she liked potpourri, because the thing smells like one of those craft stores. Runs great. Gets good mileage."

"I love it," I smile, looking from my dad back to my car. I step closer and rest my hand on top, letting my fingers run along the shiny roof.

"I can drive us around the block if you want. I told Rebecca I got it, and she's already made an appointment to get it retrofitted with hand controls with that guy she knows," he says.

"Okay," I say, swallowing again, my lips aching from the smile forcing my lips up higher than they're used to.

"I call shotgun!"

Taryn rushes around the front of the car and crawls into the passenger seat. I shake my head and laugh at her.

"I can still put her in timeout, you know," my dad says, one eyebrow raised.

"I'm pretty sure you could never put Taryn in timeout…or me, for that matter," I laugh. "It's fine, though. I'll ride in the back. I want to ride in every single seat of this thing. I…I love it so much."

I link my arm through my dad's and lay my head on his shoulder. I don't think I've done this with him ever. Not once. A day of firsts.

I made my dad drive us around the block seven times, and before I could beg for one more, Taryn faked a phone call from TK and made up an excuse to leave. I didn't mind. She didn't have the same enthusiasm I had for my car, and I imagine the loop around our disgustingly familiar neighborhood was a bit of torture when the thrill of the first trip wore off.

When she left, I sat in the car for an hour, turning it off and on, programming the radio stations, searching for all of the secret compartments inside. I found a hair tie in the space where the seat pushes against the center console. It has a small pink flower on it, and I put it around the mirror, twisting it so the flower hangs just below the reflection.

It's not a peony, but I will pretend it is.

When my dad left the house tonight, I hugged him goodbye. I watched him back out of the driveway through my window, not thinking less of him, but thinking less of me. He was actually doing something incredibly selfless, and my instincts were to blame him for keeping secrets and being an alcoholic.

For the last two hours, I've sat in the dark of my room with my back against the wall, my legs stretched out on my bed, and my phone in my lap, thinking about how wrong I was. I've been wondering if perhaps that applies to other things, too.

I've read the last text I had from Wes dozens of times.

You would have been great today. Nature just wasn't ready for you to show that girl up yet.

Half a year has passed since he typed those words, and yet I look at them constantly, hoping to see more words behind them, new texts—the sweet ones, like before.

I close my messages and open my music, finding my favorite playlist from training and plugging in my headphones. When Rebecca called a while ago to confirm my car appointment, she also gave me the date for our photoshoot and the interview with *Girl Strong*. It's next week. With heavy beats deafening my ears, I pull my knees up and push my heels deep into my mattress while I look at my muscles work. Rebecca told me the sensation will never go away. I'm making the same movements, both of my quads are flexed, the lines of definition cut deep along my thighs, and when I close my eyes, I swear I can feel both of my ankles, both of my heels, the arches of both feet. I feel the flex, just like my mind is telling my legs to do. Every time I open and look, though, only one limb is real.

"Bi-on-ic," I mouth to myself along with the lyrics of the rap song blasting in my ears.

I stretch my legs back out and lean forward, wrapping my hands around my toes on the left and the smooth fiberglass on the right. A year ago, I wouldn't have been able to stretch like this even if someone offered me a hundred dollars. My body just wouldn't do it. I lacked the drive. I can't help but smirk at that thought. I meant what I said when I yelled at Wes. Yes, I've lost, but I have also gained.

My blinds open, I see the lights roll up along the curb first. My music mutes out the familiar rumble of his engine, but I imagine it so well that I almost don't hear the music anymore. All I hear is Wes.

The songs change, the beat heavier on the next song, and my mouth starts to curve with a smile. I lean back, rolling my shoulders before falling forward again, this time my legs apart, my body moving from one side to the next and then flat in the middle. My elbows fall to the bed and I push myself more until my forehead grazes the blanket beneath me.

"I am fucking awesome," I whisper, knowing my voice is probably louder than I think with the headphones in. I smirk at the thought and sit up, prepared to scream the words in my empty house, when I notice that the lights once parked along my house are now pointed right at it.

Yanking my earbuds out, I push my now trembling body to the edge of my bed. My breath comes out ragged, and my stomach sours when the motor outside revs once. The lights are blinding, and I can't tell who is in the car—if it is a car or a truck like I thought it was.

My eyes flash when the engine revs again, and my mouth starts to salivate like it does just before I throw up. With quivering lips, I crawl to my floor slowly, my head barely above the window sill. I keep telling myself that whoever is out there can't see me in my darkened room, but the lights…they're so bright.

The rev comes again, and I bring my sweaty hands up and rest my palms flat on the wall. I'm remembering it all—my dad, his car, Wes, my life…*my death*. It's this flash that pans out, a blink that could have changed everything. I'm nine again, watching my life crumble, waiting helplessly, confused and alone and embarrassed.

I'm paralyzed when the last roar echoes. Tires screech, and somehow I feel like I can smell them burn. The two lights speed forward, swerving to the right, crossing through the dirt in front of our house, racing over the loose bricks that used to be a flower bed until the front of the car smashes into the back of mine.

Tires squeal again, this time in reverse, and sparks light up the night as metal drags along my driveway. The bumper of my new car is pinned underneath a large older vehicle that's rolling down the sidewalk and into the road. The scraping sound is louder than thunder, and the car has to jerk forward and back twice before my car's chrome loosens enough that it can drive away. Once it breaks free, the car swerves as it speeds back toward the main road leading to the highway, and I rush out front as fast as I can, just in time to see the car turn left, toward the flower fields.

My eyes flash to the totaled pile of metal in our driveway, jagged pieces of steel lying on the concrete and smoke from the friction lingering in the air. My face feels numb, and my body feels lifeless, the world growing bright, then dark, then bright again. I'm unsteady on my legs, using my hands to hold along the doorway and the walls of the hallway back to my room.

I dive for my bed and clutch my phone, pulling up my contacts. I don't hesitate. I don't doubt. I do nothing but believe. I believe it all…every last crazy piece of it, and I do the only thing I know will help.

I call Wes.

CHAPTER 12

I barely got my words out before Wes was off the phone and his truck was out front. He's standing in the middle of my driveway now, his hat in one hand, his other hand gripping his hair, trying to make sense of the mangled mess in my driveway.

I haven't been able to get myself to go back outside, and I'm not sure if it's because I don't want to see my day-old car ruined, or because Wes is there...and I called him because I got scared.

When he starts to move toward my front door, I decide I can't put this off any longer, so I rush toward it to unlock it for him and let him inside.

"Thanks for coming," I say, my voice calm as I hold the door wide.

"Are you okay?" His hands cup my face quickly, and I tuck my chin and step back. It's too easy to go back to that role—the girl he needs to save. I need his help. I acknowledge that. But I need to be able to save myself, to protect myself and find that feeling of safety somewhere in myself. I can't put all of my faith in someone else when they could leave.

They all leave.

"I'm fine. They just trashed my car," I say, shaking my head and moving our conversation to the kitchen. "I haven't even gotten to drive it yet. I had to ride because we're getting the hand gears set up next week."

"Did you see someone? What direction did they go? Did you call the police?"

Wes spits out a dozen more questions after those, and I can barely get through the first one.

"I saw lights. They were in a car, and I thought..." I breathe out and let my lids close. "I thought it was you outside."

Wes is quiet, and I'm glad.

"I haven't called the police yet. You're right. I probably should," I say, walking back to my room to find my phone. I find it on the edge of my bed, where I dropped it while I stared out the window waiting for Wes. After I grab it, I turn to go back to the kitchen but Wes has followed me to my room. The space instantly feels smaller, and his eyes begin to roam the floor, the walls, my things.

"I've been cleaner since...well..." I lift my prosthetic and nod my head toward it. "I kept tripping over shit."

Wes's mouth pulls in on one side in a crooked smile, and his eyes flit to mine.

"What should I tell them?" I say, searching for the non-emergency number on my phone as I ask.

"Everything you can remember," he says. I feel him move closer, and without looking, I can sense that he's sat down...on my bed...*where I sleep.*

The operator answers after half a ring, and I'm flustered by it, so I sit down and hold the phone with both hands against my right ear, Wes to my left.

"Hi, uh...I need to report a crash, or maybe...maybe vandalism. I'm not sure what it is, but, shit," I wince. I bring one hand to my face and pinch the bridge of my nose, and before I can regroup, Wes takes my phone from my other hand.

"Someone rammed into her car parked in her driveway. It was intentional," Wes says, and I turn my head sideways, watching him as he speaks, drawing in that word—*intentional.*

"Yes, we're home," he says, pausing to listen to more details. "Yes, the car is still here. It's not drivable...yes...yes..."

He cups the phone and glances to me, and I'm frozen, still repeating that word in my head.

Intentional.

"They need to get your information down, for the report. They'll send someone out, but it's going to be a bit," he says.

My hands are shaking and Wes notices as I take the phone from him; I give the woman on the other end our address, my name, my father's name, the insurance that I know we have. She asks me to get the numbers for our insurance company ready for the officer to include in the report, and then she tells me someone will be by within the hour.

"I'm staying," he says the moment I hang up, not giving me a chance to tell him to go. He knew I would.

I shrug slightly and look to him from the corner of my eyes briefly. He's a foot away from me, and it would be so easy to pull my legs up, lie to my side, and rest my head in his lap. It would feel so nice, but I can't seem to make myself move. I've made barriers, and I won't cross them.

Wes leans forward, his elbows on his knees and his hands linked, one rubbing the knuckles of the other, cracking them, then switching. I remain still, my hands cupping my phone in my lap and my eyes entranced with his repetitive fidgeting with his fingers.

I know what I want to ask. I've had the question held on my lips since a stranger demolished the gift from my dad. More than company, more than security—it's the reason I called Wes. My lips feel numb now, though, parted as my breath slips over their skin. I say the words in my head, and hate that I can't seem to get them to come out for real.

"I wanted to," Wes says, finally breaking several minutes of silence between us.

I move my eyes from his hands to his face, but he's still looking down at my floor. His jaw twitches and his lashes blink slowly, his focus lost in a trance as he chews at the inside of his cheek.

"I told you I *wouldn't* come home, and you were right…the way that sounded…" His eyes blink again, this time opening on mine. The connection is sharp, like a pin in my chest. "That word doesn't reflect the truth."

"Then what word does?" My voice is calm, my heart is tired, and above all, I don't want to cry.

Wes swallows, his body remains still, and his gaze stays right where it's been.

"Wanted. I wanted to come back," he says, closing his lips tight and nodding his head with a tiny movement.

"You *wanted* to come back," I say, emphasizing the word.

Wes nods slowly.

"But…you *wouldn't.*" I tilt my head as I speak, shifting to look at him more closely. Wes shakes his head.

I breathe out through my nose slowly and try to wrap my brain around where I am, how this life is mine. None of it seems fair. I've had so very few years of happiness. A child should be happy. For a girl like me, though, happy has always been defined differently.

"How does the story end, Wes?" I ask, finally able to get the words out that have been stuck for so long.

He blinks, and his jaw twitches.

"Do I die?" My eyebrows lift as I think about what I just asked. Hearing it out loud, processing it this way—it makes me start to laugh slightly to myself.

"I don't know. It's just some stupid book Shawn made years ago. I feel stupid for even thinking maybe it was real," he says, and I can tell he's lying. He still believes it.

"You mean your *dad's* book," I say, calling him that because I know Wes doesn't want to hear it. It was mean.

"Yeah," he says, a little more bite to his tone. "My *dad's.*"

His eyes remain locked on mine. I blink a few times, looking at his mouth—resting in a flat line—and his hands, now cupping his knees.

"I die in the book, don't I?" I press on.

Wes looks at me for a few more seconds before standing and moving to the window, the blinds still open from when I twisted them to wait for his truck to pull up.

"You don't die, Joss. You live a long happy life, happily ever after—alone, and bitter, and unforgiving," he says. I jerk back, flinching at his words. Wes has never been outright mean to me.

"Fuck you," I say, standing and moving to leave my room. I make it to my doorway before I feel his hand grip my wrist.

"Don't go. I'm sorry," he says.

My muscles grow tense, but I don't pull away. I stop, one hand flat against the side of the doorframe and the other balled into a fist just below Wes's grip.

"I'm not unforgiving," I say, my words raspy and my voice only at half strength.

Wes doesn't respond, so I turn to face him, and his fingers slide around my wrist, never letting go, but loosening their hold.

His eyes flit from mine to my mouth, and I feel betrayed by the way my lips respond, parting with a silent gasp, welcoming him to look.

"Take it back," I say, bringing his gaze back to my eyes. His focus shifts from one eye to the other, and his expression grows defeated and sad.

"I wanted to come home," he says, the words coming out in a slow whisper.

My chest rises with a full breath and I hold it for a few seconds before letting it go, my shoulders falling.

"Then why didn't you?" I ask.

More silence. More long looks. More blinks as his eyes drill deeper into mine, growing sadder with every breath.

"It isn't you," he says, and my brow draws in fast in response. "The end of the story. It isn't you, Joss."

It's him. He dies. Wes dies, and he's afraid. My rigid muscles relax a little and my heart beat picks up as I wait.

"It's your dad," he says, and everything in my world stops.

Wes brings his free hand to his mouth, covering it so all I have to go by is what I can read in his eyes. I search for the truth, and all I see is all I've ever seen when I hear these stories—insanity.

My mouth bends up, quivering at first and eventually shaking with quiet laughter.

"My dad," I repeat, my head leaning to the side.

Wes's fingers slide away from my arm and I take a step back as his other hand falls from his face.

"I know how it sounds, and you're right; it's probably just crazy shit Shawn drew out of spite. He always hated your dad. I know, and I get it. I…I put this together just when you did, Joss. What you know? That's what I know, and I see how the pieces fit together. I see the picture, I get how jealousy fits into this. But there have been so many things that…" Wes pauses.

"My leg," I nod.

"Your leg," he says, his eyes closing.

Of the dozens of scenes Shawn created, some elements ring close to the truth. I lean against the doorframe and tuck my hands in my back pockets. When Wes opens his eyes again, he stands and moves to my open door, resting his back on the hinges, and we're so close that the toes of our shoes touch.

"I saw someone here," he says, and I look up quickly, my mind matching up his words with what I saw a few days ago, strangers in my yard. "Before I came back for good, before you found me, I would drive by at one or two in the morning. Sometimes…I was just getting my fix. Seeing my home, your street—sometimes you."

"You saw me?"

He nods, and I lift my chin, my heart stinging.

"I wanted to come back," he repeats his words from before. "But every time I was back in your world, something from that story came true. Never exactly like it, but the damage was enough."

"You came back once, Wes. Something bad happened once, and not because you came back. It happened and you were here. That's it," I say as his eyes fall somewhere below mine. "Have you ever stopped to think that it was just a coincidence? Or maybe Shawn is forcing you into these situations because he wants his fantasy to play out so he can watch? He could never save my mom. He was always too weak. So instead, he's playing fantasy with us."

His eyes lift to mine.

"Come here," he says, taking my hand again without asking, his fingers tight around mine, his hold more confident, more like how we used to be, and I soak in the familiar for a few seconds before fighting back. He doesn't let me let go, though, instead leading me back to the kitchen, to the stove, flicking it on high and waiting while the burner's flames grow blue and heat the coils they surround.

"There are some things, Joss, that I just cannot ignore. Why can I do this?" he says, holding his right hand over the flames, while his other hand holds onto mine even harder.

"Wes!"

He pulls his hand away and holds his palm flat in front of me.

"Nothing," he says. "It's not even pink, Joss."

Without hesitation, he places his palm flat on the grates of the burner, and out of instinct I reach for his arm, trying to pull him away.

"Leave it," he growls, holding me away with one hand while he tries to destroy his other.

"I can't even feel it, Joss. No pain. It's like I'm just pressing it flat on the counter. My hand," he says, finally pulling it away and holding it with his fingers wide, palm to my face. "Something is wrong with me, Joss."

I've seen things. We've talked about his abilities, if that's what they are. I've watched him save me from things that should have killed both of us. But he's never openly shown me what he can do.

My fingers slowly reach up to his now-quaking palm, and I glance to his eyes, asking permission. He lifts his chin as his eyes fall and his mouth turns down. My touch is gentle, starting at his thumb and his pinky, eventually cradling his hand in both of mine and bringing his palm closer. I draw a soft line along the center with my finger and his fingers twitch from the tickle.

"It's cool," I say.

He swallows loud enough that I hear it without looking up at him.

"I know," he says.

I run my fingertip along the lines in his hand, then down each finger, stopping at the inside of each knuckle and waiting—for what, I'm not sure.

"Joss, Shawn always put me in a place where I could be close to you.

After the bridge, I came to him because I remembered his stories. He would read them to me, and I used to think he was just trying to be funny when he would name characters after me and what I later realized was you, but then I remembered the bridge. I remembered the water."

I curl his fingers around mine and I stare at them in my hand, covering them as they continue to shake.

"He said I'm supposed to be your hero, but what if…" Wes's other hand comes up to cover mine, and I glance up slowly to meet his eyes. "What if I'm the bad guy?"

None of this makes sense. There are things that I can't deny, though, and what I just saw—that happened. Wes is special. And deep inside, I know that he and I were meant to walk the same path. Our roads were always meant to intersect. Those reasons, though—they've changed.

I move our hands lower as I step closer to him, and the vibration in his hands begins to spread throughout his nervous body. I let go of one hand and move it up the length of his arm, stopping at his bicep, where I bring it to the center between us, laying my fingers flat against the center of his chest. His breath is ragged, and his pulse is wild. His eyes are begging me to fix everything that's broken, but just as he said—I know what he knows. I don't have any answers, but my instincts are strong.

My other hand falls away from his hold and I bring it up the length of his body, his stomach and chest warm under my touch, and his trembling almost as strong as the rhythm of his heart. I don't stop until my other hand is cupping his face, his cheek rough from needing to shave, his breath hot against my arm and hand. His front teeth are closed together tightly, but his lips are parted enough that I can hear him breathe out in tiny, painful bursts. My thumb draws a line along his cheek, and I fall into the blue of his eyes a little more.

"I don't have the answers either, Wes, but there are two things I am certain of," I say, bringing my right hand up to match my left, holding his head in my palms. He does the same to me, his timid fingers finding me with a desperate touch as his eyes close. I push up on my left toes, holding the weight of my body as I stretch to match his height. Wes bends his head down, until our foreheads touch.

"I don't need a hero anymore," I say, and I feel his face shudder at the rejection, even though it isn't one. I'm not rejecting him, I'm rejecting the idea that I'm not strong enough to fight in this along his side. "Shhhh," I say, stepping an inch closer, close enough that my lips graze against his. His mouth opens to catch my top lip, to suck in softly and taste me like I'm a drop of water in the desert, but only for a single breath.

"I don't need a hero, Wes," I say again, pressing our foreheads tight again, my thumbs both drawing soft lines along his jaw. "I just need *you*."

His eyes open on my words, and I lean back enough to look into them.

"I need you," I repeat. We stare silently at one another, and I feel how hesitant he is, his fears worn on his face, but his weakness for us just as obvious. "I need you," I say one more time. "And you are not my villain."

My teeth grab onto my bottom lip as I shake my head. I raise a shoulder and smile through my nerves, through everything that hurts— through admitting I need Wes, and I see everything inside of me reflected in him.

"I can't let you feel hurt," he says, closing the few inches between us, his hands moving to the base of my neck and sweeping into my hair.

"When my dad was at his worst, Wes. When my life was complete and utter shit, do you remember what you said to me?" My hands fall to the middle of his shirt, grabbing the soft gray cotton and holding it in a way I've ached to do for months.

"You said you couldn't let me do it alone," I say. "You couldn't watch me carry that burden without helping. Let me help now."

"But I need to protect you," he says, and I shake my head and smirk before he's done speaking.

"No, Wes," I say. "I need to protect you."

His eyes close and I follow as his mouth takes over mine, his lips tasting me as his tall frame shadows me from anything else in the world. I hold onto his shirt with my clenched fists, and slowly I begin to feel everything I've kept at a distance. I feel his worry for me, his apprehension and apologies, but I also feel the way his heart has steadied in his chest.

Whatever he thinks he does for me, it's the other way around. I give him peace.

"I'm your home," I say, not realizing at first that the words I uttered against his mouth were out loud.

His mouth draws along mine in slow sweeps, resting with my upper lip caught between both of his again.

"I think maybe you are," he says in a whisper.

"I was angry," I say.

"I know," he says, and his breath tickles my upper lip. I smile against him.

"I was angry because I love you, and I never got to say it."

"I know," he says again, his lips nibbling mine softly before he runs his nose along my cheek, the roughness of his chin scratching along my neck and sparking a rush of goosebumps along my arms.

"You know I was angry?" I say through a light laugh.

"I know you love me," he says, and I bunch my face, parting enough to look him in the eyes again. "Subtlety is not your thing," he says, pulling me close once more and kissing my forehead.

Reality chimes in without warning, the knock on my front door abrasive and loud. The screen rattles under a heavy hand, and both Wes and I shake from the calm we managed to find amid this storm.

I follow Wes to my front door, and he opens it to let in two officers. We shake their hands, but I know the moment my eyes connect with the silver-haired cop that my story is about to take another twist. I was nine, and the man in front of me was probably forty then. He took notes, and he was the last to leave. The moment I say my name, he's going to remember why this place—why this house—looks so familiar.

Another car crashed into things here once. We were both here for it when it happened. My dad was probably drunk when it happened, and I…I should have died.

"Let's see, so can you tell me what happened here? To the best of your knowledge, Miss…Miss…*Winters.*"

I expect the man's eyes to widen, for recognition to hit and cut

129

between us like lightning, but it doesn't. His name is Officer Polk. I memorized it as I stared at it printed on his shirt when I sat cradled in Wes's arms in my driveway as a child. He flips open a small book and clicks a pen, ready to take another routine report. He doesn't recognize me. The decade erased my tragedy from his memory bank. My heart thumps wildly, but with each blink of my eyes, the beat slows, and I start to retell my version of what happened tonight. I'm almost calm, relieved that I'm the only one who seems to connect the past, when the second officer holds his ear against the radio strapped to his shoulder, ducking outside away from us. I continue to tell my story, but I'm unaware of the words coming out of my mouth. My attention is focused on the officer, on how long he's outside before stepping back through my door, interrupting my statement to share something private with his partner. He mumbles something, and they both glance at me, then to Wes.

Digital paper trails will always lead back to my past, and all it took was a few keystrokes to pull up my name and address to resurrect my near-death experience here. Officer Polk remembers me now.

"Are you family?" His eyes are set on Wes. He knows who he is, too. They've interviewed him about what happened here before, and Wes always claims he doesn't remember a thing.

"A friend. She was scared," Wes answers.

"Can I see your driver's license or I.D., please?"

Wes smiles and nods with tight lips, pulling out his wallet as Officer Polk steps closer to him. He takes the license in his hand, and I hold my breath as I watch his eyes scan the details.

"Wesley Christopher Stokes," he reads, glancing sideways to his partner then back to Wes. "Mind if I hang on to this for a minute?"

Wes shrugs. "Sure."

The officers look at one another again and have a silent conversation.

My eyes meet Wes's in that brief moment, and with the slight shake of his head, I know exactly what he's going to do. He's going to lie, just like he always said he would when my dad's case came up again for review. He'll tell them his name is Wesley. He'll say he knows he was in an accident when he was little, but that he doesn't remember anything about it. He'll say he doesn't remember me, and I'll have to act surprised, as if I didn't know it was him all along.

We'll add to the mountain of lies and hope we don't die from their weight. The problems lay beyond us, though. They begin when this conversation has to include my dad—who purchased the car in the driveway—and Wes's parents, who are going to want to know what's going on. Everyone is going to realize the miraculous chain of events that somehow put the two of us back together again, and then life is going to change one way or another.

CHAPTER 13

I'm not sure what's happening, but I know that Officer Polk is pretending just like us. You can't fake reactions like he had. But he never brought it up. He asked us questions, filled out a report, and then asked me to call my father.

That's where things stand now as Wes and I wring out these last few minutes of our beautiful illusion. My father is coming home from his second job. He's worried, and he's pissed because my car is totaled. And two officers are parked out front waiting.

"I don't think there's a way any of this is going to be okay," I say, picking a weed from the hardened dirt berm Wes and I are sitting on in my backyard. I hold it up to inspect under the moonlight, admiring how pretty even an ugly weed can be in the right setting.

"This used to be my favorite place on the entire earth," Wes says, not even acknowledging my worry.

I stretch my legs out and lean back on my elbows, feeling the sharp rocks and dried bits of grass poke into my arms as I look at Wes. He pulls his hat from his head, tossing it on the ground between us, his hair a tangled, brown mess that he weaves his fingers into as he rests an elbow on his knee and looks over the barren space that is my backyard. I follow his gaze around the perimeter of our home, along the patio covered in dirt, a half-filled recycle bin, old bats and gloves that haven't been touched in years, and the barbecue my dad bought right after my mom left us. She hated meat, and he hauled that thing home in an act of rebellion. He used it once.

"I thought this place was magical," I say through a sideways grin. Wes's head twists just enough that his eyes catch mine, and his lip tugs up on the side closest to me.

"Who do you think would have won?"

I stare back into his eyes, hearing nothing but the sounds of crickets and the steady purr of traffic along the highway off in the distance. I sit up and pull my legs in, crossing them and tugging the end of my T-shirt over my chilled knees. Hugging them, I rest my head on the top and give in to the pinch of the smile my lips are dying to make.

"The day of the final race?" I ask.

Wes nods, his mouth hinting at a smile, too.

I let the quiet linger for a few seconds, blinking as I breathe out a short laugh.

"I would have kicked your ass."

The silence is destroyed by Wes's thunderous laugh, his head cocked back and his eyes shut.

"I knew that's what you'd say," he says as his chin falls back to his chest and he twists to look at me. "I don't know, though…"

"You don't know," I repeat, biting the inside of my cheek, my lips puckering in a smile.

"I mean…you never really got to race me." Wes shrugs his shoulders and lifts a brow, trying to tempt me.

"You know what I think?" I tease. He responds with a slight lift of his chin, and I move closer to him, my movements slow and smooth. "I think…if speed was your super power, then you'd probably…be able to…"

My mouth ticks up on one side as my eyes haze and concentrate on his, even though my attention is not there at all. It's on his hat, only inches from his hand, but closer to mine. I position my left foot on the ground, ready to push myself up for my escape. Wes's head tilts with suspicion, and just as his eyes flash wider, I grab his hat and sprint down the berm.

"You'd be able to save your precious hat from me throwing it out in the alley!"

I giggle as I run, ducking and weaving as Wes tries to capture me. I teasingly pretend to throw his hat over the back wall, never actually doing it, and I use the angle of the hill to push off and gain speed. I know I can't outrun him completely. That was never my goal. It wasn't even really about eventually getting caught.

It was about getting back to *us*.

"I'm pretty sure you're disqualified," Wes shouts, finally wrapping me up in one of his arms and swinging me over his shoulder.

"My race, my rules, Wesley Christopher!"

With my head dangling upside down and his hat clutched in my right hand, I tug at the waistband of his jeans and shove his hat in the back of his pants, laughing so hard my voice practically gurgles.

"You think that's going to save you?" he teases, spinning with me over his shoulder, his hands gripping the back of my thighs as the ground below me forms a dizzying circle as we go around and around.

"You've seen me throw up, Stokes. Careful what you wish for," I say, secretly loving the way my head feels lighter, the way my hair splays out in the wind and my fingers tingle as the blood rushes down my arms. "You know I won't give in. There's no way I'm losing!"

Wes circles me through the air one more time while rolling my body back over his shoulder, but catching my thighs until I'm held in front of him, cradled.

"Fine, Josselyn," he says through a smile that spans his face but slowly slides into something more intimate.

Wes's eyes paint my face in gentle strokes as he holds me in his arms, his body now still as we stand in the middle of the place where we began. My face starts to tingle from his attention, and for just a moment, I forget everything that waits for us on the other side of the house.

"I was going to let you win," I say, my eyes set on his. I could look around him and see thousands of stars. It's the one gift of living in Bakersfield on nights without a moon. But I can't tear my eyes away from him.

He's home.

"You swore that there was no way you were losing," he laughs, the vibration in his chest like hearing my favorite song, the way it feels against my body.

"Not now. Not…not just then," I say, pulling my lip into my teeth and glancing up at the stars once. I let my lip go and breathe out, feeling the stretch of my mouth as it curves into my cheeks and my eyes move back to his.

"Then," I swallow. "When we were kids. Before I got worried about everything with my parents, I decided that if you looked sad when you showed up for the race that I was going to let you win."

Long seconds pass with his gaze on mine, his mouth curved with the hint of a grin, his breathing a slow and steady wave taking me up and down in his arms, soothing me.

"Maybe it wasn't your race to give to me," he says, his smile growing crooked.

"I would have won it…for you. I wouldn't have lost," I shake my head. "It would have mattered too much to me."

Wes's forehead comes to rest on mine, and I breathe in the nearness of him.

"I haven't gotten drunk or smoked or any of it since the last time you saw me at the bottom," I say, my eyelashes tickling his cheek as my lids fall shut. I feel his fingers adjust their hold, twitching with nerves. "I knew…I always knew that you were alive, and I wasn't going to go back to that place."

His nose grazes along my cheek as his chest rises with a deep breath that he holds this time.

"What place is that?"

"The one where you found me," I say. "Where it's dark, and I hurt myself so I can feel something. Where I feel alone."

It's quiet between us, but the right kind of silence. It's peaceful, and I remind myself to remember how *this* feels. Never will I settle for anything less.

"You are never alone, Joss," he says, letting my legs slide from his grip until I'm standing in front of him. He runs his thumbs through my hair, pulling it back behind my ears on both sides and pausing when his palms find my cheeks. "There are so many people who love you in this world. I'm merely one of them."

I tip-toe to kiss him, but the moment my mouth finds the softness of his lips, my father's throat clears.

"Were you home for this?"

My fingers are woven through Wes's and I'm squeezing so hard that I may break his bones. Though his bones don't seem to break, so I'll probably just break mine. My father is standing a foot into the covered patio, the garage door open behind him. His head keeps swiveling from Wes and me to the damage behind him.

"Did the officers see you come in?" I sidestep his question.

"Yeah, they're waiting by the car. I told them I wanted to find you first," he says.

My father's face is red. He's always had a tell for his temper, but this...this is different. This is the same way he looked when the bridge collapsed and our bus rolled. It's fear.

Wes and I follow my dad back through the garage to the driveway, where the officers are both now examining the front of my dad's car. The bumper is missing, and deep gouges bend the metal at the front of the hood.

Officer Polk has quit pretending, and the moment his partner pulls Wes aside toward the house to "ask him a few questions," I know that the blissful moment I had minutes ago in my backyard is the last I might have for a very long time.

"Mr. Winters, can you tell me where you were this evening?" Officer Polk asks.

My dad's head tilts and the wrinkle on his forehead deepens.

"I'm sorry?"

"Sir, please just answer the question," the officer says.

My dad's lips part and his eyes begin to blink rapidly as he looks from the destroyed gift he gave me to his own banged up vehicle. I can see his chest shudder with panic, and I instinctually move to stand closer to him. His wide eyes move to me, though, and he holds up his hand, his fingers stiff and spread.

"No, no…it's fine. Yeah, sure…I…I have a night job. I've been working at Crane's Tack and Feed, stocking and inventory. And I know," my dad pauses to let out a nervous laugh as he gestures to his crinkled hood. "This looks weird, but I did this on my way to work tonight. Some guy backed his trailer into me and it hooked under the front…ripped the bumper right off. He offered to pay for it, so…"

"So you were at Crane's…tonight," Officer Polk says, not bothering to look up from his notepad.

"I was," my dad answers, clearing his throat lightly after he speaks. His hands fidget at his sides as he rocks from foot to foot.

"And you have someone who can verify this?"

I can tell by the way my father's breathing halts and the way his shoulders lift, his muscles tensing, that he doesn't.

"I work alone. They gave me a key, and I just come and go," my dad says in a rushed voice, his eyes darting from me to the officers now circling him. "I'm sure there's a security camera or something, though. The stuff there is all pretty expensive, and I know there's a security pad. I punch in the numbers, so that's recorded probably, right? And I have the name and number for the guy with the trailer…I didn't want to make a report. You know, screw the guy over on his insurance?"

"We'll follow up on that," Polk says.

My father exhales with relief, but only briefly.

"Mind if we take a look in your car?" Officer Polk is already circling my dad's vehicle and reaching for the handle before my dad can get out a "go ahead."

My father's forehead wrinkles and his mouth slopes down heavily, like he's going to be sick, as our cop friend makes his way to the back seat. When he pulls out a half-empty bottle of whiskey, I understand why.

Weaknesses.

"Sir, we're going to need to administer a breathalyzer…"

"Oh no, no…I haven't been drinking," my dad interjects quickly.

"He hasn't. He's in recovery, and he's been sober for months now," I defend, struggling to not believe that bottle of whiskey means anything.

Our words are meaningless, though, as Officer Polk looks up with pursed lips, his pen paused in his hand a few inches above his paper. His eyes zero in on me, and time slows down enough that I can see his pupils dilate with his stare.

"So you're refusing?" He says the words to my father, but his gaze lingers on me for a second as he speaks.

"No…no, if…if you need me to, I will," my dad says.

He looks sick, his skin pale and tiny beads of sweat kernelling above his brow.

I feel helpless, standing only feet away from him, my head turning to check behind me for Wes, then back to my dad as Officer Polk forces him to take a test he's failed so many times before. In a blink, my mind flashes through them all—from the night he spent in the county jail drying out after he threw a stool through a window at Jim's to the last time he tried driving himself home after a late-night binge. I'm expecting the words that never come, for them to inform him that he's beyond a legal limit, but my father's kept his promise. He's sober, just like I said he was.

I hear the screen door at the front of my house open behind me, so I twist to see the officer who led Wes inside standing with one foot outside. He nods to Officer Polk, and there's a noticeable pause for everyone.

"Mr. Winters, we're going to need to take you in to ask a few more questions," the other officer says, moving to the squad car. He opens the back door, where they put criminals…murderers.

"Is he under arrest?" I take a forceful step closer to Officer Polk as I ask.

"We just need to talk to him, Josselyn," he says. He's hiding things, and his tone is condescending.

"Then maybe you should call our lawyer," I say, folding my arms over my chest.

My father's eyes rush to mine and his head falls to one side a tick as he breathes out.

"Joss, it'll be fine. They just want to talk to me. You stay here with Wes, and I'll be home soon," my dad says, trying to reassure me even though I see his hands trembling.

"My father was at work. He bought me this car. It was a gift. He bought me a gift!" My voice grows louder as I follow them to their cars, but I may as well be in another dimension where nobody hears me. "Dad, tell them! Daddy!"

My father isn't handcuffed in front of me, but I know that was out of respect. I can tell by the way he walked, the way his posture fell under the weight of shame. The officer who was talking to Wes put his hand on my dad's shoulder, lowering his head to keep him from bumping it as he slides into the back seat. It's only because he's cooperating, but something is wrong. Something is terribly wrong, and we need a lawyer. I lied when I said we had one, but I'll find us one.

"What am I supposed to do?" I shout, my hands finding my forehead as I walk aimlessly between my family's two wrecked cars.

"Here," Officer Polk says, handing me a card after writing something on the back. He tears away a pink copy of the report he'd taken for my car. "If you think of anything else, or if you see anything new…if someone bothers you…makes you feel…*threatened*—call 911, then call me."

I don't speak, instead swallowing what feels like razorblades down my throat. It's only air, and it isn't cold, but it hurts. It takes me several seconds to snap out of my stupor after the car pulls away, but the last thought I had still sticks with me.

"Grace," I whisper to myself, rushing to the door. Grace can help.

Wes is standing at the edge of our kitchen counter, one hand flat on the surface. He's waiting for me. I freeze where I stand, our eyes meeting.

"My phone…I think I left it…" My words trail off, because I start to get that feeling in my chest again, like a spoon digging into the softness between my ribs. I haven't felt that pain in months, and it knocks my breath away.

"It's here," Wes says, sliding his hand to the right and grabbing my phone. He pulls it into his palm, but doesn't move his feet, so I close the distance between us myself.

"I didn't tell them anything, Joss," he says, and my eyes flit from where my hands touch his to his face. "They asked if I knew you, and I told them how we met…in January, when my family moved here. But, I could tell."

"They took my dad in," I say, and Wes breathes in and his cheek twitches in a painful wince. "They didn't arrest him, but they have questions."

I look down to the wrinkled report and business card in my hand, now noticing the writing on the back. What I'd assumed was an email or another phone number, is actually a message from Officer Polk, and it confirms everything Wes and I were worried about:

ARE YOU SAFE?

"He thinks my dad did this," I say, handing the card to Wes.

I begin to dial my phone while Wes turns the card over in his fingers a few times. I let it ring several times, eventually holding for the voicemail on my grandmother's line. When I hear the beeping tone, I fumble through my words.

"Grace…I need your help. I'm…I'm okay, but my dad's in trouble, and…no, he's not drinking. He's actually doing really well, but there's a misunderstanding I think, and someone vandalized my car tonight, so they took Dad in to ask him some questions. I just…I think we need a lawyer, but I don't know how to get one. Dad's working a night job, so I'm pretty sure we can't afford it. This is really hard for me…"

I swallow in the pause, my eyes moving to Wes's again.

"I think I need some help. Please call me back."

I hang up with the feeling in my gut stronger than ever, and I expect nothing from my plea.

"I'm not sure what to do," I say, pressing my back teeth together hard while my eyes zone out on the speckled countertop beside us. I lay my phone on it, then run my fingers along the pattern, feeling the imperfections left behind from knives used here to cut apples and cheese over the years.

"The first time I slid for softball, I cut the shit out of my knee…I didn't do it right," I say, halting my hand and splaying my fingers out over the counter's surface. I pat my palm on it twice, softly. "My dad lifted me up and set me right here. He poured that stuff on my leg that hurts like hell…what is that stuff?"

"Bactine?" Wes's voice croaks out.

"Yeah…that's it," I say.

I let the quiet take over again as I fall back into my vivid memory of that day. "My dad was so proud of me because I didn't cry. I screamed when the Bactine stung, as my dad wiped away tiny bits of sand and gravel, but I didn't cry. I gritted my teeth, and I squeezed the edge of the counter…right…here."

I feel along the bottom to the place where the vinyl is coming apart from the board underneath, and I dig my fingernails in and snap it.

"I ripped this part off," I smile, flicking the torn counter piece again. "But I didn't cry," I say, my smile falling as I look up to meet Wes's gaze. "Not once."

Wes tucks my hair behind my ear, his movement slow. When he leaves his fingertips along the side of my head, I reach up and hold his wrist, moving his hand forward until his palm is flat on my cheek. I slide my fingers up to cover the back of his hand, and I press his warm touch into me.

"I need to tell my family everything, and we need to tell your dad," he says.

My lips pull in tight, and I nod slowly.

"I know," I blink.

I hold his hand against me for minutes, and we stand silently in my kitchen, avoiding the weight of the things that lay ahead. The truths give me hope, though. My dad wasn't drinking, and the police know he wasn't…at least not tonight. My dad didn't do this to my car, either; someone else did.

Someone who is going to do something bad again.

And that's the place we are now. Me and this boy…this superhuman boy, who can hold his hand to the fire and fend off drowning, who can catch rocks flying through the air at the speed of bullets and stop cars from killing little girls. This boy who is the only thing I have loved other than the man the cops just drove away.

My phone rings, and I fumble as I scramble to pick it up from the counter, finally finding the CALL button as I bring it to my ear.

"Hi…hello…" I had calmed my heart finally, but it pounds now.

"Josselyn, it's your grandma. Tell me what you need," she says, and I bring my fist to my mouth, squeezing my eyes tight. I won't cry, but I will feel relief. I have family.

"Grandma, thank you. Thank you so much for calling me back," I say, feeling Wes's hand slide to the middle of my back. "I need your help, and it's going to cost money. And maybe…maybe you could come, too. For just a little while."

"I'll leave first thing in the morning. Now tell me about the rest," she says, and I breathe deep and start at the very beginning, telling her the side of my story that she doesn't know—the parts even my parents never truly saw.

"The day of the accident, when I was nine…there was this boy…"

CHAPTER 14

Wes spent the night, sleeping on our sofa with the front blinds open enough for him to keep watch. I doubt he slept for real, because every time I was awake and walked from my room to check on him, his eyes were fixed on that window, standing guard.

School starts in three hours. It feels ridiculous to just jump right back into normal life as if none of the crazy shit that is happening is real. But it is real, and sitting around trying to untangle it isn't going to make it go away. I'm also not going to understand it. And routine, it turns out, is my friend.

The sun isn't up for another hour yet, but I can't wring any more sleep out of the dark. My clean clothes clutched against my chest, in my arms, I walk from my room to where Wes is sitting on the sofa, his feet on the floor, his hands on his knees, his hair messy and his eyes wide—still looking out the window. The blanket I gave him is folded next to him along with the pillow.

"Tell the truth. Did you sleep at all?"

I lean into the wall as I look at him. He doesn't answer with words, instead smirking on one side and shrugging his shoulder.

"Bionic or not, you need sleep Stokes," I say.

"Bi…onic?" His brow quirks up.

I laugh lightly and shrug my shoulders.

"It's a line from one of my favorite songs. I've been listening to it a lot lately," I say, kicking my prosthetic forward. "I guess you're not really bionic, though."

Wes is wearing that stupid smile…the one that made me fall in the first place. It's this barely there curve that I can only read when he's staring at me, like it's a secret code just for me. We spend a few seconds just like this—staring.

"I love you, you know," he says. Simple words with the weight of concrete on my chest. I don't know how to respond to them, because I'm not sure I understand what love like this is. I'm not sure anyone could. What are we? Why are things happening to us? Why does the idea of *us* have to be filled with so many impossibilities and hurdles?

I part my lips to say it back, but I'm stopped by my phone ringing. I step toward Wes, setting my clothes down on the coffee table and pulling my phone from the pocket of my shorts I slept in. The number comes up UNKNOWN.

"Hello?"

I keep my eyes on the boy who says he loves me.

"Joss, it's Dad."

The sigh comes hard and fast. I didn't realize how little I'd been breathing since my father left. Hearing his voice lifts this immediate weight from my shoulders.

"Dad, oh my god. Are you okay? Are you coming home?"

I have a million more questions, as I'm sure he does. My mind is racing through everything I need to tell him—Grace is coming, Wes is Christopher, Shawn is his dad, and Bruce doesn't know. None of those things come out though, because my dad—he talks first.

"I'm going to be here for most of the day. I need you to go to the window…right now," he says, and my heart spikes its rhythm.

"Okay." My words come out breathy, and I shake my head at Wes when he looks at me with concern.

I walk to the front window and look out at the street. There's a dark car parked out front, and my stomach drops instantly.

"There's a car!" My words rush out in a panic, and Wes is standing behind me in a blink.

"It's fine. It should be a black ford, slightly tinted windows," my dad says.

I study it, and after a few seconds, I'm certain it matches his description.

"It is," I say.

"We're going to have an officer watching us for a while. It's okay…" he speaks quickly, not wanting to give me room to worry. I'm worried despite that, though. "Listen, I'm going to be fine. I'll be home tonight. We'll be fine."

"What's going on, Dad?" My eyes are fixed on the officer's profile, sitting in the front seat. I can see his movements; his arm raise and bring a cup to his lips. He's drinking coffee.

"We're going to be fine, Josselyn." He's using his stern voice, the one I get on the field, and the one I used to get all of the time until he started working on being sober. I don't like that voice. It brings out a side of me that I am trying to tame.

"There's a cop out front watching our house, Dad. Someone smashed in my car, and you've been at the police station all night because your car is trashed, and then there was the whiskey. And there were people snooping around our front yard last week…"

"Who was in our yard?" My dad cuts in fast.

"No one, or I don't know…maybe someone. It didn't seem important then," I lie. It was important then. It made me nervous, until I lied to myself that it was nothing.

"Josselyn, you need to be aware of things. I don't want you staying at the house alone, either. When I'm not home…I'd like you to go to Taryn's," he says, and my nerves ratchet up a little more. If this were nothing, if we were going to be *just fine,* then code-red orders would not be coming out of his mouth right now.

"Dad, let's get over this concept that you need to protect me from information. I think I've proven I can handle shit."

His sigh is audible, and it isn't because I swore. It's because I'm right.

"I owe some money to a couple of guys," he says, spilling the words out quickly, as if he's asking if I want him to pick up juice at the store.

"How much?"

I close my eyes and pinch the bridge of my nose. My dad doesn't answer right away, and the longer he's quiet, the more money I know it is.

"Eighty thousand."

A sour taste takes over my mouth, and my bottom lip falls as my eyes flutter. I was expecting a big number. I was not expecting it to be *that* big.

"Jesus, Dad!"

Wes nudges my shoulder so I turn to face him. I shake my head, but he doesn't back away. He knows this is something big.

"How did this happen? Why so much? Were you…gambling? Was this from before? When you were drinking? Did you slip? Is that why you had the whiskey? Or was it…Dad…was this…drugs?"

My father is quiet again, and I can no longer stand. I move back toward the couch, sitting down and holding my head in my hand, the phone pressed to my ear. I wait for my dad to tell me, to give me a response that is better than any of the ones I laid out as possibilities, but as his silence registers with me, I realize that the truth is actually much worse. That money…it was for *me*.

"I would have been okay."

I'm not sure when the tear formed, but it slices along the side of my face until I catch it at my chin, wiping away it's evidence with the long sleeve of my favorite sweatshirt. I hear my father swallow hard on the other end, I know he's trying to be strong, too.

"Okay wasn't good enough," he says, and I smile even though my face wants to cry.

"Rebecca?" I ask, wondering if the woman who has inspired me so much knows what my dad went through to pay her.

"Some of it," he says. I turn my head and look at Wes, now sitting on the coffee table across from me, his legs on either side of mine. He leans forward as his hands come up to hold my elbows, and our foreheads rest against one another as I talk to my dad.

"You should have told me," I say.

My father chuckles.

"You would have scrapped the plan," he says. "You needed this. You've always been meant to defy odds and prove people wrong. Hell…you put *me* in my place."

"I didn't need to compete again, though," I say, knowing it's a lie the moment the words leave my lips. My dad's right—I would have withered away, at least inside. My soul needed the fire to be relit, and it was more than losing my leg. It was like being reborn as a stronger version of me. I had hit bottom, and I climbed out. Without this, without having something to fight for, I may never have found the light.

"I'm not going to talk bullshit with you," my dad says, coughing through his laugh. I can tell he's tired. "And it wasn't all Rebecca. Bills have been piling up for a while."

I take that in, that word—*while*. I wonder how far in the hole we were before the accident buried us.

"They think the people you owe…that they did this? My car?"

Wes pulls back and looks in my eyes, but his mouth remains closed. He's listening.

"Most likely," he says.

"And the burn on your arm…"

My dad sighs again.

"Why would you get in with someone so dangerous? You could have asked your parents," I say, and a guttural laugh bursts from my father. "Fine, okay, maybe not, but…Grace? Why not Grace?"

"Joss, Grace and I aren't close, and while she's a good woman, I'm pretty sure she would think I made my own problems," he says.

My throat starts to close with what I have to say next.

"I called her."

My dad is quiet.

"I didn't know what else to do, and the cops took you. I was afraid it was because…"

I shudder, stopping my words too late. My dad doesn't respond right away, and I hear activity in the background—phones ringing, doors buzzing open and shut. It sounds like he's in an administrative area, which means he really is just talking to officers. This isn't his *one phone call.*

"You thought it looked like I tried to run my daughter over twice."

I hear him sniff in a short breath. Hearing him say it out loud is sobering. It's what so many people saw when I was a kid—my dad tried to kill me with his car. Then he abandoned me to alcohol. People would think it happened again except the only people who know about my smashed car are my father and Wes. At least until some neighbor sees the car and the tow truck that's going to have to haul it away, and rumors start.

"I was afraid they would accuse you," I admit. "I mean your car getting messed up tonight is a crazy coincidence, and the whiskey…"

"It was old," my dad cuts in. A quiet pause lasts several seconds before he continues. "Every day I think about throwing it away, but it's like my crutch or safety net. Knowing it's there, even though it tempts me, it also makes me feel like I have options."

"That isn't your option anymore." My tone is stern, the child scolding the parent.

My dad doesn't respond, and after a few seconds I know he's done talking about his recovery.

"So you aren't a suspect. When can you come home?" I ask.

"Soon," my dad says. "They had some other questions."

I want to know what those questions were—if my dad was so drunk when I was nine that he really did almost kill me in a fit of rage. I want to know just how close I came to dying.

"Did you answer them?"

My question isn't fair, and I don't mean it to sound as hard as it does.

"I'm sorry…" I begin to retract.

"Don't be. I did. They had the breathalyzer, and I was able to get the time stamp from work on video. And the questions from the time with Kevin, when I…"

"I know what time you mean," I cut in, not wanting to hear him say *when he almost hit me* again.

"Right, well...anyhow...those questions were the same as they always were," he says, and I wait thinking about how many times I've tried to change that day in my head. I come home a little later, we don't have the races, and my dad has to work, so he never sees my mom...or Kevin...or any of it.

"Except for one thing," he says, snapping me out of my own head.

"Yeah," I breathe, my forehead crinkling.

"They asked me why Wes was there."

I laugh out once. "Were they trying to tell on your little girl having a boy at the house when you weren't home? Because I called him and that's why he came," I say.

"No, no...not that," my dad says. My laughter fades back to silence. The unraveling is beginning now. "And not tonight, Joss."

He means then—years ago. They asked him why Wes was there both times, which means my dad now knows that Wes is the boy he owes my life to, the one who kept him from becoming a monster.

"Oh," I say in a hushed tone. My eyes are locked on Wes's, and I can tell he knows what we're talking about without hearing the words. There's a shift in his expression, a slight tilt in his eyes.

My dad knows I won't say more about it now, and he doesn't wait for me to fill in the gaps.

"What time is Grace coming?" he asks.

"Noon. She's going to take a taxi to the house, and I'll run home from school to let her in," I say.

"Have Wes drive you...if he can," my dad says.

I nod slowly, then speak. "I'm sure he can," I say.

"All right, then. I better go. They need me to get some information to their detectives, meet with a few other people. I phoned in for a sub, so I won't be at school. And I guess..." he pauses, letting out a fast and heavy breath. "I guess let Grace know I'll be late. And make up my bed for her. She'll be more comfortable in there. I'll take the couch."

My eyes roam to the right, to the blanket Wes barely used, and I smile.

"Okay," I say.

I hang up with my father and sit still, my legs touching Wes's, my eyes now looking a little below his.

"He's okay," I simplify.

I blink a few times and leave my focus on Wes's neck and chest. He ducks his head after several seconds, catching my gaze and bringing my head up with widened eyes.

"Really, he's okay," I say. "He's not in trouble. I mean...other than owing some lunatic eighty grand," I laugh out.

Wes's chest fills and he leans back a little.

"Yeah, maybe not...*okay.*" I give Wes a wry smile. "But he isn't arrested. They know he didn't crash into my car."

"Good," Wes says, his shoulders falling a little as he relaxes slightly. I look down at his chest again.

"They asked about you," I say, expecting him to tense up again. He doesn't.

"I thought they might," he says.

I catch his eyes again, and I hold onto them for a breath or two before standing and moving out from the small space trapped in front of him.

"I should shower. We have school, and you probably need to get home so your family doesn't freak out," I say.

"I told Levi I was here," he says, holding up his phone. "He texted me after I left. When you share a room with two other dudes, you sorta notice when one kicks around a pile of clothes on the floor looking for a shirt so he can race to his girlfriend's house."

My lip rises on one side. *Girlfriend.* I don't tease. In fact, I don't draw attention to it at all. I don't debate it, or rehash that we still have a long way to go since he left and came back. I push down thoughts on how I'm filled with trust issues because of my father, and how absolutely fucked-up crazy our lives are with Wes thinking he's been put here to save me. I don't talk about how I waver from believing in that damn book of predictions and thinking the whole thing is a load of crap. Instead, I just let the moment wrap itself around my heart, because *girlfriend.*

"All right, well...I'll be a few minutes, and at least we can get you into some fresh clothes," I say, taking a step or two down the hall before pausing, tapping my fingers along the wall and looking over my shoulder at him. His eyes are waiting for me, and his lip is raised on the same side as mine. I let the energy of that one look settle into my chest and warm me from inside, then I head the rest of the way down the hall and shut the bathroom door behind me.

My eyes take in my reflection as soon as I rest my back against the door. I haven't looked at myself in a long time, and the last time I did—the last time I *really* looked—I didn't think the girl looking back at me was good enough. This girl, though—she's strong. My mouth is still curved in the same smile I gave Wes, and it grows as I step closer to the sink, setting my clothes and phone on the counter.

My blonde hair has gotten lighter from the summer sun. It used to be dark and lifeless, hidden by late nights and a bedroom where I never once let the light in. It's longer, too, the ends twisting down to my elbows. I lean in, studying the grayish blue of my eyes—which, while they've never been bright and vivid like Wes's—are unique on their own. The color looks like a storm.

I no longer hate the freckles that sprinkle from one cheek to the other, and the pinkish tone of my cheeks, kissed by sun like my hair. My shoulders are bronze, and I tug my shirt sideways at the neckline and run my opposite finger along the light line drawn over it where the strap of my tank top has become a permanent pattern on my body.

My shoulders are strong, but still feminine. I lift my shirt up over my head, dropping it to the floor, and I run my hands down the front of my body, over my breasts to my stomach and hips, hooking my fingers in my shorts and underwear, dropping them to the floor as well. I look back up and take all of me in, at least to my waist where I can't see below in the mirror.

Somehow, over the last six months, I've become something more than just a girl. I look at this person in the mirror, and she's a woman. My leg is not perfect. My thighs are thick from running and working the muscles hard as I train. My nails are short from playing ball and chewing at them, and my skin is dotted with light bruising from workouts and missed grounders on the field. But my imperfections make me smile more.

I glance down where my phone lays by the sink, and I pull it into my palms and open a message to Wes. Without hesitation, I type what I feel right now. No second-guessing and no doubts or worries. Just this one thing that, while I've said it, I don't think it's been heard by him enough.

I love you, you know.

It's exactly as he said it to me minutes ago, and I mean it with the same depth and emotion as he did. I set my phone down and watch the screen with a pounding heart, waiting for him to type something back, but instead, the bathroom door pushes open slowly.

I don't turn at first, instead just watching through the mirror. Wes's eyes meet mine in the reflection, and I swallow slowly, my pulse gaining speed and my lips tingling.

Wes steps fully inside, shutting the door behind him, but he doesn't look down at my body—he holds his gaze right on mine in the mirror. As he steps closer, his hands move to my elbows, then slide down my arms to where my hands are resting on the counter, his fingers threading with mine. Almost as if a reflex, my fingers open and invite him in, squeezing tight at his touch.

His head turns slightly and his eyes fall shut as his mouth moves close to my neck, stopping a breath away from actually touching my skin, and my body drowns in shivers when he opens his mouth and his bottom lip grazes me. I tilt my head to the side, giving him more access, and his eyes open to meet mine again in the reflection.

Lips curve before opening slightly to kiss along my neck, and his hands follow the lead of his mouth, running up my arms and over my shoulders, into my hair that he pulls up and grabs fistfuls of as his mouth tastes more of me, traveling from my neck to my shoulder.

"I know," he whispers, and I turn into him, his eyes taking me in now, seeing all of me and roaming slowly up my body until they meet mine again. His chest rises and falls rapidly, and his mouth hovers open without words and his breathing grows ragged. I can read his thoughts behind his eyes, and I can practically taste his hesitation. My boy is bashful. He's also beautiful, the way he looks into me, seeing my entire story—the broken parts and the pieces he's managed to repair.

"I know that you love me," he continues, his hands moving to either side of my face, cupping my cheeks as he leans in and presses his mouth to mine. I open to him, and I taste him, moaning when his tongue touches mine, his lips sucking my upper one as his body takes a slow stride back, ultimately leaving me breathless.

His eyes don't move from mine except for the brief second when he lifts his T-shirt over his head and adds to the discarded clothing on the floor. I lean into the counter behind me and watch as he steps toward the shower and turns the water on, holding his hand in the stream to test its warmth. Turning to me, he unbuttons his jeans and slides them, along with his boxers, down his body, kicking them away before holding a hand out to me, his palm up.

I know I should be nervous, but I'm not. I should be afraid of him seeing me, but I've never wanted to be seen more. And Wes isn't afraid either. He isn't waiting for me to reject him, and he isn't doubting the words I said, just as I don't doubt his. This is that rare moment where a girl and a boy are ready for something, in a way it was probably always supposed to be. Those other times, those other boys—those were all regrets now, because this…*this* is special.

"I have to take off my leg," I say, stepping toward him and taking his hand.

"Okay," he says, lip raised enough to form a dimple on his left cheek.

Of everything that I've prepared for in my physical therapy, this was the one thing that I tucked to the depths of my mind. There isn't therapy for this—a course or a manual that helps me navigate being intimate with someone else, someone…whole.

When Wes was missing, I didn't have to think about how my body looked to someone else. I wasn't interested in a near-future, or a distant one for that matter, that included a scenario like the one I'm in right now.

I feel vulnerable. I *hate* feeling vulnerable. And I can feel the sureness leaving my body in waves with every breath I wait through to do it.

I step forward and balance myself, holding onto the long bar my father had installed near the shower entrance. It's a move I make every morning and night all on my own, one I've gotten so good at that I'm able to perform it in seconds. My hands are shaking now, though. Wes notices, and his hand quickly slides along my arm, under my elbow, to support me.

Swallowing, I don't let myself look at him, instead imagining that he isn't looking at me with pity, or wanting to step in and make this small task easier for me. Perhaps he isn't, but it's a risk I can't take. Nothing is easy for me. It's that resistance I get with everything I do, though, that I thrive off. I need it to survive, and if I ever want to feel what it's like to love someone, wholly and completely, I need to overcome this push, too.

I detach the socket and twist my knee, feeling the pressure release as I set my leg to the side and roll down the silicon sleeve and layers of padding. I place them on the counter near the sink and take a deep breath. The air feels heavy in my chest, and my pulse radiates through my core.

"This is what I am," I say, my eyes blinking slowly as I force myself to look him in the eyes. His gaze is waiting for me, along with the sweet smile that is exactly as I left it. My lips pinch in at the corners, quivering with the want to smile and cry all at once.

"No," Wes says, moving into me until our foreheads touch. "This is only a fraction of what you are."

His hand sweeps behind my body to the small of my back. My balance is lost in a flash of a second as his other hand runs down the side of my body and lifts me under my good leg. My body held close to his chest, our heads still touching, his eyelashes tickle against mine as he steps with me in his arms into the steam from the shower.

Wes lowers me slowly, holding me tight until my foot finds it's balance between both of his. My arms drape over his shoulders, and my hands feel the warm stream of water that cascades down his neck.

I have never done something like this. The other times, with other boys, it was always a dare I gave myself—an act of rebellion. Those times when I showed my skin, bared my breasts, and discarded clothes were all in darkened rooms swirling with the scent of alcohol or the back of pickup trucks parked just behind the drive-in. Bonfires, basement parties, and the abandoned shed where the football team's equipment is stored—I was that kind of girl. But not anymore, and never again. Wes has taught me what tender means, what love is, and what self-respect deserves.

I tighten my hold around his neck and pull myself to him, my lips finding his waiting. His kiss begins softly, taking slow passes along my bottom lip then my top before sucking me in and parting my lips enough that he tastes me completely. We move together under a blanket of water. My hands roam along his arms, around his back, my fingers daring to move to his chest and stomach. I pause with my fingertips just below his waistline, curious, but not wanting to be forward—wanting to be pursued.

His hands wash down my shoulder blades and trace the curve of my back until he finds my butt, squeezing as he lifts me up into him, holding my thighs and kissing me harder.

In a breath, my back is against the wall, and Wes's body is pressed against me with my legs wrapped around him. I've forgotten completely about what my body is missing; instead, every inch of me feeling alive and whole as his mouth covers my jaw with kisses. His lips dive into my neck, and I feel the sharpness of his teeth as he grazes my collarbone. Every kiss, every touch, tears away one more layer of worry and doubt that I'll ever be more than I was. Wes pauses, his head resting on mine again, his eyes looking down at my breasts, silky with beads of water, and I feel his body pulsing with every heavy breath he takes.

He wants me.

I need him.

I am more than I was. This body…it's sexy.

"Take me to my bed," I whisper against his lips. His fingers pulse against my legs where he holds me, and his body feels harder.

"I'm not leaving," he says, and I nod against him.

"I know," I say.

"Before, I only stayed away for you. Everything…it's for you. I came back for you, I was born for you." His breath hitches and his body shudders and he pulls me tight against him and turns in the shower, leaving the water running.

He kisses me as he carries me to my room, our bodies dripping water along the carpet. Wes pushes the door open with his elbow and kicks it closed with his foot. My body finds the softness of my blanket, and I push myself up until my head rests on my pillow, not caring that my hair is soaking the sheets. Within a blink, Wes's body is hovering over me, his weight held up by arms that somehow look stronger than they ever have, even though they've saved me from so much—even though they've done impossible things.

His head drops forward and his eyes close. I run my hands up his chest and neck until my hands hold his head, my fingers in the wet strands of his hair, drops hitting my body and leaving a chill in their wake.

"I love you, Wes. The kind of love that makes my chest hurt and makes me feel afraid," I say.

"Don't be afraid," he says, his nose grazing along the side of mine.

"I'm not...not really. I just want you to know that you, that this..." I say, stumbling with my words.

"I know," Wes says for me. "It's like for once we're in charge and this is exactly how our story is supposed to go."

"Yes," I smile against him, my lips dusting his, then taking hungry passes over his mouth until I'm lost again in his kiss.

Minutes pass with his lips on mine, my mouth raw from his stubble, my body hot from desire. I let my hands be brave, tracing every muscle of his body, down his stomach, until I find him hard against my thigh. His body reacts from touch, a sharp breath drawn and a moan escaping his lips.

"Josselyn," he says my whole name, slow and seductive.

"I have something...in that drawer," I say, my hand falling to the right of my bed.

Wes's eyes meet mine, his lids heavy, his lips parted. We hold our gaze through pants and unexchanged words that pass as thoughts from my eyes to his and back again. He leaves his gaze on me as he moves to the right, reaching with his hand and sliding my drawer out enough that he can touch the contents inside. When I nod, he looks away, finding a condom and a discarded pack of cigarettes. He pulls them both out and smirks at me, his head tilted waiting for a response as he holds the half-filled pack between us.

"Emergency pack." I offer a wry smile—one that says *guilty*.

"E-mergency…pack?" He repeats the words slowly, teasing me.

"Yeah," I say, grabbing it and throwing it back in the opened drawer. "You know, for those times when your superhero boyfriend goes missing in a river, you ride a bus over a broken bridge, someone tries to ram your house with a car in the middle of the night, or—"

"I get it," he chuckles, lowering his head enough to kiss my lips lightly, smiling against me and holding himself there for a few extra seconds, until I smile back.

"I didn't smoke them," I say, shrugging one shoulder against the bed, his eyes go to the movement of my arm, and he falls forward, holding my eyes as long as he can until his lips hit the bare skin of my shoulder.

He lifts himself completely, sitting between my legs on his knees—*all of him*.

"I wouldn't blame you if you did. I was just kidding," he says.

"I know, but…I didn't. It's…" I shrug my shoulder again, and his eyes glance at it, his smile growing just a little. I love the way he looks at me. "It's just important to me that you know I didn't give in…that I'm strong enough."

His smile falls slightly, still there, but his expression softer now. If I had to give it a word, I would say he's amazed—he's amazed by me.

His eyes sweep shut in patient blinks as his focus turns to the small packet in his hand. I wait as he tears it and slides the condom on himself, tossing the wrapper to the side. Wes lowers himself on his elbows, caging me in underneath his powerful body, and as his eyes meet mine, I nod again, letting my knees fall open just enough that he easily finds me ready, guiding himself with his hand until I feel him sink inside.

We both breathe deeply, our chests growing, our eyes shutting—as his head falls forward, mine falls back, my body arching with his movement. Wes pushes in deeper, sliding forward against my skin, and I roll with the sensation.

"You've done this before," I say, not meaning it as an accusation or a jealous statement. It's naïve to think I've slept with guys, but Wes has never had sex. His eyes meet mine, his mouth a hard line as he nods slowly. My lips curve and I let my eyes close with my grin.

"I'm okay with that. So have I," I say, tilting my head forward. "It's never mattered before, though."

My eyes lock with his, and I feel him pulse inside of me, leaving me hungry and full all at once.

"This more than matters," Wes says, and I nod, holding his gaze.

"It does," I whisper, pulling my bottom lip between my teeth.

Wes dips down, tugging my lip loose gently with his own teeth. He pushes into me again, and I gasp, arching and wanting him to touch me everywhere. My lips part and I ache so much that I'm unable to make a sound.

I crave.

Wes moves into me, then backs away.

I beg, my head coming forward and my eyes finding his.

I demand.

Wes pushes into me, rocking his body against mine as his hand pulls my thigh up around his hip.

I cry out, bringing my hand to my mouth and biting my knuckle.

Wes reaches for my wrist and moves my hand above my head, holding it down as his body continues to move him in deeper before falling away.

My hips roll, and Wes grunts. His guard is down, and he's showing me his selfish side. I want him to be greedy with me, so I arch against him again until his mouth covers my breast, warming the cold peaks with his breath, his lips, his teeth and his tongue. Every pass of his mouth against me accompanied by the smooth stroke of his hips, the fullness of him creating a building sensation that I have only felt a few times in my life—

and never during sex.

I'd been drunk. I was stoned. The guys were temporary, and they used me like I used them. Some I didn't know well, others I never saw again. I pretended, and I cried out with pleasure like I thought I was supposed to, like I'd seen in those late-night movies at Kyle's house—the way the boys would tease when they'd follow me in the halls at school.

I see now, though, all that I'd been missing. My body quivers with every movement of Wes inside. My lips hum with sounds of pleasure. I whimper and pant, my body moving faster with every stroke Wes takes.

His eyes open on me, and his chin dips, trapping me in a look that tells me I will never experience something quite like this again. This is special—a rare fusion of first love and lust. I feel beautiful, and I never want to climb the peak that my body seems to be racing toward, but it's inevitable. I am the girl who wants to dive over the edge, the girl who demands to taste the wild side—and when I feel it's close, I let it take me completely.

"Oh my god, Wes," I cry out, my hands finding his back, my arms holding him closer as my legs squeeze his thighs.

Every pulse builds until finally it's nearly unbearable, and I become his—my body dependent on every push, every touch, every wave he lets me ride as his mouth falls into the crook of my neck, his lips parting with his groan as he pushes again and again. My nails dig into the skin on his back, and his hips rock forward a final time until his muscles relax and I'm drowning in the weight of his body.

We lay like this for minutes, Wes still inside me, my body listless, arms draped over chests and tangled legs. I want to thank him. I want to tell him something important. But there's nothing that can do service to how I just felt, and we've been through the fires of hell together. Words would fall short, and this feeling…I think maybe it's enough.

His fingers begin to trail along my arm, long slow drags to my shoulder and down to my wrist until my fingers curl and his thread through them, our hands a perfect fit. I get lost in the way they look.

"Do you think you held my hand? When we were little kids," I ask.

I feel his body shrug in response before he speaks, so I turn my head enough to look at him.

"I don't know," he says.

His eyes flit to mine, then back down to our hands. I don't look away. I study him, watching his light brown lashes as he blinks, his nose wriggles with an itch, and his pupils open with the light.

I think of the picture I saw of Wes and me, the one in the album, at Shawn's. I make a silent promise to myself that if I'm ever at Shawn's again, I will collect all of the things Wes deserves to see. I hold his gaze, feeling the weight of guilt that I know a piece of him that's been kept from him.

His head shifts more, and he lifts himself enough to look at me more directly. The feel of our bodies, still naked and sticky, makes me blush. Wes notices, smoothing out my hair with one hand as he leans in to kiss the side of my face.

"Hey," he says, a nervous swallow as he looks away, moving his body away from mine, closer to the edge of the bed. I wait, allowing him this change in subject. "We still have hours...and this drawer of yours," he says, pulling out another condom.

Wes puts the packet between his teeth and rolls back toward me, dropping the package between my breasts and resting his chin just below it as he looks up at me.

I breathe out a giggle, but my body begins to tingle at his suggestion, and within seconds, my hands have woven themselves into his hair, and his mouth is leaving a trail of kisses down my body, lower...lower...*and ah.*

CHAPTER 15

Wes went home to pick up his brothers before the sun was fully up and they were awake, slipping in as if he'd never left. Even though his brothers knew where he was, he didn't want his parents to see him not home and worry. It doesn't take much to trigger the panic now. I felt it—the moment he left. It's this irrational rush of adrenaline that leaves behind a sour taste and strange feelings I may not see him again.

I ate my Pop-Tarts by the front window, and when I was done, I sat there with the empty packet in my hand watching the car outside my house with the officer inside whose job it is to babysit me—babysit *us*, I guess. I sat there until Taryn's car pulled in my driveway and life picked back up as it normally does, only it was nothing close to normal.

If it ever was.

I filled Taryn in on everything on the drive to school. It's hard to hide an unmarked police car in front of my house. It's also hard to hide the smile on my face. I shouldn't have one—my tiny family is being threatened. But I smile anyway. I did it with my head turned away as we drove here, and I smile now in the gym, as Wes and I exchange quick glances and speak to each other with single looks and lingering touches. His fingertips ran over mine when I hung my jump rope as he reached for it, and his knuckles brushed against my thigh while bending down to adjust the weights on the bench press I was standing near.

Every touch shocks those parts of my body alive that he now owns, and my grin can't be helped.

"Hey," Taryn says, kicking her toe toward me and knocking me out of my trance. I've been lifting the same light weight in a bicep curl for minutes, poorly masking my stare at Wes.

"What's up?" I turn away from her and walk a few steps away from the training table she's sitting on. It's a move to avoid her that she calls me on the minute I walk back.

"Heyyyyy?" The awkward *hey* slides slowly from her mouth, and I can't help but silently laugh at it. "Are you okay?"

I suck in my lips and think of the best way to answer her. I shouldn't be okay, and a lot of me isn't. But then…

"I don't really know. I…I slept with Wes."

This isn't anything shocking—not to Taryn, not to anyone really. For most of my small world, this is just a less-than-hushed rumor being whispered about Joss Winters sleeping with a guy.

But this—what happened between me and Wes—it's different to me. I wouldn't be able to put it to words, other than *love*, and it feels so cliché and hokey to say that he's special because I love him, and this means more, but it's the truth.

This…it means more. Wes Stokes means more than anything ever has, other than my own dreams. And right now, the two run parallel.

I stare at Taryn, my lips closed, wanting to curve, but also not wanting to draw any attention to our conversation. I slide up on the table to sit next to her, and she quirks a brow, puckering her lips, ready for juicy gossip, I'm sure. I don't need other people hearing my stories, though, because it will just become this joke with the rest of the guys in here. I've always been treated differently by the guys at my school—somewhere between being one of them and being this conquest they want to tame. But Wes isn't a joke. There is no game. There's only *us* and trying to survive this story we're in.

"When?" Taryn says, her voice hushed.

"This morning," I answer. "He stayed over…and I woke up early. I know how it sounds, but the time was just…I don't know…right?"

I avoid her stare, though I feel it hot on my cheek. Instead, I look out to Wes, standing with his brothers, as they should be. I haven't thought much about Shawn and his relationship since we briefly talked about it, and I think maybe that's for the best, because these boys…they are his family. There's a difference between biology and real love, I've learned. My own mother has taught me that.

"All right," Taryn says. I don't turn in response, even though her reaction surprises me. I half expected her to make an off-color joke about how only I could find time to let a boy get in my pants when my world was falling to shit again. But she didn't, and I think it's because she knows just how special this thing between me and Wes is, too. Instead of talking about the details, we both sit with our backs against the wall watching the two boys we love—brothers—spot each other on the bench press while their third brother and Kyle sit close by, laughing.

"Sometimes I can almost see us all as kids," my friend says.

I hum, picturing it for myself. There's so much of the little boy who saved me in Wes, but I think maybe I'm the only one with the ability to see the subtleties masked by the man he's quickly become.

"Do you think we would have been friends?" Taryn asks.

This time I look to her, and she turns enough to meet my gaze.

"You mean all of us?" I ask.

"Yeah," she says, rolling her head along the wall to look back out at the boys who, I know in my heart, any one of them, would do anything for us. I turn to do the same, and think about her theory, picturing smaller versions of ourselves, knowing what I know about who I was then, who Taryn and Kyle were—*who Christopher was.*

"I don't think so," I say. Seconds pass before she speaks.

"I don't think so either," she says.

We don't dissect the conclusion we both came to, but I know our reasons are the same. Kyle, me, Taryn—we were this close-knit threesome that sometimes…*sometimes*…allowed Kyle's brother Conner to make us a group of four. I've always thought it was just me, that *I* was the hard bubble to crack, but I was never in it alone. None of us were. No kid is. We fought just to be the kids that weren't noticed for being different. We couldn't let the different kids ruin the picture we'd worked so hard to paint for everyone just to be nice to them.

But we got older, and I'm disappointed in my younger self.

"I could have found him...Christopher?"

I feel her shift, but she remains silent, her eyes on the boy full of secrets.

"I think about that a lot," I say, pausing to suck in my lips. "I replay the day at my house...the races. I wasted too much time; I was never *really* looking for him. And I bet he was alone. At the hospital, and later with the Woodmansees. He didn't have any friends, and his foster family was so awful."

My eyes move to my knees as I chew at the inside of my cheek, thinking about how deep that story goes—the details only I know, about Shawn being Wes's real father.

"We were kids," Taryn says, trying to soothe my conscience.

I shrug.

"He was a kid," I say.

It's what I always come back to. He was just a kid, but he still chose to save me rather than look on at the horror like everybody else. I wonder if I would do the same.

"You had a lot going on," Taryn says quickly, not letting me slide into guilt too deeply.

I feel her hand brush against my thigh, so I turn to her.

"You never really answered," she says.

My brow pulls in.

"Are you okay? You didn't really answer."

I hold my friend's gaze, my insides still feeling twisted and uncertain about almost everything.

"It's because I don't really have one," I say. "But..." I pause, nodding back toward our boys, laughing loudly at something Kyle said. "I love him, T. I love someone, and that has to mean I'm okay in some ways, right? Like...some ways I never thought I'd be okay again?"

"Yeah," she says, and I can hear her smile in her tone.

I push off from the training table to walk back to where the boys are standing, and I make it most of the way before my brief moment of feeling good is shot to hell by a dick football player.

"Dad try to run you over again, Josselyn?"

I barely have time to register the chortle of laughter from a meathead who amused himself. The words come out of Zack Ramsey's mouth in one breath, and before I can turn to face him, Wes's fist is crashing into Zack's nose, sending a gush of blood to the concrete floor. The slap of flesh pounding bone comes hard and fast followed by the rush of feet along the floor and young testosterone shouting, sliding heavy metal weights back to the walls, giving Zack and Wes space.

I don't want this. Wes doesn't need it in his life, and the kinda shit Zack said is really nothing I haven't heard before. People around here can be assholes. I would know—I was one of the assholes.

"Wes, stop!" I shout, moving close to the brawl where Wes is straddling Zack on one knee, his punches falling into him hard.

Zack pushes Wes's hands out of the way, grabbing his wrists with every blow, rolling his body loose from the hold Wes has on him until his leg breaks free enough to fly at Wes's face and hit him square in the eye. His face should be bruised or swollen—but it isn't.

"That's enough!"

Mr. Wilshire's booming voice fills the room, and most of the boys step away, but Wes and Zack keep attacking one another.

Our school's wrestling and football coach, Mr. Wilshire splits time up in the gym with my dad. He's twice my father's size, but my dad's authority rules with a heavier hand. He can crush a kid with the right words, and fights—they don't happen in front of my dad. I wish he was here now.

"Wes…Zack…stop it!" I shout, grabbing the end of Wes's T-shirt and holding it in my fist so tightly that it rips as his body lunges forward.

"Please! Please just stop!" My voice shrills, and Wes swings his arm with half strength at Zack, getting up from the floor and tugging his shirt, ripping the strip I tore from the bottom and throwing it on the ground between him and Zack.

"You don't say shit like that!" Wes's eyes are wild as he paces, taking long strides toward Kyle then back to the ground where blood now spreads. This time, he points before he speaks. "That's not okay. You don't say shit like that. Not to her."

Zack's chest heaves, his eyes wincing with the deep breaths. I wouldn't be surprised if one of his ribs was broken.

"Wes, it's okay," I say.

"No," my boy says, turning to me with the sharpness of that word. His eyes hold mine and he pants as his muscles start to relax until the fist at his side finally uncoils. "No," he says again, the word quieter this time.

"You're right," I say, stepping closer until I can touch him. I move my hand to his arm slowly, my fingers eventually grasping around his bicep, hot from having been so filled with rage. "It's not okay, but I'm used to it. And I don't care about Zack. I don't care what he thinks about me, about my dad. Zack's an asshole who can't catch a ball—so they made him a lineman, even though he's too small to stop anyone."

"Fuck you, Joss!" Zack shouts, finally standing from the floor, spitting as he moves to the other side of the weight room.

"No, I'm pretty sure today it's fuck *you*, Zack. In fact, fuck you all," I say, backing from the room, dragging my finger through the air and pointing to the people in here who know nothing about me other than the stories they heard and memories of one afternoon in my front yard when we were all kids.

"Office," Mr. Wilshire says, tugging on the shoulder of Zack's sleeve. "Both of you...now!"

Waving his bulging arm, the man armed with a whistle and a six pack turns red in the face as he ushers all of us out of the weight room, throwing out threats he has no intention of following through on, like closing the weight room for good.

My dad will just open it again. And closing it won't stop people from being assholes. It won't even slow them down.

My friends and I all follow Wes and Zack to the office, and we wait outside, taking turns staring through the slender window in the door that stands between us and the dean's office.

"Can you see anything?"

I've had my face pressed to the glass the longest, my eyes straining to look around the corner where the dean's office door is open.

"No, but he's been in there for a while. Zack is still sitting in the hallway," I say.

Zack flipped me off the first time he saw me looking at them. I ignored him, like my parents always told me to do with bullies. It's the only time I've heeded that advice, and I only did it because I have no use or time for Zack.

Kyle's shoulder rubs against mine, so I move an inch or two to the left to give him room to look on with me. We both stand in silence while Wes's brothers and Taryn whisper, replaying everything as they saw it, getting their stories in order to make sure none of this lands on Wes.

"He deserved it, you know," Kyle says.

"Probably," I respond.

"No probably. He *did*. And Wes was right. You don't say things like that…" he says, swinging his arm into me. I turn just enough to catch my friend's eyes. "Not to you. People don't get to say things like that to you anymore. I shouldn't have ever let them get away with it in the first place."

The right side of my mouth tugs up in response, and I lean into him.

"I can take care of myself," I say, and Kyle lets out an airy laugh, his eyes flitting from me back to the glass in front of us.

"He's coming," Kyle says, backing away.

I freeze for a second, and Wes stops where he is, his eyes finding mine through the small window. Blood stains are on his shirt, and I know they aren't his. I bring my hand up in front of my body, resting the tip of my finger on the glass as my head falls forward against it, and Wes's eyes sweep shut, opening when his head dips down and his focus drops to his feet. I back away, letting my finger draw a short line down the glass as I move.

Wes pushes the door open, and everyone stands the moment his hand curls around the door's edge.

"Let's get out of here."

His head turns slowly, his eyes catching his brothers' first, then stopping on mine. His lips are a flat line, and his face is void of emotion, but his eyes tell the full story. It's time.

"Okay," I say, reaching my hand out to grasp his.

My step falls in with his as he lets the door close behind him, and I catch the glares from our friends as we walk past them toward the exit. They aren't sure what Wes means, and they don't understand if they're supposed to stay or come.

I nod my head toward the open hallway and level them with my gaze, trying to invite them without saying the words. After a few seconds, they follow. We all walk quietly through the silent hallway, classroom doors closed, the only sounds from muffled lectures as we pass each room.

Wes pushes the door wide, and I step through with him, holding the edge long enough so Kyle can catch it to let Taryn, TK, and Levi come through next. Wes walks silently all the way to his truck, opening the passenger door for me. Our friends stop a few paces shy, brows furrowed and confusion scribbled across their faces.

TK is the first to break the silence, "Are we...ditching?"

"Yup," Wes says, taking my hand to help me inside. I give him a crooked smile, and he shoots me one back, leaning in enough to brush his lips on mine before stepping back to shut the door.

Our friends pile in the back, and Wes climbs into the driver's seat, watching in the mirror until everyone's sitting down and holding on. He fires the engine up, pulls from his spot, and drives timidly through the lot and out to the main road. Once the school is in the distance, though, his foot grows heavy on the gas, speeding us away from the weight room, from the dean's office, and from dick holes like Zack.

"Did they suspend you?"

My voice is hoarse. I slide my hand along the seat until my fingertips graze his jean-covered leg, and he glances down, moving his hand to cover mine and giving it a squeeze.

"No, just a good warning," he says, quirking a lip and laughing once. "Being the missing boy who finally came home has its perks, I guess."

I smile, but it fades quickly. My heartbeat picked up the second Wes leapt at Zack, and it hasn't really slowed down since. His secrets aren't mine to tell, and I know that what he's about to do is harder on him than it is me, but I have this selfish worry nevertheless. Things are going to change.

Wes drives us beyond our neighborhood, rolling through stop signs until he turns off on a dirt road that winds behind the drive-in movie theater. His tires kick up dust, and my eyes search people who may see us. We're out here alone, though.

"Why here?" I ask, thinking about our last trip here, and what I did.

"I came here a lot when I was gone," he says, turning the wheel hard and parking the truck in the shadow of the largest movie screen. After breaking, he shifts to park and kills the engine, sighing hard as his hands fall to his legs and his back rests heavy in the seat behind him. His head rolls to the side and his eyes meet mine. "I had this fantasy that you'd come here to think too, and then you'd see that I was okay, that I was watching you, and you'd understand and be okay with what I had to do."

"You know that's crap, right?" I respond.

Wes's chest lifts with a short laugh.

"Yeah, that's why I said *fantasy*," he says, his mouth resting in a tight-lipped smile.

A heavy pound echoes about our heads, and we both twist in our seats to see Levi's face as he squats behind the back window in the bed of the truck.

"Did you bring us all out here to watch y'all make out? Or are we going to blow off some steam?" Levi's head swivels, his eyes shifting from mine to Wes's. I glower at him eventually and reach for the handle on my door.

"You better run," I shout, and Levi's eyes flash wide.

"Oh shit!" he shouts, kicking his legs over the edge of the truck bed just as I rush out of the cab.

I sprint after him for a few steps, grabbing the bottom of his T-shirt, but losing my grip as he spins around, laughing loudly and feigning to be genuinely scared of me until his feet tangle underneath his body and he falls into a tuft of weeds.

"She didn't even have to touch you, dude!" TK says, stepping forward and holding his hand out to his brother to help him back to his feet.

"I know my place, man. I know Joss could kick my ass. I'm not like you, all delusional and shit, thinking I'm a better ballplayer than she is," Levi says, not quite fully standing as he speaks. TK's smile contorts into a grimace and he pulls his hand away, sending his brother right back to his ass, which makes us all laugh hard—even Wes.

I walk over to where Wes is leaning against the side of his truck, and I fold my arms over my chest and lean with him. We both watch his brothers and Kyle take turns kicking dirt at each other while Taryn sits on the truck's hood, pointing and shouting out insults to them all. It's the first time in forever that we've all felt young and stupid, and I let the feeling brand itself on my insides, because I know how fleeting it is.

Eventually, his brothers stop wrestling, and an edge settles over us all. No one wants to be the first to ask what this is about, and I don't want to break the ice until Wes is ready to share, so we all wait, uncomfortable silence ruling as we do things like kick at the tire of the truck, pick ragweed, and blow pollen into the breeze.

"What are we doing here, man?" Kyle finally asks. His eyes remain steadfast on Wes, and I know that he has an idea of what this is all about. It's why he's not looking at me. My friend is playing along for the good of the rest of us. He's playing along to make me feel okay, and so feelings aren't even more hurt that I've shared the most with him.

Wes breathes in long and slow, but exhales fast, his lips closed tight as the air escapes through his nose. His arms fall from their hold over his chest, and his hands find his pockets as he kicks a rock forward near where he stands, crossing his ankles and looking down at his feet. His hat hides his expression from our friends, but from the side, I see him struggling. His mouth hangs open, and his eyes blink while he searches for words.

"I'm sorry that there are news trucks parked outside our house sometimes," he says, looking up and bringing a hand to his face, his fingers scratching at his cheek while he draws his mouth in on one side and pinches his brow.

"It's all right, man," TK says, shaking his head and shrugging.

"No…it's really not," Wes chuckles, shaking his head and eventually covering his face with both hands. He rubs as he laughs, then stops instantly, his face tilting to the sky as he stretches his arms out, looking for answers.

"Just tell them," I say as his laughter dies down. Wes's chin falls and he turns his head to me, his eyes heavy with uncertainty. "They're your family. We all are."

Wes closes the small distance between us and cups my cheeks, pulling my head toward his and resting our foreheads together. "I love you something fierce," he whispers, and for the first time in an hour, my pulse begins to slow.

His lips brush against mine before he backs away, walking to the tailgate of the truck and flipping the hitch, lowering it so he can climb inside. All eyes are on him as he steps up along the rim of the truck's bed, then climbs to the roof of the cab, his black Vans heavy as he steadies his feet. I can see his muscles twitch with nerves, and his hands go back in his pockets on instinct as his eyes scan the back lots of the drive-in.

"When the bus rolled into the river and I jumped in to save Joss's dad, I didn't drown," he says. The ground near me rustles as his brother's shuffle their feet and fidget with their own arms. I glance to the side and catch them looking at each other; Kyle and Taryn are looking down.

"I guess that's obvious, because…ha, right…I'm alive," Wes says, stretching his arms out to his sides. "What I meant, though, is…yeah…I got banged up good along the rocks, and I was caught in the undertow for…" He pauses, pushing out a short breath from his nose and smirking. "I was underwater for a long-ass time. I should have drowned. I should have been bloody, cut to shit from the rocks and glass, metal and branches…hell, the pieces of bus caught in the undertow with me. But I wasn't. My body fought the current for miles."

"How many miles?" TK says, looking up to meet his brother's eyes.

There's a long pause as the two of them stare into one another. Finally,

Wes answers.

"Maybe a hundred," he says.

TK's chest lifts slowly, and I never see him exhale. Wes continues to look at his brother as he speaks.

"When I climbed out, I went straight to Shawn's," he says, pausing to let his words really register. Both Levi and TK breathe out, and when I glance to their faces, I catch the way both of their jaws grow rigid with hurt and confusion—with resistance. "Not because I didn't want to come home."

Wes swallows.

"I just…"

"You just what? You wanted to make us think you were dead so we could watch mom not eat for a week? Watch dad fumble trying to keep things normal, even though we could hear him consoling mom at night while she cried herself to sleep?" TK shouts, walking to the back of the truck and climbing into the bed.

Wes shakes his head and turns, preparing himself to take whatever his brothers need to lash out with. I was in their shoes not so long ago. This path they're on—it has to be walked.

"Was this some fucked up joke then? I don't understand Wes!" TK climbs to the rooftop to stand facing his brother, his hands to his sides, both in fists. He shakes his head slowly and his eyes narrow on Wes, and I step in closer, catching Wes's gaze. He shakes me off, but I stay close. I'm pretty sure he's not handling this smoothly, and no matter how invincible he is, it's still hard to watch him get knocked down. And he's going to.

"You better make this make sense really fuckin' fast, bro," TK says, stepping forward and pushing at the center of Wes's chest with both of his palms. Wes's feet stumble a little, but his face never drops his resolve. He'll take it all.

"TK, let him talk," Levi says, walking to the front of the truck, his palms on the hood next to Taryn, whose eyes are wide and darting from mine to her boyfriend.

"Let him talk? We thought this asshole was dead, and instead, he was just having a sleepover at Uncle Shawn's," TK says, turning to face Wes again.

"At my dad's," Wes responds, and TK's eyes slit even more, his mouth closed tight, puckering.

Wes's feet are steady, but his body is relaxed, his shoulders sloping and his thumbs hooked in his pockets. TK's nostrils flair with every breath he takes until he starts to shake his head, chuckling. Without warning, his arm lunges forward and his fist strikes Wes in the jaw, sending him back on his feet, his balance faltering and his body falling flat to the dirt ground by the driver's side door.

TK walks to the edge of the roof to look over at him, his eyes red and his fist still formed, ready to strike again. But when Wes stands up easily and brushes the dust from his jeans, rolling his shoulders a few times from the fall, TK's face softens. This time, he's the one who takes a step back.

"I was at my dad's," Wes repeats.

He and TK lock eyes for long, quiet seconds.

"Shawn…" Levi starts.

Wes looks over to his other sibling, shifting his jaw from side to side slowly before finally nodding once, a small lift of his chin. TK's legs falter, so he kneels on the truck roof, finally sitting with his feet dangling over the edge. Kyle comes closer to me, leaning on the truck's side and waiting patiently, never once letting on that he knows everything that's coming. If only he did. There are so many things that I would never be able to explain. Only Wes can do that.

"Shawn Stokes is my dad." The words stumble out of Wes's mouth slowly, almost as if he's still trying to convince himself by hearing his voice say them.

Levi's eyebrows raise, and he blows out air as he pinches the bridge of his nose.

"How?" he asks.

Wes's mouth grins on one side, but his eyes sag. He lets out a breathy sarcastic chuckle.

"He paid a hooker to sleep with him. Knocked her up. She wasn't the mothering type, so…" He swings his arms out to either side, presenting himself. I don't care how he was made; I'm just glad that he was.

"Okay, so Uncle Shawn…" TK begins.

"Is my dad," Wes finishes.

The three brothers all stare into the same emptiness between them for several seconds.

"Fuuuuuck," TK says, breaking the brief silence, but only for a moment. They all go back to it, and while they stare at nothing, Kyle, Taryn, and I flit glances to one another.

The air around us grows warmer from the rising sun. Fall in Bakersfield isn't much of a fall at all—the temperatures rival most summers for everywhere else. It'll be in the eighties today, and we're all beginning to perspire from the stickiness, but no one dares to suggest we leave this place. Wes came here because he knew no one would come looking. He's only just begun to share his story, and he needs the comfort of being somewhere secret. I knot my hair on top of my head and roll the sleeves of my T-shirt up over my shoulders.

"Tell them the rest," I say, bringing Wes's attention to me first, and within a breath, everyone else's along with it.

His eyes lock on mine as he opens his mouth to speak, staying with me the moment the words come. All I can do is smile faintly as he begins, but it seems to be enough. He doesn't hesitate; he tells them everything.

"He never called me his," he begins, his choice of words hitting my chest. How long did he go through life belonging to no one? "I'd always get taken back to him, though. You know…when things didn't work out? I figured that was just how the system went."

His eyes flit down briefly, and his lip rises with a short laugh.

"I guess I thought it was like with a puppy from a rescue or something. If the dog wasn't a fit, you just brought it back to the rescuer," he says, his mouth falling as his eyes come back to mine. "Only he wasn't rescuing me. Whatever is the opposite of that word…sabotage, maybe? *Using* for sure—definitely using me."

TK slides from the roof of the truck, his feet crunching on the ground, and everyone begins to make small movements to settle their nerves, now rattled with Wes's story.

"There's a reason Mom and Dad never take us over to his house," he says, looking back to the ground, his feet kicking at the loose dirt and gravel, hands back in the safety of his pockets. His brow creases. "He's sorta nuts."

"What do you mean?" Levi asks.

Wes chews at the inside of his cheek and scrunches his eyes, searching for the best words.

"When I was a kid, I thought it was cool. He had all of these comic-book things, and he would always call me *hero*. He had this one book..."

His eyes scan up from the ground, back to mine; my breath pauses.

"It was filled with sketches, most of them color. He drew them," he says, his hand rubbing against his chin as he smiles, his eyes glazing over with thoughts of his past. "The art is actually really good."

The smile evaporates, and a heaviness regains control of his shoulders and chest.

"Maybe that's part of the problem," he says. "Those drawings were so good...so...*real*. He always told me I was the hero in them. He said he drew me because he knew my story, and I thought it was cool, because it looked like me. I guess anything pretend felt a hell of a lot better than where I was—a boy who didn't belong to anyone."

He smiles on one side of his mouth and glances at both of his brothers.

"You know...the hell that is foster care?"

TK and Levi both snort out a small, sad laugh and look down as it fades, burying this common *hell* they all share.

"It was all just this fantasy that I'd get to visit when I was with him, in-between the miserable families—if you can even call them families—that Shawn placed me with. I'd go to hell then come back to this world where I had powers, where I saved the day—"

Wes stops with his front teeth together, lips parted. His forehead dimples as his breath picks up just before his eyes meet mine again, and for the first time since I've learned the truth, I see just how terrified he was of not being able to stop the painful things his father predicted would come my way.

"And then a car came racing at this girl I liked more than anyone in the world, and without flinching, I dove in front of it to save her...just like the book said I would."

I look inside him, my eyes boring so deeply into his that I can actually see the boy who lives inside. I see us, and that day, and all of the days that came before and after. We are forever connected. Shawn may have put us together, but the fact that we belong that way has nothing to do with him. Wes would have found me on his own; I'm sure of it.

"She's the girl," Levi says, his voice hushed.

"She's the girl," Wes echoes.

He looks at me with this unfathomable love that I never quite feel good enough to deserve. I'm starting to think that loving each other is a curse. Maybe that's the moral of our story—we suffer and overcome, then risk again.

Levi runs his hand over his face, dragging his eyes down as he leaves his palm over his mouth.

"She's the girl," Levi says again, nodding this time.

Understanding.

"He has so many stories," Wes says, his eyes not leaving mine. He wants me to see through him, to grasp all of the whys that kept him away. "I've lived so many of them. Catching dad when he fell from the ladder last year at Christmas, or stopping the truck from falling on my face when the jack slipped out last spring..."

Wes turns his head slowly with that last one, his eyes catching TK's. His brother was there for that, and Wes said he slid out in time. He holds his brother's stare through several deep breaths, the only sounds from buzzing insects and the humming highway miles away.

"The bridge collapse," Wes continues, and TK's head falls to the side slightly in response, his eyes sagging with sympathy. "Joss..." Wes continues, quieting for a moment to suck in his lips and shake his head, blaming himself still.

"Her leg," he says.

Our collective stillness puts me on edge. The only other person who knows nearly as much as I do is Kyle, but hearing Wes speak openly about the fucked-up destiny his father swore him to—that he and I share—feels raw and new.

"I thought if I just stayed away, then the predictions would stop playing out," he says, his gaze sliding back to me. "But what if it's worse without me here? I figured maybe the real point is I'm supposed to stop something from killing *you*."

"Nothing is going to kill me," I say, feigning my confident self as I shake my head and look at my boy. I'm not entirely confident—not when loan sharks know where I live. But whatever is coming for me…for my dad—it's nothing compared to the things I've survived.

Wes's lips form a sealed line, and he breathes in deeply through his nose.

"You're right," he says. "Nothing will. I won't let it."

My lungs fill and my mouth is overcome with a sour taste because what Wes isn't telling them is that the story never says I die—my father does. And while Wes is determined to protect me, I'm just as determined to save my tiny family.

"So what you're saying is…" Levi begins, pushing away from the truck and stepping closer to his brother, stopping just out of his reach. He points a finger at Wes from his folded arms. "You can stop bad things from happening."

"Some of them," Wes says, a slight lift in his shoulders.

"Because you're…like…"

This is where Levi stops. Saying anything more out loud feels childish and fantastical. I avoided it for a long time. In many ways, I still refuse, because underneath the strange things that Wes can somehow do…is a young man with a soft heart and a capacity to love that I once thought didn't exist. Wes isn't weird. He isn't alien. He's a gift—rare and mine.

"Because I'm like this," he says, walking toward the front of the truck and holding out a hand to help Taryn slide down so she can stand next to TK. Wes lifts the hood high, propping it up with a metal rod I can tell he or his brothers or dad added to the truck themselves. Rubbing his palms together, he studies the engine, looking for just the right place to make his point, pausing once his gaze passes over a rounded metal box lodged on the right side of the motor. Wes reaches forward, his fingers outstretched, inches away from the searing-metal piece, but before he grips it, TK grabs his wrist.

"Dude, you'll burn yourself. Don't!" his brother says.

They both stare at one another for a few seconds, neither of them blinking, until one at a time TK's fingers let go of Wes's arm, as if he somehow knows what's coming next and just isn't sure if he's ready to witness it. The moment he steps back from the space radiating with heat under their truck's hood, Wes returns his attention to the part that would leave blistering, and likely debilitating, burns on anyone else's skin. Without pause, he falls forward, gripping the box hard and flexing to make sure all of his hand is exposed.

We all watch breathlessly, and I glance to my side, catching the expressions on Kyle and Taryn's faces. Their eyes, mouths, the paleness of their skin and the wash of disbelief that colors their cheeks—it's exactly how I'm sure I looked the first time Wes showed me just how different he is. After a dozen seconds, he pulls his hand away, curling his fingers into a ball that he holds in front of his chest.

"It's not that I don't feel it, it's just that…" He pauses for a deep breath, turning to face us all. He rolls his wrist, slowly opens his fingers, and unveils a slightly pink palm, and skin that looks like it's never been harmed. Lips part and words hang on the tip of his tongue, as if even he is amazed at what he can do despite living with it for eighteen years.

"It's that it doesn't hurt like it should."

No one moves for nearly a minute. Wes holds his hand open, on display for us all, and I know the urges that are kicking at everyone's insides. Wes does, too. It's why he doesn't make eye contact with any of us. He simply waits until we're ready—until one of us is brave enough to say something out loud.

Kyle is the first to move, only his first step isn't toward Wes, it's toward the open hood where he rests his elbows on the rim of the open cavity and rubs his palms together as his eyes narrow on the part Wes just touched.

"That's your exhaust manifold," Kyle says, reaching forward and holding his palm several inches away. "That should have puckered your skin and smelled like death when you touched it."

He pulls his hand away quickly and rubs the back of it with his cooler palm, wincing as he does.

"A foot away and I'm pretty sure I singed away the hair on my knuckles," Kyle says, looking at me first, then to Wes.

More silence follows—everyone is processing. Nobody knows what word to use to describe what we've witnessed, and I refuse to buy into Shawn's story, to label Wes as he always has—as something *super*. But it's hard not to go there when he does things like this. He's human and whole. There's nothing about him that's otherworldly, other than these things he can do without getting hurt.

"You can touch hot things," TK says, finally, pacing around the front of the truck, stopping next to Kyle and leaning in to point to the proof. "You don't get hurt."

Wes lifts a shoulder and blinks in acknowledgement.

"That's some of it," he says.

"Some of it," TK repeats.

"I can take an impact, like say getting knocked on my ass by my brother from the roof of a truck seven feet up," he says through a faint smile.

TK's eyes haze and they shift from the rooftop down to the ground where Wes landed.

"A'right…what else?" he asks.

Wes pulls his lips in tight and breathes in through his nose, thinking.

"I can get hit by a car, straight on, going forty miles per hour, and come out with nothing more than a little temporary memory loss. I can roll down the highway, catching someone mid-air, at about the same speed, and walk away with a few scratches. I've held up cars for minutes at a time, even our truck…when I'm working on it alone and you guys aren't around to see it. My reflexes are fast, too…like…I can catch things in the middle of the air at high speeds."

"Like what?" TK continues, his face contorted. I think he's waffling between a world of skepticism and one of awe.

"Rocks…" Wes says, his eyes swiveling to Levi's. "Hit from a metal bat at twilight."

Levi's chest rises fast, his memory kicking in. It wasn't long ago that we all played a game of makeshift baseball on the beach as the sun went down. Levi was pitching a rock, and Kyle's brother Conner was swinging the bat. Wes saved me from being hit, and nobody noticed.

"You catch rocks," TK says, smirking on one side of his mouth, letting out a short laugh. "That's so unimpressive," he adds, rolling his eyes.

He keeps the act going for a few seconds, spinning on his feet and wandering a few steps from us all before turning back, his hands in his pockets and his chin tipped up.

"So that fight in the weight room…when you went all caveman on Zack for saying that shit he said to Joss…"

"Yeah," Wes says quietly, chewing at the inside of his mouth as he waits for TK's real question to come.

His brother looks down at the ground as he steps forward, closing the distance until his nose is inches from Wes. TK tilts his head, and their eyes meet, but he lets everyone simmer in anticipation for a few more seconds.

"You hold back on that asshole?"

Wes's mouth twitches with the urge to grin, but he holds it off for a beat, finally giving in and letting his lips curve up on the right as he nods once to his brother.

"I'm not the one bleeding," he says.

"Joker, you just full-on felt up a steaming piece of metal in our crappy 1980s engine block with your bare hands. Don't give me any of that '*I'm*

180

not the one bleeding' shit. You held back, you douchebag," TK says, laughing through the end of his speech before hooking his arm around Wes's neck, rubbing his head, and working to wrestle him to the ground.

Levi and Kyle start to laugh, too, and my chest fills completely with a breath I've been dying to take, each intake of air coming a little easier as what began as wrestling between Wes and his brother morphs into an embrace. TK's hands move to Wes's head, and with his eyes closed, he rests his forehead on his brother's, rocking gently side to side on his strong legs. His jaw flexes in his fight not to cry.

"You're my brother," he says, and all Wes can do is nod, his eyes closed and his hands clinging to TK's elbows. "Nothing ever stops that, you hear? Nothing. You and me and Levi—Mom and Dad. We're family. No matter what."

"I know," Wes says, his words coming out through a hoarse whisper.

"You do now," TK says. "You don't have to handle things alone. You've got us…you've got me."

Wes nods again, their heads still resting on one another. Their family makes me wish for a sister or brother of my own.

"So this book thing…" Levi says, breaking the peace and cutting through the air like a hammer through water. My mind flashes to my dad, to the situation we're in, to that crazy trailer parked near the lake filled with answers and questions.

Wes and TK break apart slowly, and my boy's eyes catch mine in short passes. His hands go back in his pockets, and my chest grows tight again.

"What comes next?" Levi asks the question the others all want to know.

Wes hitches his shoulders high and wobbles his head side to side, downplaying the unbelievable things he's just shared.

"I don't really know. They're just stories, and it's all probably just coincidence—like things I'm reading into, maybe remembering wrong…"

Wes's words trail off as he looks at his brother. Levi steps closer, his posture a mirror to Wes's, hands in his pockets, too.

"Family," he says again, as if he has to remind him of the huge mountain of trust they've just climbed together.

Wes's eyes shift to me again, and I exhale slowly, my eyes falling closed.

"It's my dad," I say, opening my eyes when my chin is tucked to my chest, so my focus is away from the stares I know I'm now getting.

"Like when we were kids?" Taryn asks in a whisper.

I shake my head *no*.

"Not his drinking, or anything happening to me. Something bad will happen to *him*. At least, according to the guy who kept giving his only son away to strangers just so he could watch over me," I say, sharing more than I'd planned, but unable to hold back the pressure of it all inside.

I spare a glance up, and the faces are all as I expected—wrinkled, frowning and breathless. I suck in air fast, pushing it out just as quickly, but the tension in my body only squeezes tighter.

"I'm pretty sure Shawn was in love with my mom," I say, my gaze moving to Wes. "He hates my dad. It's not all that crazy that he fantasized about bad things happening to him."

TK and Levi lean against the truck, arms folded over their chests, and Kyle kicks at the ground. I recognize where they are in their heads—they're caught between calling the bullshit card and believing that some of this might just be for real. I'm caught there, too, honestly, but the one thing I'm certain of is that Shawn is pulling a lot of the strings, even if it is just by messing with all of our minds.

"Hey," Kyle says, nodding his head up and squinting with one eye from the rising bright sun shining in his face. "You think next time we ditch we could go back to doing fun shit? You know, like swimming at the lake or pushing shopping carts around with the front of our trucks? Not that watching Wes try to hurt himself isn't loads of fun, but for the most part…this morning's been a bit of a downer."

Our collective laughter starts quietly, but picks up fast, and soon Wes is rushing toward Kyle and lifting him over his shoulder, carrying him toward the truck.

"How about we push your ass around in a shopping cart in front of the truck?" he shouts through laughter.

"Atta boy," Kyle yells, slapping Wes's back hard before he puts him down.

Their eyes meet and make a silent agreement, and nothing else is said as we all climb into the truck and Wes drives us back to school. We'll get dinged for being late, and I'll use the car crash at my house as an excuse to buy us a little leeway. I'll also probably prop a nail up underneath the back tire of Zack's Camaro, because I found one in the pickup truck bed a minute ago and something told me I should put it in my pocket. Zack will know why it's there, and he won't say a word.

And Grace will be here soon.

My father will be home.

Everything will be just fine.

CHAPTER 16

Wes drove me to pick up Grace from the airport during lunch. We didn't talk about the morning, about my dad and the money he owes, or about the truth Wes finally shared with his brothers. We talked about unimportant things, both of us craving a little normal, I think. Wes asked what I planned on wearing for my *Girl Strong* photoshoot, and I talked about how maybe the photographer will show me a few things I can use for the next assignment due in my photography class.

Wes isn't in the class anymore. He's got study hall instead, partially because he registered so late and also because his counsellor insisted that the school find ways to "ease his transition."

They have no idea how long Wes's transition has been going on. It started the day Shawn paired him and me together. From that day forward, he would never just be a boy on his own, he would be the boy responsible for the girl his caretaker made him believe was important. Somehow, though, over time, we've both become important to each other for real.

I knew Grace understood who he was the moment Wes shook her hand. I caught the flinch in her face, and the small tick of her nerves when recognition hit. Her eyes caught mine on their way to the curb where Wes's truck sat, and her hands laid flat on her lap, fingers rigid, the entire drive to my house as I sat between her and Wes.

She and I didn't have much time alone before I had to rush back to school, and my father was waiting in the school lot to take me to my physical therapy as soon as my last class let out. He didn't talk much either, and I'm beginning to wonder if I'm the one somehow commanding everyone to silence, or if people are just under the delusion that not talking about what's happening will actually stop time from marching forward.

Unable to take it anymore, I turn in my seat as my dad drives us home, lifting myself and dropping my body into the vinyl with a heavy *thud*.

"Yes? I see you're pouting about something, Josselyn?" My dad blinks to glance at me sideways, then blinks again, his eyes back on the road.

"I'm not four, dad. We need to talk about what's going on…I need to be a part of plans that impact our family," I say.

"You mean like when you called Grace and invited her to stay with us? I really enjoyed the way we discussed that," he says, his words dripping with sarcasm, his sentences clipped.

"That's different. I had no idea why you were being hauled away in a squad car," I explain.

"I understand you were freaked out from the car crashing into yours, but…"

I cut him off.

"Not freaked out, Dad. I was afraid. Fear—heart-pounding worried," I say, my voice loud. I relive not just the sounds of the car crashing into metal, the lights racing closer to my house, and the roar of the engine, but the absolute panic that rushed my system when I saw the suspicion in the officers' eyes, when I knew they suspected my father of doing it. I was so certain that we were going to get torn apart. We'd only just gotten back together, despite living under the same roof for my entire life.

"You were afraid that they were arresting me?" He glances at me from the side again, eyes wide and brows raised, this time studying me for a few seconds longer as we idle at a stoplight. When I was a kid, I would get excited at this light because it meant that we were only four minutes from home. Today, though, I hate how close everything is in this stupid small town. I'm in no hurry to get to a place where people want to hurt us while we live under police surveillance. It's only a matter of time before the entire school knows the latest chapter in the saga of my life.

I don't answer my dad, and eventually his brow falls heavy and he turns his attention back to the light about to change to green.

"Borrowing money, even from the lowest form of people...it isn't illegal, Joss," he says, and I can't help but watch his face closely for some sort of tell—a little slip that lets me know he's playing at this, that he knows what I'm really getting at when I say I was worried about him being taken into custody. But he never gives me one, and that's because he honestly doesn't have a clue. "That's all I did, Josselyn. I borrowed money from the wrong people. I knew the cops would see I was at work when the car was smashed and realize my alibi is true. And there's no law that a man can't damage his own property, so I wasn't worried about that, and you shouldn't be either. We'll get this figured out. And Grace..."

He rolls his neck, his hand grabbing at it as he wiggles his head side-to-side with a pained expression. "It's not that I'm mad you needed help and felt close enough to her to call her, it's just that...look—she's never really cared for me. And here I am, her granddaughter's dad, borrowing money because I can't take care of what's mine. She's just going to see a failure; she'll judge. It's the last thing I need."

His nostrils flair with irritation even though his voice is trying to put out a calm vibe. It's the same way he is on the field when one of his athletes isn't listening.

"This is how you were when Mom left," I say, regretting it the moment the words leave my mouth.

My dad stops the car hard at the stop sign near our house, and my palms flatten on the dash as I jerk forward. All I want is for my dad to drive through the intersection, to continue on pretending he didn't hear what I said, but that won't happen. I'm just like him, and I wouldn't be able to let something like I just said go either.

"Is that what you think this is about?" he asks, shifting the car to park and leaning with his back against his door. I glance behind us when a car honks and zooms around us, but my dad doesn't bother to.

"Just take us home. Grace is waiting," I say, barely making eye contact with him as my head swivels to look in front of us then over my shoulder to the next car approaching that will no doubt honk and pass, too.

"You think all of this…the money borrowing, me talking to the cops…the trouble we're in…is what? Me acting out? This…*issue*…it has nothing to do with your mother and how I feel about what she did to us." He laughs through his last few words, but it isn't the humorous type of laugh—it's laced with fury.

"That's not what I think at all, Dad. I think you were trying to take care of us, and things got out of hand…and when the cops had you, I wasn't…they were…" I stammer, not sure what to say next, when my dad talks over me.

"They were what, Joss? What possibly could they be taking me in for? Did you actually think for a moment that I was the one who totaled your car? Do you know how ridiculous that sounds?"

"You were drunk!" I shout, my hands flying out in front of me, fingers stiff and hands like claws, as if I'm choking the air between us.

The wrinkle between my dad's eyes deepens and his mouth contorts as he looks at me like I'm crazy.

"I was at work, Joss. I came home immediately. I haven't had a drop in months. They gave me a goddamned breathalyzer…"

"I'm not talking about this time, Dad! I'm talking about then!" I interrupt, freezing his expression briefly until the words soak in.

My dad's lips part with a heavy breath, and his chest shudders.

"Then, Dad," I say, my voice quieter now.

His eyes remain on mine, but the fury and self-righteousness quickly erodes into regret—his for the past, and mine for the present. Clearing his throat, my dad turns back to face the wheel, rolling his window down and gesturing with his arm for the car behind us to pass. He doesn't drive forward, instead watching for a few seconds in the rearview mirror to make sure no one else is coming.

"Who told you that?" he asks, his voice about a dozen decibels lower, confidence deflated and anger turned to shame.

I don't answer him, and when he looks at me, my eyes dart to my lap where I tangle my hands. Wes's story isn't mine to tell, but in this case, our stories are aligned—they're the same story with the same tragic end.

"That boy…" my dad says, almost in a whisper.

I glance to the side and our eyes catch for a moment, then we both look away.

"Christopher," I say, chewing at the side of my cheek for several more seconds before I speak the connection my dad's already made. "Wes…"

My father covers his mouth and chin with his hand, rubbing his patchy stubble with his rough fingers and tilting his head to look out at the road.

"I was trying to quit," he says after what felt like a minute of silence. My eyes study him while he continues to look straight ahead. "When your mom left, I had been going to meetings, trying to stop. The night before that day…that's when I found out Kevin was real, and not just some ugly suspicion I had."

He leans forward until his forehead rests on the top of the wheel, the collar of his shirt flipped up in the back. I reach over and straighten it, leaving my hand on his upper back when I'm done. We sit like this for a long time; nearly a dozen cars pass us, and each time I hold up a hand so nobody thinks we need help.

They can't help us. All the heroes in the universe couldn't help the Winters family. We're a clan of beings who can only help ourselves. I come by my faults quite honestly. They're in my DNA.

When my dad's shoulders begin to shake, I move my hand from one shoulder blade to the other, feeling his muscles underneath my touch. He used to be so much stronger. This life—it has worn him down.

I wait until his shaking stops before I talk.

"Wes was almost suspended today," I say.

My dad brings his arm up to his face as he leans back in his seat, running his palm over his eyes as he sniffs in the last bits of evidence that he was ever emotionally weak.

"What did he do?" he asks, his eyes flitting to mine briefly before he looks over his shoulder and shifts the gear to pull us forward.

"He beat the crap out of Zack Ramsey for saying something pretty awful to me," I say, deciding not to give my dad the details of what Zack said. It would make him feel worse to know some people think the fact that he almost killed me with the car once is something that they can joke about.

"They let him off, though? Even though he was fighting?" My father's attention is back to the road, and his face is hard and stoic again. It's his mask, and I know he needs this.

"They did. Probably because the entire world knows Zack deserves to get his ass kicked," I say.

"You know he scored in the wrong end zone freshman year?" my dad says, a slight smile highlighting his lips. Even if he's making this story up, it's nice to hear.

"For real?" I ask.

"Uh huh," he says, chuckling as our car jiggles over the curb leading to our driveway. "It was his one shot, and that idiot picked up a fumble and ran the wrong way. He tried to come out for baseball after that, and I just crossed his name off the list the second he wrote it. Told him that was my first round of cuts."

I laugh to myself as my dad gets out of the car. His story may be embellished, but I have a feeling most of it is true. I climb out of my side, my body tired from my workout but my heart and head overcome with a calm feeling that somehow, we're all going to be okay. My dad's waiting for me at the front of the car, and he holds his arm out for me to slide into the comfort of his embrace as we walk. We're getting better at things like this.

"That's probably why Zack attacked you. Kid hates me," he says.

"I can handle him," I say, letting go of my dad as we reach the door. He holds it open as I slide by him and step inside.

"You can handle a lot of things, Joss," he says, his hand falling to my shoulder and halting me. Our eyes meet, and I exhale in response, knowing that those words were meant as an apology for the things I've had to handle because of him.

"I hope you all are okay with eggplant. I had this new recipe, and I walked to that store up on the corner and bought a few things," Grace says, busying herself with our mismatched pots and pans—our kitchen full of activity it hasn't seen since my mom left, and even she rarely cooked.

"Since our dinner usually gets handed over through a window, I'd say eggplant sounds awesome," I say, leaning over a pot with bubbling sauce. Grace waves her hand at me, shooing me away.

"Don't touch; you'll burn yourself," she says. "Go wash up."

Wash. Up.

I smirk at my dad as Grace turns back to the stovetop, and he shrugs his shoulders.

"You heard the woman," he says. "Go wash up."

We both laugh silently—never really having had a grandmother in the house to say grandmotherly-like phrases—but I obey, leaving them to sort through the things I know they need to say to each other alone. I spend a few minutes in the bathroom, then I hide in my room in silence, listening to my dad and Grace talk. I can't hear everything, but the bits I do make out are respectful and kind. My dad explains about the trouble he's in, and Grace offers to help with what she can, insisting, even after my dad refuses her money at least a dozen times. He takes it eventually, but even with her help, he's only halfway there. And I have a feeling that loan sharks don't work like banks, letting you make payments in good faith.

My room is growing darker as the sun falls to the back of the house, so I twist open my blinds to take in the view I'm still not used to. It's a new guy tonight—older. *Much* older. I bet he's a volunteer. I wonder how long they'll watch over us before they'll give up and just chalk things up to a one-time incident. My only hope is that whoever these people are my dad owes are wanted for a whole lot more, something that will make them worth law enforcement's time.

My phone buzzes in the side pocket of my backpack, so I drag it across my bed to see who's texting, smiling when it's from Wes.

Two news trucks for me. You?

I breathe out a laugh, moving to the floor and dragging myself close to the window, framing my phone between the slats of the blinds and taking a photo of my geriatric bodyguard. I send the picture to Wes, zooming in so he can make out the gray-haired details.

Just this guy.

Wes writes back in a few seconds.

Calling in the big guns, huh? Joss Winters will only work with seasoned professionals.

I run my thumb over his words on my screen.

There was this one time, when I was parked at the drive-in, where we were today.

There's a pause at the end of his text, but I can see he's still typing. I let my other leg fall to the carpet alongside my good leg, and I slide down until my head is propped up on one arm, my phone clutched in my other hand.

I texted you to see if you wanted a Coke. I thought if you knew what I meant, and showed up, that maybe it was a sign that I was supposed to come home.

I read his words several times, each time wondering if I would have done the right thing—if I would have known what he meant and followed the clues that led me to him. I think I would have. Another text from him buzzes in my hands.

I never sent it. Too scared to. I saw you on that road near Shawn's trailer two days later. I figured that was probably my sign.

"Joss, dinner," my dad says, drumming his knuckles gently on my door.

"Be right there," I say, sitting up and pulling my phone into my lap for one more message.

I don't do subtle. I make my signs nice and obvious.

I wait for a few extra seconds to see if he writes something more, but when he doesn't, I plug my phone in its charger and I join Grace and my dad at the kitchen table.

"So this is where you're supposed to eat?" my dad says, winking as he slides a chair out for Grace to sit.

She laughs with her lips slightly puckered, lines around them from age and sun.

"I remember when you and Kristina bought this table, before the house…in that tiny little apartment. Thing filled up most of the space and you had to squeeze around it just to get to the bathroom," Grace says.

My dad and I stare at the woodgrain cut in half where the table folds, both of us faking smiles. Grace sees right through us.

"Sorry, I didn't mean to bring up..." she begins, but my dad holds out his hand.

"It's fine," he says, pulling the side of his mouth in tighter, forcing a bigger smile that's still just as phony. "It's been a long time."

"It has," Grace says, staring at my father and waiting until he looks back at her.

There's something exchanged between them on that glance—a little understanding, maybe a peace made between two outsiders both hurt badly by the same woman they loved—a daughter and a wife.

"How about you say grace, Josselyn," my grandmother says. Her request sends a bolt through my body, and I can hear my father sniggering under his breath, glad he wasn't the one asked. We aren't religious, and I didn't get the sense that Grace was with my short visit in Tucson, but I don't want to be disrespectful either.

"I'll...try," I say, my voice crackling through the words.

I clear my throat and begin to pray for something to get me through this. I'd almost take another car driving into our house just to buy me time. My father awkwardly reaches his hand to grasp Grace's open palm, and I do the same, meeting his gaze and shrugging slightly before we both reach across the table. Grace smiles at us and dips her chin, closing her eyes.

"Right...okay," I breathe out, closing mine. "Heavenly Father..."

My prayers answered, a light knock interrupts us, coming from the front door. Without masking my joy, I untangle my hands and leap from the table.

"Oh...got it...I'll get it," I say, racing toward the front window and pulling the shade out to the side.

A bright light blinds me temporarily, and I let the shade fall from my hold and rub my fist in my eyes.

"Who is it?" My dad's joined me near the door.

"I can't tell. Our rent-a-cop is lighting up the house with his spotlight," I say.

My dad's eyes close a little and he leans over my shoulder, peeking for himself, but also unable to see anything. He holds his arm across my chest, as if he's shielding me, and slowly unlocks the door, opening it just an inch or two, his arm flexed and ready to slam it shut again fast. I don't say anything to argue with him, but if someone's willing to drive a car into our things, I'm pretty sure they're prepared to bust through my dad's fifty-year-old bicep.

"It's Wes," he says, pulling the door open completely.

"Hey, Coach. I'm sorry I just showed up. I…umm…do you think you could wave to the cop guy out there? That light's really annoying," Wes says, his smile crooked to match the tilt of his hat. His clothes are wrinkled, and I can tell he probably threw them on and raced out of his bedroom the minute we finished texting.

My dad waves his arm, which results in rent-a-cop waving his light a few times, but eventually he turns it off and mutters something before getting back in his car.

"I hate this so much," I say under my breath. Only Wes hears me, and I'm glad.

"Come on in, Wes. We were just sitting down to eat. You should join us," my dad says.

My heart pounds nervously, because as much as Wes and my dad are comfortable together, there's a new layer over all of us now that my dad has linked the past to the present. And even though we haven't talked about it yet, I know that layer is there for Grace, too.

"Are you sure?" he asks, one arm hidden behind his back. I lurch to look, but he catches me and turns his body, grabbing my wrist when I try to fight my way in.

"I'm sure," my dad says, his eyes catching Wes's touch and his mouth falling flatter.

My dad moves back toward the dining table, but Wes and I stay near the door, a cool breeze cutting through the screen door and the sounds

193

of crickets marking what's left of the sun.

"I uh...I sorta did a thing," Wes says, dipping his head so all I can see is the brim of his hat and the hint of the shy smile dusting his lips.

His hidden hand comes between us, clutching a small bouquet of pink flowers, tied together with a ribbon, a wet paper towel wrapped around the cut stems.

"They aren't peonies. I think they're called phlox. My mom grows them in a pot in the backyard," he says, tipping his hat up. I catch the bashful wrinkle to his eyes, and I fall for him a little more. He holds the flowers higher, pushing them closer to me. "She said I could. I was just trying to follow your signs, and I'm pretty sure you were giving me the flowers vibe."

My hand covers his as I take the bundle from him, leaning forward to smell the petals, already wilting slightly. It's a sad bouquet, and Wes knows it. I love it, still.

"Thank you," I whisper, my lips resting in a flirtatious smile. Wes's eyes dim and his lip curls to match mine. "And *phlox* is a really stupid word for a flower."

His chest shakes with his quiet laugh, and I bring the drooping bouquet up to my nose. They smell sweet.

"Grace...she's going to want to talk more than we did earlier, when you drove from the airport," I say, leading Wes across the living room, to the dining table filled with steaming pots and plates and napkins and silverware. It feels like a holiday, but it's only Monday. "I'm pretty sure she knows who you are."

Wes's chest lifts as we approach, and he draws a quick breath, nodding slightly to me and straightening his shoulders before reaching a hand out to my grandmother.

"I'm sorry for just showing up, ma'am," he says, and I catch my dad rolling his eyes at Wes's formal greeting.

I fill a glass with water in the kitchen for my bouquet. When I return to the table, Grace is holding Wes's palm in both of hers, covering the top and patting, just as she did with me when I showed up in Tucson. Her eyes narrow in on Wes's face, her head tilting a little to the side before she reaches up with one hand and pushes the brim of his hat up just a hair.

"You shouldn't hide eyes like that," she says, her mouth curved slightly, as if she knows a secret. I'm certain she does. "It's been a while since I've seen eyes like that, you know."

Her hand comes to cup his face with familiarity, and her eyes dazzle looking at him. Her attention is making him nervous; I see it in the way his jaw flexes and the way he swallows slowly, trying to hide his nerves from the rest of us.

"Yes, ma'am," Wes responds, pulling his hat off completely, setting it on the counter behind him.

"Grace, Wesley. You can call me Grace," she says, using his formal name, just as she likes to do with me. She holds a hand out to encourage him to sit.

He does, smirking as he looks down at his empty plate.

"Grace is one of my favorite names," he says through a smile, glancing at me sideways. My heart beats a little stronger for just a breath. With just a subtle look and a few words, he can take me back in time to when we were children.

"Speaking of my name...Joss was about to *say* grace," she says, and without warning, my mouth and attitude kicks in, and I breathe out a sigh that makes my father laugh and makes my grandmother twist her mouth with disapproval.

"Sorry," I say, clearing my throat, pursing my lips and gnashing my back teeth together. "I've never done it before...is all..."

"I can," Wes cuts in.

My hero in all ways, I swear.

"Thank you," Grace says, smiling at him, but letting her mouth fall straight when she moves her gaze to me.

Glancing at me in the seat next to him, Wes gives me a closed-mouth smile and slides his hand toward me along the tabletop, lifting his fingers just enough for me to slide mine under his palm. He does the same to my grandmother then looks across the table to my father, who is just as awkward as I am at this. I wait for Wes's cue, dropping my chin to my chest but not closing my eyes right away. I can see my dad from my periphery, and I notice he's doing the same—his open eyes blinking as they stare at the table's edge.

"Dear Lord, please excuse the poor etiquette I'm about to display. I've never really done this…said grace at a dinner table with friends. My family isn't much for the formalities of religion, but that doesn't mean that you and I don't talk. We do. I've talked a lot lately about the people I need in my life. I've prayed for their safety and health…I've prayed for their forgiveness."

His hand squeezes mine with a gentle force, and I feel the pang of his words in the center of my chest. I squeeze him back.

"You've given me more than I deserve, and I thank you for this day…for this evening, here at this table with three other people I know would each give of themselves completely just to make sure the others would have one more dinner like this. We're grateful for the food and for the shelter, but above all, we're grateful for the relationships—for the people who make us better, and who lift us at our worst. Thank you…for this life. Sometimes it feels as if it may be more than we can handle…at least it does for me. Doesn't mean we won't try, though. I promise I will try."

At some point during Wes's words, my eyes fell closed. We all sit silently for a second or two, and eventually Grace leads us by saying, "Amen." We all repeat her words, and everyone lets go of their grasp on the hand next to them. I let my hand fall below the table to Wes's knee, and his eyes lock with mine.

"That was lovely, Wes," Grace says, holding a large plate weighed down with stuffed eggplant. She scoops one onto Wes's plate, but leans toward him before handing the platter over to me. "I've never given thanks before a meal either," she admits, her eyes sliding to mine briefly, teasing me before moving back to Wes. "I'm pretty sure the last time I heard someone give thanks, in fact, it was you. You were three, and you lived in that house right over there," she says, turning her head and nodding to the house next door, where Shawn used to live. "Even back then, you were thankful for her. 'Thank you for Joss,' you said. The words came out with a lisp, and you followed them up with a cookie. We all thought it was cute, but I had this feeling that you really meant it."

My boyfriend and my grandmother stare into one another, both holding the heavy plate of food between them, slight smiles drawn from cheek to cheek. I glance to my father, and his brow is heavy, dimpled with the weight of dots he hasn't quite fully connected.

"I remember you now," Grace says, finally taking control of the plate and passing it to me. I hold it, but remain focused on the quiet conversation next to me. "And I remember the things you can do."

CHAPTER 17

"What can you do?"

Really, it's a question I've held on the tip of my tongue since the first time I witnessed Wes do something extraordinary. It's why I tested him for so long. I wanted the truth, sure—to know for certain he was Christopher. But I also wanted to know what he could do.

We've been sitting out on the curb in front of my house, about a dozen yards behind rent-a-cop, taking turns throwing small pebbles at the sewer cover in the center of the street. We never discussed the rules, but we both know that the closest rock to the center of the cover wins. So far, Wes has me beat by about six inches.

"Is this because of what Grace said in there? At dinner?" He leans forward, propping his arms on his bent knees, and looking at me with one eye squinting.

"It's a little because of that…yeah," I say, shrugging then lining up my toss, shooting the small rock with basketball form, landing it right next to his. I twist to face him and lift my brows once.

"Couldn't just let me win, could you?" he chuckles.

"Aw, Wes. I'm sorry, want me to start throwing left-handed?" I push my lips out in a pout and he rolls his eyes.

"No," he sighs. "With my luck, you're better at this with your wrong hand."

On a whim, I fling a rock in the direction of our target with my left, skipping it along the road, and it lands next to the other two we've both landed there. Wes's mouth curves slowly, his tongue caught in his back

198

teeth as he shakes his head.

"I swear that was an accident," I say, giggling.

Wes exhales, pretending to be a sore loser, and tosses the few pebbles left in his hand out into the road. The lights from an oncoming car cast shadows along the ground, glowing underneath the rent-a-cop's car, and I hear his door open in response. I hold my breath, and I draw my legs in close, preparing myself to stand—*to run*. The car passes slowly, turning into a driveway about six or seven houses past mine, and I slowly unravel the grip my fingers had on my knees.

"He had his radio out, ready to call someone," Wes says, nodding toward our watchman. His door closes again, and he resumes the comfortable position he was in, bringing a large Styrofoam cup up to his mouth and tilting it to let the ice slide out.

"He's had sixty-four ounces today, I swear. I wonder when he pees," I say, hushed.

"Joss," Wes says.

I turn to him with a, "Hmmm?"

He reaches for my fingers, still gripping my leg, and he pulls them into his hand, revealing the small indents left behind from my fingernails. Shifting slightly to the side, he keeps my hand in his, running a finger from his opposite hand along the marks on my leg.

"I don't like how nervous all of this makes you," he says.

My eyes focus on my leg for a few quiet seconds while I think of the right words to say. I am scared, but I'm also done letting fear tell me what I can and cannot do.

"You know what's weird?" I begin, my gaze shifting from Wes up into the starry sky. "The more nights I sleep with the idea that this is my life, the more okay I am with it."

His forehead creases.

"Not just since the car being totaled, but since…I don't know, my leg maybe?" I say. "It started out as a sort of coping mechanism—some piece of wisdom I picked up from one of the dozens of doctors who tried to tell me the best ways not to be depressed, because of their medical expertise, of course. Not that a single one of them had ever lost a limb…when they were seventeen."

Wes nods slightly, sympathy coloring his cheeks and sloping his eyes. He rests his chin in his palm, waiting for me to explain.

"I go to sleep and tell myself that this is just what it is—my life is this. And in the morning, it will be there waiting for me, and I'll get up, and I'll go to school, or to my job, or to the field, or…wherever. And I'll be in this body, with Eric Winters as my dad, and with sour memories of my mom," I say, breathing in and holding the air in my chest, puffing it out as I turn to look Wes in the eyes again. "But then there's also you."

My mouth quirks, and his eyes squint suspiciously, his mouth hinting at a smile.

"I'm not under the same delusions that Shawn is, Wes. I've tried to accept them as real, but they just aren't. This is my life," I say, holding my finger up in the air between us. "I decide to get drunk, and it goes this way," I say, lowering my finger to my knee. Wes covers my hand with his and pushes my finger down to the ground, and I look at him sideways, even though I know he's right.

"My dad makes an effort, and my life does this…" My finger begins to draw a slow slope back up in the air between us. I stop when it's at my shoulder's height, and I leave it there.

"The state of California can't afford to fix a bridge," I chuckle, dropping my finger back down, this time to the sidewalk we're sitting on. "I meet Rebecca," I say, raising my finger again, slowly as I continue to speak. "I work hard. I train. I get a magazine story. I meet my grandmother. I *love* my grandmother."

I shake my head, my mouth forming a crooked smile. Then I draw my hand into a fist and let my fingers stretch back out as my mouth makes a quiet explosion sound.

"My dad racks up some serious debt," I laugh.

I hug my knees to my chest and rock back a little, my face tilted up and my eyes moist from laughing.

"There's a reason for every dive and climb, Wes. There just is. And my life, it depends on my choices, on my dad's decisions…on some government vote…*on you*. I wake up smiling now, because of you. And not because I think I need you to save me, or because of the weird shit you can do," I say, shaking my head. "I don't Wes. I can ride the waves, and I know I'll be just fine. Because of me. I can count on myself, and that…*that* is a pretty fuckin' healthy place to be, don't you think?"

His eyes on mine, Wes's mouth puckers into a slight smile as he leans in and pulls my head toward his lips, kissing me as he sweeps the tiny loose hairs from my skin. His fingers touch my chin next, and his mouth dusts mine with a brushing of a kiss.

"I can fly," he whispers against me, pulling away just enough to look me in the eyes. My lashes lower and my focus shifts from his left eye to his right, my heart beating faster the more milliseconds that pass. My stomach starts to dive, and my eyes begin to widen just as Wes's mouth twitches into a curl.

"You ass!" I shout, pushing him until he rolls into a ball along the curb, his laughter echoing off our garage door.

"I couldn't help it…and you called me weird!" he teases, righting himself and poking my side where I'm ticklish.

"You are weird!" I say back, pushing him again.

He catches my wrists in his hands this time, tugging me close and kissing my lips a little harder than before.

"I'm yours," he says, his head falling against mine.

"Yeah?" I ask.

"Yeah," he says. "I'll be the reason you wake up smiling. That's hero enough for me."

Wes stands, holding a hand out to help me to my feet. We both dust our legs off, and I walk with Wes toward his truck parked on the other side of where rent-a-cop sits. Our guard looks up as we pass, so Wes holds up two fingers to wave. Our watchman nods, grumpily, then goes back to reading something on his iPad.

"Must be a good book," Wes jokes.

"I bet it's porn," I say.

Wes shakes his head and pulls me into his arms, swallowing me completely in his embrace. "It's not porn," he says, pressing his lips on top of my head. "You can't get a strong enough signal out here."

I smack lightly at his back then find bliss in the raspy laughter that echoes in his chest.

"Take you to school in the morning? TK and Levi are riding with Taryn."

I hold on to the front of his shirt and nod *yes* while he pauses with his driver's side door open, his keys dangling from his thumb.

"Good," he says, nodding over his shoulder toward my house. "You better get inside. I can see your grandmother at the door."

"Good night, Wesley!" Grace calls out.

I tuck my head into his chest, embarrassed, but Wes only responds with more raspy laughter.

"Good night, Grace," he says, waving over my shoulder then sliding back into his front seat. His thumb brushes over my bottom lip, and I feel it seconds after he drives away, all the way inside my house.

"That young man grew into some gentleman, didn't he?" my grandmother says.

"He did," I say, my mouth falling closed into a grin. My dad busies himself with the dishes in the kitchen, and I notice that he's whistling lightly. My body grows warm inside hearing it, and even though I can't remember a time my dad whistled like that before, I know he has, and I know I heard it somewhere. This feeling—it's the kind that prickles from memories—good ones.

I walk into the kitchen to kiss my father goodnight, then do the same to Grace, thanking her for dinner. On my dad's orders, I gather up the spare blankets and make him a bed on the sofa, my fingers kneading at the sheets I laid down for Wes.

"I'm just fine sleeping here, you know," Grace says, already kicking her shoes from her feet and pushing them to the side of the couch.

"I insist," my dad says, drying his hands and leaning on the counter as he picks up the TV remote. "Unless you want to join me out here for the

Motor two-fifty. I recorded it this weekend, and I managed to avoid hearing who won, so I'm gonna sit back and watch every lap."

"Well I could tell you who won," Grace says, my dad's eyes flashing wide instantly. She sniggers and winks at him. "I'm kidding. You enjoy your race. I'll have Joss help me get settled in."

We both head down the hallway to my dad's room, and other than a few stray dirty shirts and a pile of papers from his visit today to the police station, my dad's room is pretty clean and bare.

"There's an extra quilt in the chest," I say, lifting the lid to show her. "And if you don't like his pillow, I'll switch you with one of mine. We share the bathroom…oh…and Dad has one of those air-filter things. If you like to have white noise, or whatever."

"I'm sure I'll be fine," she says, sitting on the bed's edge, her small suitcase open on the floor near her feet.

"All right…well…goodnight," I say, my eyes lingering on hers as she says the words back. I turn to leave through the door, but before I enter the hall completely, I give in to temptation.

"What can he do?" I ask, turning to face her swiftly. Her head jerks up and her brow furrows. "At dinner. You told Wes you knew what he could do."

She chews at her lips for a few seconds, almost as if she's deciding whether or not I can be trusted with this information.

"I didn't know him well. I mean, I wasn't around that much, and you both were very young." Her voice lifts at the end, and her brow bunches again as she drops the nightshirt back into her open suitcase. "You two were glued at the hip," she continues, grinning slightly, her eyes set on something invisible to the side of me. "I can't say it was you more than him, or the other way. We all thought it was this adorable first best-friends thing. But I do remember one thing that really stood out."

I lean back, looking down the hallway, seeing my dad's arm now resting in his favorite chair. Mumbling comes from the TV, which means he's distracted. I look at my grandmother again, her gaze beyond me one moment, then on my eyes the next.

"It's like he could predict the future," she says, her voice almost laughing out the words. She waves her hands and stands again, lifting her nightshirt from the ground. "Oh, it's just silliness."

"No…I don't think it is," I say. She turns to look me in the eyes again, slowly. I shake my head with tiny movement, my eyes flitting to her hands then back to her face. "What made you think that he could see things? Before they happen…"

Her breathing slows, and I notice the way she swallows, a glassiness forming over her eyes. Instincts tell me to brace myself against the wall near the door, so my hand grips the doorway behind me, holding on.

"Your mom…she had troubles, which I told you about," she says, and I breathe in deeply, holding it as if I know somehow whatever Grace says next is going to choke away the rest of my air. "I was parked out front, waiting for her to come home from a doctor's appointment she had taken you to with her. Your dad was at the school, so I was just standing out front, talking to that nice man who lived next door…the one in that picture."

"Shawn," I say, the sound barely audible.

My grandmother smiles as she nods, but her eyes aren't smiling at all. They're red and the first tear slides down her cheek just before she quickly swipes it away with her palm, trying to erase it existed.

"He and I were talking about nothing, probably the weather that day. I don't even remember what we were saying, but I will never forget when that little boy came running out of the house and tugged on Shawn's pant leg then patted on his cane to get his attention," Grace says, sliding her right palm to the center of her chest, a heavy breath leaving her nose. "He told us that you were in the garage next door, and that your mama was in there with you. He said you were sleeping in the backseat and your mom was sleeping in the front. And then he told us that he saw it in a dream, two nights before. In his dream, Shawn and I were standing out in the yard talking when he came running up. He said that's how he knew he was right, because everything in his head looked just like this."

My gut twists as I add the facts to the only sickening conclusion. My mom was trying to kill me; she was trying to kill us both.

"I had left my car running at the curb, even though I parked, and I couldn't hear the engine in the garage," Grace says, falling back to a sitting position on the edge of the bed, her hands needling at the shirt. "That boy ran to the garage and began banging on it, and when Shawn didn't know how to get it open…Wesley jammed his fingers underneath and lifted, bending the bottom panel near the ground until he could slide more of his hands underneath and lift the garage door completely. I told the police he was the one to save you, but Shawn laughed it off and told them he had made the discovery and lifted the garage. Even with his lack of mobility and muscle coordination, it was far more likely that the adult did the rescuing…but I knew better. *I knew better.*"

Through it all—my life—I have never felt as hollow as I do right now. No heart beats inside of my chest, and my lips are numb and cold, which is all right since I'm speechless, too.

"Your mom wasn't well, Joss. And you were so young, there's no way you would remember," she says, her words rushing to fill the quiet. She's speaking normally, and I don't even care if my dad hears any of this now. "Your dad and I thought it was best that this was something you didn't learn about. Your mom got help after that, and for a while, she was better."

"She literally never wanted me…" My eyes are wide, but I can't really see anything. The room is all a blur, and Grace is sitting motionless, not sure whether she's supposed to hold me or wait for me to accept and move on, all on my own.

"This is what my life is," I whisper, and my grandmother shakes her head, her brows lowering, questioning what she heard. "I'm sorry…I was…coping."

I crack a laugh, and the sharp sound burns my chest. I stop breathing again and feel the pain.

"She wasn't well, Josselyn," she repeats.

"I know," I nod, still not looking Grace in the eyes.

"That was the last time Shawn and she spoke, too. He moved away, and I don't think they really kept in touch," she says.

"He wrote her a letter," I say, almost in a trance. Without thinking, my eyes act on their own and my gaze locks to Grace's. I stare at her in silence through several breaths, my inner voice repeating over and over "Shawn was in love with her." I never once say it out loud.

I leave Grace, promising that I'm okay, despite being the farthest from okay I think maybe I've ever been. When I get to my room, I close the door gently, overcompensating for the urge to slam things and punch holes with my fists. I remain calm, and lay down on my bed with my phone in my hand. I try to figure out whom I need to talk to—who can make this hurt go away.

Kyle will listen and enable. Wes will try to fix. Taryn won't understand, but she'll sympathize.

Several minutes pass and none of my options ever feel right, so I make the only choice I have left—I call Shawn. I find his number quickly, and he answers within the first few rings. He isn't surprised to hear my voice at all, and it's either because he's intuitive or because he's an exceptional faker. I think, maybe, he's a little of both.

"Wes is the one who sees things," I say, and his only response is silence.

His silence is enough.

CHAPTER 18

I didn't call Wes with the latest revelation I learned about his life. I simmered on it, spending hours trying to make sense out of everything Grace said. It isn't so much the part about Wes as it is the part about what my mother tried to do.

When Grace came into my room to comfort me, I let her. I acted the part—broken daughter who is trying to understand that her mom wasn't well. The only thing I really understand is why nobody told me. I'm glad they didn't, but I'm also glad I know. I think *now* was the right time for me to find out. As much as it hurts, it slides so many of my puzzle pieces in place, and the picture of me and my mother that was fuzzy for so long is so much clearer.

None of this was me. It wasn't that I wasn't wanted, or that I was some experiment to see if my presence would fix all of the broken things in my parents' relationship. Nothing was going to fix things for my mom. She would never be happy—her mind and body simply wouldn't let her. And as much as I mourn the joys I missed out on because of it, I feel this odd sense of closure on all of those painful wounds I carried around for so long.

None of it was my fault.

I slept; I think because of the peace. I dreamt of things that didn't make sense—a new candy machine in the school hallway, a speech I was supposed to give in English that I wasn't prepared for, and some chalk drawing in my driveway that looked like hopscotch. In my dream, I had both of my legs, and I hopped all the way into my garage.

Even now, as Wes pulls up to the curb and I finish the last bite of my Pop-Tart, I don't feel anger or resentment. This is my life...and *that* was my mom's. Neither could be helped.

"Your dad's back in the gym today?" Wes asks as I climb into the passenger seat.

"Life as usual. That's how we do things in the Winters house, we just mow right through the crap and pretend we never saw it," I laugh, buckling my belt as Wes pulls away.

My phone buzzes just as I'm bending forward to tuck it in my bag, so I bring it back to my lap and see Rebecca's name. Wes turns his stereo down so I can hear.

"Hey, it's me," I say, pulling the phone away from my ear for a second just to check the time. "Were we supposed to work out this morning?"

"No, and I know it's early. I figured you'd be on your way to school?" she asks.

"I am," I say.

"Good. Do you have your equipment?" I glance to Wes and he slows the truck down as I hold my finger up.

"I'm right by the house, so I can get it," I say, swirling my finger in the air and asking him to turn around.

We're back at my house in seconds, so I get out of the truck and continue to talk while I gather my things from the garage. There's a new stain on the concrete in the middle of the ground, and I stop to stare at it while Rebecca explains that the magazine wants to get some shots today of me working out at the field. She says she's cleared it with the school. I respond with automatic "okays" and "uh huhs," but my focus is on that stain. It's oil from the car I owned for less than a day. The last bit of proof that my dad's gift to me was parked right here before police hauled it away as evidence.

"Do you think my dad can be in the shots with me?" I ask, snapping my focus back to Rebecca. I've interrupted her, and I'm not sure what she was saying. "He's just been an important part of my progress. People should see the value of family."

I spin it for her to sell to the magazine, and it works. She agrees and we hang up as I shut the garage and carry my things out to Wes's truck. I didn't ask because of the family element to the story. I asked because my dad is trying so hard, and because I want to show him that I see it—I feel his love, and I love him back.

So very much.

"Sorry," I say to Wes as I climb in after dropping my things in the back. "The magazine is going to take some shots today out on the field."

Wes grins on one side of his mouth then looks to the road, shifting and pulling us forward. "That's awesome," he says.

"My dad's going to be in the photos with me," I say, my eyes watching his face for a reaction.

Wes's lips rest in a slight smile, and the longer I watch, the deeper his dimple becomes. I mimic his expression, and we don't talk about it anymore. Wes is proud of me for this, but that's not why I did it. I did it because at the end of the day, my dad's earned it, too.

At least a dozen times during our drive, I try to find a natural way to bring up what Grace told me to Wes. There really isn't a natural way to tell someone you found out your mom tried to kill you when you were little, though, much less add in the part that your superhero boyfriend had a vision and stopped it. By the time we pull into the school parking lot, I'm giggling at the very real absurdity of it all.

"All right, what's funny?" Wes asks, resting his left arm on the wheel as he turns to look at me. I glance to his hat, the way it's slightly crooked, shading his left eye from the sun, and just to tease him, I reach forward and tug it down low, over his eyebrows.

"You sure you can't fly?" I ask.

He punches out a short laugh.

"Pretty sure," he says, twisting the other way and fixing his hat as he leaves the truck.

I leave, too, knowing I need to talk to Wes about what I've learned, but deciding now isn't the time to dissect more of Shawn's lies.

Taryn and Wes's brothers haven't gotten to the gym yet, so Wes goes to work doing the exercises he doesn't need a spotter for, and I grab a jump rope from the wall. My dad is flipping through a stack of papers at his desk in the corner, and he doesn't notice me when I walk up. I glance at them, upside down, and recognize the name of our insurance company.

"For the car?" I ask, and my dad jumps a little in his seat. He sets his pen down and leans back in his chair, scratching at his chin.

"Yeah, looks like we'll be able to replace it. Picking insurance plans is the one thing I didn't screw up," he says, shaking once with a laugh before he lets his palms fall flat on his desk as he stares up at me.

"You didn't screw up a lot of things," I shrug. His eyes hold onto mine for a few seconds before he responds.

"Thanks," he says, quiet so only I hear.

My pulse picks up, not from nerves, but more from anticipation. I glance around to make sure we're alone enough to talk without obnoxious football players eavesdropping. I notice Zack isn't here, and I'm pretty sure he got suspended for yesterday's fight with Wes. A few of his friends are here, and they're watching Wes while whispering, I'm sure just waiting to text Zack about how the golden boy got off easy. What they don't realize, though, is Wes really is made of gold—light, and gold, and something more. I'm not entirely sure he's human sometimes, but I don't care.

"Speaking of things you're good at," I say, sliding into the open chair at the side of his desk.

"Well this list oughta be short," he chuckles, turning in his swivel chair and folding his arms over his chest. My dad reaches into his middle drawer and slides it open, pulling out a pack of gum. I see about a dozen half-ripped open packs in there. He takes out a stick and holds it out for me to take one. I shake my head *no*, but smirk as he puts the pack back in his drawer.

"I know, it's a lot of gum," he says, leaning back again as he unwraps his stick. "They don't like me spitting seeds in here."

I nod and smile while he pops the gum in his mouth and begins to chew.

"I haven't had a chance to tell you about something," I start, and my dad's head tilts to the side, curious. "It's a good thing. I know my track record might make you think I'm about to tell you I'm failing, but I'm not. My grades are pretty good so far, actually. I mean…it's early still, but…"

"Screw track records," my dad says, snapping his gum before smiling through tight lips.

"Exactly," I say, laughing lightly. I glance around once more, satisfied that the few people in here with us are absorbed in their own worlds. "I'm going to be in a magazine."

My dad's eyebrows raise and his hands loosen around his chest as he sits up a little straighter.

"Yeah," I smirk, my cheeks blushing with pride. I look down at my hands, twisting nervously in my lap. As much swagger as I claim to have, having someone see something in me still feels extraordinary.

"When? What for? How many copies can I buy?"

My dad's face has never been so bright. He scoots his wheels closer to the desk and rests his elbow on the top, propping up his head as he stares at me with what looks like wonder.

"I'm sure they'll give me copies, but you can buy a hundred," I joke.

"Done," he says fast.

Our smiles settle on each other and I let his eyes dazzle around my face for a few seconds, warm under his glow.

"It was going to be a story on Rebecca at first," I say, pausing to raise my eyes and suck in my lips, still not used to the idea that I'm somehow important enough to do something like this. "She told them she knew of a better story…or not better, but just…"

"Horseshit, your story's better," my dad says, a little too loudly. A few people in the gym look over, but they go back to their workouts quickly.

"The story is going to be on her post-injury work as a trainer, and on me as her client…athlete…I'm not sure what they'll call me. Client sounds so weird," I say.

"They'll call you amazing," my dad cuts in fast.

I blush again and let my head fall to the side.

"Thanks, Dad," I say softly.

"What's the magazine called?" he asks.

"*Girl Strong.* You've seen it," I answer.

"You've gotten it," he confirms. I nod *yes.*

My dad lets his hand fall flat on the desk again and he continues to stare at me, his smile never shrinking this entire time.

"There's another thing," I say, butterflies back in my chest. I'm excited for this, and I hope he's okay with it. My dad nods at me again, ready for more. "They're coming to shoot my workout on the field today. My workout...with you."

"With...me..." His head cocks slightly, and his lips twitch, uncertain what I mean.

"I could not have done any of this without you, Dad. The photos need to be with me and you. You're part of this success story. Pushing me to be my best...it's something you're good at, turns out."

My dad's mouth closes, a hint of a smile on his lips, and he swallows hard, his eyes misting. His breath hitches, stuttering through his nose, and after a few seconds, his eyes close in a slow blink. For a moment, I think he might not open them, but he does. Leaning close, he reaches his hand toward my head, his palm caressing the side of my cheek and hair, covering my ear. He pulls me close and I bend forward as he kisses the top of my head.

"I'll be there. Right after school. With whatever you need," he says, his voice cracking halfway through his words.

He backs away and stands, flashing me a quick smile and holding up a thumb before he steps through the door, letting it swing closed behind him. He's gone for a walk, to be alone. I let him, because I know he's outside reveling in what a win feels like, and not the kind he's earned thousands of out there on the field, but the kind he's fought for with me...for months. Perhaps even for years.

"Are you sure you don't want to make this about you and your hot best friend? I bet *Girl Strong* readers would really like a story about that,"

212

Taryn says, swaying her hip into mine as we throw our backpacks over our shoulders and fall in step with the crowd that fills our main high school hallway.

"You know, that was my first pitch, but funny...they weren't interested," I say.

"Fools," she says back fast.

Taryn and I walk down the hill toward the boys, and I notice a few other people hanging out with them. My eyes dim the closer I get to them, and I decide to question Levi first. He's always been the weakest of the bunch.

"I know Wes told you guys, but who did you tell?" I say, giving him a sideways glance.

"Dude, this was all your dad. Don't even look at me," Levi says.

I take in the seven or eight guys standing and talking behind my friends and then glance out to the field where my dad is dragging the dirt, trying to make our field look better than the cheapest-per-ton spread of thin gravel and eight-year-old bases ripping at the corners. He's almost manic in the way he's working, rushing around in circles, the chains kicking up dust behind him.

"He's proud," Wes says, his arm falling around me as his lips graze my cheek.

"I know; I'm just not all about audiences is all," I say.

"Pretend they're fans. You're just taking infield and hitting. Shit, Cherry...showing off is your thing!" TK teases, laughing at himself.

I roll my eyes, despite kind of agreeing with him, and I step in his direction.

"We're going to have words about this *Cherry* nickname thing. You know better," I say, pointing at him and trying to hide my smile.

"Yeah," he says, waggling his head and sniffling confidently. "I do, but I wanted to piss you off so you'd get off your dad's back. Worked, didn't it?"

"Oh, I'm pissed all right," I say, turning around. I smile to myself as I keep going into the locker room, knowing that TK is several feet behind

213

me now, not sure if I'm joking or not.

I grab my things from the locker, where I stuffed them this morning, and I sit on the bench looking at my sliding pants, the socks I've cut and sewn to work with my leg, my favorite practice shirt.

"Want me to braid your hair?" I smile hearing Bria's voice.

"For once, yes…yes, Bria…I want you to braid my hair," I laugh, turning on the bench and letting her pull the band from the base of my neck.

Bria and I haven't talked much since the bus accident. I didn't really see her over the summer, but she's been spending a lot of time with Levi. They like each other, but they're both being stupid about it.

"Levi tell you about this photoshoot thing?" I say, my head jerking as she tugs my hair to make it smooth. "Yeah. Don't be mad; he was excited."

"I'm not," I say.

Her hands work along the sides of my head, finger combing the loose ends into her hold, and she begins to weave and pull, making a braid.

"I know you don't like people staring at you, or whatever," she says.

"It's okay. I figure if it has to be anywhere, at least it's out there. I get lost when I'm playing," I say, thinking about that part rather than the eyes that will be on me, watching me be the focus of something other than a rival team or a girl I've threatened just because she looked at me funny.

We're silent while Bria finishes working on my hair, wrapping the end with the same band she pulled from my hair and running her fingertips along the weave to make sure every piece is tucked in where it should be.

"Is it one of those French kinds?" I ask.

"Yeah," Bria says, stepping back to admire it.

My mom gave me a French braid once. She took a picture of it because she was proud of her work. There were times when she could be such a great mom.

I turn and stand from the bench, taking a few steps to look into the mirror that stretches along the back wall.

"Thanks," I say, my mouth tugging up on one side.

If I still had a mom, I think I'd wear my hair like this more often. I actually like it.

"It's really great that you're doing this," she says, her voice smaller behind me.

I turn with my prepared smile plastered in place, but it isn't necessary. She's looking down.

"My mom can't make it out to our games, so you've probably never seen her, but she's in a wheelchair. She was actually born without both of her legs. I can't wait to tell her about what you're doing and give her a copy of the magazine."

She looks up at me with a blink, breathing in deeply through her nose. She didn't tell me that because she wants me to say I'm sorry about her mom. She told me because, while half of the people out there waiting for my photoshoot are interested in the celebrity idea that comes along with photographers and magazine stories, Bria is actually interested in my message.

I have a message. That sunk in when Rebecca first brought this idea up for me, but it really cuts at my heart now.

"I don't know how I feel about being a role model," I shrug, showing an honest side of myself to Bria.

She shrugs back.

"I know," she says, standing from the bench and backing away slowly, stopping when her hand is on the door to go back outside. "But there's pretty much nothing you can't become the absolute best at—so I feel pretty good about you figuring this role-model thing out."

I chuckle as she laughs lightly on her way through the door, and the smile remains on my face when I'm standing in the locker room all alone. I look down again at my pile of clothes and my gear, and I inhale, readying myself to be the best, and to forget about the people watching.

It takes me a little longer than usual to get dressed, mostly because I pay attention to things like how well my shirt is tucked in, how even my pants are below my knees, how straight the seams are on my socks. Covering the prosthetic is actually easier than my normal leg, mostly because it only wraps up the socket.

I've gotten better at working with the blade leg. I've gotten faster, thanks to Rebecca. There's a tinge in my chest, though, and I hate that I feel it. As good as I'm going to be, I'm still never going to be as good as I was. I've resolved myself to that, too. But right now, all I can think about is what the people out there are expecting to see. I'm afraid I'm going to disappoint them.

My phone dings, so I push the rest of my things into my locker and grab my gear, palming my phone, reading the text as I walk past the crowd that's now doubled outside. I refuse to acknowledge them, and I walk behind a few of the storage sheds on my way out to the field so people won't follow me or want to talk.

I slide open a message from Rebecca.

Just got here with Seth, the photographer. Anita Welton is writing the story, so she came to ask you a few questions before Saturday's studio shoot.

I pause, still shaded by the shed where they store most of the track mats and hurdles. Anita Welton went to the Olympics. I watched her pitch for USC, and I watched her pitch for Team USA. I swallow hard and type back *okay, on my way.*

It takes a few more seconds for me to regulate my breathing and continue out toward the field. Wes is helping my dad carry out his equipment bag, and he's holding the catcher's mask, pads that are too small wrapped around his legs. They're pink; I think they're Bria's.

"You look ridiculous," I say when I'm close enough for him to hear me.

He slides the pink mask on over his head, his hair poking through the sides and the straps on the top.

"I look awesome," he says, pounding his fist into his glove a few times.

"Ha!" I laugh hard, and my voice reverberates off the dugout walls.

"Who cares what I look like. Cameras are here for you, babe," he says, walking slowly backward toward home plate.

"Babe, huh?" I say, dropping my bag down into the dust and pulling my batting gloves from my back pocket.

"You prefer Cherry?" he chuckles.

"You just keep that glove up, Stokes. I might need to foul something off and I wouldn't want to hurt your pretty face," I say, a little sway to my head for extra attitude.

Now behind the plate, he lifts the mask up and smiles crookedly at me.

"You love this pretty face," he winks, sliding the mask back down and crouching.

I watch my dad talk with Rebecca and a man and woman I am pretty sure are from the magazine. My dad's nervous; I can tell by how much he's laughing at everything the other three say. My dad doesn't find people amusing, and I know that he's like me with this—we won't be comfortable until we're in the zone, doing our thing.

Rebecca calls me over, so I pick up my bat and jog to the mound. She introduces me and we all shake hands. Seth says something about lighting and his position, and what he'll need from me, but the only takeaway that sticks is that he wants me to just do my thing as if he isn't even here.

I think I can manage to forget about him and his lens. But the bleachers have filled, most of the people in them have faces I've known since I was six. I'm not sure I can tune them out.

We wait for a few minutes while Seth finishes setting up one of his lights, taking a few test shots from different angles to see how they turn out on his screen. Every picture he takes shows a preview on a laptop, and Rebecca waves me over to look. I call Wes to come look with me.

"This is going to look amazing," she says, and I gaze over her shoulder at the screen. The color reminds me of the prints from the old camera my dad used to use. He said he had gotten it from his parents.

"You should have him show you some of his techniques," Wes says, his arm brushing mine.

I close my eyes and let a wave of nausea pass.

"Maybe at the studio," I say. "I'm trying not to pass out right now."

"You'll be fine. Once he starts shooting and you're working, it's going to be great," Rebecca says.

I nod to her and walk back toward the plate. I feel Wes's fingers brush against mine on the way, and I grip his hand hard.

"Just pay attention to me and your dad. Pretend this is a game," he says.

"People don't show up for our games," I chuckle.

"They will now," he says, pounding his glove again and crouching behind the plate.

A smile tugs at the corner of my lip and I look down to the spot where my bat bangs against the plate. I haven't done that since I was a kid. I saw a baseball player do it once, and I thought it made him look tough. It somehow helps now.

"We'll take it like normal. Bunt a few, then I'll throw you some fastballs to swing away at," my dad says, already settling into his role as he waves a ball in his palm and points to Wes. "Let me find my rhythm."

I back away and adjust the Velcro on my gloves, watching as my dad's arm windmills, delivering the ball to Wes with a snap. My dad's always been a good softball pitcher, better than I ever was. He gets about seven or eight pitches in and rolls his shoulder a few times and points to me, then gives me a thumb up.

"Swing away, Cherry," Wes jokes, and I breathe out a laugh.

"Foul tip, Pumpkin," I sass back, soothed slightly at the sound of his laugh muffled by the mask.

Someone in the crowd behind me whistles, and I hear a few people cheer my name.

"Let's go, Joss!"

I dig my feet in, twisting the blade until I find a stance that feels right—my balance just like before the accident, and I nod to my dad.

This is a game. The scouts are here. They will notice me.

My eyes lock in on the threads of the ball as it flies from my dad's hands, and I load my arms, my weight just right, my inner voice chanting with joy because my dad could not have started with a better pitch. I take a hard cut at it, missing the ball completely.

My breath hitches and I grip the bat in front of me, my front teeth pressed together hard as I try to ignore the laughter behind me, the sarcasm and heckling from untalented assholes who think even though they bat ninth or ride the bench that they're still better than me because I'm a girl.

"Damn it," I grunt out, loud enough for only Wes to hear.

"You're playing for them. Stop that," he says, patting his glove against my leg. "You do this for you; like you always have."

I step back into the box and let my bat hover over the plate, feeling the weight of it.

For me.

I turn my head slowly, my vision narrowing on my dad, his eyes squinting from the sun, and I nod to him to throw again. This time, the background noise mutes. My dad tosses the ball in his hand a few times, clearing the distractions on his own, and he holds it up for me to see he's ready to pitch.

His arm winds the same, and this one is coming in a little higher. On a normal day, in a game, I'd let this pitch fly by, but today is too important. Failure is not an option. Through the rapid fire of camera clicks and the muffled chants and sneering behind me in the bleachers, I load my weight again, feeling the pressure on my thighs and quads, my blade digging into the loose dirt as I twist, my hips first, my hands last, the bat flying at the ball, catching it dead center.

I send this one deep over the right-center fence, farther than I think maybe I've ever hit a ball here before, and my dad spends a few seconds with his back to me watching it.

"Damn," Wes says from his position below me.

"Right?" I say, dangling my bat over the plate, readying myself to do it again. "I told you I was stronger now."

Wes's only response is to pound his glove and ready himself for my dad to pitch the ball again.

After about a hundred swings, including a few on the left, we move onto the field, and my dad hits me hard grounders, some that I have to dive for, before I can gun the ball to Wes at first base. Back in my element, I sometimes forget that I'm on a stage, and I let my mouth get ahead of me, dropping a few F-bombs when I don't make a play, or when I want to razz my dad for not being able to get a ball behind me. Nobody stops me, though. They let me do my thing on this stage that I was built for—the one place that I have always owned.

Exhausted, I pull my visor from my head and wipe the sweat off my brow with my arm as I walk toward the dugout from the dirt area around short and third. My eyes begin to focus on the people still sitting in the bleachers, and though it's been more than an hour out here under the warm California sun, almost every single person who came, expecting a spectacle, has stayed.

"I think you might be more popular now," Wes whispers at my side.

My brow furrows and I twist my lips.

"Uh, I'm not expecting to win homecoming queen," I joke, but mostly because I'm uncomfortable with the idea that people suddenly see me differently.

"You shut people up," he says, pulling my attention away from the slow exit in the stands. "It's not a bad thing. And you're going to make someone reading this magazine believe they can do something that looks really hard."

I squint a little at his words, but as I step into the dugout, I really think about them, and I start to smile.

"Joss, that was amazing," Rebecca says, pulling me into a sweat-filled hug.

"Thanks," I say, still a little out of breath. I flip open my water bottle and drink nearly a third of it down while my dad, the photographer, and the writer join us in the dugout.

I glance to the side, toward the stands, and feel a little relief that everyone has finally left.

"Joss, if you can hang out here for just a little bit, I'd like to ask you some questions about your training—everything you did out there. Mostly workout stuff today," Anita asks.

I stammer out a response that sounds sort of like, "Sure," then insist that my dad and Rebecca stay with me, since they were such a huge part in my training. Then I spend the next five minutes rehashing every key moment in Anita Welton's career to her face. I'd feel guilty, but she engages me on every point and question I ask, and by the end of it, our interview turns into a conversation between two women who like to play in the dirt and rule the boys. We cover my training, my climb back mentally and physically, and when they need to, Rebecca and my dad both insert themselves to give Anita the details on my recovery, or as Rebecca likes to call it, *rebuild.*

The sun is beginning to set by the time we quit talking, and I hug Anita before she leaves. My dad finishes picking up the gear and equipment on the field, and Rebecca makes a plan to meet with me tomorrow for our workout and to plan what we'll bring for our joint photo session at the studio. With only a sliver of light left in the sky, Wes and I sit in the dugout, me between his legs, lying back against his chest in the corner.

"You ever see a firefly?" he asks.

My face scrunches and I laugh lightly.

"No," I respond, wondering why this is the first thing he says when we're alone.

"We had them in Nevada, near the water. They'd glow with this short and tiny flash of light that maybe lasted for two or three seconds. I would catch them in my hands and stare at them, trying to figure out how they were made," he says.

"Are you comparing me to a bug?" I tilt my head up, lifting my chin to see his face above me. He winces a little and smiles, biting his tongue.

"You're ruining this," he says.

"I'm pretty sure it was already ruined," I say.

I pretend to pout, but rest comfortably against his chest, loving the way it shakes with his laugh. His arms wrap around me tighter, and his lips dust the top of my head.

"My point is, I could never figure out how they worked. I mean, I get the science, but it just seems like it's more special than that," he says, taking a small breath as he rubs his hands along my tired arms. "You defy science."

My head falls to the side against him and I think about his words, about where I was less than a year ago, even before my accident, and I think maybe he's right. I'm sorta super, too.

"I can fly," I say, my tone serious.

Wes's laughter erupts instantly, and his arms hold me to him again as he rocks me side to side, eventually lifting me in his arms as he stands and starts to jog around the bases. Our laughter overtakes the chirping from the tall grass behind the field and the rustling in the trees from the breeze, and for that brief moment, everything in my world is simply perfect again.

One perfect day that lasts all the way until the end. I deserve this.

CHAPTER 19

It's a new rent-a-cop outside this morning. I wonder if we're part of an overtime shift? Maybe people are fighting to get the hours. Seems like a pretty easy gig for a full day's shift of overtime pay. The new guy looks like a real cop. He even has a pair of reflective sunglasses that reek of the old cop shows on cable. He also chews; there's a stain growing right outside his door where he keeps spitting. Even when I smoked, I picked up my shit. I didn't mar the world with my habit.

"New guy outside," I say to my dad, yawning and stretching my body as I meander into the kitchen for my Pop-Tarts.

"I'll make you eggs. We're out," my dad says, stepping away from the laptop open on the kitchen table and pulling a pan out from the bottom drawer below the stove.

"Thanks," I say, moving to the stool near the counter. I curl my good leg up, lodging my heel close to me on the seat, and I watch my dad take eggs from the fridge and crack them against the sink.

"What's on the computer?" I ask, noticing the page that's open filled with job listings. A rush of adrenaline numbs my spine briefly from sudden worry that my dad's lost his job at the school.

"Just seeing if there's something that pays better than the feed store," he says over his shoulder.

I get up and click through a few of the postings, most of them night jobs that won't add up to much and will leave my dad too exhausted to be able to coach come spring.

"What if I take on more hours…at the Jungle Gym. I could work a little more, cut back on training…"

"Joss, this isn't your problem," my dad cuts in, never looking at me. His hands remain busy at work on my eggs.

I look back at the listings, glancing to my dad a few times. A year ago, something like this would stress him out to the point of benders and bar fights. I scroll through a few more, then minimize the search window, revealing an open folder underneath. A few of the file names catch my attention—words like DELINQUENT and FORECLOSURE.

"Are we losing the house?"

The words fall out of me in a panic. I probably should have eased into it, investigated more…something. But this place is my home. As crappy as it is, it's the one place that has always been my identity. Everything awful and wonderful has happened here, and while I've spent my life wanting to run away from it, all I can think about now is how badly I don't want to let it go.

My dad moves the pan on the stove, setting it on a cool burner while he takes a plate from the cabinet above him. He slides my eggs from the pan onto the plate and turns to face me, setting my breakfast down on the counter near the seat I just left. His palms rest on either side of the plate and his eyes stare right back at me, his look not wounded, but definitely tired.

"At one point…yeah…we were," he says.

I'm not going to be able to eat those eggs. I feel sick.

"At one point?" I question.

My dad nods, nudging the plate forward. I shake my head at him.

"We're not losing the house now, so eat your damn eggs," he says, a touch of hostility to his voice.

"Don't do that," I say, standing and moving to the seat, pulling the plate to me to humor him.

"Sorry," he says, hushed.

I pick at a few pieces with my fork, and eventually I put one in my mouth. It's tasteless, but my stomach growls so I know I'm hungry. I force another bite down, then lay the fork flat and fold my hands together on the counter, waiting for my dad to give me the entire story.

"It's been tight ever since your mom left," he says, shrugging once as his eyes flit down to our scratched and glued counter that we've never once talked about replacing. His hand runs along the rough surface. "Every year I'd run a little short, and they'd make threats, and then I'd get things paid somehow. But the more I drank…"

His eyes raise to meet mine, and I blink slowly, puffing out a breath from my nose and looking away.

"You drank away our mortgage," I shake my head.

"Yeah, I did." He doesn't deny it, owning it—part of the whole recovery process, I've learned. I still resent him over it now, though. Fair or not, I do.

"Is that why you borrowed money?" I ask, letting my legs dangle against the bottom of the stool, glancing at him sideways.

"It started out as just a little bit…enough to get us through, and I could keep up with it. I took out loans from one of those same-day places. It was working for a while, but then the gap started to get too big—between what I owed and what I could pay back."

"How big was the gap?" I ask, knowing nothing can shock me quite the way the eighty-thousand number did.

"Maybe ten…eleven thousand," my dad says.

I nod.

"It went to collection, and that's when things started to get away from me," he says, stepping back, his hands sliding along the counter. My eggs are cold now, so I stand with the plate and walk to the trash, sliding them inside and dumping the plate in the sink.

"There was this guy who worked at the loan place…" My dad closes his mouth, pushing his lips together tight and locking eyes with me as he takes a deep breath.

I flit my eyes to the side, blinking quickly in disbelief.

"He's the one you owe the money to now."

I wait for my dad to nod, and eventually, he does.

"Him and another guy. We were at the bottom, about to lose the house, and no place would loan to me...*legitimately*. I couldn't fail you like that..." My dad looks up at the ceiling, his shoulders sagging as his breath leaves his chest. "I'd already failed at so many things, the least I could do was keep the damn roof over your head."

I'm not even mad. I try to let my chest shudder, and I can't. I think maybe I'm tired of everything, and I feel sorry for my dad—not in a pity sort of way, but genuinely sorry. I hate that this is his life, and I wonder what it would have been like if we had nothing but days like yesterday rather than moments like right now.

I move to my backpack hanging over one of the chairs at the table, and I unzip the front pocket, pulling out my last check from Jungle Gym's for $187. It's wrinkled from being stuffed inside for the last two days, but it cashes just the same. My dad starts to turn and shake his head as I get closer, but I grab his hand in mine and stuff the check inside, folding his fingers around it.

"It's change compared to what we need, but take it. I want to do my part, too," I say, and our hands stay folded together around the envelope and measly contribution. "The loan guys...they saw the new car in the driveway, didn't they?"

My dad's eyes are on our hands still. He takes a short breath and flits his gaze to mine, nodding once before looking away again, finally backing off and taking the check I insist he have.

"Instead of paying them, you were spending the extra money...*on me*," I say.

"Joss, this shouldn't impact you...that was the point. I never wanted any of this to touch you," he says.

"I know," I respond, folding my hands behind my neck and turning in a slow circle with my face to the lights above. "I know you didn't, Dad. But it has, and we're in this together like it or not. Does Grace know how bad it is?"

My dad lifts his left shoulder and rolls his head back and forth.

"She knows enough," he says. "She's giving us money, but even with that, it's not enough."

I stare at him, knowing it doesn't matter if we still owe fifty, sixty…seventy thousand dollars. It doesn't matter if that number's only ten. The people my dad owes are never going to stop until he pays them back, and any number is impossibly more than what we can scrape together, even with everyone we know.

My phone buzzes with a text from Taryn telling me she's out front, ready to take me to school. I close the space between my dad and me, stretching up to kiss his cheek, and he grabs hold of my hand, letting my fingers slip through slowly as I walk away.

"We'll figure it out," I say, looking at the folded blankets on the sofa where my dad slept the night before. I wonder what came first, the drinking or the regrets? They're forever intertwined, but I wonder which was the trigger. I wonder where I fit in that picture.

Slinging my bag over my shoulder, I leave through the back door, ducking under the half-opened garage on my way to Taryn's car, trying not to let anything show on my face. Taryn begins talking the second I slide into my seat, telling me about some fight her parents had this morning over who put the keys in the wrong place. She's complaining about how unreasonable her dad can be, how selfish her mom is with the car—needing to have the best one while her dad drives a truck that breaks down constantly. I let her vent about her unhappy morning in an otherwise spotless family home filled with warmth, support, trust and love, and I keep my mouth shut about how much worse things are in mine. I'm done winning the pity-party contest. I doubt the universe will even let me play anymore, given the unfair advantage I have over everyone when it comes to who's got it worse.

We get to the parking lot at school, and Taryn is still letting out her frustrations, content with my sporadic "uh huhs" and "totally not fairs." I'm not looking for signs at all. I'm not even looking for Wes yet. I'm just thinking about my code, my mission to get to the next thing—to class, to training, to work, to home. I'm focused on the speed bump that's lodged in-between every destination for me now—the one that costs thousands of dollars and is guarded by killers. And then some freshman falls from his BMX bike right in front of me, a dangling strap from his backpack lodged in one of his spokes, sending him spilling to the ground and dumping his bag's insides all around the front of Taryn's car.

His knee is bleeding, a hole torn through his jeans, and he's red with humiliation. I start picking up his things, just wanting to do someone right today, maybe jack up my karma a little, when I realize his bag is filled with comics. I stand, sliding one behind the next, looking at the familiar covers—most of them wrapped in plastic, labels taped to the bottom with dates and notes written in letters I recognize. The curve of the *G*, the crosses on the *Ts*...the *Is*.

"Where did you get these?" I ask, no longer worried about the kid's bloody knee or torn pants.

"Some dude posted about them on the Internet. He's giving everything away. Why...do you...are you into comics?"

There's a geeky look of hope in his eyes, and I dash it quickly, handing the stack I've picked up to him as I walk toward the school, my phone in my hand.

Taryn calls my name, and I wave at her, pointing toward the main building.

"Library day," I lie, just needing to have time alone.

She nods and walks to the weight room, and I scan the parking lot for Wes's truck. It's parked at the bottom of the hill, so I keep it in my periphery, changing direction and walking to it the moment the gym door closes behind Taryn.

I text Wes without a second to spare.

Don't tell anyone you're leaving. You have to drive me somewhere. Now.

His door is unlocked, so I crawl inside, dumping my bag on the floor and lying low in the seat. Wes jogs out of the gym in less than a minute, slowing his steps when he sees me in his truck, then jogging again after checking to see if anyone's behind him.

"What's up?" His face is tight, mouth pursed and eyes worried.

"We need to go to Shawn's," I say.

Wes breathes in deep, half of his body still outside his truck. A crease forms between his eyes, and I instantly wonder if he saw this coming.

"I think he's up to something…maybe disappearing. And he's the only person who can help my dad," I say, pleading, my mouth hung open as I search for what to say next. "He owes me this, Wes. He owes me."

I can tell he agrees with me by the way his breath slows and his eyes dim, blinking as his focus moves to my leg—the one thing that, no matter how hard I work, will always define me in some way. Wes nods and shuts the door, turning the key and buckling up as he backs out of the lot.

He drives faster than normal—urgent—like he knows something. I wonder if he had a vision of Shawn leaving, or if he knows that this debt is what will kill my dad. I wonder if he knows whether or not we make it there in time, if Shawn will help us change the future, if he'll give us a warning so we have a fighting chance, if any of it will matter.

I keep trying to get myself to ask, but even if Wes did, his answers wouldn't stop me. Whatever anyone thinks they see about my future…is their version.

My dad's voice echoes in my head, and I smile.

Screw track records.

CHAPTER 20

Everything looks exactly as I remember it, and nothing like it should. There's a certain quiet that practically stuffs my ears and mutes all other sound when we get out of the truck. The van is gone. There aren't even tracks in the dirt to prove it ever was. My heart sinks.

"We're too late," I say, my teeth gnashing as I march forward anyhow.

Wes doesn't leave the truck, and I don't ask him to. This place isn't dangerous, and I get why he has mixed feelings about being here. The way I felt about losing my home earlier isn't something he would understand, because he never really had a place. He has a family now, though. And he has me. But this...it's just a trailer that once held a bunch of old junk.

I glance back at him when I reach the ramp leading to the door. His hands are resting on the wheel, and he lifts one to raise his hat to let me know he's watching me. I turn back and climb the slope, not sure whether to expect it to be unlocked or not, knowing that my knock will be useless. I rap my knuckles on the door anyway, and it rattles from my touch. I can see a light shining through the crack, so I twist the knob and pull, the door opening easily.

"Hello?" I call into the space before the door is fully opened, a small sliver of hope still alive in my chest that Shawn will call back, that he'll be smiling and welcome me, and tell me that he was wrong, that the police are wrong, that my dad was mistaken, and we're not in any danger. I give myself exactly one breath to swim in the fantasy, and then I push the door wide.

The room is empty, except for the coffee table that we set our water on when Kyle and I visited Shawn the first time. The walls are freshly painted in a bright white, and the smell is strong throughout the trailer. The costumes are gone, and the framed memorabilia that filled the wall behind where the sofa once sat has disappeared as well.

I spend a full minute soaking in what's left—the nothing that I'm surrounded by, as if it's all been erased. Eventually, I move into the kitchen area, opening the fridge hoping there's some sign of something, not even a bottle of water left inside. I grow manic, and I begin to pull open drawers, flip through cabinets, peer through the small space where the fridge butts against the cabinet wall. The place is spotless, ready to sell.

The small bedroom in the back is the same—closets bare, the floor clean. Carpet probably never existed in here given Shawn's mobility, but the vinyl floor that is there looks almost new. If I didn't have Kyle with me when I came, or Wes outside waiting for me now, I could easily believe I was going mad.

I leave nothing unopened or unsearched, even floor vents and light covers. I tap on the walls, and I run my hand along wood panels hoping to find something loose, but eventually I'm forced to give up. I leave the lights just as I found them, the one in the living room on, and I step back outside into the morning sun. I'm sure I'll get a detention for missing first and second hours, and I'm surprised my dad hasn't lit up my phone wondering where I am yet. He was planning to leave our house minutes after I did. It's been a long time since I've spent my day in study hall though, and I almost look forward to it. I won't have to talk to anyone, I'll get to catch up on the things I didn't get done last night. The only sad part is missing photography, but my heart's not even in that today.

Turning to push the door closed behind me, I take my phone from my pocket and open my camera, snapping a shot of the pretend world left behind. Maybe I'll do something with it in class, or maybe I'll just use it to remember that this is the crazy shit that happens to girls like me.

I push the door shut, not bothering to lock it, then move down the ramp toward the truck. Wes hasn't moved much, his hands resting on the wheel, his head still cocked to one side. He didn't expect to find answers here either, and I suppose he shouldn't. All he's ever found here are lies.

My shoulders lower and my energy is drained as I cross over the concrete walkway leading to the ramp, into the dirt and back to Wes's truck, happy that at least I have him waiting for me. We make eye contact briefly when I get inside, but only long enough for me to shake my head and confirm what he already knows.

I tug on the strap for my seatbelt as he starts his truck and begins to back away from the trailer, but it's twisted, so I turn in my seat and release it to get more slack. Wes drives slowly as I pull the belt away again, my eyes adjusting from the inside of the cab to the tall weeds and electric posts clustered outside. Standing tall, the only thing not obscured from overgrowth, is a bright-red mailbox, so shiny I'm sure it was recently painted, too. The flag on the side is flipped up, and in a weird paradox, the flag…it's not painted, but rather rusted and original—one small detail left behind.

Mail.

"Hold on," I say, letting the belt slip back through my fingers.

Wes stops and shifts into park, turning toward my now-empty seat as I run the dozen or so yards to the mailbox, not even hesitating to push the flag down and flip open the front. This mail—it's for me. My hands find a bundle inside, the contents nearly the same size as the box itself, and I have to work to slide the paper out without ripping anything. Thick rubber bands hold it together, and I don't take it apart until I get back to the truck, setting it on my lap as I unbind everything.

Wes leans close, his hand in the middle of the seat between us, and he catches a few loose papers that threaten to slip to the floor as everything opens on my legs and between my hands. I recognize the book immediately—the sketches drawn by Shawn that I saw during my last visit. A small note is clipped to the top, and folded in the center of everything is a thick, yellow envelope, bound by more bands. I slide them away and bend open the flap to find a stack of hundred-dollar bills pressed tightly together. I check the date on one, expecting it to be new, but it's not. I wonder if Shawn ironed them, or kept this money somewhere flat, like between heavy books.

"That's a lot of money," Wes says, taking the full envelope from my hand and thumbing through the bills, counting quietly.

I turn my attention to the note, folded perfectly in half, and I slide it from the clip recognizing Shawn's writing.

"He wrote this to me," I whisper, my finger tracing my name at the top of the page.

Wes moves closer to me, taking the note from my trembling hand then glancing at me, waiting for direction.

"Yeah…read it," I say, afraid of what it says as much as I'm oddly hopeful about it.

Wes clears his throat and smooths out the fold in the paper, holding the note in one hand while his other palm massages the back of his neck.

"Josselyn, I'm confident you'll find this. You are the girl who does not give up. You never have been, and I'm counting on that now. You were right…Wes is the one who could see things…"

His reading stops and his hand lowers an inch or two as he takes in what it says. His eyes shift to look at me, and I breathe steadily as I look back into his. Biting my lip, I let my lids fall closed, my chest tightening, knowing I'll have to tell Wes not just about my mom and the garage, and how he found us, but about what else he can do.

"Keep reading," I beg, my eyes still closed.

A few seconds pass, but eventually, I hear the paper crinkle in his grasp, and he speaks again.

"I never believed until the day he proved what he could do, the day we found you and your mom in that garage. You said Grace told you the story, and I'm sorry you had to hear it. I never wanted you to know."

Wes stops for a second, adjusting his position where he sits, and I glance to his face, his lips turned down and his brow low.

"That's when I started writing all of his dreams down on paper," Wes continues to read. "It started as little notes I kept in a small spiral notebook, but then Wes started to forget the things he'd told me about, lose the details. That's when I began drawing them, making them into stories he would be interested in, ones he couldn't forget. He saw things until the day he was hit by your dad's car, and whatever damage it did to his brain erased it all. He saw your life all the way until that last picture—the one on the cover. He saw it until your dad's death, and then his dreams just started to become normal dreams. And I'm sure if you asked him now, he would tell you that he can never remember his dreams anymore. I don't think he has any."

The paper falls to his lap along with his hand and Wes stares out the front window.

"I don't see things, Joss. If I did, you would know," he says, his head falling to the side, his eyes sweeping to mine.

"You don't anymore," I say, the words coming out slowly.

His eyes don't blink as he studies me, his jaw working, his neck muscles tensing.

"He lies, Joss. This is all just to get your hopes up. He'll hurt you," Wes says.

"I love you," I say to him quickly. They're the only words I think will work right now. I love him, and he protects me. And he's right that Shawn lies. But he's not lying about this. I look down at the paper and eventually Wes holds it in his hand again, ready to read.

"Grace told me you saw things," I say now that his eyes are off me. "You've saved me more times than you know...than you remember. The first time, we were three. My mom was depressed...suicidal."

I let the facts burn inside my chest for a breath while Wes digests them.

"You found us in the garage, and you told Grace your dreams told you to," I say, knowing Wes is going to want to reject everything I just said, less because of what it means about him and more because of what it means about me. I'm the girl who almost died at the hands of both parents. I'm the girl who probably shouldn't be here, and it's quite possible the only reason I am is the boy reading me a letter from a man who ruined him.

Almost a full minute passes without a word between us, and eventually

Wes begins to read again, his voice even softer this time.

"Before your mom had you, I promised her I'd keep you safe. I loved her. And because of that, I love you, as if you are my own. The money in this envelope should be exactly enough. The drawings on the cover and the last page should help you know what to look for. This is all I have left to give…I give you this, and I give you my son. You are both better off with each other. And in the end, just remember, Joss—you are just as special as he is."

Wes stares at the page, slowly turning it over. Just like me, he hopes there's more on the other side. There isn't. In typical Shawn form, the letter is filled with mystery and half-answers. It's also filled with hurtful things. I shouldn't have let Wes read this. It was never meant for his eyes.

"He didn't love me more than you," I say, not believing a word, and knowing Wes won't either.

"It doesn't matter," he says, his eyes flitting down to the space between us, his teeth scraping across his bottom lip as he hands the paper over to me. I stare at it, my eyes zeroing in on the hardest words—*I loved her…I love you.*

"I don't think he's coming back," I say, turning back to look at the empty trailer, not a trace of Shawn Stokes left inside.

Wes nods slightly, pulling his lips in, his mouth a straight line as our eyes hold onto this sad moment, staring into one another.

"We should get back to school," Wes finally says, breaking our gaze as he restarts his engine and shifts the truck into drive.

I watch in the rearview mirror as the trailer and the red mailbox blend into a blur, obscured by the overgrowth and eventually shadowed by the mountain. The truck rocks along the dirt and gravel, and when the wheels find the smoothness of pavement, Wes drives a little faster—not nearly as fast as he did on our way. Urgency is no longer necessary. We're both in no rush for time to march on.

About halfway through our drive, I begin riffling through the things Shawn left for me again, rereading the note, hoping for some paragraph that got skipped. I shake the envelope out, wishing for a card to slip through the folds with a phone number or a clue—anything other than the pile of "cross your fingers and hope for the best" Shawn left us with.

By the time we're about twenty miles out from school, my phone rings with a call from my dad. I hold it up for Wes to see, and his eyes slide to mine briefly.

"You should answer," he says.

"It won't be good," I say.

"Yeah, but it'll be even worse when you have to talk to him in person if you don't answer now. Blame me—tell him I needed you to help with something," he says, waggling a finger toward me, urging me to answer now that my phone is on the fourth ring.

"He'll see right through it," I say, and Wes's shoulders slump as he sighs. I'm being stubborn.

"I'll answer. I'm not going to lie, though," I say, swiping my phone and pressing it to my ear. I don't get the first words out, and I didn't expect to.

"Please tell me that you're just holed up in one of the school bathrooms sick, or that you accidentally fell asleep in someone's locker. I just lied to the front office and said you'd be in class in twenty minutes, that you had to run home for personal things. Jesus H Christ, Joss...I said the word *period*. Where the hell are you?"

"I'll be in class in twenty minutes," I say, turning to look at Wes. He sighs, but pushes the pedal down more, the truck lurching forward.

"Good. You didn't answer my question—where the hell are you?"

I open my mouth, half under the delusion that I'll magically have something to answer him with, but no matter where I begin, this conversation is too long and unbelievable to have over the phone while Wes and I race back to Bakersfield. My bleak future, drawn in pictures, sits in my lap, and I breathe out a laugh as my eyes roam over the details in the drawings. Then I see the envelope with the money.

"How much do we owe?" I ask. My dad breathes in slowly, and I hear the frustration through the phone. "I'm not deflecting."

"You are," he says, and I grit my teeth, just as frustrated with him.

236

"Fine, I'm on the road between the lake and Bakersfield; Wes is driving. We went to a trailer where Shawn, his uncle who helped the Stokes adopt Wes, used to live. Shawn, who is actually Wes's real dad, disappeared, but he left a bunch of money behind. I'm supposed to use it, and I think I'm supposed to use it to pay your debt. Oh, and don't talk to Wes about the Shawn thing, because it's sucky for him. And don't bring this up to his parents either—let him tell them when he wants to, if he wants to, not that you talk to anyone's parents, because you're like a hermit or whatever, but damn it, Dad…can you just tell me how much money we owe now?"

My dad's quiet, and I worry that I've stunned him with information. I'm also pissed.

"Are you high?" he asks. I grip the phone in both of my palms and hold it in front of my face, staring at the screen as I groan.

"No, Dad! I'm not high!" I shout into it. I exhale hard and bring the phone back to my ear. "I'm telling you the truth. I'll pee in a friggin' cup if that's what you want! Just tell me how much money we owe."

I can hear my dad swallow, and it's silent for a few more seconds. I close my eyes, ready to fail.

"After your grandmother's money, I'd say we still have maybe…about forty-seven thousand to pay," he says.

"Forty-seven thousand," I repeat, looking to Wes. His eyes leave the road for a moment to meet mine.

"Forty-seven thousand, two hundred and two," Wes says, leaning his head toward the envelope.

I repeat the number to my dad, and after a few more seconds, he tells me that's how much is left on his debt—down to the dollar.

"It's exactly enough," I hum, using Shawn's words. "I'll find you after lunch. Thank you for lying to the school. I love you, Daddy."

I hang up before he can question me anymore, and I begin to flip through Shawn's comic book feverishly, memorizing everything and feeling the familiar images in the center of my chest. Things in here have happened. My friends are in here. Everyone's names are different, but that's probably because Wes didn't know us yet when he had these dreams. There's only one name that stands out among the fictional ones—it's for the heroine, the one on the cover being dragged somewhere by a pair of strong arms and dirty hands.

"Grace," it reads.

My middle name.

The name Christopher knew—his ticket into the race.

"Shawn sold it all to pay my dad's debt," I say, holding the stack of cash up in my fist. "It's exactly enough."

My mouth aches to curl, and I give in the smallest bit, smiling and laughing quietly, my head a little crazy with relief, possibility, and fear. I can see Wes's mind working behind his eyes when he glances at me, his expression guarded, not ready to celebrate. He's looking for the flaw—the trick that will somehow backfire. For once, I don't think there is one. Shawn gave me a hero, and he gave him the pieces to help me fight. That crazy man might just save my father.

CHAPTER 21

There have been a few moments over the last few years, before he got sober, when my dad was really a dad. The night before my fourteenth birthday, he told me exactly what present I was getting the next day. He was buying me a new glove, an expensive one with flexible webbing that would translate well no matter what base I played. His eyes lit up when he talked about it, and he told me that it was a special order from Fresno, and the shop was breaking it in.

That night, I didn't sleep. I laid awake with my old glove on my hand, the fit small and the webbing brittle. I pretended to toss a ball and catch it as I stared at the ceiling, bathing in the warmth that flooded my chest because my dad really did love me. I couldn't focus on a thing, and I knew that my life would live on pause until I got that new glove in my hands. The glove never came. I remember hating him then, thinking it was a cruel joke he pulled, promising me something he knew I'd want so badly that I'd lose sleep imagining it, just to take it away in the morning.

Time gives perspective on things. For me, it took four years to understand that my dad wasn't playing a joke. He was deluding himself for a moment, too—believing that he could afford to give me a gift like that. A four-hundred-dollar glove is half of our mortgage. We never talked about it, but I'm fairly certain he was just as crushed telling me the glove wasn't going to happen after all. I got a used one a few weeks later. For a while, I abused it—left it on the field hoping it'd get stolen, let it bake in the sun or soak in the rain. Eventually, I forgot that I resented it. It's the glove I wore for the photoshoot, and it's the one that's been on my hand for every diving play I've made out on my high school field. I still thought of the expensive one, though. I thought about it often. I still wanted it.

Obsessions work that way.

I can feel the weight of the money Shawn gave me in my bag. My mind will not stop trying to conjure an image of the people my father owes. I don't know what they look like other than the rendering the police sent home with my dad. My dad calls one of them Mike; he's the guy who works at the loan store. He's not the one who loaned the money. He just knew a guy who knew a guy. According to police databases, the guys Mike led my father to don't even exist. They're ghosts.

With the bundle from Shawn stuffed in the bottom of my backpack, I rush out to the parking lot to meet my dad where he's waiting to take me to my session with Rebecca. I find him leaning on his car, his arms folded as he's ready to scold me for ditching this morning and spouting off things I'm sure he thinks are crazy. His foot starts to tap and his head dips, like it did when I used to hide my report card from him only to have him find it under my mattress weeks later and still unsigned by a parent.

"You drive, I'll talk," I say, not letting him lead the direction this all goes. I keep my bag with me, tucking it between my knees as we both get into the car, and the second my dad pulls out of the lot, I unzip the bag and remove the envelope of money.

"Forty-seven thousand, two hundred and two."

I toss it into his lap and he jerks a little, his head swiveling to look at me while his left hand picks up the thick packet of bills.

"Where did you get this?" he says, scanning around the intersection we're stopped at before peeking inside to see that I'm right about money being in there.

"I told you, Wes and I went to a trailer by the lake, where his dad-slash-uncle lived, and…"

"Joss, I know who the hell Shawn Stokes is. The man can't stand me; why the hell would he give you money to bail me out of trouble?"

My dad tosses the cash back to me, almost disgusted by it, and I stare at his face as I pull it into the safety of my lap. This cash is the key—it's all I have. It has to work, and we can't afford to lose it.

"He wanted to help," I say.

"Bullshit," my dad says, looking both ways before turning left and hitting the highway. He chuckles as he shakes his head. "I bet that money's stolen, marked or something, and the minute I hand it over to someone I'll be caught in a big sting operation or something."

"You're being crazy," I say, my voice growing louder.

"Psh, I'm crazy. Listen to you…with this whole Shawn and Wes, and he's really his dad, and he secretly left this money for you, and it's exactly the right amount. Did you even count it? I bet it's not even real money."

My dad's face is growing red, and I'm not sure if it's because he knows the real reason Shawn would bail him out or because he's genuinely mad and suspicious. I decide to quit pretending I don't know the truth, though, and I toss the envelope back into his lap, infuriating him for a brief second before I speak.

"He left this money for you because he was in love with mom, and he loves me because she told him to. It's all there. Wes counted it. There's no way it could be the exact amount you need if what I'm telling you wasn't real. Wes is Shawn's son, and for some strange reason, this universe has decided he needs to protect me. He was the boy who saved me…he saved me when you drove the car at our house…"

I take a deep breath, still not used to saying this next part, but knowing it's the part he needs to hear. He'll know I'm right then.

"He saved me when I was three, and mom was home alone with me, in the garage…the motor running…"

My dad's eyes close just as he pulls to a stop at the red light. His fingers work around the wheel, his grip tightening and relaxing, the tension falling from his face and his mouth sloping down on the ends.

"I know she was sick. I know how hard it was, for you…for her. I know that it wasn't about either of you not wanting me. But Wes knew I was in that garage, Dad. He saved me. Shawn knew this trouble was coming, and he left money for me to find. Sometimes, Dad, you have to just believe in things. If you don't pay these guys off…"

I feel my eyes start to burn, and I push my right fist into them, refusing to let them tear.

"I'm afraid they're going to really hurt you, Daddy. I can't…I…"

"Okay," my dad says, his own voice choking up with his words. He looks down at the money envelope clutched in his left hand, and he reaches toward me with his right, squeezing my palm tightly. "Okay. I'll give them the money. We'll end this. Okay," he says.

My body starts to float, a thousand pounds rising from my bones, my lungs filling completely, my throat opening up.

"Thank you," I say, letting my dad accept it all quietly as he drives the rest of the way to my training session.

He holds his hand over his mouth, his elbow propped on the window, and all I can see are his eyes darting around the landscape in front of him. I'm almost positive that underneath that palm he's talking to himself, trying to undo what's been done to me, to undo what he has to do now. I'm just like him—I talk to myself, too.

But in the end, we walk the paths we must. It's never been easy.

My dad pulls near the curb and I get out, holding the door open to look him in the eyes. I don't ask him to promise, but he says the words anyway.

"I'll end this," he adds on to the end. "I'll be back by five."

My dad starts to pull away as I flip the passenger door closed, but I wave him down before he reaches the end of the curb. I open the door again, and hold up a finger before he can ask what I need. I reach into my other backpack pocket and pull out a new bag of sunflower seeds, pickled, and I toss them into the seat I just left.

"I bought you a present today…at the gas station on our way back into town," I say, my lips puckered in a smile.

My dad turns the bag in the seat to read it.

"Pickled?"

"It's good. I promise you'll like it," I say.

"You're a thoughtful daughter, making a special stop while ditching school just to pick something up for me," my dad says, nodding through his words and lacing them with sarcasm.

"I think the words you're looking for are 'Thank you, Josselyn. I'm sure I'll love them,'" I joke.

"I'm pretty sure the words I should be looking for are 'get your ass to work, and quit horsing around.'" He gestures to the building behind me, and I push the door closed again, stepping backward onto the curb.

I watch my dad drive away, and just before he turns, he holds up the bag of seeds and gives them a shake—his way of saying thanks.

Rebecca is already setting up obstacles and weights for me inside, so I put my things away and jump right into work. We train me for faster side-to-side movement, and spend the last hour of my workout completely shredding my obliques.

"My six-pack is going to put Kyle's to shame!" I say, lifting my T-shirt and flexing in the gym mirror after my last set.

"Those are baby muscles, girly-girl," I hear Kyle's voice boom behind me.

I roll my eyes as he pretends to tear away his shirt, catching the bottom in his teeth so he can run his fingers over his well-defined abs.

"Are you inviting me to punch you there?" I tease, and the shirt falls from his mouth.

"Just flaunting the goods, Joss," he says, his eyes flirting with the two girls working with a personal trainer to the right of us. They blush, and I know they were watching my friend perform. Unable to pass up the opportunity, I wait for the perfect moment to make sure his fans hear me.

"The hair plugs look like they're taking. Still amazing how they can take hair from…" I wiggle my finger, pointing toward his crotch, and smirk when his bold smile collapses into a flat line, his eyes hazing and his head tilting with a hint of disappointment over the fact that he didn't see that coming.

The girls try to hide their giggling, then move on with their workouts. I step closer to my friend, reaching forward to tickle his stomach and lighten his mood. I feel bad for razzing him, but I'm not sorry I did it. We've come full circle, Kyle and me—and public embarrassment has always been a part of our friendship code.

"Tickles aren't going to make this better," he says, sneering at me. I tickle harder because I know he's joking, and pretty soon he lifts me over his shoulder, locking my legs down with his arms.

"This one about done?" he asks Rebecca.

"She's done for today. Just don't break her before the photo shoot Saturday," Rebecca says, handing my towel to me while Kyle lifts my bag from the floor.

I grunt a few times with the movement, his shoulder pressing into my stomach, and as soon as we clear the doors to the sidewalk, I swat him with the rolled towel in my hand, snapping his calf hard enough to leave a mark.

"Ow!" he shouts, lowering me from his hold before hopping around and grabbing his stinging skin. I laugh so loud it echoes in the alcove of the gym, but I stop when I realize that Kyle is here instead of my dad.

"Why are you picking me up?" I ask.

"Your dad called me, said he had something he had to do," Kyle says, nodding his head toward his truck and leading me out into the lot.

I trail a few steps behind, my stomach tight with worry. I was going to be anxious whenever my dad went to pay off our debt, but I expected to have a day to prepare for it, at least a night to sleep on it. I know it's where he went, and I feel helpless not knowing where that place is physically.

I tell myself this is the right move over and over again as Kyle drives us home, some country song blasting through his speakers, barely drowning out his poor singing voice. I manage to give him a smile, and I fake a laugh whenever he looks my direction and sings to me, elbowing me to try to get me to sing along. I can't think of the words, and my mouth has lost its feeling.

By the time we pull up to my driveway, my heart is aching from the quick beats, and my mouth is drowning in saliva. My palms are sweaty, my neck is cool, and I can't hide the fact that something's wrong anymore.

"Joss, you don't look good," Kyle says, quickly turning the music down and pushing the button on my seatbelt to ease the slack. I slump forward and catch myself on the dash, my head resting on the rubber above the glove box while I stare at my blade leg and shoe, my vision starting to get yellow around the edges.

"I just overdid it." It's a half-lie, because I'm sure that's part of the reason I feel sick right now, but the trigger is definitely panic.

"Your dad's here," Kyle says, leaving his door open while he rushes around the front of the truck and opens my side. He puts an arm in behind me and helps me from my seat.

"My dad?" I ask.

"Yeah, his car's here. He must be home. And it's Gerald's night tonight," he says, pointing to rent-a-cop.

"Gerald? You know his name?" My forehead bunches, and my skin is rushed with cold as relief sets in.

"Yeah, me and Ger…we had a little…thing," he says, his hand sliding away from me slowly as I hold up a palm to assure him I'm steady on my legs.

"Thing," I repeat.

Kyle winces and bites his bottom lip.

"I might have made pig noises out the window when Conner drove by the other day. Douchebag brother stopped the car, put it in park, and got out just to make sure we didn't get away. Did you know Gerald was a Marine? Retired…but still…dude's strong."

I stare at my friend with my mouth open, then breathe out a laugh as he holds up a hand to wave to Gerald, who flips him off in return.

"Don't piss off the bodyguard," I say, punching Kyle in the arm. I let him carry my bag into my house, through the garage, stopping in the kitchen to pull the bottle of orange juice from the fridge door, unscrewing it and tilting it back to guzzle down without a glass.

The top of my dad's head sticks out from the back of his chair, and my grandmother is sitting across from him on the couch, the reading light on as she flips through a tabloid magazine she got at the grocery store.

"Grace made stew. It's in the crockpot. I didn't know we had a crockpot," my dad says over his shoulder. I stare at the normalcy in front of me, then swivel my view to Kyle, then to the corner area near the fridge where a mustard-colored pot sits on the counter, boiling with carrots and beef.

"You wanna stay for dinner?" I ask.

"I'm good," Kyle says, kissing the top of my head then lifting his shirt to rub his belly as he backs away. I grimace and pretend to gag, and my friend laughs his way back through the door. I follow him out and close the garage, coming back in to serve myself up something homemade and deliciously foreign. If Grace keeps making food like this, my dad will not want her to leave.

"So did you do it?" I ask, topping off my bowl with one more spoonful before putting the lid back on the pot. I'm vague, because of Grace, but my dad knows what I mean.

"I did," he says, and I grin, salting my broth, anxious for Gerald to get to go home.

When I turn, his back is still to me, so I walk into the living room and take the seat next to my grandmother.

"I'm really glad," I say, the words tumbling from my mouth soft and subtle, the hidden meaning behind them—*I'm so relieved.* My dad looks at me after a full second and smiles with tight lips.

"It's best when it's hot," he says, pointing to the stew cradled in my lap.

I sit briefly with my family, slurping the hot vegetables and waiting for my dad's favorite part of the news—when they show the week's biggest sports blunders in under a minute. He and I laugh, and Grace looks at us like we're crazy. I'm setting up at the Jungle Gym in the morning, so I excuse myself when the show ends, rinsing my bowl and dropping it in the dishwasher.

I stop to kiss my dad and Grace goodnight, then drag my heavy bag into my bedroom, pulling my phone out just before my body hits my sheets. I dial Wes as I roll to my back, and he answers on the first ring.

"I was totally waiting for your call. I can't even lie about it," he says, the familiar laugh that echoes in his chest filling my ear.

"I like making you wait," I tease.

"Hmmm," he responds.

I blush through the brief silence, grabbing one corner of my blanket and rolling with it, covering my arms and good leg.

"Did you talk to your dad?"

I glance through the sliver of space left open in my door, the hallway illuminating with the changing lights from the TV. The house still smells of Grace's stew.

"I did. He said it was taken care of. I don't know what happens now, or if we still have to be watched for a while, or if the cops will be mad that he paid them. I don't care; I just want to feel free and happy for once, you know?"

Rolling to my other side, my eye catches the reflection of something tucked in the space under my dresser. Kicking the blanket from my body, I move to the floor and lay flat, feeling with my fingertips, recognizing it the second I touch the cool metal and grooves on the side.

"You're not going to believe what I just found," I say, sitting up and pulling my drawer out completely.

The can is dented, and the shape is deformed. I'm sure I shoved it underneath years ago to clean my room, and it's been lodged under the heavy wood furniture ever since. The paper has yellowed, and the tape is brittle and dry, but the label is still there.

"Joss and Taryn's Race, put tickets inside," I read, feeling my fingers into the bent space, hoping to find more treasures.

"No way!" Wes says, as I feel around the can. The only thing there is a nearly empty bag of chalk shavings.

"The powder is still here."

"Powder?" he asks.

"I made my own chalk for the race lines. I used mom's cheese grater and pieces of chalk my dad brought home from school, or the big chunks I used to draw on the sidewalk with Taryn," I say, smiling as I hold the rainbow dust up as I flip on my nearby lamp.

"That must have taken you forever," Wes says.

"Days. No...weeks," I hum, my eyes getting lost in the memory. "I wanted it all to be perfect."

For a moment, in my memory, it all *was* perfect. Those races were everything to me and my friends, and that last one brought me Wes. As horrible as that day was, there will always be this small silver lining.

"You know you probably could have just spray-painted the lines," Wes says.

I chuckle to myself. I'd actually never even considered it. I'm sure my dad would have bought me a can. He would have done anything to let me compete back then, even in stupid skipping races around our shitty backyard.

"I like the way it was," I say, setting the can down on my night table and tucking the dusty bag inside.

"I talked to my parents," Wes says, the change in subject fast, my mind slow to catch up. My eyes widen in surprise when it does.

"Wa...wow," I stammer. "And it went..."

He laughs, the phone rustling against the stubble on his cheek as he moves.

"It went well. Levi and TK helped. Mom was more freaked out than Dad. They both said they knew I was different. Dad's seen me do some things, like touch hot parts on the truck. I did the stove thing, and Mom got a little hysterical," he says.

"She doesn't want her baby to get hurt," I say.

"Ha, no. She doesn't. She forbade me from 'parlor tricks.' Her exact words. She also told me I'm not allowed to join a circus or go to Vegas. I'm not sure what the Vegas part was about," he says.

"Chris Angel," I respond. "She doesn't want you to become some sideshow."

"Chris Angel is dope," he responds, "and rich."

"I'm with your mom. No sideshow," I say. "And dope? Really?"

"The man is. No way around it," he says, the vibration of his laugh soothing me.

It's quiet for a few seconds—just his breath, then mine.

"I'm proud of you, Wes." I like saying his name. I like feeling proud of him.

"I didn't really do anything, but thanks," he says. I correct him quickly.

"You did. Telling your parents about who you are...and I know you're still just their son, but this part of you...these things? They're also who you are, and I know it was scary," I say.

"Hmmm," he agrees, sighing lightly.

I hear one of his brothers in the background, and he moves the phone, muffling the sounds while he says something about looking in the truck or in the garage.

"Sorry, TK can't find his cleats," he says.

"Oh."

I wait through more silence, my gut telling me there's more he wants to say, something else that's bothering him. I can sense it in the quiet.

"Maybe I can fix it," I say.

"Huh?"

"Whatever it is...whatever's wrong or making you, I don't know, a little off. Whatever it is, maybe I can fix it. Sometimes I do know how to fix things," I say, smiling to myself. "I fixed your change-up, didn't I?"

"Slider," he laughs.

I open my mouth to correct him again, like I always do, but instead, breathe out a short laugh and shake my head, deciding tonight he gets to think he's right about it. Next time I'll insist, but tonight, the debate is his.

"I heard from Shawn," he finally says.

His news doesn't surprise me. That man may disappear, but he'll never be completely gone.

"He called?" I ask.

"Yeah," Wes says, his deep breath turning into a yawn.

I can hear the crickets from outside his window through the phone. I'd open my window, but that will only make Gerald get out of his car. I like him where he is.

"What'd he have to say?" I can't help but want to know.

"Same old cryptic shit he always says. Told me he would be in

249

Texas...Midland. Some doctor there who specializes in spine and nerve degeneration. He's part of some trial that's supposed to recalculate the way things fire from your brain by forcing you to learn to move pictures around on a computer. It all sounds like science fiction to me," Wes says.

"Some might say you're a lot like science fiction," I joke, trying to make light of something I know deep down bothers him. I let the quiet settle in a little more. "Did you tell your parents? Not that he called, but that he..."

"They don't need to know," Wes answers without pause. "I talked to TK and Levi about it a lot. I don't need anything from him. And I have no plans to ever go to Texas."

"How about Chico State?"

I ask as a joke, knowing I might not even get in or end up there. As always, though, Wes believes in me most.

"I'll follow you anywhere. But remember, screw them, and go to Stanford," he says, his laugh delayed, but beautiful. He yawns again, this time sparking one of my own.

"I should probably shower," I say.

"Your dad's home, otherwise..." His voice is seductive, and I close my eyes, remembering him here. My bed still smells like him, and I may never wash my sheets because of it.

"But he is, so I guess you'll just have to ask one of your brothers to shower with you," I tease, getting a rise from him quickly.

"And on that note..." he coughs.

I laugh along with him, until the sounds on both sides of our call fade into a comfortable silence. I could sit like this with him for hours, not speaking, but just knowing he's there. There's comfort in knowing someone is thinking about me at the exact moment I'm thinking about them.

"I love you, Wesley Stokes," I say.

"I love the way you say my name, Josselyn Winters," he says back.

I nuzzle my face against my palm and the phone, wishing it was him.

"Good night," he says, and I say the same, counting the seconds before either of us hangs up. I get to twenty before he's gone.

CHAPTER 22

I heard it in my sleep. Just a fraction of a second before I woke up with a hand over my mouth and an arm holding me down. It was a loud pop—gunfire.

My heart is near exploding in my chest, the beat so rapid I can feel it in my fingertips as my instincts kick in and I grab at the hand suffocating me.

"Joss, shhhhh!"

The whispering in my ear is hot, and the room is dark. My legs kick, my mind filling in the parts of my body that are missing until I come fully to, realizing that my right foot doesn't exist, and I'm kicking no one.

"It's me, shhhhh!"

The hot breath is back, but the tone is more familiar this time. I blink wildly, desperate for my eyes to adjust as my breath rushes in and out through my nose. My hands run up the arms holding me down, my fingers feeling along the neck, the chin, his face.

Wes.

I grab at him differently this time, holding onto him and knowing in my gut that the sound that woke me up is exactly what I thought it was. My body is shaking with tiny tremors, and I keep my lips closed tightly, knowing I must stay silent. When his hold on me loosens, I slip away from him and move to my window, lifting the slat of my blind just enough to see the car out front, the one I was so anxious to get rid of, surrounded by broken glass and blood, Gerald's body slumped against the driver's door. He was halfway out of his vehicle before the bullet caught him.

My breath quivers, and I cup my own mouth as I turn back to Wes, who is now on the floor, pulling me in to him.

"Where's your leg?" he whispers.

I look over his shoulder with wide eyes, but keep my hand over my mouth. He nods, stretching over my bed to the other side where my prosthetic rests. He hands it to me, along with the socket, and I work to make myself mobile as quietly as I can.

"I was dreaming," he says. I pause, the silicon fitting rolled halfway up my leg. I look up at him, and our wide eyes stare into each other. "I saw this. This is it."

"My dad…" I choke out the words, my voice louder than I know it should be. I look beyond Wes, to my closed bedroom door. I listen to the quiet on the other side.

"You need to get out," Wes says, his hands flexed on either side of my face, forcing me to look at him.

My eyes flit from his to my door and back again with indecision. I know Wes won't give me a choice, but I can't leave.

"My dad first," I whisper.

"No." His lips are tight and he shakes his head, holding mine in place still. "We get out. The cops are on their way. I called when I saw them shoot…"

He nods toward my window, and I follow his motion, replaying the picture I saw on the sidewalk out front. I'm grateful for the darkness and half moon lighting the scene. I don't think I can handle the color right now.

"How did you get in?" I ask, my eyes still on my closed window.

I feel the pulse in Wes's hands.

"Your back door was open…to the garage," he says.

My eyes slide back to his as I try to understand how. There aren't many places to hide in this house; the only place someone could be is…

"Grace!" My voice is definitely too loud this time. Wes winces, sweeping me into his arms quickly and pushing my window open fast, stepping onto the dirt outside.

"We can't leave her," I grit through my teeth, pulling against him as he tugs on my arm.

"I know," he says, his grip on me less tight, but his hand still wrapped around my wrist. "Listen to me."

Wes pushes me close to the wall of my house, his forehead on mine and his hands squeezing my shoulders.

"I'll go in. But you have to be out," he says through panting breath. I've never seen Wes tired or out of breath. His body is reacting to something different. He doesn't know what to do. "The police are coming. They'll be here in minutes. You wait in my truck. Here…here…the keys."

He forces them in my palm, wrapping my fingers around them, as he backs away, moving along my front yard toward the gate at the side, to the door he came in through. I rush to catch up to him, but my prosthetic catches on a loose brick leftover from a garden that's been dead for years. I fall toward Wes, and he catches my hand in his, my body almost flat on the ground. I lose my breath from the sudden rush of adrenaline, and just before I stand, I catch the shadow on my roof—a man, looking down on us as Wes drags the girl with one leg across the lawn.

It's coming true.

My mouth trembles as I try to speak, my words nonsensical, but begging for Wes to see what I see in time to do something about it.

"Behind you!"

The shouting isn't coming from me, and I realize too late that the voice is from the man on my roof. A second man rushes from the side of my house, a gun in his hand that he presses to my temple in a blink. He knew I would be the weak point. He could manipulate Wes by putting me in harm. He'll manipulate my dad and Grace.

"Inside," the man growls, his face shadowed by a hat pulled low, his body dressed in all black.

My eyes roll up, glancing at the man on the roof as I'm dragged inside by gunpoint, Wes walking backward in front of us. The roof watcher sits down low again, on lookout. He'll see anything coming seconds before help arrives.

I'm dropped on the sofa, next to my father, his hands and feet tied with plastic zips and cellophane wrapped around his head like rope, gagging him.

"Nooooo," he whimpers, his eyes red, and his cheeks wet. "Not herrrr," he says, words barely legible through the choking of the plastic through his lips.

"You should have thought of that before you stole my money," the man says, nodding to someone behind us. I can't see the man's body, but a fist flies at my dad's jaw from the side, whipping his head to the left, blood spilling from his lip as he moans.

"I didn't steal anything. I paid you back. All of it. The money's with Mike…"

"Mike's in fucking Mexico," the man cuts my father off. "And that money…it wasn't Mike's to lend you. He stole it from me."

"I didn't know," my dad cries. "I swear, I didn't know…oh God, please…let her go. Please…she didn't do anything…"

My dad's cries and pleas make my eyes sting with hot tears, my selfish heart pounding, wanting to be set free, but my nerves numb knowing the cost. Wes sits on the other side of my father, his body teeming with strength, ready to strike at any opportunity. He won't, though, until this gun is off my head.

"Where's the woman?" our captor asks, glancing to whomever stands behind us.

"She's secured in the room," the man responds, tossing the empty roll of cellophane onto the table in front of us. I'm relieved Grace is in my dad's bedroom, despite the shape she's probably in.

"Here's how this is going to go," the man says, standing, but careful to keep the end of his gun pressed into my skin so hard I know there's a bruise. "Someone in this room owes me eighty thousand dollars," he says. "Plus the hundred more that fucker stole from me—plus the amount he took in cocaine."

"I paid you what I owe…" my dad argues, his words frightened and desperate, hard to understand.

"No…you paid *Mike*. And remember? Mike's in fucking Mexico! And if I recall…*you* bought a fucking car!"

I whimper when the man moves the gun as he speaks, his finger on the trigger. His head tips down and his eyes fall on me with my sound. His tongue makes a clicking sound, as if he's calling out for a cat, and he curls his finger at me, urging my chin to lift so I have to look into his eyes. It's dark in the room, and his face is shadowed still, but the white parts of his eyes glow like a demon.

"I warned your father that he needed to pay once already. How's that burn healing, old man?" His lips curl with his words. "Can't…hear…you!"

"I keep it wrapped," my dad croaks, his mouth struggling to speak through the plastic.

"Under here?" the man behind me asks, reaching forward and gripping my father's forearm that's been wrapped for weeks. My dad writhes in pain, trying to escape into the depths of the couch, knowing there's nowhere else to go.

"Don't," Wes says, grabbing the man's arm with just as much force as he's using on my father.

"*Tsk, tsk, tsk.*" Wes's grip loosens as the safety clicks and my torturer pulls my chin to the right, forcing my gaze on Wes. "My gun means you're outnumbered."

Wes lets go of the man's hand, and he squeezes my dad one more time in retribution. My father growls loudly. I can see him forcing anger instead of pain on his face.

"I want my money. And I'll get it," the gunman says, his gaze shifting from my father to me.

"You will," I answer, my heart pounding while my mind races through options, hope, escapes, words I could say. Agreeing to demands is all I can come up with.

"I will," he says, his mouth curving slightly as he breathes out a short laugh. "I'll make sure you don't forget who you owe."

"I won't…*we won't*," I say.

The demon eyes sear into mine so long I start to think he's going to leave, that this is it—this was his warning and now we have to pay, even though it's again. I start to believe the cops will arrive, just as the bad guys are leaving, and they'll catch them. I see myself cutting the ties from my father's arms and legs, my grandmother's, Wes holding me—life being okay.

"Choose," the man says.

My eyes flinch, my brow lowering. He laughs through his nose.

"Last time I burned him, and it did me nothing, so you choose who dies," he says, and my lips part as I suck in air. "Do I shoot you?"

He twists the gun, his mouth contorting at the same time. He enjoys being powerful.

"Or do I shoot one of them? I'm sure you'll say shoot the boyfriend, because…*dear…old…dad,*" he chuckles. "But the boyfriend…oh…he's so young. He has his full life ahead, and Dad…he's already lived so much, hasn't he?"

My jaw twitches and my body grows more rigid, fighting against the fear rushing through me. This is a dream. It's going to end. This isn't real.

"Or do you sacrifice yourself?" He looks back down on me, his smile wicked and dirty. "You're already damaged."

He kicks my prosthetic leg, and Wes moves to get up.

"Ah, ah, ahhhhhh," the man says, smiling on the side closest to Wes.

I look to my left without turning my head much, wanting to keep the man in my line of sight, to know what's coming. I swallow what feels like razors, and I look at the faces sitting next to me, the faces I love. Both mouth to pick them—my father nodding, despite the terror in his eyes. I flit between them, my eyes finally stopping on Wes's. He doesn't nod or move at all. He stares at me, his lids lifting just enough that I can read his eyes.

"Him," I say, staring at Wes, ignoring my dad's muffled protests, my breathing calm, my heart having faith.

I'm special too. I don't have superhuman strength. I'm bullheaded and tenacious and arrogant—*stubborn*. But I believe in what I've seen. I'm special because I'm brave. I'm brave enough to believe this choice is right. I'm brave enough to believe Wes will be okay.

My eyes close slowly and I search for every bit of resolve in my body. The gunman's quiet through my breath, but when I open my eyes again, his smile is back—a ruthless mask cast over his eyes as he chuckles louder than he has yet.

"That seemed like you're hiding something. I'll shoot him instead," he says, pointing the gun at my dad and firing at his center, the bullet sinking deep, cutting into him.

"Noooooooo!" I shout, squirming to get to my dad, arms holding me down from behind, my ears drowning in evil laughter.

"Relax, sweetheart. It's a belly wound. He'll be just fine…maybe," he says, stepping back a little, rolling his shoulders and cracking his neck. I continue to fight, my eyes on my dad's face, his body shaking with shock as he presses his tethered hands against his stomach.

"Now if I wanted to kill someone dead, I'd aim…for right…here," he says, holding the end of his gun about two feet from the center of Wes's head. I gasp out loud now, my mind spinning without a place to stop.

Even being Wes, a bullet that close will kill him. He won't survive. Any longer, and my dad will bleed out. My eyes dart everywhere, my ears muted by the whooshing of blood over my eardrums with every pump of my heart. I have a second, maybe two, to answer, to stop this from becoming something none of us can come back from.

Like an angel, a blue glow hits the front window of my house, followed by a red. My roof pounds with feet, and shouts echo from out front. I look back to Wes, his eyes still on me despite the gun held to his head. The cops are here, and everyone's time is short—even the demons'.

"Doors are locked. They won't get in," the man behind me says. The gunman gestures with his head, urging his partner to check the front window, instructing him to tell the police they have hostages. I look from him back to Wes, his eyes moving for the first time in minutes, just a hair to the left. He does this twice.

I sit as still as I can while the man leaves his post behind me. He rounds the couch, passing by our center console where the bat my dad used when he played still lays. We keep it where most people keep speakers or DVRs. I wait for the perfect moment, for my guard to be several steps away at the window, timing our gunman's eyes like a girl playing double-dutch as he switches from staring at me to Wes. I wait for the perfect in, the only one that's going to happen, a fault in the story—an edit that wasn't made.

Everyone looks up when there's a sound on the roof, officers taking down the man who was up there, and I have my moment.

I grab the bat with my right hand and stand in one motion, swinging as hard as I can at the gunman's head, my bat at full speed just as he turns to see it coming. It connects with skull as his arm flails higher, his hand pulling the trigger and firing fast. Red colors the carpet and walls as he stumbles back on his feet, smoke spilling from the gun, and I swing again, this time knocking him to the ground and hearing a *crack* in the wood in my hands.

His body falls flat as SWAT officers break down my door, dropping the only man left on his knees before forcing his shoulders to the ground, too. My hand uncurls, letting the handle of the bat fall to the floor as I turn to my dad, only to see him holding Wes in his arms, his body limp and his head wet with his own blood.

My mouth fails to make sound, words fail to exist, my dad screams for help as more uniforms and sirens rush in. My legs weaken and my body hits the floor, and someone lifts me just as I begin rocking. I'm carried outside, to a stretcher, where I fight to see what's happening to everyone else. My grandmother is walked out in a blanket, a firefighter's arm around her, leading her to me, and I try to get up.

"My family!" I shriek, kicking at the medic who touches my knee. He holds my shoulders down and calls someone from behind me, and my mind tangles, expecting more bad guys, more guns, someone to strike me in the face just like that man did to my father.

The needle is fast, and the scene grows blurry as I strain my neck, fighting to see as I recognize Wes's shirt, his shoes…his body. My dad's

258

next to his. The rushing as they work. The hurt.

The peace.

CHAPTER 23

I wake up in a white room, monitors beeping, but no voices. My hands move tentatively as I expect them to be strapped to the bed. When they're not, I hold my arms above my head and squeeze my fists, feeling the pinch from the needle taped to the top of my right hand.

"You're okay."

I twist fast to see Kyle sitting forward in a chair, his hands gripping themselves, elbows on his knees. His head leans to one side.

"They sedated you, just to make sure. But you don't have any injuries. Your heart rate was…" He smiles slightly and holds his palm up above his head, drawing a line. "But you're okay."

"Wes…my dad," I say, my throat hurting to speak. I push to sit up, and Kyle walks to the space next to me, handing me a cup of water and pushing a button on the side of the hospital bed. He glances out the door before looking back at me and smiling. It's forced.

"Your dad's in surgery," he says. My dad. Not Wes.

I try to swing my body around the bed, but his hand stops my knee, and he shakes his head.

"Do this the right way. Let them check you out and tell you when and where to go. For once…play by the rules," he says, mouth curling.

I glare at him, but nod as the nurse walks in. I let her push her table close and run me through the tests, checking my blood pressure, listening to my heart, checking my fluids I know I don't need because I have to pee so bad.

"Looks like you can get dressed. Your grandmother is here, so your friend here can take you to her, if you want to change in there," she says.

I hold up my hand, showing her the IV.

"Right," she smiles, rounding the bed to my right arm, sliding the needle out and covering the only proof I have on the outside of what happened with a Band-Aid covered in monkeys.

"I'll wait for you," Kyle says.

I meet his eyes and nod. They left my leg intact, so I scoot from the bed, my gown gripped in one hand in the back, and I take the bag of clothes from him with my other. I slip into the bathroom and set everything in the sink, holding the sides and looking at the circles under my eyes and rats in my hair. My stomach aches, and my head pounds, but I know it's only from everything that's unknown, the things I can't control. I'm afraid to ask, and that's the only reason I haven't. I flush and wash my hands, then leave the safe feeling of four tiny walls without a window, stepping back out to the place where lives dangle in the hands built just like mine, but somehow better.

Wes's hands are like that. Like mine...only better.

"They flew him to Texas," Kyle says the moment our eyes meet again.

"Texas," I echo, my voice still barely audible.

"We weren't sure they were going to clear his transport at first...because of the case. I feel like a hostage taking shrapnel in the head sorta wins over detectives needing to have witnesses handy." Kyle whispers an apology when he sees my face contort hearing the graphic details.

"A piece of one of the bullets pierced him. Even though it was small, because of the force and depth there's some damage and swelling...I don't know the details beyond that," Kyle says, his voice quieter. "I didn't understand a lot of what TK said. But he and Levi told his parents...about Shawn...being Wes's father."

My breathing gets faster, and I move to the end of the bed, sitting while my head feels light.

"They think his organs may begin to fail, and Shawn's the most likely match next to Bruce, so they called him. What makes this all so much crazier is this place he's at in Texas…"

"Specializes in brain trauma." I stare at the door when I speak, seeing it all in the blur as nurses rush by in various directions, phones ring, people laugh and chat about lunch breaks. Their lives carry on, and all the while Shawn was covering the possibilities. The money. Texas. The call to Wes.

Knowing I would be brave when I had to, and I'd believe in what Wes could do.

Planning for the fact that as much as I'm Wes's reason, I'm also his biggest weakness.

"Can I see Grace?"

I look up to Kyle, and his eyes are full of helpless sympathy.

"Sure, Joss. Come on," he says, holding a hand out for me to take. I grasp his fingers in between mine and keep his arm close to my body, expecting the ground to fall from under me at any moment.

We walk down a long hallway to a dark waiting room, window shades still drawn and the smell of burnt coffee strong.

"What time is it?" I whisper to Kyle as he pulls the door open for us both.

"Four thirty. The police have been waiting to talk to you. They've already talked to Grace. And there's an advocate waiting downstairs, too. They said with things like this, people usually need…help?"

"Ha," I breathe out. "I've needed help for years."

My friend chuckles, then lets go of my hand as my grandmother pulls me close and squeezes tightly.

"Kyle says Dad's in surgery?" I sit quickly, feeling the trembling in my legs return.

"We should know more soon. I have faith," she says, taking my hands in both of hers.

I let her soothe me, and I sit quietly, my head on her shoulder. I don't tell her my faith is gone. This is where my story ended. My dad dies here. I lost my leg. A bus rolled from a bridge. Every bit of it was right.

I'm not sure what to have faith in anymore.

The minute hand travels slowly, and I start to count the seconds, suspicious of time. I feel like it's cheating, taking longer to pass. Nearly thirty minutes passes, and someone comes into our quiet room, where the sleepy and desperate are waiting with faith and hope.

Everyone but me.

We all sit up tall because the new person is wearing scrubs, but she's only here to raise the window shades and declare a new day in the room where time moves slowly. I get up when she leaves and pull a cup from the stack, filling it with hot coffee that's as dark as chocolate, and just as thick. I dump five containers of cream inside and four packets of sugar, and I stir until the concoction turns into a thick tan soup.

"That looks awful," Kyle says as I sit back down across from him. I take a sip, my face showing how bitter it is.

"It is," I say, taking one more and offering the cup to my friend.

He shakes his head and sits back.

"Suit yourself," I say, drinking one more gulp before giving up and abandoning it along with all of the others piled on the end table near our row of chairs.

I return to the clock, and I watch the hour hand move this time. It's slower, of course, which is more frustrating. I stare hard, wondering if I have the power to make it move. My teeth gritting in the back so hard that my jaw slips when the door opens to a woman in a white jacket, a mask in her hands. I bite my tongue as I stand.

"Miss Winters?"

"Yes," I move forward. I spend that second trying to read her face, bracing myself, knowing it won't matter how prepared I think I am.

"I'm Dr. Delaney. Your father's in recovery. You should be able to see him in forty minutes, maybe an hour," she says, and I feel myself start to fall. Kyle's hand steadies me, and Grace squeezes my arm.

"He's okay?" A tear runs down my cheek quickly, and for once, I let it be.

"He's got a lot of pain, and it's going to be a while before he's on his feet and doing anything like driving or…"

"Or yelling at players on the ballfield," Kyle butts in.

"Yes, or that," the doctor says. "He'll need lots of rest, but…he was very lucky. The bullet lodged in part of his lower intestine, not severing it completely, and we were able to remove the bullet and repair the tear."

"Do you have the bullet?" My question surprises me. I don't know why I want it, but I feel like I need to hold it. I need to feel the weight of it in my hand. I need to know what cut Wes, what sent him to Texas.

"It was given over to Bakersfield PD," the doctor says.

I nod; of course it was. Police will want to talk to me. Soon.

"I'll be sure someone comes to take you to his room as soon as he's awake," she says, leaning forward and touching my arm. I expect a coolness here, like the doctor who handled my amputation—more excited about his work rather than sympathetic to my long road ahead. I get none of that though. She doesn't say anything more. She just touches me, in a way that speaks volumes, and looks me in the eyes to make sure I know this is real.

We all stand as she rounds the room and talks with a volunteer sitting at the desk near the door, signing something, then leaving to save someone else I suppose.

"So I guess…it looks like your dad…dodged a bullet?" Kyle says.

Grace and I both turn to look at him through unimpressed, lowered eyelashes.

"Too soon?" he winks.

I can't tease him back. I'm too weak, too empty from everything inside me that I've spent. I fall into him and hug him tightly, my face buried in his chest. He circles his arms around me, his hands flat on my back, and he stands with me like this for minutes until Officer Polk clears his throat, and I have to go tell them everything I know, leaving out the bits about Wes being Christopher and having abilities that no one can explain.

I talk with police and the advocate for almost an hour, until Kyle knocks softly on the door of whichever doctor's office we commandeered and tells me my father is awake. I'm excused quickly, and my legs find the strength to run.

My dad's face is puffy, a tube taped to his nose, more linked to his arm and chest. The beep is constant, and the nurse turns the volume off when I walk in, pushing a chair close so I can hold his hand.

I grab it instantly and wait while the nurse checks his vitals, moves a few bags and drops his chart in the bin attached to the wall next to the white board that lists his daily goals. I read a few as she shuts the door.

"Looks like I'm going to get to coach you for a while," I say, moving my gaze to the man I almost lost.

"I'll knock that out tomorrow," he says, coughing halfway through his words, then grimacing from the pain it causes in his gut. "Damn."

"Let's give ourselves a break with this one, huh?" I cover his palm with my other hand and watch him breathe. I think I'll sit in this chair until the sun comes up again doing just that, making sure that his lungs work, that his eyes open when they should, and that his skin is never too cold.

"I told them I didn't want the morphine," he says.

"You can have morphine, Daddy." I shake my head and bring his hand to my cheek.

"I've worked too hard," he says, his eyes barely open. His lips part and he licks at the dryness.

"I'll see if you can have water," I say, moving to stand. He stops me.

"No, I'm going to sleep. I just wanted to see you. They won't let me dehydrate," he chuckles, coughing again before another painful moan.

My head falls to the side. I hate seeing him like this.

"I'm an alcoholic, Josselyn. No morphine," he says, pushing his voice as loud as it will go.

I hold his gaze for a moment, then blink as I look down at my hand on his.

"Yes, sir. No morphine," I promise.

A weak smile paints his lips and his eyes flutter, each blink lasting longer, until his eyes are barely slits that I kiss close as I pull his blanket up to his chest. No phone to type a message with, I walk the length of the hallway to where Kyle and Grace are waiting.

"Taryn called," Kyle says, pushing his phone in his pocket. "She and her parents are at your house. They're helping with whatever the police need, arranging for cleaning or…"

"Tell her thank you," I interrupt, not wanting to think about what happens after something like this.

"She said they've set up a rental for you. It's close by," he shrugs.

"Can you take Grace? I'm going to stay the night. I don't have my phone, so can you come pick me up in the morning? Maybe bring it?" Kyle inhales slowly, and his gaze falls to my chin as he nods, looking up at me again before he pulls me in for another hug.

"He's not going to text," he whispers. I'm not delusional, but it hurts to hear anyhow.

"I know," I say, my voice quiet at his ear.

I know Wes won't write, but even still…what if somehow…he did?

CHAPTER 24

My dad can be stubborn.

I suppose I deserve it.

For the last week, I've come home from school to find him doing something he's not supposed to yet. Usually, it's something I can just snap at him for and get over, like showering without the walker or thinking he can climb the ladder to change the batteries on the smoke detector. Today, though, he's taken it up a notch.

"Deeper!" my dad shouts, waving his arm, bat in his hand, ball in the other.

There are houses lined up on either side of him, and our street is narrow, but my dad refuses to worry. It's been a while, but back when I was just learning to read fly balls, he would hit them to me in the street. I'm a little worried about his record of no broken windows now.

"You are the worst patient ever!" I shout as I pick up my step, my bag slung over my shoulder.

My dad turns to look at me over his shoulder, and even though he's too far away to read his expression, I know it's a cocky smile, and I know he's about to turn back to Kyle and wave him even deeper.

"Shit," I say to myself, striding into a slow jog as my dad tosses the ball to himself and swings hard with his right arm, sending it deep, but straight as an arrow toward Kyle's open glove at the end of our street.

Kyle shouts, "Woo!" as he jogs in a circle with his glove over his head, but closer to me, my dad stumbles to his side, putting his weight on the bat and clutching his side, where his injury is still nowhere close to healed.

"Stubborn idiot," I say, rushing to grab his elbow.

He just chuckles.

"Still got it," he says.

"Yeah, you also got yourself a trip back to the ER if you keep this up," I lecture, taking the bat from his hand. Kyle boos me and calls me a fun killer as he jogs back to us from his spot about eight houses away.

"You're not helping!" I point the bat at him.

I get my dad inside, but once our feet hit the kitchen, he shirks my hold away, waving me to head on to my room.

"I know my limits, Joss. I just got tired of sitting on my damn ass," he says as I rifle through Jungle Gym shirts on my floor, not finding a single one that's clean. Sighing heavily, I open my closet and push my clothes to one side so I can get to the shirts with my name spelled JOSE. I wasn't going to keep these, but Wes told me they were special.

I re-tie the band in my hair as I walk back into the living room, stopping to kiss my dad's cheek and warn him not to start a street hockey league while I'm at work.

"You ready?" Kyle asks, his keys dangling from his thumb.

I nod and follow him to his truck so he can drop me off at work. We get to the end of the street and turn the corner before he stops and puts it in park.

"I swear to God, Joss, if you ever tell your dad I let you do this, I will kill you," he says, hopping out of the truck and rounding the front as I slide into the driver's seat.

"You won't kill me," I say, buckling up and shifting, my left foot lined up to do the work the right is supposed to. I look to Kyle and smirk. "You'll already be dead."

"Ha, ha," my friend says.

Checking all of my mirrors, I shift the gear and get a feel for the truck with my left foot, starting out slowly before we hit the big streets. Kyle's been letting me drive for about a month. He said *no* the first two times I asked, but when I asked on the third day, he knew how relentless I would be and gave in. Other than a few scary turns where my left foot laid heavily on the gas, and one small issue with a parking lot block, I've had a pretty clean run.

"You hear anything from them yet?"

I shake my head *no*.

Kyle doesn't ask every day. He knows I'll tell him as soon as I hear, but he's also anxious on his own. Wes has been in Texas with his family for six weeks. TK told us that it was bullet fragments that actually struck Wes, and thanks to the freak luck that only exists in this world that Wes and I live in, it damaged the same part of his brain that my father's car did the day he saved me in my driveway.

They had him in a medical coma for about a week, and the next few were spent slowly regaining his coordination and speech. But as fractured as his memory was the first time he went through this, it seems it was completely erased this time around. I can tell it hurts his brothers. I've been talking to them every few days, hearing about the exercises the therapists are putting them all through to slowly reintroduce Wes to key memories and familiar faces.

Wes's mom is determined. She came back to Bakersfield to collect photo albums, music, pieces of clothing. She asked me for a few things, so I helped her pick songs for the playlist she made, and I gave her the picture I had, with the note written on the back, and the ticket he sent me in the mail. Our ticket. I didn't give her the full story, instead just telling her it was part of a sweet love note he'd left me once. She tucked my things in one of the album pockets and carried them back to Texas.

It's getting harder to hold onto hope. Routine helps, though. On days I don't train, I work at the Gym. I've started helping with the books, balancing out the night's deposits and prioritizing the inventory. It's really only working with gallons of cheese and bleach wipes to clean up gross things from the slides, but it feels a little more like a grown-up job. There's a Jungle Gym's near Chico, and I've thought about asking for a transfer if I manage to somehow pull off a miracle and get in.

I pull right up to the front door and put Kyle's truck in park, tucking my phone in my pocket and giving my friend knuckles as we exchange positions.

"I'll be here at ten, sound right?" he asks.

"Maybe a little earlier. And bring burgers," I say.

"Got it, nacho cheese with a side of screaming birthday boy," he chuckles.

I shake my head and narrow my eyes at him as he drives off.

The next few hours of work pass quickly, and before long, Kyle is texting me for my order on his way back. I drag a stool over near the register and begin cashing out, counting deposits. My phone buzzes again, and I expect more questions from Kyle, but I lay it on the counter and see it's a video call—from Texas.

My palms sweat, and my heart races. It's the same every time they call. It's never been video though. I pile the money back in the drawer, pushing it closed to lock it and I hold the phone in front of my face as I answer. Within seconds, I'm staring at Levi, TK standing behind him.

"Cherry!" TK shouts.

"Tiny!" I shout back.

"Tiny? What's that…oh…" TK turns his head, one eye closed more than the other and Levi laughs.

"Damn we miss you," Levi says.

"Same," I smile, pushing close to the counter and propping my phone up against the register.

"I see you're Jose tonight," Levi says, pointing close to his screen, probably touching my incorrect name where it shows on his phone.

"It's throwback Thursday," I shrug.

He laughs quietly and lifts his chin just a little. TK slides into the space next to him, their faces sharing the screen.

"We have someone who wants to talk to you," Levi grins.

My throat closes, and the only sound I can make is a frail, "Oh," as I swallow and press my palms against the beating in my belly.

"Don't expect much. He's been making a lot of progress this week…with places, and a few dates. But people are still hard," Levi says, leaning his head to one side and pursing his lips. "It's like he knows that

I had a birthday party when I turned eleven, but he doesn't remember that I was there. Doctors say it'll come, or at least the basics will come."

"What about the rest?" I ask, trying to keep myself from expecting Wes to see my face and return to the familiar.

"I guess he learns those parts all over again," Levi says, his lip raised in an apologetic smile. "TK sees it as a positive—figures maybe he'll find a way not to let Wes know about his fear of the dark this time around."

I lean back with a slight laugh, gripping the front of my stool.

"Of course…now *I* know," I say.

"Shit," TK punches Levi's shoulder.

The phone moves, the picture buffering for a few seconds, picking up when Levi is mid-sentence and walking down a hallway. They've been staying at a nearby hotel, but this place looks more clinical, like a rehabilitation center.

"Are you ready?" he whispers.

I breathe in deep and nod, a quiet, "Yeah," coming from my throat.

I catch glimpses of Wes's form as Levi carries the phone close to a setting that looks like a comfortable apartment living room. His legs look the same, and he's wearing my favorite pair of jeans he owns, the ones with tattered bottoms and a tear in one knee. I was with him when he ripped that part, sliding while helping me practice.

This is going to be hard, and my finger hovers over the END CALL button while the picture jostles, Wes still not in the frame. My hand falls flat the instant his eyes hit mine. It's like something is missing behind them. The blue just as beautiful as it always is, but the boy I love lost underneath. My lip starts to quiver so I bite down hard on my tongue.

"Hey," he says.

My hands form tight fists, because that small word sounds the way it has over the phone for dozens of late-night calls.

"Hey," I say back, smiling tentatively.

"I'm sorry if this…if this gets weird." He scrunches his face as he talks, just one more small gesture that's so familiar I ache to touch the face that's making it.

"It's okay," I say. "Weird's kinda your thing."

He laughs, and I hear the right timber in his chest.

"TK and Levi have been telling me about your dad...about...Coach," he says, the word rehearsed, like he's reading it off a flash card.

It hurts.

"He's doing a lot better," I say. "I...I don't know what things you remember, but my dad is sorta stubborn. *I'm* sorta stubborn," I pause, drawing my brow in and letting a sad laugh escape. "You always called me stubborn...sorry."

"No, that's good. Things like that...they help," he says. He leans forward, adjusting the angle of his phone, and I wonder if everyone's watching us talk on the other side. I don't like the audience. I feel like there are things I want to remind him of, and I don't know if I should or not, if someone would stop me. Maybe they should stop me.

"Anyhow," I continue. "My dad's been doing things he's not supposed to. Today, I caught him hitting a fly ball to Kyle in the street."

Wes tilts his head back and smiles, but it doesn't reach his eyes. He doesn't know who Kyle is.

"Kyle's one of our friends. One of my best friends, and you and he..." I stop, knowing in my gut it's too much. "You guys were friends too, is all."

A silence sets in, and we stare at the small images of each other, our eyes darting to other places then coming back. I don't know how to talk to him, what the rules are and where they start and end. He doesn't know what to ask. All of the triggers that lead back to us...they're just...*gone.*

"I should probably finish up at work, actually," I say, sniffling to mask the cracking in my voice. "I'm working the night shift, and Kyle's going to be here to pick me up soon."

Wes nods.

"Yeah, totally," he says, looking up at someone on the other side of the phone, probably his brothers. His eyes settle back down on the screen. "You work a lot of night shifts?"

"A few times a week. It's peaceful, and it lets me train. I play ball." I stop there, not knowing how deep to go.

"Yeah, TK and Levi told me about that. You're...you're good," he smiles.

"She's better than you," I hear TK say in the distance.

We all laugh.

"Apparently, you can hit my fastball or whatever," he says.

"Change-up," I correct, the weight of this conversation sitting heavy in my chest. It sinks to my gut when he doesn't react.

He shifts again, this time picking the phone up in his palm, and I get my finger ready to end the call again, perhaps even more anxious to close this window so I can hide how much this just feels. Goddamn does it feel.

"Hey, Joss?" My heart kicks and I focus on the screen.

"Yeah?" I say.

"Maybe we can do this again, like...a few times a week? Maybe during your night shifts or..."

"I'd like that," I answer fast. I answer before I'm sure if I really *will* like that. It's torture, but maybe I like that, too. I think I need this. Even if nothing comes of it beyond whatever it is now.

"Good," he smiles, his mouth straightening just a little. "And be careful. I don't think I like you working alone at night."

My right hand trembles, so I move my phone to my left.

"Okay," I smile, holding on for as long as I can, saying goodbye to him, to his brothers, and ending the call just as Kyle taps on the front door. I pretend for about six seconds when I let him in the door, and my friend reads right through it, setting the greasy bag of food down and pulling me into his embrace. I have a feeling he's going to be doing this a few times every week, after my night shift.

After Wes calls.

CHAPTER 25

What I never thought would get easier somehow did. Christmas came, and Bruce and the boys came back to Bakersfield in time for the baseball season. For the last two months, Wes and I have talked by video about three times a week. He's been continuing his therapy and studying with his mom, almost like being homeschooled, but away from home.

I've taken less shifts at the Jungle Gym, instead spending most of my extra hours working with my dad and Rebecca on the field.

The *Girl Strong* magazine story came out two weeks ago, and the attention from it has been a little overwhelming. I don't have the news trucks Wes had when he came home after going missing, but I've had a lot of phone calls from sports journalists wanting to tell my story their way. I've shared with a few, because...ESPN, and I'm not stupid. I've gotten a lot of calls from colleges, too. It was hard for me to hear, but my dad was right when he said a lot of them were just interested in me as human-interest piece.

I'm not a sideshow.

I'm more than that.

Chico thinks I'm more than that.

The most recent call, however, came from Stanford, which of course made me think of Wes and his ability to see the future.

Fuck 'em, and go play for Stanford.

I don't talk to him about his special skills. I've asked Levi and TK, though, and they both say that those parts of Wes seem to have disappeared with his memory. As special as they were, they weren't what made him special.

I've started to have dinner with the Stokes once a week. Sometimes my dad comes, and sometimes we even bring Grace. She's stayed, and I don't really see her going back to Tucson anytime soon, if ever. She's found a place I think—maybe she longed for with my mom, only with me—and I crave a mother like her. She's talked about finding a place nearby, maybe a condo, but my dad doesn't rush her. She's moved into the living room permanently, insisting he take his room when he was recovering. The sofa has been exchanged for a pull-out, and she seems fine with it.

I'm fine with it. If I get a legit offer from a college to play ball, I'll suggest she takes my room when I'm gone. I'm keeping this plan to myself for now, but I think everyone will like it.

The men who held us hostage were just one link in a long chain of people who passed money down the coast and across the border in exchange for drugs. When the man my dad trusted broke that link, getting lost in Mexico with what ended up being nearly a million from various drug runners, the *really* bad guys started to notice. My family's trauma is now documented in several pages of a DEA file that spans nearly a decade, and while we've been told that a trial will come and we will need to cooperate, I have this feeling that in the drug world, the bad guys vastly outnumber the good ones. The only silver lining is our debt is now considered extortion, like the drug lords committed fraud by not counting the money my father had paid. The only amount we can prove is what Grace lent us, because of the bank records.

Shawn called me the day after New Year's. For the first time since I've known him, there was nothing cryptic in his words. He was, instead, rather direct. He told me never to tell Wes about him. To never remind him, and if he started to feel like there was something there, a memory that was foggy about a man in a wheelchair, an uncle—a father, Shawn wanted us all never to nurture it along. He said the same words to Bruce, to Maggie, and to TK and Levi.

I was angry at first, and I never promised. He didn't ask for one though. He knew I'd follow his wishes. He knew he was going to die. And on a Tuesday in the middle of January, in a small apartment just on the border of Texas and Oklahoma, he did just that. The notice in the paper was small, almost invisible. Bruce assumed a neighbor must have submitted the obituary because he never did. He got the call that his brother had passed from a sudden cardiac arrest. It was deemed natural even though we all know there was nothing natural about Shawn at all. He left his brother everything left to his name—a red cape once worn by Christopher Reeve, and a 1991 Chevy van. Bruce sold both for four hundred and twenty dollars combined. TK and Levi spent it on catcher's gear and a new bat.

I'm three months away from graduating. I'm going to graduate, and that alone, as Taryn keeps reminding me, is a miracle. My GPA is pitiful, but so far this spring, I'm hitting the ball hard. It isn't fair, but I'm getting noticed more than those kids buried in books every morning at the library.

It's my first weekend completely off from everything. My dad's too. Finally back to work fulltime, he decided to spend his day napping, and I'm beginning to think he's onto something as I unlace my running shoe from my good leg. I get the knot halfway untied when I hear a gentle knock at the screen door. I glance out my window and recognize TK's shoulder, so I start to put my shoe back on as Grace answers the door.

"There's someone here for you," she says, meeting me in the hallway on my way out.

"I saw. They probably want to watch movies here or something," I say, moving past her. Her hand grasps my shoulder, and she turns me just enough that I stop. My eyes meet hers, and all she does is shake her head and smile.

It had gotten easier, because it was distant. He was in Texas. I was in California. It was like nightly interviews that sometimes turned into me telling him about my day, him telling me about his. I labeled it *long-distance friends* finally, but now someone is here to see me.

My hands instinctively move to my hair, sweeping it up into a knot. I cut it recently, wanting to keep it out of my eyes when I ran. I hadn't cut it in years, and the ends were starting to look shaggy. Wes won't remember anyhow, but for some reason I wish my blonde waves fell further than my shoulders.

He's standing behind his brothers as I approach the open door, maybe nervous too. I push open the screen and invite them inside.

"We were actually thinking maybe you could come hit some balls with us," Levi says.

My gaze shifts from him to his brother behind him, and I wait for his blue eyes to flit up under the shadow of his hat. His mouth is flat, his hands in the pockets of a pair of black shorts that fall just above his knees. His body is so mature, and as grown up as I thought he was before he left for Texas, there are phases I've clearly missed. He's an inch taller.

"Let me get my stuff," I say, closing the door behind me and rushing out to the garage.

Grace opens the door just as I push the garage button, and her eyes glance out to the driveway, seeing the legs of the Stokes boys standing out front waiting for me.

"Tell Dad where I went, if he wakes up while I'm gone," I say.

"I will," she says, her eyes soft on mine. She doesn't want me to get hurt. I feel her message in my heart.

"Give 'em, hell," she winks as I back out under the door as it's closing.

The truck running by the curb, Levi jumps in the driver's side and TK hops in the back.

"You should sit up front, Joss," he says, making obvious eye contact with me that makes me blush.

I hand him my gear and slide in to the middle of the seat as Wes climbs in on the other side. When he shuts the door, his knee brushes against mine. I stare at the place we touch until we reach the end of the block, but Wes doesn't look at it once. I dare myself not to look at our knees again—sitting so closely—for the remainder of the trip.

"When did you get in? Or...are you and your mom just visiting?" I stare straight ahead as I wait for his response.

"It's been a couple days. And yeah, we're back for good. I'm starting on Monday," he says.

Monday. So soon.

"Funny thing, Joss," Levi cuts in, smirking as he looks sideways to me. "Seems the one thing that Wes can remember about you is the fact that you hit his *slider* out of the park when we first met."

"Change-up," I deadpan, glancing to the side at Levi, catching the way his lip raises a little higher. "And I didn't hit it out of the park, just hard and down the line."

"Now see, Wes here thinks it was a slider," he says, his voice clearly taunting his brother.

"It doesn't matter what he thinks it was, Levi," I say, biting the tip of my tongue and turning to my right to look at Wes's profile. His lips are forming a tight line, holding back a smile, and his eyes refuse to look at me. "And it doesn't matter what he pitches to me. I'll hit it. Because he still hasn't learned how to hide his pitch."

I cock my head a hint and pucker my lips, which finally gets Wes to look sideways with his eyes.

"Or did I?" he says, slowly.

There's a familiar fire in my belly, and I'm careful not to make more of it than it is, but it feels good. It's that competitive edge I love, but it's also that small piece of us—perhaps my favorite piece.

Levi drives us right up to the fence for the field, and we slip through the space where the gate is locked poorly, the gap wide. We spend a few minutes throwing balls around, warming up our arms, and I continue to remind myself that this is just one more day, in a series of days, where my friends and I are doing something we love.

But then Wes makes his way to the mound and turns his hat, lowering it just a little on the right, the shadow drawing a dark line across his cheeks and nose. I get lost in his routine while I unpack my bat and slip on my hitting gloves. He digs the metal of his cleats into the dirt, kicking out the edge of the rubber, where my father told him to. He swings his glove loose on his wrist, adjusting the tightness, then feels the ball in his mitt, compressing it with his hand, forming his fingers to the threads and finding the right touch.

It's all familiar, but it's also what every pitcher does. I write it off as coincidence and nothing more. And then he bends down, and with his thumb, he wipes away the dirt from the tops of his shoes, until the white curves at the front of his feet are no longer covered in dust.

"You're home," I hum to myself.

I'm breaking Grace's rule. This may hurt. I won't care.

Levi pounds his glove, urging Wes to throw, and I study him carefully, watching as he works the ball and presents it before delivering snap after snap to his brother's mitt. He throws seven or eight fastballs, and I count at least two curves. But there are no sliders, and he hasn't shown me his change-up.

"Batter up!" TK shouts from the other dugout.

I push my helmet tighter and step up to the plate, tapping my bat on the end of Levi's glove.

"No catcher interference now, you hear?" I say.

"No ma'am," he responds.

I find my footing, feeling the weight even out on my blade and my front foot, my bat ready to strike just off my shoulder. Wes pulls his hat lower and brings the ball to his glove in front of his face. He thinks he's hiding it, but I can see everything in the way his arm flexes. His forearm is turned in slightly, which means he's feeling for laces, so it's a fast ball. It takes him almost a full rotation, so my guess is four-seam instead of two. I adjust my weight, so my attack will be fast but level, and I see things in slow motion as his leg lifts, his elbow flexes and his wrist flicks, sending the ball soaring seam over seam toward me. I'm a little early, so this line drive shoots right over the third base line and into the weeds.

"You sure you still don't want to marry me?" Levi says, chuckling and tapping his glove into my leg.

"Better luck next time, Wes!" he shouts to his brother.

Wes shakes his head, but as he turns, I catch the smirk on his lips as the sun unmasks him from the shadow of his hat. TK tosses him another ball from the dugout, and he starts his routine again. So do I.

I watch his hands work, his arm turn, the inside of his arm showing me more. His grip comes fast, but he continues to pretend. My father taught him this, but he still needs work. I see it coming, and he's going to say it's a slider, but it's not.

It's not, because it's about eleven miles per hour slower, and that time feels like forever as I wait. I keep my bat back, letting the ball travel right to the sweet spot, releasing my arms and casting them through my zone knowing that sweet feeling of perfect contact is coming.

Until it doesn't.

The ball drops fast, Levi blocking it at the edge of the plate, his laughter breaking through in an instant. I swung and I missed because that shit was a slider. My chest beats fast with my pulse, my arms tighten with the rush from the adrenaline I get when I'm mad. I am mad. I pound my bat on the plate then point it at Wes, holding it out like the end of a rifle. His smirk grows bigger, spreading from cheek to cheek, and lighting up his eyes.

"Slider," he says, winking.

My expression softens fast.

He remembers. If he can remember something like this…maybe he can remember more someday. Maybe…I can make him.

Afraid of making a slip, of saying the wrong thing, of doing something that will chase this away, I keep up my act and I drum up my emotions to make myself feel the fire of competition again. It comes naturally, but this time it battles with something else. I want this to be real; I want him to remember this. If he remembers this…

Wes pitches to me for nearly an hour, taking time between each one, and fooling me about half of the time. He's gotten stronger, and his speed is up. I can keep up with it, but it's not as easy as it was. I'm almost proud, but I also take it as a sign that *I* need to work harder.

As the afternoon sun starts to bake us from the west, we slow down, and soon we've piled back in the truck, in the same spots we came in. The drive back to my house feels fast, and I waste that time not speaking to Wes. My mind pretends we're having conversations—meaningful ones—

but it's all pretend in my head. Whatever this was, this last hour, I'm not going to make it more than it was. I'm also not going to make it less.

"Tell your dad Wes is coming out to our practice this week, if he wants to stop by and watch after yours," TK says, handing me my things as he climbs from the back of the truck and slides into the cab.

"I will," I say back, my eyes catching Wes's for just a moment.

I wait until they drive away, then I open the garage and drop my gear by the door, glad to see my dad's car inside. The house smells like Italian food when I enter, and my dad already has a bowl of something in his hands as he passes by.

"Grace said Wes came by," he says, and I can tell he's practiced this move, trying to act natural while mentioning something to me that he knows takes up a serious amount of real estate in my head. I play along, too.

"He did, with his brothers. We hit some balls. He got me with his slider," I say.

My dad pauses in eating and looks at me with a flash of a grimace, his mouth stuffed with pasta that's hanging out, draping over his fork.

"That's something we'll only let happen once," he says, continuing to shovel.

I laugh and grab a bowl of my own.

"He's starting school on Monday," I say.

Neither Grace or my dad reacts. They know the words I'm not saying.

"He's going to start playing with the team, too," I add.

"Good, they need help. When you graduate, I'm taking that job back. Those fools don't know what they're doing. They may as well be playing coach-pitch."

My dad plays his personality up, partly to distract from the important piece in everything we've both just said—Wes is here. He's back, yet he isn't.

We don't dwell on it. There aren't any parent-daughter talks about not getting my hopes up or about not losing myself to a boy. We're past that. I'm not. I'm going to play Division One ball, as an amputee. What Wes does or does not remember won't change any of that. It never would have.

But my *right now* is still hopeful that he will remember us. That he and I will have to talk about things like long-distance relationships, visiting girl-only dorm rooms, gas money to see each other, and how jealous he's going to be when I'm far away and I have to beat the guys—from whatever college's baseball team—off me with a stick. I amuse myself at that last thought.

My dinner done, I escape to my room, pulling out my government book to study. For most of my peers, this last semester is meaningless, but for me, a few more decent grades in my average might be the difference between a partial athletic scholarship and a full one. We just got out of debt, and I'm not so anxious to dig new holes.

My eyes glaze over the text, and I shake my head to focus several times, finally giving in after an hour of trying to memorize the passage of various bills and amendments, matching them to their years and their sponsors. I close my book and let my cheek rest on my pillow, aware of everything on the other side of my eyelids for about a dozen seconds before it all fades into background noise and I fall to sleep.

When I wake up, my room is bright from my lamp, but I know it's late. I rub my eyes and glance to my clock to check the time, struggling to focus to read it at first, and finally seeing it's a little after two. A knock comes at my window, and I roll my head to the other side, looking at the perfectly sealed space I made my dad cover in shutters.

I click my lamp off and wait a few seconds for my eyes to adjust, my phone buzzing while I wait.

It's me. I know it's late.

Seeing Wes's name has me standing quickly, and I circle my room as I type.

I'll be right out.

I search for something nice, finally giving up and walking outside in the same smelly shirt and joggers I played in this afternoon. He's standing at the end of my driveway wearing the same thing he wore, too, and it makes me laugh to myself.

"Hey," I say, closing the door behind me quietly.

Wes's hands are in his pockets, and his eyes are down, glancing up to me briefly as I approach.

"Hey, sorry," he says, his voice low, almost a whisper. "I know it's late. And this is probably...I don't know, maybe not a good idea or whatever."

His eyes scrunch and he brings his hands from his pockets pressing his palms on either side of his head as he paces a few steps to either side.

"It's okay, really," I reassure him. He stops where he's at, his arms relaxing, and his hands falling to his sides as he studies me, his body turned to the side.

He shakes his head slowly, his hat backward and the ends of his hair curling at the base of his neck. His mouth has the tiniest curve, and I start to focus on it more than I should as he takes a deep breath through his nose. My mouth parts, but I'm not sure what to say, so bite my bottom lip and wait. His eyes notice, and I feel it in my chest when he blinks slowly.

"I found this...ticket," he says, pulling his right hand from his pocket again, holding it out for me to take. I look at it and smile faintly.

"That's yours. You should keep it," I say, my heart caught in the present and the past, with a little boy wanting to be accepted and have a friend, and a younger me wanting to be nicer than she ever really was.

He holds it out for a few more seconds, his hand finally dropping and holding it at his waist, where he stares at it a little longer.

"I know something about this ticket, but it's like it's caught in a fog," he swallows.

"Yeah," I say, my fingers tingling anxiously, my mind screaming at me to finish the puzzle for him. I know I can't.

"I found it as soon as we got home from practicing. It was in with a bunch of my things, in this box with my socks," he glances up and his eyes meet mine. "I knew it had something to do with you."

I nod slowly.

"It does," I say. My heart booms loudly, and I start to sway on my legs, needing to ground myself.

"Before I came here, I just drove," he says, pushing the ticket back in his front pocket, leaving his hands there when he's done. "TK called me, freaked out. I guess driving around a place I only slightly remember at midnight worries the fam."

He laughs on one side of his mouth and I smile.

"I can see that," I say.

His chin lifts and his eyes meet mine again, and our eyes lock for longer this time. My legs steady, and I remain perfectly still.

"I didn't know where I was going, but I just drove. I took turns because they felt right, I stopped when something told me to. I went to this place."

His brow draws in and he takes a deep breath, his lips relaxed, but pulling at the corners, trying to decide whether to frown or speak. Eventually, he moves toward his truck, and I follow for a few steps before giving him space. He reaches inside and pulls out a messy cluster of flowers, some of them still showing their roots from where he pulled them from the ground. He takes deliberate steps toward me, lifting my hand in his and wrapping my fingers around the bunch of peonies, my eyes focused on the perfect one in the very center.

"These are your favorites," he says, and I look up into his eyes over the tuft of pink we both grasp between us. "I don't know how I knew that, but I knew these were your favorites. They're important."

My lips part and I gasp a quiet breath before nodding slowly. I feel his other hand cover mine, closing over my knuckles, squeezing my grip tighter on the flowers. His feet take tiny steps forward, inches closer to me, as he holds my gaze hostage.

"You're important," he says.

My eyes break rank first, the cool tear finally giving way to gravity and sliding down my cheek before stopping and waiting for more.

"You're important," I say back to him.

The words barely leave my mouth before his right hand is cupping my face, his thumb drawing a gentle line under my eyes, sweeping the tear to the side but not extinguishing the proof that it existed.

We existed.

We exist.

"I can't fly," he says, his forehead falling against mine slowly. We both laugh silently through breaths as I let the flowers fall to the ground and I bring my hands to his shirt, grabbing it in bunches.

"It's overrated," I say, tilting my head enough that his lips graze mine, the feel of them like breathing fire into an icy, dead soul.

"I loved you," he says.

"You did," I nod, my head rolling against his with the tiny movement.

He pulls back enough to look at me, my face cupped in his hands, my tears filling my eyes, and my favorite flowers at my feet. Wes begins to nod, and I stare into the blue illuminated by the moon, and I see the shift the moment it happens.

"I love you still," he says.

It doesn't come all at once, but like glitter blown in the wind, the boy I knew begins to come back to me a piece at a time.

Until I have him all.

EPILOGUE

"All right, racers! Before we can start, I'm going to need to see everyone's ticket!"

Taryn stands on top of the berm in my backyard as she paces and shouts, dressed with socks pulled up to her knees and short red shorts that make her look like a roller derby princess. Behind us all, my patio is dressed up with lights and mismatched chairs borrowed from neighbors and friends. I didn't want a party, but my dad said the fact that I graduated was worth celebrating. I'm still not entirely sure if he was joking about that or not.

"Any forfeiters can step forward now! Or you can all just concede to my athletic superiority, give me the last corner piece of cake, and then we can all get out of here and head to the drive-in where the rest of our class is already drunk," Kyle says.

"Sit your ass down, Kyle!" my dad shouts from the back porch.

"You really had to yell the drunk part?" Taryn slaps Kyle's hat lower as she scolds him. "Because of that, you race in the outside lane."

"Aw, come on!" he whines.

"Wow, was he like this for every race?" Wes asks, bumping his knee into mine as we sit side by side along the back wall of my yard where we stood so many years ago.

"That boy was born this way," I chuckle, turning to Kyle and saying a little louder, "entitled and always mistreated!"

"Guess he's going to really throw a fit when he loses, huh?" Wes stretches his legs out and pushes his folded fingers outward, cracking his knuckles.

I smirk at him.

"I guess you both will," I say, holding the tip of my tongue at the front of my teeth. Wes and I stare at each other with mouths hinting at smiles, like two poker players facing off, each with aces in their hands.

Nothing is perfect. There are fractures in Wes's memory still, but every day, something new seems to come back to him. Sometimes it's something as simple as remembering that he liked to put a pack of gum in the ashtray of the truck he shares with his brothers. Other times, it's something big—like our first real kiss, in that treehouse at Jungle Gym's. I helped that one along a little, inviting Wes to my work after it closed, just like he used to do. He helped me climb up, and we sat there for hours just so he could feel the moment.

He and his brothers are staying together for college. They're the first set of three brothers to all play for Pepperdine at the same time. They'll be seven hours away—five the way Kyle drives. My heart was always in Chico. Kyle won't be far—he couldn't resist the lure of Stanford. He's starting to freak out about the academics, but I've assured him that he'll find a nice, pretty tutor that will be happy to take care of him. Taryn will be right at home in L.A. We're a band of troublemakers sprinkled along the coast.

We have the summer together. A summer to find old memories and make new ones. I'm okay with the distance. This is all I wanted, to have to experience this—*a long-distance relationship*. I'm not naïve. I lost all of that youthful romanticism a long time ago. But I do believe if there were any two people in our position who were ever destined to survive this, it's Wes and me. We've survived so much.

My dad gave me a new glove for my graduation gift. It's almost exactly like the one I was going to get when I was a kid. I didn't mention it when I opened it, but I know that's why he got it for me. It was important to him.

It was perfect.

Wes gave me his favorite sweatshirt before everyone showed up for the party. I wanted this shirt a year ago, but now I think I kinda need it. Somehow, it feels like security, and not because the boy who wore it saved me so often. It feels that way because it reminds me of my year—of everything I can do if I have to. It reminds me of the things I want. Wes just happens to be one of them. I plan on bringing it with me any time I see him so I can force him to put it on to pick up his scent.

I wasn't sure what to give him. Everything I came up with seemed so cheesy, or like it wasn't enough. I didn't know what I was going to give him until an hour before he showed up at my house today. I found the perfect gift tucked in the bottom drawer of my dresser. The pages were flat now from resting under my jeans and sweaters, but the drawings were still clear—the color bright. I took Shawn's book into my father's bedroom and promptly put it through the shredder. My father had never seen it, and he wasn't home when I pulled the cut-up pages from the bin and ran them through again, until I was left with nothing but confetti. I stuffed the pieces in a jar and glued the lid on tight. I've been waiting for the perfect time to give it to him, and I wanted to wait until we were alone, but something about now just feels right.

"She's going to go over the rules for minutes. Come with me," I whisper to Wes, leaning into him.

Taryn snaps at us for leaving in the middle of her speech, threatening to disqualify us, but I counter her fast.

"As co-founder of these races, I overrule you. No majority vote," I laugh as Wes takes my hand and we walk down the hill.

"I don't know what that smart business was you just said, Joss Winters, but it's not going to get you any favors. Now *you're* in the outside lane!" Taryn shouts.

Kyle pumps his fist as I shrug.

"I'll win from wherever you put me, T," I say. My friend tries to hide her smile, but her tight lips eventually let out a laugh.

Wes and I slip through the sliding door, and he follows me to my room, his finger looped in the back pocket of my denim shorts as we walk. He closes the door the moment we're inside and holds my face in his hands, his thumbs at my chin as his mouth covers mine. I smile through his kiss; I love these stolen moments that are only ours.

"Do you want your present or not?" I giggle against his lips.

"I always want my present," he says, tugging at my shirt teasingly, pulling it from my shorts. I know he'd never take it that far with my father just outside, so I let him go as far as he's willing before he stops on his own.

"All right, what's this present you have for me?"

He sits on the corner of my bed with his eyes closed and his hands held out in front of him. I slide the small jar from under my pillow and step in front of him, laying the glass in his hands. He feels it for a moment, his lips curled as his thumbs run over the curves and the metal grooves on the lid.

"Jelly," he laughs, opening his eyes and rotating the jar around in his hands. His teasing smile straightens a little and his brow pinches in. "Uh…"

"It was the book," I say, hesitating before I tell him more. Wes remembered the book early on in his recovery. He asked about it, but I'd forgotten amid all of the other things he started to remember.

He shakes the jar in front of his eyes, the bright colors changing like a kaleidoscope trapped inside that glass forever.

"It's almost pretty like this, ya know?" he says, rolling the jar slowly along his leg.

"I thought so," I smile. I sit next to him and take it in my hand, holding it up against the light coming in through my window. "I didn't really think about it. I just did it. It seemed like…I guess it just seemed like our story was done, so we didn't need this anymore."

Wes stares at the jar in my hand for a few seconds, sliding his fingers along my wrist until his hand grasps it and he takes it back from me. He holds it on his knee then slowly moves his gaze up to mine. An amused grin takes over his mouth, pushing faint dimples into his cheeks as his eyes close just a little, his left a little more than his right.

"And here I thought our story was just getting started," he says.

The corners of my lips rise.

"You two are up! You're racing TK and Kyle, so get your shit together!" Taryn shouts through the closed door.

"I guess we gotta go do this race thing," I say, my eyes not leaving his once.

"I hope you'll still love me when I leave you in the dust," he smirks.

I get up and hold out my hand, his fingers finding mine after he leaves the jar on my desk for later. I lead him back down the short hallway, through the living room and to the patio where our parents are joking and Taryn is standing on the hill. We hold hands all the way to the faint chalk line Taryn made me draw with pieces I had left in the bag I found from when we were kids. Wes digs his front foot into the dirt, twisting it to get a good grip, then places his hands on his upper leg as he leans forward, his eyes now on Taryn, his muscles poised to go.

I do the same, turning my head to face the short dirt track ahead that used to seem so big when I was a kid.

"You know I'm not going to let you win, right?" I say as Taryn raises her arms and watches to see when we're all ready.

"You never have," he says.

My cheeks round as my smile grows, and the second Taryn shouts "Go!" the earth rumbles with our heavy feet, clouds of dust growing with every gallop and laughter slicing through a shared will to be the best—to win.

Wes and I take the lead immediately. We both push, and leap, and kick until the very end, sparking a debate that lasts until the sun goes down over whose body crossed the line drawn in the dirt first. Everyone else needs to have a winner. But Wes and I—we've already won. We've found our place again, among races, and tickets, and dares…and kissing.

We've come home, to the beginning.

Our story starts again.

And nobody writes it but us.

THE END

ACKNOWLEDGEMENTS

Thank you for taking this ride. Thank you for embracing my strange little story that's a little different. Thank you for holding these characters' hands, holding them tight, as they battled and fought through the things life threw at them.

It's safe to say now, that you've read the end, that yes, I love superhero stories. I love the idea of origin stories, and of the responsibilities that come with power of any kind. This story brewed in my head for quite some time. I wanted to write a story about a boy who was just a little bit different—maybe even a little bit better—than the rest of us. The *Like Us* duet isn't just Wes's story, though. It's very much about Joss, too, and the things that make her super. My goal, which I hope like hell I achieved, was to write a superhero story that felt real, that felt like this…*this* is how it would really be if someone like this existed. Our hero wouldn't save the world. He would save *his* world. And the damsel, if you can call Joss that— she would be tough as nails. While Wes's powers are a little more magical, Joss's are tangible—rooted in overcoming adversity, defying odds, believing when it feels impossible, breathing when you feel dead inside. Villains abound in real life, too. And this time, the good guys win.

I don't know that I'll revisit their world, but I will never say never. I loved living here too much. I hope you liked this trip to Bakersfield, too.

I have so many people to thank. Tim and Carter, my boys…my world. Thank you for rooting me on, and leaving the house for hours when I needed to focus, and high-fiving me when the covers came out so dang good (I'm proud of them, at least). BilliJoy and Tina, thank you for making sure my words hit the mark. And my amazing beta readers – TeriLyn, Ashley, Jen, Bianca and Shelley – oh how you keep me sane and in line! Thank you so much!

For me, when I write, I like to make goals along the way. Sometimes it's a deadline to my betas, and other times it's the end-goal to my editor. But what I look forward to most is when I get to reach out to you, Autumn. You are my ambassador of confetti, waving at the finish line, ready to help me celebrate, then push out my latest work through Wordsmith Publicity. I'm so grateful for you.

I wouldn't be able to tell stories like this if it weren't for the passionate readers out there. Many of you blog, but even if you don't, you share your passion for books you love wherever you can. If not my books, you share your love for others, and I speak for all of us trying to be noticed in this rough and tumble bookish world—thank you! Thank you for taking the time to post our covers, teasers, excerpts. Thank you for leaving reviews. Thank you for making this dream of mine real, and for putting a smile on my face. And Ninjas, members of my group—ohhhhh you guys, you know…you are everything!

I'm going to breathe for a day or two, but I've already got notebooks filled with outlines and characters, ready to dip into another world. I hope you'll make the trip with me. I promise to be one hell of a guide.

ABOUT THE AUTHOR

Ginger Scott is an Amazon-bestselling and Goodreads Choice Award-nominated author of several young and new adult romances, including Waiting on the Sidelines, Going Long, Blindness, How We Deal With Gravity, This Is Falling, You and Everything After, The Girl I Was Before, In Your Dreams, Wild Reckless, Wicked Restless, The Hard Count, Hold My Breath and the Like Us duet.

A sucker for a good romance, Ginger's other passion is sports, and she often blends the two in her stories. Ginger has been writing and editing for newspapers, magazines and blogs for...well...ever. She has told the stories of Olympians, politicians, actors, scientists, cowboys, criminals and towns. For more on her and her work, visit her website at http://www.littlemisswrite.com.

When she's not writing, the odds are high that she's somewhere near a baseball diamond, either watching her son field pop flies like Bryce Harper or cheering on her favorite baseball team, the Arizona Diamondbacks. Ginger lives in Arizona and is married to her college sweetheart whom she met at ASU (fork 'em, Devils).

Ginger Online

@TheGingerScott
www.facebook.com/GingerScottAuthor
www.littlemisswrite.com

BOOKS BY GINGER SCOTT

The Like You Duet
A Boy Like You
A Girl Like Me

Read The Complete Falling Series
This Is Falling
You And Everything After
The Girl I Was Before
In Your Dreams (spin-off standalone)

The Waiting Series
Waiting on the Sidelines
Going Long

The Harper Boys
Wild Reckless
Wicked Restless

Standalones
Blindness
How We Deal With Gravity
The Hard Count
Hold My Breath